PROOF

A Thriller

Jon Cowan

GALLERY BOOKS

NEW YORK AMSTERDAM/ANTWERP LONDON

TORONTO SYDNEY/MELBOURNE NEW DELHI

G

Gallery Books
An Imprint of Simon & Schuster, LLC
1230 Avenue of the Americas
New York, NY 10020

First Gallery Books hardcover edition June 2025

Interior design by Kathryn A. Kenney-Peterson

Manufactured in the United States of America

10 9 8 7 6 5 4 3 2 1

Library of Congress Cataloging-in-Publication Data has been applied for.

ISBN 978-1-6680-5113-9
ISBN 978-1-6680-5115-3 (ebook)

For my parents, who filled our house with books.

For Lexie, Caitlin, and Spencer, who fill our house with life.

And for Jennifer, who fills my life.

"The law does not pretend to punish everything that is dishonest.
That would seriously interfere with business. . . ."

—Clarence Darrow

PROLOGUE

"We're all guilty. Of *something*."

Jake West fixes a knowing look on his face as he locks his eyes on the jury box. This is probably the key thing he's learned in his decade and a half of trying cases. You need to remove the wall between the jury and the defendant. You need to make them feel they're not standing above the accused in judgment. If they're going to make the harsh decision to take away the freedom of another human being, they need to be forced to sit in the shoes of that person. They need to feel what it's like to be judged. Who among us wants to be judged on what we've done? Not Jake, that's for sure.

"Don't get me wrong," he continues. "I believe in the system. I believe *you* believe in the system. And I know people say lawyers are liars, and most of us are. But what I've just told you? It's the truth. You know it. You *feel* it."

He pauses to let the jury feel it. To let their minds wander to all the things each of *them* are guilty of. When he's satisfied that he has ignited the flame of their guilt, he offers absolution.

"I'm not judging you," Jake assures them. "I'm no different. Let me tell you my truth."

Jake takes a longer pause here. It's calculated, crafted to make them lean in. He milks the moment as he approaches the jury box. Twelve chairs walled off from everyone else by a light maple half wall. It's a modern design, and Jake doesn't like it. He prefers courtrooms cast in walnut or mahogany; he feels that gives the proceedings the gravity they deserve. The light wood is businesslike. Perfunctory. But he's in performance mode, so it doesn't matter. It's up to him to bring the gravitas. And to do that, he must make it personal.

He stops at the edge of the box and fixes a stare on a singular juror. Camila Cortez. Like any good lawyer, Jake knows things about his jury. His audience. He knows Camila is first-generation American. He figures her parents came to have her born in the U.S. of A. Maybe they came legally, maybe not, but either way it speaks to reinvention. Leaving the past behind. She's a few years younger than he is, but there are stories in her face, probably stories about that past. Doesn't matter what the stories are—he can use that.

"Me—I've cheated on my wife, I drink too much, I work too much, I inhaled in college, and after that—" Jake stops himself, realizing he can't admit to a felony here in court. He sheepishly grins at Camila. "Well, I really don't want to jeopardize my career, so that's as far as I can go. But you—I bet *you* slept with someone you shouldn't have. Took something you shouldn't, smoked it, shot it, inhaled it."

Sitting in the jury box, Camila Cortez can't help but feel the words are directed at her. Jake West isn't so much talking to her as looking into her soul. Lord knows she can't count the number of things she's guilty of. Not the least of which is what she's thinking right now. What she's thinking about Jake right now. Forget about the fact that his hair is rumpled, or that his suit is wrinkled, or that he didn't shave this morning. He's mesmerizing. She thinks she could listen to him talk all day. She would sit cross-legged at a campfire and listen to him spin a yarn.

"Tell me you never walked out of a store with something you didn't buy, just to see if you could, just to feel the rush."

Camila's mind goes to the jewelry counter at Woolworth's, not that that was the only time. Jake watches her, and she senses he can see what she's thinking. What she's done.

"So if I put *your* life on trial, you'd feel guilty. Because you've done *something*. And if you sat in that witness box and started squirming, a jury of your peers would see it. All I'm asking of you today is to consider that. To consider that what you see as guilt may be guilt about something else entirely."

Eye contact is the key in any trial, so Jake's eyes remain locked on Camila's. You believe people who can hold your gaze. People who look away—they're liars. So Jake's gaze never wavers, and he's pretty sure he has her. But he can't rush this, so he loosens his visual grip on her and walks slowly back to the defense table, knowing her gaze will not leave him. There's a glass tumbler waiting for him. Clear liquid and ice. He sips it like it's not water. It's *not* water. He feels it burn. It energizes him, gives him strength to continue.

He turns back to Camila. Eyes her black dress with a red floral print; the fabric looks like silk, though odds are it's polyester. It's a wraparound with a tie, and all Jake can think about is pulling the tie loose. Maybe that's the liquor seeping into his brain, but experience has taught Jake to hide those kinds of thoughts. He can't keep them at bay, but he can conceal them. He needs focus. He's got to be perfectly sure he's sold his audience. His audience of one. Because you only need one juror.

"You gonna let me have some of that?" Camila says, breaking his train of thought.

This might be the time to mention they're alone in the courtroom. At night. Even so, Jake admonishes her: "You don't get to talk. Yet."

Camila leans in, working her own magic. "I won't talk. I'm enjoying the performance. But I'd enjoy it more with a little taste."

Jake considers the juror's request and decides that it's rude to drink alone. He takes out a small, silver flask from the breast pocket of his suit. Pours more of the Casamigos Blanco tequila into his glass, then carries it to the jury box, dangling it like a carrot.

"You're not playing by the rules, now, are you?" he chastises her, holding the drink just out of her reach. Almost daring her to come get it.

"Are you really a lawyer?"

Jake leans in. "It's been said I can persuade *anyone* to do *anything*."

Camila knows it's a line, but she's a lost cause as she stares into those eyes. Deep green, with flecks of brown. Without taking her eyes off his, she reaches for the drink, her hand slithering over his until it's grasping the tumbler. She slides the drink out of his grip and puts it to her lips. Takes a sip. It's strong. It's nicer than what she usually drinks.

"What's the verdict?" He means the drink, but she's not done playing.

"I don't know. I'm thinking guilty. You think you can change my mind?"

Damn, but Jake likes a challenge. He leans in even closer.

"Here's the thing you have to understand." His voice is soft, intimate. "Being guilty of something doesn't mean you're guilty of what they say. So the question isn't, did my client lie? It's, what did they lie *about*? What did they *really* do? And whatever it is, did the other side *prove* it?"

Jake sits on the edge of the wooden railing. He's almost straddling Camila.

"You understand guilt, don't you? What do *you* feel guilty for?"

"Not for what's about to happen, that's for damn sure," she says.

And just like that, he's won the case. Or rather, he's achieved his end goal, which in this case means he slides his hand behind her neck and pulls her into a hard kiss.

Camila revels in it for a moment, then pulls away. Something isn't right. She studies him. The dark hair hasn't started to gray. Neither has the stubble, which would be the tell if he was coloring it out. His general air of bad-boy charm had been working for him, but in the kiss, she felt something dark, angry. Now, sitting back, she sees the darkness has crept into his eyes as well. Maybe it's just the liquor taking effect, but what seemed like charm thirty seconds ago is all at once clearly revealed as damage. Damage buried under a shitload of booze.

"Something tells me you understand about guilt yourself, Jake."

She's beautiful in the damaged way Jake is always drawn to. The damage makes her more attractive. As does the fact that she sees his darkness and she's still here. Jake drops over the side of the railing, grabs the tie holding the dress together. He doesn't pull, just slips a hand through the opening in the fabric and—

"Counselor!"

At the now-open double doors of United States District Court, Central

District of California, Western Division, courtroom number 5D, a heavy-set security guard stands with Richard Kaplan, a lawyer in a suit that looks far better than Jake's, with hair that's far better than Jake's, and a face that's shaved far better than Jake's. None of which hides the fact that Kaplan seems weary and wary, staring with mixed emotions at what was once his best friend.

"Hey, Richie."

Jake doesn't remove his hand from inside Camila's dress. He's enjoying this unexpected turn of events.

"What the fuck, Jake?"

"I hadn't gotten to the fuck yet."

At that, Camila removes his hand from her dress. Liquor or no liquor, amazing eyes or not, she's not going to be put on public display.

Kaplan comes closer, digesting the depths to which his friend has sunken. "You really wanna get disbarred?"

"I have been working at it pretty hard."

Kaplan sighs. He wants to be angry, but all he feels is sad. He used to look up to Jake. He used to want to *be* Jake. What a joke that turned out to be. Over the past year he's watched Jake cut off, one by one, everyone he cares about. He tried to break through Jake's misery, to be a good friend, to be there for Jake. And that only made Jake work harder to push him away, to say things he probably didn't mean, but they had enough basis in truth to sting. Then he watched him behave that way to others, and he just couldn't take it anymore. He gave up.

But tonight he has a job to do. He walks over to Jake and tries to put his emotions in check. "Jake. Seriously. What are you doing here? You don't have any cases—you don't even have any clients."

Camila is surprised by that; she thought he was a big deal. He implied as much.

Jake shrugs an apology to her as he answers Kaplan. "I was doing a closing. Fact is, it was pretty good, wouldn't you say?"

He silently wills Camila to render the verdict he needs. She sees that the security guard at the back is looking the other way; clearly he wants nothing to do with this shit show, so there's no legal jeopardy here. As for Kaplan, she instinctively doesn't like him. He seems uptight, very unlike Jake, who, now that they've been interrupted, seems back to himself. The darkness has passed. And despite having been lied to and perhaps used, she still finds Jake attractive as hell. So she decides to play along.

"I'd say . . . he was gonna get his client off," she teases.

Camila and Jake are both amused. Kaplan can't say the same.

Kaplan and Jake head down the steps of the First Street U.S. Courthouse, a glass cube ten stories high, almost floating above the sloped downtown street. Kaplan's BMW 750i—with custom Donington Grey Metallic paint—is parked in a red zone right in front. It's more car than Kaplan needs, but it's worth its price for how his clients admire it if they hit the valet stand at the same time.

"This how you pick up women now?" Kaplan asks.

"No. I picked her up at an AA meeting."

"And which step is this?"

"Hah. Funny. I don't remember you being so funny."

"And I don't remember you being so stupid. Oh wait—yes I do."

Jake stops and tries to assess what's really going on. For as long as Jake has known him, Rich has never had the guts to step out of line. He lives vicariously through Jake's penchant for it. So what's different tonight?

Rich is on a similar train of thought. Thinking how Jake used to amuse him. But now, at forty-one, what was once charming, almost enviable, is overwhelmingly sad and pathetic. Was Jake *always* sad and pathetic? Did Rich never see him for what he was?

"Do you even want to be a lawyer anymore, Jake? Or are you done with it all?"

"How could I be done? My name is on the door."

"It's your father's name on the door," Rich says bluntly.

"True, but I try hard to forget that," Jake says. It's his cross to bear, sharing a name with Norman West, the feared leader of the esteemed firm of Thompson & West.

Rich sees the paternal callout got under Jake's skin, but it's hard to have sympathy when having the shared name has bailed Jake out of trouble more times than he can count.

"You think I like this? Being your babysitter? You don't think I have more important things to do tonight?"

"Gotta run home and redline some clauses? Adjust those profit definitions?"

Beneath this attempt at banter, Rich is aware this is exactly what Jake thinks of him as a lawyer. Hell, it's what *everyone* thinks. Forget that his billings bring in 60 percent more income to the firm than Jake's do; what he does is viewed as grunt work. He'll never be at the top of the food chain because his work has no glamour. And tonight of all nights, this pisses him off.

There's a lot Rich wants to say, but instead all he offers is this: "Fuck you, Jake."

"No one asked you to come here, Richie."

"Actually, someone did. The guy whose name is on the door."

Interesting. Is his father keeping tabs on him? How the hell would he know to send Rich here? As Jake ponders that intrigue, Rich opens the passenger-side door, trying to move this along. An invitation for Jake to serve his penance. But Jake feels a deep, gut-level instinct to run. To bolt the other way, to fall in with the homeless contingent downtown, find some guy with a bottle in a plain paper bag and make a new friend. He envies them, really. No responsibilities. No one to disappoint. He is acutely aware that thought makes him an asshole, but the idea holds a strong appeal.

Then he sees the beaten-down look on Rich's face—it reeks of disdain and pity and disappointment. And the liquor is wearing off, which means Jake's just noticed it's cold out. LA cold, maybe fifty-two degrees, but like everything, it's all about context and expectation.

Jake takes the easy way out—he gets in the car. Rich closes the passenger door and slowly walks around to the driver's side. He's gotten the job done, retrieving this human baggage, but the emotional toll it's taken is quite high. He feels an intense need to sleep. For a week.

This night should be a good one for Rich. He's on the verge of proving he's more than what people see. He may fail; he's well aware that the case he's taken on is either a way out or a way to destroy everything he has, but it's the way people like Jake look at him that makes him know he's done the right thing.

In a sudden burst of inspiration, or maybe it's fear, he thinks he should tell Jake everything. Enlist his help. But then his senses come back to him. He can see exactly how that would play out. Jake wouldn't marvel at what Rich had done, he'd step in and do what he always does—make it better and take all the glory. Richard Allen Kaplan would once again recede into the background, and no one would remember he was ever there. He thinks about *Chicago,* the musical. "Mr. Cellophane"—that's him. People look right through him as if he's not even there.

Fuck that. It's time to change. And he will allow Jake no part in it. He'll take him home and be done with it. He climbs in and settles in the cushy leather seat and marvels, not for the first time, at what $131,878 can buy. He turns the car on, but then he takes in Jake sulking in the passenger seat, and he softens. In spite of everything, he loves Jake like a brother.

In his 2L year at Boalt, UC Berkeley's renowned School of Law (now simply called Berkeley Law to remove the connection to its racist namesake), Rich had spent so much time reading and studying and prepping, trying to keep up with others whose brains seemed to work faster than his, or digest material faster than he could, that he didn't notice that his first real girlfriend, Emily Towne, the girl he had designs on marrying, had been around less and less. So when he found out he got an A plus plus on his Con Law final and showed up unannounced at her apartment to celebrate, he was stunned to find she'd been in bed with a 3L he knew and hated. Rich hated the 3L more, seeing him wearing a T-shirt Rich had left there. A T-shirt and nothing else.

Rich had wanted to sulk and brood and cry, but Jake was having none of it. Jake instructed him to burn every last item that had any emotional connection to Emily, then they went up to Tilden Park, made a bonfire at an empty campsite just below the steam trains, and drank until they passed out. A week later, Jake found Rich a date for an end-of-year party who was so hot, and draped herself all over him all night, that it made Emily insane. A crass stunt—but man did it make him feel better.

So now, he decides to give intervention one more try.

"Is this really what you want, Jake? To use your legal skills to get laid?"

"Kinda makes winning more fun."

Beneath Jake's repartee, Rich sees he isn't actually having fun. He's miserable.

"Look, I get what you went through—"

"No, Rich. You really don't."

That thought drives Jake to take the flask from his coat pocket. He unscrews the cap, tips the flask to his lips, and swallows. The Casamigos feels good going down, but it's not going to fix the problem, and that just makes him want more. So he takes another long pull.

Rich watches, shakes his head. It's hard to witness someone's self-destruction. Jake then offers up the flask. Kaplan despises himself, but in that moment he wants it. Needs it. He takes it and downs a big swallow of his own, which gives him the nerve to ask a delicate question: "You seen Cara?"

"Nope."

"The kids?"

"Every other weekend. Tuesdays. Gives me a reason to sober up once a week. Not that they want to see me anyway."

Jake really believes this. They've never told him so, but they don't have to—he feels the deeply rooted truth of it. He embarrasses them. He embarrasses himself, which drives him to take the flask back. Rich sees the pain, the *real* pain, in his friend's face, and it's hard to stomach. Is part of it Rich's own fault?

"Come on, Jake—"

BAM-BAM-BAM. A hard knock on the passenger-side window with a flashlight. Jake and Rich both startle, but neither can make out the figure with the flashlight beam shining directly in their eyes.

"Cops. Always there when you need 'em." Jake rolls down his window. "Good evening, Officer, I'm—"

The matte-black barrel of a .44 Magnum appears in the open window and, almost simultaneously, a gunshot explodes. Rich Kaplan's head explodes too, blood and brain spraying onto the laminated safety glass of the windshield, onto the glass-reinforced polypropylene of the dashboard, onto the black merino leather, and all over Jake.

Jake is paralyzed. The sound has detonated the world into an altered state of reality; he can't hear, everything is underwater, he feels warm and wet, and he's not sure if he himself has been shot. He looks at what's left of Rich slumped against the driver's door. There's no head there anymore—there's flesh and bone and lots and lots of blood, but no discernible face. He looks back to the open window and sees nothing. No one.

Then Jake's eyes go to his lap, where the .44 Magnum now lies; he can feel heat from the discharged barrel through the mouliné wool of his suit pants. How the hell did it get there?

Panicked, he fumbles for the door handle, the blood making his hand slip off the polished metal. He manages to flick it open, kicks the door, and gets out, desperately trying to wipe the blood and brains off himself, like there's a spider on his body he can't see. Finally, he steadies his breathing, searches every direction. Unlike his ears, his eyes are fine, but all his retinas take in is darkness. No movement at all, not even a homeless person sleeping, no car creeping by. How is that possible?

Then he sees a hooded figure at the top of the block, ducking into the

Metro station. There's a fractional instinct to give chase, but his feet don't leave the ground. His instinct to avenge what just happened is at war with the very real uncertainty of what would happen if he caught up with the shooter. What if they have another gun, or there's an accomplice Jake never saw? He could end up with no face like Rich.

He looks back to the blood-soaked Beemer, his dead friend slumped sideways. And his choice of inaction is made. Then he sees the .44 Magnum again—he's inadvertently knocked it to the pavement.

Yet all he can wonder in this moment is: Where the hell did his flask end up?

1

The guy looks like an asshole.

Sioban McFadden knows the type well. It's not a species unique to Los Angeles. Back in Dublin, the haircuts were different, the clothes warmer, and the accents more appealing, but there were Irish Jake Wests just like there are Jake Wests the world over. Wealthy, entitled, spoiled assholes who think they can get away with anything. The world has taught them that they can. And while more often than not the assholes are right about that, it doesn't stop her from trying to change things.

She stares through the one-way glass at Jake; he's barely cleaned up, blood spatter still evident. He's trying to appear composed, but he's fidgeting. How much of his agitation is because of what's happened and how much because he needs a drink is hard to say. He looks up at a wall-mounted video camera.

"So, guys, I'm softened up—would you get in here?"

Sioban is enjoying his discomfort. She wonders how many times in his life he's made people wait, let suspects sit and squirm, either because he was too busy to show up or because it served some manipulative purpose he had in mind. Let the shoe be on the other foot for a change.

She's already biased against the man she's watching in the box because she's come to hate lawyers. She understands that some are good people, but the process teaches them to cheat and manipulate. It actually *rewards* such behavior. Sioban wonders if there is any place in the world where justice truly is blind. Where the system endeavors to do what's right. Where you don't have to fight so damn hard to stop people like Jake West.

In the box, Jake's mask is slipping. He's barely holding it together. His hearing has thankfully come back, but he still feels underwater, like everything is unreal. And while usually he enjoys being the center of attention, this is not one of those times. He wants to be alone, to drink, to shower, to drink again, and to forget.

He can't take it anymore—he gets up, paces. He feels like one of those lions at the zoo. How do they stand it, being watched and studied, day after day? He knows he shouldn't do this; he's supposed to be calm and nonchalant. But his best friend, or at least ex–best friend, just had his face blown off right in front of him, so maybe a little pacing is the norm in such circumstances. Maybe that's what they're expecting from him to demonstrate he's a witness and not a suspect.

Jake walks up to the glass. He assumes they're watching, and he tries to demonstrate his innocence. He fixes a look on his face, the same one he schools his clients to use, particularly the guilty ones, in the courtroom. But from his side of the glass, all he can see is his own reflection, and he can't help but notice his appearance. Bloody, scared, sunken eyes. Is that from lack of sleep or the drinking or the trauma?

Then he sees something that makes his heart race.

"Shit. Is this . . . brains?"

He tries hard to control his breathing as he gingerly flicks the organic matter off his shoulder. Watching it hit the floor, he's struck that what he's just done is awful. This piece of Richard Allen Kaplan, his friend with whom he was sharing a drink hours ago, flicked aside to be swept up by the janitorial staff. Jake suddenly feels sick. He has to end this.

It occurs to him they may not be watching through the glass at all—they may be in a back room having coffee and congratulating themselves for having locked up someone who's helped guilty people go free. But he needs their attention. *Now.* So he turns to the camera and says for the record: "I know you're out there, and I know you need me to talk, so let me make a deal. I need a drink. I understand you have to keep my flask, it's evidence, whatever. Bring me what you've got. Gin and tonic. Easy on the tonic. And not some cheap, tasteless shit. Someone around here has to have some Tanqueray or Magellan stashed in their desk." And then he smiles. "Pretty please?"

At this point, Sioban has what she needs. She feels she knows this man, how he likes to play people, how he uses what he's been told is his charm to his advantage. That knowledge is all very useful to her. Let him be charming. She's immune to it.

Jake has settled back into the intentionally uncomfortable chair, essentially having given up, when the door finally opens. He's expecting a grizzled veteran, someone like Adrian Hernandez or Dan Flores, someone twenty pounds overweight and jaded and excited to get a chance to come after the asshole attorney who's torn them apart once or a dozen times in various situations where they were either sloppy or corrupt or just had the bad luck to draw a case in which Jake needed to mercilessly beat their story into a lie.

The woman who enters is a welcome surprise. He pegs her in her thirties, very fair, a red tangle of hair providing all the color that's needed. She offers him a lowball glass. Intrigued, he takes the drink. The glass is heavy. Belongs to someone who understands having a drink isn't just about what's in the glass—it's the total experience. You feel it in your hand. You smell it. Only then do you sip. The glass is a fine start. Now he smells. Then sips. His eyes betray nothing.

"We were out of the gin. But the tonic's top of the heap."

Her Irish accent is the second surprise. She must be new. He would remember her.

"Your blood alcohol was 1.6, Mr. West. You've probably had enough anyway."

"I wasn't driving."

"Well then, I guess the world is safe." She extends her hand. Very friendly. "Detective McFadden. Sioban McFadden."

"You draw the long straw or the short?"

"You think you're worth drawing straws?"

Touché. Jake just might like this one. "You bother to check the security cams at the Metro like I told them?" he asks.

"Guy wearing a hoodie goes into the Metro. Very descriptive."

"Was he there?"

"Sure. There was a guy. A hoodie. But he wasn't running, wasn't panicked. No blood, no gun, no nothing to help. And rest assured, we even went a step further. No CCTV footage with an angle on the car. We see you and Kaplan leaving the courthouse, that's it."

"So do you have any leads at all, Detective?"

"Yes. We do. Actually, we think we may have the shooter in custody."

Her eyes drill into him, making her point clear. Wouldn't that make their lives nice and easy? One lawyer murders another. Get rid of two for the price of one; that's how the joke would go.

"Really? I'm the best you can do?"

"Gunshot residue on your hands—"

"I was opening the window—"

"Blood all over you—"

"I was sitting right next to him—"

"You were holding the gun when the patrol car drove by."

"I was going to give chase," Jake explains, though that's a complete lie. He doesn't know why he picked the Magnum up. It was a mistake. But he was in shock. Scared. It's why he hasn't asked for a lawyer yet; he wants to remedy that mistake. He wants to play concerned friend, co-victim of this attack. Asking for a lawyer before the police have asked a single question runs counter to that goal. He takes a sip of the drink, forgetting that it's just tonic. So disappointing.

"How pissed were you, Jake? That Richard Kaplan ruined your night?"

Jake expected this play; it's the obvious first move. He's not sure if she really believes it or just wants to, but this is how they were bound to game it out. His history wouldn't be lost on them. A drunk train wreck of a career, a history of violence—at least that's how they would spin it if they found out about his minor lapse. Or major lapse, depending on how the event was viewed. Regardless, everything she's saying makes sense. If he was prosecuting himself, he would have a field day in court. Again, why the hell did he pick up the gun? He has to defuse that bomb.

"I get you have to start with the standardized playbook, but you're wasting your time. If you actually knew anything about me, you'd know Rich Kaplan was my friend."

"I know exactly who you are. I know you pissed away your career, you've been drinking, wife left you, you're a walking cliché. I'm thinking Kaplan stepped into the void, took your spot at the firm, became your father's go-to. That had to hurt, right?"

Sioban gives him a minute. She wants to let him stew in the evidence that two hours has brought to light. He'll understand it's just the tip of the iceberg. She's sure there will be more.

"So no, this isn't your average playbook, Jake. I hope it's okay, calling you Jake. Mr. West seems so . . . formal. Like we're talking about your father. Who, I hate to tell you—he can't help you now."

If it weren't his own life on the line, Jake would enjoy this performance. It's a familiar pitch, but she's selling it well.

"So you know the drill," she continues. "This can go two ways. And I understand what your instinct will be, but before you lawyer up, let me suggest there's an easier way. Cut a deal, make a plea. Save the taxpayers some money, save your wife and kids the drawn-out heartache, and get this off your chest."

She pauses to let him digest. He knows the game, but the words have to land differently now that he's a suspect. She doesn't get a fast rebuke, which is a good sign.

"At least think about it, Jake. People say I'm easy to talk to."

"Sounds like a line from someone trying to get you in bed."

"Sounds like a remark from someone who has to *use* a line to get someone in bed. Or has to use the federal courtroom to get someone in bed. That's what the security guard had to say, and I'm sure the lucky woman who turned you down will confirm it. Seems she left before the shooting."

That's good, Jake thinks. No reason to drag Camila into this. But he's gonna have to find a new AA meeting. He doesn't want to face her again. Which isn't really an issue; he doesn't have a drinking problem, he only goes to an occasional meeting so he can be honest when he tells Cara he's going.

He sees Sioban watching him and realizes his mind has gone down another rabbit hole. He's losing track of where they are in the questioning. He's not disoriented; what he's really feeling is tired. And the truth is, while the detective is his adversary in the moment, he's growing to like her. Maybe talking *is* the answer. Why not just tell the truth?

He takes another sip of the nonalcoholic drink, which still does nothing to help how he feels. She must see him struggling, because she presses: "What's it gonna be, Counselor?"

"I'm going to shock you, Detective. I have nothing to hide. And I want you to do better than this pathetic attempt to close a case. Maybe this plays well in County Cork, but here in LA you have to do better. So I'm going to tell you exactly what happened."

And maybe he would have, but at that moment the door opens and a regal man in his late sixties strides in. He's got a sharp suit and a sharper mind, but in this moment, he uses brute force and bombast.

"Shut the fuck up, Jake."

Behind the newcomer trails a weathered police sergeant who's just putting in hours until he has his twenty. He looks sheepish because he's just been raked over the coals by this older man, and he fears Sioban will not be happy. He shrugs a lame apology.

Jake misses all this, as his focus is only on the man in the Brunello Cucinelli suit that probably cost five grand. He feels no relief at the arrival of the cavalry. Just dread. But he forces a smile.

"Hey, Dad. Good to see you."

The view from Mulholland Drive, facing south over Los Angeles, is impressive. On a clear night—and let's face it, that's not all the time—one can see 180 degrees, from the ocean to downtown, and from some angles to the San Gabriel Mountains far to the east.

There had been almost no talking between father and son all the way from the Central Police Station on Sixth, up the 101 to Barham, then up Woodrow

Wilson to the lookout. Norman West parks the Bentley, sits for a minute, then gets out and walks to the cliff's edge. Jake stays put in the warm car, in the comfy sweats Norman insisted the cops provide him, desperately yearning for a drink to make his insides also feel warm, and to help him discern the message of this little outing his father has concocted.

Finally, reluctantly, he joins his father at the edge of the cliff.

The sudden temperature change hits Jake like a knife. With the wind blowing, it feels colder than what the Bentley's supremely accurate gauge says it is. Even so, his father seems impervious to the cold. But then, his father is impervious to most feelings.

Norman West grew up in Los Angeles. Not the ritzier side that he now lives in, but in North Hollywood. They call it Valley Glen these days, but no fancy name can change what it is—a stiflingly hot, run-down part of the city you'd avoid unless you're searching for granite countertops or flooring or what might euphemistically be called a massage. Norman went to UCLA, not because he was driven to have a better life, but to avoid the draft. Law school was merely a way to avoid figuring out what to do with his life. But once there, he took to it. He didn't "love the law" like some. Norman appreciated how he could mold and manipulate it to his benefit, and eventually to that of his clients. It was a tool he wielded like a sledgehammer. And what he loved best was going up against the bigger firms, the ones with lawyers from Harvard and Yale and Stanford, with lawyers who grew up in Brentwood and Bel Air and the Palisades. He enjoyed kicking their asses, taking their money, and making them look stupid in front of their clients—who'd then become *his* clients, in some cases.

After growing his reputation in the real estate boom of the eighties, Norman and his friend Archie Thompson took their top clients and opened their own shop. He didn't want to be big like O'Melveny & Myers or even like Manatt—he wanted an elite team of the best. Never more than fifty lawyers, more than enough to service any case he wanted, and small enough to prevent any factions that would try to challenge him for power. And the crowning achievement for Norman would be bringing his son into the firm. An heir apparent.

When Jake graduated Berkeley Law, he certainly had other offers. But the more he met with other firms, the more he sensed their goal wasn't to hire him, it was to get under Norman's skin. Jake could understand that—it was an activity he enjoyed regularly, but he had no desire to play that role for others. What he wanted was distance, so he took a job at a public interest firm. That had been a fine, fine day, telling the legal patriarch he was passing on Thompson & West to work for under a hundred grand a year.

But then Jake made a tragic mistake—falling in love. He met Cara, fell hard for her, she got pregnant, and suddenly a job that paid mid-six figures seemed like a reasonable choice to make. It wasn't like his father could make him do anything he didn't want to.

Hah—the folly of youthful idealism.

Much clearer now on what Norman West is capable of, Jake wonders: What is the plan up here on Mulholland? He doesn't ask that—Jake knows well enough to wait his father out—but it does occur to him that perhaps having his only begotten son freeze to death is his father's idea of punishment.

"It's a big city. A lot of shit goes down out there. And our job . . . sometimes our job is to clean it up."

Though he has finally deigned to speak, Norman just keeps looking out into the distance. Jake has to concede it's a masterful performance. Not the dialogue, but the delivery is solid.

"Thank you, Raymond Chandler. But can you make your point less abstruse? I'm freezing here."

Jake thinks his fingers might actually *be* frozen, fifty-two degrees or not. Still, his father doesn't take his eyes off the view of the city lights.

"My point is, I don't care what happened tonight. Whatever you did, I'm behind you."

A sentiment that might be touching, if not for what it implies.

"You actually think I killed him. Jesus, Dad, he was my friend."

"He was sleeping with your wife."

For one of the few times in his life, Jake is rendered speechless. Assuming this is true, which his father's tone and pitying look suggests it most definitely is, this is a shock to him. He feels a pit form in his stomach. He fights a sudden need to throw up. He fights putting an image to this betrayal, which some might say is not really a betrayal at all because he and Cara are separated, and what's more, Jake's own betrayals obviously predate hers. But that logic doesn't change how it feels. Nor his need not to visualize it.

His first accessible feeling about this isn't anger, it's hurt. It makes him sad, both for himself and for Cara. Next comes embarrassment as he realizes that clearly others know about this. Then his legal brain takes over. This gives the police a motive that'll play very well in court and the press. Jake wasn't taking the case against himself seriously, and their decision to release him without charging him bolstered that, but now he needs to rethink.

He starts by replaying everything Rich said tonight, trying to see it through this new prism. But now the anger floods through him, thinking about Rich with his wife. Until the visual of his faceless face intrudes and the rage turns to regret. He shudders at the grisly image, one that will haunt him for a long time to come.

"You had to know. It wasn't a well-kept secret."

"It was from me." Jake is still struggling to digest this double betrayal.

Norman finally turns to look at his son—the remnants of blood on his neck, the police-issue sweats, the usual unshaven thing made worse by the hours in lockup. How has his son come to this?

"What'd you expect, Jake? That Cara would wait around for you to get your shit together?"

It doesn't matter how old Jake is, how much he's told himself he doesn't give two craps about his father, that *look*, that withering look of utter disappointment—of *disgust*—still stings. Jake turns away. All he can see now is Cara naked in Richie's arms, and that's infinitely worse than his friend's exploded face.

"How much have you been drinking?" Jake hears disdain beneath his father's even tone.

"Enough."

"Enough to forget who you *are*?" Norman snaps. "You were gonna talk back there, Jake. What the fuck? You know the helpful gambit never works. It doesn't get you sympathy; they'll just think you're playing them."

Norman West, he who has no emotion and can eviscerate his opponents with a quiet knife they never see coming, is absolutely livid. Which plants a new thought in Jake's mind.

"Do you really think I did it? Or do you just want me to think it wasn't *you*?"

His father takes a moment. No visible reaction, but when you don't have feelings, it's easy to hide your reactions. He says simply: "I have no motive. Why would I have done it?"

Jake tries his father's tactic. He doesn't react. He just waits him out. It works.

"I'm your father."

If that's meant to soften Jake, it doesn't work. Instead it stirs up countless years of resentment. And between that and the murder of his best friend, who also happened to be banging his wife, and the alcohol, and the fact that it's too fucking cold up here for this little Raymond Chandler–esque lecture, Jake decides to let his father in on a little secret.

"I used to lie awake and think: I must be adopted. They must've switched me at the hospital with some other kid. And somewhere out there is a forty-one-year-old uncaring asshole stuck in a family that actually has a heart."

Jake lets that land, then moves around his father to the car. Norman doesn't move, just turns back to the city—the distant, innumerable lights doing little to cut the darkness.

2

Cara West didn't sleep much last night, but that's nothing new. Trazodone and melatonin with a NyQuil chaser put her into a haze, but she never went deeply under. She still hates being alone in the bed. She should love it—Jake snores, tosses and turns and wants the room to be arctic, while she prefers a warm cocoon. But now she feels the emptiness. It isn't so much that she misses Jake—at least not the way he's been this last year—but despises being alone.

She opens the window to let in air and takes in the second-story view that once filled her with a sense of success, of having arrived. Just east of UCLA, Little Holmby is everything she ever wanted. It has trees and wide streets and a park within walking distance. She knows the neighbors, their kids, their dogs, their cars, and with a few of them the problems with their husbands, though she tries to avoid that kind of talk so she doesn't have to reciprocate. She has what most people yearn for—a place one could live in for their entire life. But the FOR SALE sign on the front lawn suggests that ain't happening here.

In her late thirties, Cara runs, she hikes, she's in better shape than she was when she was younger, and when she actually gets a good night's sleep, her face is still smooth. She keeps her blond hair at a middle length, rejecting the short "mom" cut so many of her friends have adopted. She loves being a mother but refuses to let that define her. And it works—if she's out alone, she still gets hit on. She would never pursue it, but it's not bad for her self-esteem. In fact, someone meeting Cara West might just think she had everything. They'd certainly think she was happy. They'd be wrong. The truth is, there's a wounded part of her, and an angry part of her, but she keeps both well hidden.

She pads down the dark, wooded hallway and knocks on a bedroom door. "Chloe . . ."

The response is both groggy and annoyed all at once. "I'm up. Jesus."

Cara tries a second door. Her voice is gentler—she doesn't mean it to be, but it is.

"Aaron . . . Time to be up."

"I am." He's cheerful. At least one person in this house is.

In the kitchen, Cara goes straight for the coffeepot, desperate for some jump start to her system.

"I miss your coffee."

She nearly drops her mug as she turns to find Jake sitting on a barstool at the counter. He's holding his own mug—WORLD'S GREATEST DAD. As always, the master of irony. Cara has competing simultaneous reactions—fury at the intrusion and comfort at Jake being exactly where he belongs. The latter thought makes her angry at herself. No, he doesn't fucking belong here. Not anymore.

"Sorry. Didn't want to wake you."

"You can't just come in here—"

"We need to talk."

Cara reads something on his face. Whatever he has to say, it's not bullshit. It's real. Still, she doesn't trust him. She takes his coffee, smells it—it reeks of alcohol. Of course it does. Which makes how he's doing worse than she imagined.

"It's six thirty in the morning."

"Rich is dead."

Almost immediately, Cara feels she is outside her body, watching herself receive this information. Every time she watches some movie or TV show where someone delivers world-shattering news, the reactions always strike her as false. She's not sure what the right reaction should be, but each time she sees a version, all she can think is: nope, not like that. But here she is, living the moment, and all she is is frozen. There's a gnawing in the pit of her stomach, and whether it's lack of sleep or her alcoholic husband or the unthinkable words he just said, it's all she can do not to vomit.

Jake's trying to read what she's thinking. He should be kind, help her get through this, demonstrate he is still someone she can count on. Her rock. Instead, he takes the low road.

"Must come as a blow to you," he says pointedly.

He knows. Shit, Cara thinks. The least of her problems right now, but still—shit.

"What . . . happened?"

"He was shot."

"Jesus. By who?"

"If you ask the police, they'll tell you I did it."

Jake studies her reaction and hates what he sees. Doubt.

"That's sad. My father believes I did it. My wife believes I did it."

"Did you? Kill him?"

She doesn't really think so—this is more a deflection from her guilt about Rich. And fury at what Jake has become, that he's become someone so lost and unreliable that this question actually needs to be asked.

But all Jake hears is her anger, and he responds in kind.

"Did you? Sleep with him?"

Cara can't believe this is what they're talking about. She can't believe the judgment written all over his face. *Well, fuck you, Jake. Yes, I slept with him. And I hated it.*

Okay, she didn't hate everything about it. She liked that it would piss Jake off if he knew, but at the same time she desperately never wanted him to find out. She certainly thought less of herself for doing it. In spiteful moments, when she'd had too much white wine, she was actually glad she'd done it—it made her feel less a victim of Jake's chaos. But mostly, she hated that she'd allowed it to happen in the first place. The irony was she didn't even really like Rich. That said, she can't fight the urge to throw this in Jake's face.

"If that's why you killed him—trust me, one fuck wasn't worth it."

Jake stares at her. He's not sure he knows her anymore.

"When did you become so cold?"

"When I had to. So you couldn't hurt me anymore."

The day he met Cara, Jake was putting in hours at a legal aid clinic, but only because of the Stanford grad he had his eye on. She'd interviewed to join his firm and mentioned that's what *she* was doing, and he wanted an excuse to ask her out. But when he arrived to show the lucky grad just what a noble guy he was, he'd been introduced to her wife. So he was stuck. He couldn't leave without looking like a jerk. *What a waste of a day*, he'd thought.

And then in walked Cara. She came in with a twenty-year-old Latina girl, the daughter of her parents' longtime nanny, who was trying to get her mother citizenship. From the moment he saw her, Jake was done. Everything else went out the window, all thoughts of the Stanford grad forgotten. He had to find a way to impress Cara, and none of his usual methods would do. So he took her case, volunteering for a full month, allowing him to guide them through the process, building a real relationship with Cara as he did so. Sure, he probably could have made it happen faster, but he knew then that Cara wasn't someone he just wanted to sleep with. He *did* want to sleep with her, but he wanted much more than that.

Within a year, he'd asked her to marry him. He knew guys who felt they *had* to marry their girlfriends—they wouldn't choose it, but they succumbed to the pressure. Jake actually wanted to get married. He was himself with Cara—a better version of himself. She knew he had demons, that he had a dark side—you didn't grow up with Norman West without developing that—but she loved him anyway. And the truth is, when he was with her, he didn't go so dark anymore. He wanted to be present with her. Sober.

But that was a long time ago. Before he screwed it all up.

Sitting on the barstool he still remembers picking out with Cara in the up-scale showroom at the Pacific Design Center, Jake is unhappy with how this conversation has gone. He isn't sure how to move forward with Cara. But he wants to. Even now, having just witnessed a murder, having just learned about her infidelity—okay, it's a stretch calling it that since they're separated—he still wants her. What would happen if he walked over and kissed her, held her, told her he'd stop drinking?

"Dad!"

Aaron bounds into the room and runs over for a hug, almost leaping into his father's arms. Eight is a pretty great age for boys—old enough to have real conversations, too young for the all-out resentment that's sure to follow when he realizes just who his father is. Jake holds his son tight, infusing into that hug all the emotion and love and loss he's suppressing in other ways. And why not? Aaron represents the best of Jake: love of Little League, an endless fountain of useless statistics, full of fun and enthusiasm, a zest for life and adventure. For Aaron, this is just a morning like any other, but Jake can't let go—he holds on for fear of everything he's about to lose. Fear that Aaron in turn will lose all of those great attributes before Jake knows it. He's sure he'll find a way to screw Aaron up and make him cynical and bitter and perpetually angry and he'll probably start drinking, and it'll all be Jake's fault.

"Hey, champ." He tries to keep it light.

"You taking me to school?"

"No." Cara draws a clear line in the sand, her eyes laser-focused on Jake's coffee mug, and he knows she's right. He's not even qualified to take his son to third grade. "Get your shoes on before breakfast, Dad and I need a minute."

"Okay." Aaron starts out, then turns back to his father. "See you tonight?"

Shit. It's Tuesday, which means it's Jake's night. He'd forgotten. Again. He'll have to pull himself together. He'd counted on spending the day drinking himself into oblivion, but he can't. At least not *all* day.

"Wouldn't miss it," he says with a wink, overselling it.

Cara rolls her eyes as Aaron bounds out, calling out, "Chloe! Dad's here!"

The reply from upstairs is all attitude: "Great." But his daughter doesn't come down. Jake feels the sting. He wonders how much is typical thirteen-year-old attitude and how much is disdain that he personally has earned. He fears it's more the latter.

Cara watches him. Pities him. Then the emotion of what he's just told her hits, and she realizes she needs answers.

"What happened, Jake? Really?"

"I . . . I don't know."

He takes a long gulp of his drink. Fuck that—she grabs his mug out of his hand and dumps the contents in the sink.

"What. Happened." She refuses to let him look away, something she learned from him.

"Rich and I were sitting in his car, outside the courthouse. Someone knocked on the window with a flashlight, and when I rolled down the window, whoever it was shot him."

She blinks multiple times, as if to make the words clearer. It doesn't help, because something doesn't add up. "You didn't see the person right there?"

"It was dark, there was a light in my eyes." Jake sees this answer isn't enough. "It happened so fast."

"They didn't steal anything?"

"No."

"Say anything?"

"You're sounding like the detective who hauled me in."

"Yeah, about that. You said your father thinks you did it. You said the police think you did it. You're officially a suspect?"

"More like a person of interest, at the moment."

"Why is that, Jake? What did you do?"

"I was just . . . there. The shooter dropped the gun, and I picked it up and I had it when a police car drove by and saw me, and suddenly I was on the ground being cuffed."

She tries to digest this. The details aren't making any more sense than the obfuscations.

"As for why dear old Dad thinks I did it? He knew about you and Rich. He figured I found out; that gave me motive. But the thing is, I didn't know. Until he told me."

There's so much information to process, but all that Cara's brain filters let in is the digital clock on the stove telling her she's late. An excuse to get away from this horror.

"I have to get the kids to school. You need to go."

"Cara—"

"They'll see you tonight. If the police don't lock you up first. Or you don't find some other reason to bail."

He'd argue the point if it wasn't based on recent history. He can't stand the disappointment he sees on her face. She starts to walk out of the room, then stops herself. Not sure she should give him this, but—

"For what it's worth? We both felt bad about it." She sees Jake is confused, that he doesn't pick up on her meaning. "Me and Rich. It was one time, and it was wrong. I think we both just felt lost without you."

After she goes, Jake sits there on the barstool, taking in the house that isn't his anymore. The Swedish prints Cara got from her grandparents. The cabinet doors just slightly misaligned because he eyeballed the reinstallation instead of using a level. The whiteboard with the kids' schedules. Cara doesn't need the whiteboard to know who goes where and when; it had been designed to keep Jake in the loop, but even in his absence it's fastidiously up-to-date. His eyes fall on the coffeepot just beneath it, which gives him an idea. He knows he should go, but instead he retrieves his WORLD'S GREATEST DAD mug from the sink, rinses it out, and refills it with black coffee, no alcohol this time. It was so much better with the WhistlePig eighteen-year double malt, but it's hot and it's strong. It'll have to do. He has a big day ahead.

3

For the most part, Kendall Clark loves her job. She gets to wear nice clothes, sit in an air-conditioned office on the thirty-seventh floor in Century City, and she's paid very well for answering the phones and greeting the guests. She is aware she got the job primarily because of her appearance—this is Los Angeles, after all. It isn't fair, but it also means she's underestimated here, as she has been her entire life. Her long brown hair and deep blue eyes have always helped her get away with things, but the trade-off is she has to work twice as hard to prove she has worth beyond what her mother always called her "God-given beauty." As for the inevitable men flirting with her, for the most part she finds the endeavor entertaining, a little like watching a nature documentary on the mating habits of meerkats. She has no qualms joining in the banter, knowing it'll never go anywhere. Kendall isn't one of those people who takes a job like this to meet someone rich. She fully intends to get rich herself. She just hasn't figured out how yet.

There are inevitably assholes who step over the line, who don't understand the rules of the game, but she always feels safe behind the oak-paneled bank that separates her from those who come in to have the lawyers at Thompson & West hide their millions, or make them millions, or bury their crimes. And for those who refuse to take no for an answer, she casually makes sure they see the security camera, maybe drops a hint that an external microphone sits on her side of the desk recording every word, should it ever be required in a court of law.

The attorneys who work at the firm are a mix—cutthroat, boring, condescending, dismissive. But the few who actually talk to her and treat her like a person and not a decoration, those she likes. Richard Kaplan was one of those. And though she's sitting here being professional and answering the phones this morning, there is a heaviness in the air she can't shake. Someone she knows, knows very well, was *murdered,* and having to sit here and go about business as usual makes it worse. Thompson & West should have closed. At a bare minimum, brought in grief counselors. But no—too much business to be done. People to be fucked over.

Which is why seeing Jake come through the glass doors is so welcome. He isn't like the others. He knows her name, knows she's from San Diego, he was extra kind to her parents when they came in for lunch, asked about what they did as if he actually cared, then said nice, acutely observed things to them about her. So Kendall has a soft spot for Jake. And seeing him as he is this morning—in a custom-tailored Tom Ford suit, perfectly pressed, his hair in place, clean-shaven—is a huge relief. She's heard stories of his debauchery, most of which she assumes are exaggerated, but before he stopped coming in altogether, she'd seen enough to understand he'd fallen deep down the well. So this change is welcome. Most acutely because he, at least, will feel the gravity that this day should have.

"Good morning, Kendall. Miss me?"

"I did. What are you doing here?"

"I work here." Jake's claim is technically accurate, as he still receives paychecks and his partner shares haven't changed.

"Right, of course, I just mean I heard. About Mr. Kaplan. Rich."

"I didn't kill him, if that's the rumor."

She freezes for a second, then manages a horrified: "I know that."

"But you don't dispute that's the rumor." Jake says it with a grin, not intimidating her. It's not a question—he's just confirming what he suspects. Someone will have had a source in the LAPD, and while they probably don't have details, there will be intimations of Jake's guilt that will have made it from lawyer to assistant to front desk and likely to the parking garage at this point.

Kendall isn't sure how to answer. She has indeed heard fifth-hand rumors, but she puts no stock in them. She knows there are those at the firm who mock

Jake—he's a nepo baby, a hopeless drunk, and his absence this last year only fueled their disdain. So they're ripe to gossip and speculate. But for Kendall, it doesn't hold water. There are attorneys at Thompson & West that she might think are capable of murder—Jake just isn't one of them.

He notes her discomfort and lets her off the hook. "It's okay. Long as *you're* clear on the truth, I can handle the rest of the assholes around here."

Despite what's happened, despite what he's been through, he's trying to make her feel better. She leans in and whispers: "We *are* outnumbered by them, though."

"That we are, Kendall. But if any one of them gives you trouble, you know who to call. Day or night. An affront to you will not be tolerated." Jake has a knack of doing this, and it never seems like he's flirting or wants anything. "Do me a favor, though—buzz Asshole Number One and tell him I'm back."

"I assume we're talking about Mr. Gibson?"

"We are indeed. And let's have a little fun. Tell him I need to be brought up to speed on everything Richard Kaplan was working on."

Jake is asking her to drop a bomb, and Kendall will relish that job. "Done. And Jake . . ."

She nods subtly with her eyes, and Jake follows her gaze. Across the lobby, Daria Barati is ostensibly checking messages, but really, she's watching Jake. He loves it—the ripples of his return are starting. Parking garage probably called up a warning. Daria inadvertently meets his eye, then caught, heads off down the hallway, pretending to read her messages.

"Hang in there," he tells Kendall. Then he goes to take the bull by the horns.

Jake's never quite known what to make of Daria. In her late thirties, she is what Jake would call striking—tall, dark hair, impeccably dressed. Classy. Her Iranian parents moved to California to give her the best education a girl could have, and she had it. Harvard-Westlake, then actual Harvard, both undergrad and law school. She is quiet but tough, maddeningly inscrutable, and she wins her cases—pretty much all of them—which has made her a rising star at Thompson & West; she's a senior partner, technically Jake's equal. He assumes she's trying to find meaning in his sudden reemergence at the firm, and he decides to use that, to pretend they're close and see where it gets him.

"Daria. How the hell are you?"

But she's not one to be played; she's ready to parry his move as he falls in step with her.

"Question is, how are you, Jake? Sober?"

"Three hours without a drink. You think I get a chip for that?"

"Seriously—what are you doing here?"

Jake has a ready answer for this. As with Kendall, his strategy is to be flip. He wants to project that he's the same old Jake. And by that he means the old Jake, before the alcohol and failure or, in a more accurate order, the failure and the alcohol consumed him.

"Why does everyone keep asking me that? I work here."

"We've learned not to expect much from you."

He stops and she thinks he's ready to feign offense, but he surprises her.

"That's fair. Maybe I can change that, though." Jake smiles warmly, or rather, Jake fakes a warm smile. This comment actually seems to unsettle her, so he decides it's time to let her stew. "Have a good one, Daria."

He starts to peel off down another hallway, but she puts a soft hand on his arm.

"Jake—what happened? Really? With Rich?"

He studies her, gauging her intent. "You mean why did I kill him?"

"I didn't say that."

"No, but you were thinking it. That's why I'm here. To prove you're wrong."

With that enhanced punctuation to their little talk, he leaves Daria wanting more. Exactly as he intended.

Jake enters his dark, wood-paneled office and flips on the light. The office is neat; it's likely no one's been here in almost a year, but the cleaning staff has done their job of keeping it pristine, awaiting a return that seemed unlikely. On the desk, the lie of his life—photos of Cara, Chloe, and Aaron, separately and together. They look like such a happy family. They'd have you over for a barbecue. They'd be great fun if you shared a beach house for a week. These are people you'd want to be part of your life. Jake wonders if it was always a façade, the photos just a lie to sell his clients.

On the walls, black-and-whites of Jake with some of those clients he sold the lie to. Many well-known, others just rich. And then, prominently, Jake and his father. Norman West appears proud. Another lie.

Beneath the photos, the one immutable truth of his life: a fully stocked bar. Jake's pleased to see nothing has wandered off in the intervening months. It's all here. The Glenlivet XXV Single Malt. Yamazaki. A Pappy Van Winkle that had been a gift for winning an eight-figure settlement. These are his true friends. His comfort. Tempting. Really fucking tempting. Three hours feels like an eternity. And he's unlikely to get that flask back anytime soon.

Jake goes to the bar, takes in the colorful array, and then lifts a favorite—a porcelain container of Clase Azul Reposado. So smooth it goes down well at any hour. It would make this day in particular go so much smoother.

"Breakfast of champions?"

Jake turns to find Stephen Gibson at the door. Gibson is in his forties, his dark hair definitely coming out of another kind of bottle; it's as fake as his attempt at collegiality. This is a man who is driven by one thing: naked ambition. He tells himself it's okay because he's on the right side of things. His self-deception is astounding. He thinks he's a good guy. He's wrong.

"Stephen. You here to bring me up to speed? Don't we need some files?"

Gibson closes the door behind him. With the blinds down, it gives the room the cast of seriousness, of mystery—which is intentional. Gibson takes a seat on a comfy leather couch the firm had imported from Milan. Puts his feet up on the coffee table that, nice as it is, might be less expensive than Gibson's shoes.

"This is a bad idea, Jake."

"Coming back to work, or trying to find out who killed my friend?"

"Who are you kidding—you weren't friends anymore. No one has seen you in ages. And if you think hunting his killer puts you in the clear, you haven't read enough Grisham."

"I'm thinking this is more Scott Turow. Less big conspiracy, more just people being what they are—self-serving, self-interested creatures who eat their young and anything or anyone else in their way. But they're found out in the end."

Jake delivers the last line like he's pronouncing a sentence.

Gibson's unimpressed. "You haven't practiced in a year."

"Which means I have a clear calendar. I'm the obvious choice to take over Rich's caseload."

Jake is aware this is bullshit—he's not the obvious choice, certainly not from the firm's point of view—but he's going to force the issue. The part about an open calendar is a solid argument, but his goal is to use this access to Rich's cases to clear his own name. A selfish goal for sure, but he's also a highly skilled lawyer, so he reasons it'll be good for everyone.

"I'm sorry, Jake. No."

"I wasn't asking you. I'm telling you."

"And *I'm* telling you *no*. I'm the managing partner—"

"And I'm a *senior* partner. You can't keep me from accessing his files."

"You are not touching those files."

"Afraid of what I'll find?"

Just the slightest hesitation on Gibson's part before he shoots back: "I'm afraid of the damage you'll do. What happened to Kaplan changes nothing. You were censured, Jake."

"And I have you to thank for that."

"Still not taking responsibility for your own actions, I see. But it doesn't matter. You nearly cost this firm a top-three client. You're a hazard. The answer is no."

"You sound like my father. How's he treating you, by the way? I know

Archie Thompson handed you the whole 'managing partner' thing. I know you think your name is going up on the wall. But between you and me, that's *never* gonna happen. My father may be many things, but he is *not* stupid. He knows you don't have what it takes. Just a friendly heads-up from someone who knows the guy a little bit."

The probable truth of that gets through Gibson's armor. He eyes Jake with a deep hatred. He's always despised Jake's arrogance, his sense of being untouchable, that he didn't have to abide by the same rules as others. He doesn't care if Jake is Norman West's offspring, he's an anchor dragging the firm down, and Gibson's job is to cut anchor. If it were up to him, he would have done so a year ago. He had grounds. Norman wasn't ready.

Gibson is clear he can't make the first move to oust Jake, but perhaps this little impasse is actually an opportunity. While he waits on Jake to be charged with murder—a prospect almost too good to be true—let Jake dig his own grave. He inevitably will. So even if Gibson doesn't want Jake on any cases, he'll give him a little rope.

Maybe the rope is all he needs.

Gibson gets up from the couch and walks to the desk. He picks up Jake's PBX phone and punches two buttons.

"Grace. Bring all of Richard Kaplan's files to Jake West's office."

He places the receiver back in its cradle. Jake doesn't like this, doesn't like Gibson at his desk; he feels violated.

"Sure, Stephen. Make yourself at home."

Gibson wants him to be unsettled by his power move, but what Gibson doesn't grasp is that his need to make the move shows weakness. As does his need to try and spin his concession to give Jake access to the files as a victory.

"To be clear: You can *look* at Kaplan's files, but the clients will choose who they want in their corner. And in case it's not obvious, I will *not* be recommending you."

"I'm good with that."

Jake doesn't give Gibson the fight he was expecting, so he's not sure what to say next. They're left with something of a stare-down. Two warriors sizing each other up. As primal as in the days of Spartacus. Jake should leave it alone, take the win, but he can't help himself.

"So how are things, Stevie? This murder aside. Anne left you yet?"

"Anne wouldn't know what to do with herself."

"Wow, and they say true love is dead."

"Well, yours is. At least that's what I hear."

Jake should have seen that one coming from a mile away and he's pissed for leaving himself open like that. He tries to come up with a rejoinder, and no doubt one would have come to him if not for the knock on the door.

"Ah. That'll be Grace." Gibson smirks.

"Grace is fast. I always liked Grace."

"I bet your wife didn't."

Hard to argue *that* particular point. Gibson's on his game today. Clearly Jake's been away from this snake pit for too long. He's out of practice.

"No. No, she didn't." Jake sighs, then tries for an upbeat tone with: "Come in."

Grace Jamison opens the door, and Jake's stomach flutters; he suddenly remembers why what happened happened. Grace is in her late twenties, blond, a Southern girl by birth, but transplanted to LA for so long you wouldn't spot it. She's a paralegal, but that doesn't give proper due to her role in the company. She does more work than many of the associates. Her legal reasoning is sharp and sound and out of the box. That's what Jake always saw in her—the talent.

"Mr. West."

"Hello, Grace."

Gibson enjoys the awkwardness. But Jake is struck by an oddity—Grace is holding just one file folder.

"Rich's caseload is that small?"

"No, it's just that if you're taking his cases . . ." She hands him the file. "You have a hearing in a half hour."

Gibson interjects. "No need. We have an associate there already."

But Jake sees a flicker in Gibson's eyes. Fear? Some other kind of obfuscation? This reaction interests him, and he decides to push it a little further. He turns to Grace. "A hearing on what?"

"Plea agreement," Grace says as evenly as she can. "Double homicide."

Gibson steps in again. "Kaplan already signed off on a plea; the case is over. Feel free to peruse the ones that are still active. Knock yourself out."

Gibson was never a great liar. Jake is onto something. "Richie was handling a double homicide? This I gotta see. I am definitely going to that hearing."

"Jake—"

"Not to mention you're having an *associate* handle a double homicide? That's irresponsible managing, Mr. Managing Partner."

That part might be true, which is what makes Gibson pause again, just a fraction, before pronouncing: "I have full faith in our team."

"That's good to know, Stevie. And I can reassure you that, as you said, the client will be free to choose—to choose the legal counsel of whichever fine associate you sent, or to choose me. But you know clients always choose me."

It irks Gibson because it's true. Still, he doesn't want to give in, so he finds a side way out; he sighs as if it's just a nuisance. "Fine. Even you can't fuck this one up. Kaplan did the hard work. So let's call it a test run. See if you're *really* ready to come back."

With that, Gibson leaves as if he's had the last word. Jake can see Grace is barely holding it together as she watches Gibson leave. And as she turns back to Jake, it occurs to him there are multiple reasons for her obvious distress.

"You okay?" he asks gently.

"You should go."

"Don't you think I should read the file first?"

"I think you should settle this. Fast."

He reads something in her face. Something that definitely seems like fear.

"Something you want to tell me?"

Grace looks around as if the place is bugged. "No."

Whatever she really wants to say is not what comes out of her mouth next. "But you should know—the hearing? The judge is Eleanor Merrin."

That's not good. That's not good at all. Jake glances over at the office bar. The Clase Azul Reposado is still incredibly tempting.

"Don't even think about it," Grace says sharply.

"Not thinking about it," he lies.

Shit. Into the fire. Stone-cold sober.

4

Eleanor Merrin sits on the bench much as Bloody Queen Mary once sat on her throne—with impunity. One might think she's taken the "Judge" title literally and begun to exude judgment like a virgin female silk moth casts off pheromones. Not so. Merrin has been this way since she laid out the case to her elementary school principal that her nemesis Bruce Anderson needed to be suspended. Bruce's transfer to a new school a week later was something she'd viewed as not just correct, but her right. That was the first time she passed down a sentence.

Jake had his first case before her a year ago, and he made the fatal mistake of thinking he could charm her as he'd done with countless other judges. Had he been sober at the time, he never would have made the misstep. Now, Jake has a hard time understanding how he missed all the signs. Like Kathy Bates's iconic Annie Wilkes in *Misery*, she could seem tame, but fuck with her and she'll take a sledgehammer to your legs.

Getting the junior associate to bow out had been easy: a simple, earnest lie that his father had asked Jake to personally handle this case, coupled with a promise of the firm's Dodger tickets, which had become a prized commodity since the signing of Shohei Ohtani. But the harder task lies before Jake as he moves to the defense table and Judge Merrin registers just who is entering her throne room. Jake unconsciously tenses his leg, bracing for the pain of the metaphorical blow he's sure is about to fall.

"Your Honor—"

"Mr. West. I knew one day I'd get my apology. Is this my lucky day?"

"I'm here on Tiana Walker. You may have heard that my colleague Richard Kaplan—"

"We *have* heard. And for that I am deeply sorry."

At the prosecution table, Deputy DA Austin Bell feels compelled to add: "I'm sorry for your loss, as well. I liked Rich."

Jake turns to his opponent in this matter with irritation. The gallery's fairly empty, yet this guy can't help playing to the press. There's no way Kaplan was "Rich" to him, but Bell wants to project a certain image. If not to the gallery, then to the judge. Bell is Black, in his thirties, tall and slim. He's Hollywood handsome, with huge political aspirations that will no doubt pan out because he's charismatic, polished, and deadly smart.

The judge ignores Bell—she's laser-focused on Jake.

"I have a question for you, Mr. West. I understand you're standing in for Mr. Kaplan, but are you fully cleared to practice law?"

Jake isn't sure if this is a question or a chance to throw his failings in his face.

"It was just a censure, Your Honor. My license to practice remains intact."

"*Just* a censure? That's an informative perspective."

Not a good start for Jake. But much as Bell enjoys watching his opponent's rebuke, he decides to bail Jake out. He wants this case over with. "Your Honor, the late Mr. Kaplan and I negotiated a settlement. This'll take five minutes, tops."

Bell holds up papers to illustrate his point. Dangling that rare gift—a simple dispensation. Merrin considers, then reluctantly waves them both up to the bench.

"Approach, Mr. West. I want to smell you."

Jake feigns flirtation. "I didn't realize you were interested."

It's a bad habit—quipping is not going to help his cause. But Merrin's need to dominate, like a disappointed mother, brings it out in him. That said, Eleanor Merrin is *nothing* like his mother.

"You know what I'm interested in, Mr. West? I'm interested in making sure sobriety is not an issue in my courtroom."

Jake obliges—he breathes on her. Which she finds irritating, but in fairness, she asked for it.

"Of course, if it was vodka, you wouldn't smell anything. Perhaps you'd like me to pee in a cup?"

He's pushing her to the limit but can't help himself. Bell tries to bail him out once more. "Or you can sign off on this and he'll be out of your hair, Your Honor."

Much as she hates Jake, Bell's argument wins out. "Let's just get this done."

She motions for the paperwork. Jake watches carefully as Bell magnanimously hands over the documents. They say don't look a gift horse in the mouth, but Jake knows this particular horse never gave anything that didn't serve his long-term self-interest. And the deal on the table—eight years for voluntary manslaughter—doesn't seem to serve Bell's interests. It's the kind of light sentence for which a DA can get crucified. There are mitigating factors, so this alone wouldn't be a red flag to Jake, but there's also Stephen Gibson sending in an associate, telling Jake *Even you can't fuck this one up.* And most pressing on Jake's mind is Grace's anxiety, her urgent exhortation to take the deal. All of it, cumulatively, doesn't sit well.

He's aware of his own history with paranoia, thinking there are grand conspiracies out there that explain your case—that's backfired on him before. But sometimes with paranoia, they really *are* out to get you, so Jake makes his move.

"I'm sorry. I understand you both have pressing matters to get to. But I'm not sure I can make this deal."

Judge Merrin looks up from the papers. Her cursory glance has made it clear this is an unusually lenient deal, which suggests to her that Jake West is once more behaving recklessly. But her displeasure is nothing compared to Bell's—he's furious.

"What are you talking about? This was negotiated. This deal is a *gift*."

"I do love a nice gift," Jake says genially, "but you seem so eager to wrap it up, I think the situation warrants talking this over with my client."

From the bench, Merrin watches the two men metaphorically stomp their feet and pound their chests. Nothing makes her angrier than having her courtroom be used as a venue for other people's machinations. This is *her* battlefield, and she calls the shots. "Gentlemen—I do not like my time being wasted while you play games."

"Of course not, Your Honor," Jake says as earnestly as he can muster. "But last I heard, the code of ethics suggests I shouldn't make a deal I don't think is in the best interests of my client. I've done a lot of reading on those ethics, Your Honor, as you so eloquently directed me to the last time we met. So as kind as Mr. Bell's offer is, I'd like to double-check my late partner's work. I'd like to at least take a few minutes to talk this over with Ms. Walker. If it's all right with you."

Jake keeps his eyes fixed on Judge Merrin. Working hard to demonstrate his sobriety and soundness of mind. She takes a long time before making a concession.

"If you're going to do it, do it right. Talk to your client. Study the case. We meet back here tomorrow, and either this gets done or we're going to trial."

Austin Bell is not happy with this turn of events, but her tone makes it clear further argument is moot. Round one to Jake, who holds his glee in check and nods solemnly at the judge. "Thank you, Your Honor."

Jake resists his urge to gloat at Bell, because this is just step one. Now it's time to figure out why the hell everyone wants this case settled so badly.

Tiana Walker's eyes are closed. She spends a lot of time that way these days because she can't bear to actually witness what her life has become. She doesn't want to see the six-by-eight room that she couldn't leave if she wanted to. She doesn't want to see the green jumpsuit that marks her as having been charged with murder. She doesn't want to see the shackles that suggest she's a danger to others. And the truth is, if you put something dangerous in her reach, she doesn't know what she'd do. Because she's lost everything.

She hears the hard click of the door to the holding room as it's opened and feels a rush of cool air that comes in from the hall outside. She's not sure if they keep these rooms too hot on purpose, to make defendants sweat and thus appear more guilty when they're taken into the courtroom, but she suspects it's no accident. Certainly when it comes to defendants with her particulars: early thirties, Black, poor, and labeled a killer.

The bailiff who brought her in, the one who actually loosened the metal pinching her wrists when she asked, opens the door wide for a man she doesn't know. She sizes him up instantly as unimpressive and, more importantly, as unimportant to her.

Jake reflexively extends his hand. "Jake West."

Tiana stares at him, part who-the-fuck-are-you, part my-hands-are-shackled-asshole. But Jake moves on; he has to quickly assess whether helping her means taking the deal that's too good to be true or risking her life on his genius.

"I'm sorry to tell you Mr. Kaplan was killed last night."

He's hoping this will make it clear why he's there, but Tiana doesn't register this news as having any meaning. At least that's Jake's take on it. He thinks she's not following.

"Your lawyer, Richard Kaplan. You know who I'm talking about?"

Yeah—she knows. The information doesn't make her sad; it makes her anxious. "He said he was getting me out. *You* gonna get me out?"

Jake should know better than to be irritated by her attitude, but his best friend, or what was once his best friend, is dead, and while he's come to save this woman's life, she doesn't seem to give a shit. Sometimes, he really hates criminals.

"I see you're all broken up about it."

"I don't know the guy. He just took my case. He said he was getting me out, so my question is still—are *you* getting me out?"

If Jake wasn't fighting his deep desire to self-medicate with any possible form of alcohol, he might admire her bravado. He might see they both have the same goal. He might recognize that the system has probably failed Tiana her entire life, and he's just the latest to come in and pretend to care. The truth is, Jake *doesn't* really care about her—he doesn't know her at all. Despite all that, it rubs him the wrong way, which is why he's taking a moment to answer.

"Shit. I'm screwed, aren't I?" She closes her eyes again, willing it all away. Maybe the next time they open, it will all have been a dream.

"Ms. Walker. You set fire to your house with your three children inside—I think you were screwed long before I walked in the room."

It's harsh. It's cruel. But Jake has little time to assess his game plan, and the truth is, the file he studied more carefully before coming into the room has made him question his whole conspiracy theory. The investigation appears sound. He doesn't see much upside in going to court. The deal is outrageously good. So if he's going to do anything other than say yes on her behalf, he has to know what he's working with. That's why he needs to push her, a little too far maybe, but this is what'll happen if the case goes to trial. She has no idea how the system will *really* push her, in totally inhumane ways. That's what the system allows, for lawyers to take someone who's already been destroyed and crush them even further.

But Jake sees something that surprises him in this moment. In her utter devastation, he finds something familiar. It's familiar because he understands what it's like to fuck up your own life and see no way out. He softens. "I'm sorry, let me start over. What I came to say is this: I worked with Mr. Kaplan. I'm here to represent you now, but only if that's what you want. But you should know, my two cents, going through your file? He made you a good deal. Voluntary manslaughter. Eight years. You should take it, Ms. Walker."

"No. No, we're going to trial. He said he's getting me out; I'm getting my son back."

He sees her utter desperation. Which he understands. She had three children—Mariella, Quinton, and Reggie. Now she has one. A tragedy. An unthinkable tragedy, but her desperation doesn't equate with innocence.

"I'm innocent." And there it is. She delivers the line well. It's a good performance. Jake's certainly heard it countless times, and she's definitely in the top 5 percent, but still . . . it's not enough.

"Every bit of evidence points to you."

"That's not true. He said he found something."

Tiana is trying to make him understand, but it's as if he's deaf. *What the fuck is wrong with this lawyer,* Tiana wonders. "The lawyer. The dead guy? He said he found something. *Yesterday.*"

This is the thing Jake was looking for, and yet he fights the impulse to believe her. *She* seems to believe it, but he's seen Rich's file, and there's nothing there. No smoking gun, no notation of misconduct, nothing circled seven times in red pen to denote its importance. And Rich Kaplan, God rest his soul, wasn't a criminal attorney. Clarence Darrow, he was not. So even if Jake wants this case to be some crazy explanation as to what happened last night, it's difficult to believe Rich discovered something Jake isn't seeing. Jake is in alcohol withdrawal, so it's hard to accurately judge, but he's pretty sure nothing Tiana has said changes his legal advice. "I hear you. I do. But all I can tell you is, if he found something, it's not in the file."

"So?"

"So if I were you, I'd take the deal."

Hatred is radiating off her. "Would that make your life easier? Me taking a deal, admitting to something I didn't do? Would you lose any sleep over that?"

"I don't sleep much anyway. But it's not about making my life easier. It's about making *your* life easier. And this file—it says if I go to court, I lose. By that I mean *you* lose. Because I'm not the one who's going to be locked up for the rest of my life."

"The file is bullshit," she says. "They never *looked* at anyone else. They had me. I was easy. That doesn't mean they're right."

He's heard this argument before, but for some reason, her words resonate with Jake. Even so, it doesn't change his mind.

"I lost two of my kids! I have one left; he needs me," she pleads.

This has gone far enough. "Ms. Walker. Tiana." His tone cuts through—strong but not harsh. He's sympathetic but not encouraging. As gently as he can, he tries to make his point crystal clear. "It's a good deal."

She takes a long moment. She knows he's saying it's over. She knows arguing with this man is likely futile. But she has Reggie to think about. Her surviving son.

"Maybe it seems good to you, but like you said, you're not the one who's going to be doing the time. You can move on to your next case, but this is my *life*."

"And this is my job," Jake says. "To tell you to take the deal."

"Then you have a lousy job."

"Don't I know it." He means that. Jake truly doesn't like being the final arbiter of a person's fate, so he offers both of them an out. "Look, this hearing has been rescheduled for tomorrow. If you don't want me to represent you, you can certainly find another lawyer, or the court can appoint one." He's trying to be helpful. If she wants to tilt at windmills, who is he to stand in the way?

Tiana considers this. Knows the answer to her final question but asks it anyway. "Another lawyer going to say any different?"

"Not a good one. A good one will tell you to take the deal."

Leaving the courthouse, Jake decides to do what he avoided when coming in. He walks the block from the Clara Shortridge Foltz Criminal Justice Center to where Rich's car was parked last night in front of the First Street U.S. Courthouse. The whole area is a four block–by–four block mass of courts and courtrooms—federal, state, civil, criminal, appeals, small claims. Something to accommodate every wrongdoing, grievance, and all levels of crime imaginable. Jake passes the Gloria Molina Grand Park Playground, a small green oasis in the concrete jungle of justice. He sees kids and mothers, or more likely kids and nannies, playing happily, oblivious to the abject misery playing out in the buildings that tower over them.

When he gets to First Street, Jake searches for signs of... anything. Standing in the gutter, the symbolism of which is not lost on Jake, he sees there's nothing here. The blood was mostly spattered inside the car, and anything that hit the street has been washed clean or just blends in with years of oil and garbage and dirt. He glances up to the Metro entrance where he saw the hooded figure disappear, but all he sees is the normal activity of midmorning downtown. He can almost talk himself into believing the whole thing never happened. Maybe a drink or three would help him actually forget, but that feels wrong. His friend is dead. A man he got raging drunk with and cried with and partied with and competed with is dead. A man who slept with his wife is dead.

A horn blast shakes him from the thought. Someone trying to park where he's standing. Jake flips off the driver, who leans out the window. "What the fuck, asshole? You're in the middle of the street!"

Jake sighs—he *is* an asshole. Sure, the legal advice he gave Tiana Walker is sound, but if he wasn't an asshole, he'd do better. Rich Kaplan told Tiana he found something, yesterday, and he was murdered that very evening. Jake has one single day to figure out the connection. While it's a connection that may not exist, it should be worth a try. Yet his plan now isn't to do that. It's to do the one thing he knows will make him feel better.

5

The amber liquid has such a high alcohol content that Jake almost gets a contact high from the aroma. But he doesn't drink it just yet—he sits in the dark booth and stares into it as if it has all the answers. He always feels like the answers will come somewhere in the middle of the glass. They don't, but by the time he gets to the bottom, he's stopped asking the questions.

Maybe this time will be different. Maybe ordering it will be enough. Tempting himself, luxuriating in the bouquet, then finding the inner strength to put his money on the table and walk out. But who is he kidding? His inner strength has been lacking ever since he took his first sip.

He was nine. Norman had won an important case, some big client got away with something that would've cost them a fortune if they'd been held to account, and a couple of Dad's asshole colleagues came over to sample the five-thousand-dollar bottle of Rémy Martin Cognac that was sent as a token of thanks. Having sipped a bit, they felt cigars were in order, and the boisterous group went outside to smoke by the pool. Which is when Jake came in and smelled booze—real, hard booze—for the first time. It made him dizzy, but the feeling came with an undercurrent of adrenaline. Like he was putting on armor; it strengthened him. Outside, Dad and the assholes were laughing about something, and it pissed him off to see his father so happy. He'd been cruel to Jake earlier about who knows what, and Jake felt having some of the liquor might just be an appropriate *fuck you*. So he took the glass. Only he didn't know that you weren't supposed to *drink* it, you were supposed to *sip* it, so he took in way too much and it burned like hell.

But after the burning subsided, after he realized he wasn't about to die, he decided he liked the burn. He liked the pain. It was numbing. Emboldening.

So he had a little more. Finished Dad's glass. Then two more. Then he stumbled upstairs and slept for thirteen hours. Which is why his taste in liquor has always run to the high-end. When you start with expensive, the cheap stuff tastes like rubbing alcohol. Jake is glad about that—he prides himself on the fact that while he may be a drunk, at least he is a drunk with *taste.*

And right now, he could use a taste. A little something to take the edge off the fact that he just left a woman locked up in jail and he's likely to make her shitty life even worse. Not to mention the fact that he's a suspect in the murder of his best friend. Either one of those alone calls for a drink. But when he pulls the glass to his lips, what happens is more like a deep swallow, one that would've burned his nine-year-old throat to hell, but now it just slides down like a warming balm.

When he lowers the glass, he sees that Grace is now sitting across from him. He wasn't sure she'd come, and frankly, she doesn't seem happy to be here. Her eyes ask a pointed question. Jake understands what she's asking, but he just shrugs, so she takes his drink and sips. It burns, too strong for her taste.

"It'll grow on you. Knob Creek. Single Barrel, 120 proof."

"It's not even lunchtime."

"Think of it as an appetizer." Jake takes a sip to sell its virtue.

"Is that really a good idea?"

"It's what the doctor ordered."

"I think you need a new doctor."

Jake doesn't like the judgment in her tone—because she has a point. He tries to banter his way out of it.

"You know the origin of the word *proof*? In the eighteenth century, British sailors were paid with rum. They wanted 'proof' it wasn't watered down, so they doused gunpowder in it. If it ignited, boom. There's your proof. At less than 115 proof—it won't ignite. It won't explode away whatever you're trying to forget."

"What are you trying to forget? Rich?"

"The client's face."

Grace closes her eyes. This is what she had feared. This is why she came.

"She claims she's innocent."

"Jesus, Jake. They all claim they're innocent."

"I know. And looking at her file, nothing backs her up." Jake pauses here. He needs to focus on Grace, study her reaction to what comes next. "But then I started thinking—the prosecutor is pressing for a deal on a case he shouldn't care about. Gibson pressed me to get it done. And then there's *you*. You told me this morning to settle. Like you knew something. Something that scared you."

Her pause is only a fraction of a second before she lays into him. "Do you hear yourself?"

"Of course I do. Why do you think I'm drinking?"

There's still no tell in her reaction. Jake sighs. Maybe it's all in his head. Maybe he should stick with his advice to Tiana Walker, make it clear there's nothing to be done. That's why he came here, after all—to make peace with that. But then he called Grace.

"I am well aware I can't cry wolf again, that'd be the end for me. And yet . . ." He pauses with purpose for a second time. He's forcing her hand.

"And yet what?"

"And yet if she *is* telling the truth? Doesn't someone have to fight for her?"

Grace's resolve starts to buckle. This is what Grace has always found irresistible—he believes in things. He fights the good fight, and when he loses, it hurts him. Deeply. Some would call it a weakness, but it's exactly why she broke every rule she had and slept with a married man, her boss, someone way too old for her. Fuck—he was forty at the time. But he represents everything she loves about the law. Not the practice of it—that, she's come to see, is corrupt and filled with awful people willing to do terrible things. No, what she loves is the *idea* of the law. The concept that when life shits on you, there is someone out there who will fight for you. Someone to give you hope.

As an undergraduate at Wesleyan, Grace was a psychology major. As she'd said in her application essay, she wanted to help people, and working for a year in the university's Center for Prison Education, where she tutored remote students actually serving time in Connecticut prisons, she certainly saw the role mental health played in their situations. But it was talking at length to one man, who swore he was innocent, and whom she truly believed, that led her to think about pursuing the law instead. Because what could mental health do for the man other than validate his anger at the world? Not to mention the fact that getting coverage for mental health was a complete scam; the insurance companies love to find ways to minimize coverage, regardless of what is supposed to be a system of parity.

She finished her psych degree anyway—she was too far along to change her major without incurring another year of steep tuition fees—but in her senior year she charted a new path. Law school.

Problem was, her grades weren't good enough. Not for a top-ten school, and she loathed the idea of a second-tier school because she wanted to work for the best. So she graduated, went to UCLA Extension for eleven months, got her paralegal certificate, and was hired at a top local firm, Thompson & West. She knew it would pay well, and when she was ready, it would boost her application for Yale and Harvard and Michigan and Stanford. And for UCLA—the actual law school, not Extension.

She quickly became the go-to person at Thompson & West, but one year became two, and then six. As for why she hasn't taken the LSATs? Well, that's a question she's not very good at answering. To her mother or herself.

The man sitting across from her is part of the problem. Jake represents both what she wants to be and what she's afraid of becoming. He also represents what she desires and hates herself for desiring. All of it makes her want a drink of her own. As does what's happening across the table from her. She has to do something to stop him.

"You were supposed to settle," Grace says as evenly as she can manage.

"You really think people should settle in life?"

"It's not funny, Jake—"

"Don't you believe in due process? Giving the client her day in court? We have a system here—"

"Fuck the system. You know it's corrupt, I know it's corrupt, everyone knows it's corrupt."

"Quoting me—nice. I'll drink to that."

And he does. After which he looks down at the bottom of the glass. No answers. So he waves for another round, pointing at Grace to indicate one for her, too.

"I don't want to drink with you."

"And yet you came." She's reeling from that truth, which is the perfect moment for Jake to see how she reacts to another one. "The client. Tiana Walker. She said Richie found something. Yesterday."

Grace doesn't flinch. Did she already know this?

"Don't do this, Jake. You have to settle."

"Why? What aren't you telling me?"

Grace tries to hold his gaze. She does for a moment, and he sees the truth in her eyes before she turns away.

"What did he *find*, Grace?"

He's too loud this time. Grace looks around, nervous, then leans in and lowers her voice. "Rich called me last night. He wanted me to come up with everything I could find about . . . exceptions to attorney/client privilege."

Jake's stomach roils in a wave of excitement and fear and nausea. He sees where this is going, and it's a minefield. His first step is tentative. He doesn't want to push her too far, too fast.

"He say why?"

"He wouldn't tell me. But he seemed like a kid in a candy store."

Jake has to proceed cautiously; jumping to conclusions has been his undoing before. "You *sure* this was about Tiana Walker?"

"That's what he'd been working on just before he got the call to rescue you at the courthouse. And it fits with what the client told you, with the fact he had a hearing today."

Shit. This is both good and dangerously bad. Jake picks up his glass, not remembering it's empty. "For the record, I didn't need rescuing." He expects a flip retort, and when it's not forthcoming, Jake realizes she's still holding back. "What else?"

She's afraid to answer. The arrival of their fresh drinks is a welcome respite. But when they're alone again, just the two of them and the booze and whatever she isn't saying, he tries a gentler approach.

"Grace? I can't help her if you don't tell me."

She takes a sip of her bourbon to dodge the question. It burns as much as it did the first time, but this time, the heat feels good. It gives her courage.

"He told me to get the privilege precedents and meet him this morning. *Outside the office*. That he'd explain everything. And he told me to bring one more thing that he needed—client billing information. For Reagan Hearst."

A jolt of rage shoots through Jake's temples. He knows that arrogant asshole scion of one of LA's wealthiest families all too well. And if Reagan Hearst is in the middle of this . . .

Grace sees all that going on in his head, and it scares her. "Jake, please, you have to listen to me, something bad is going on."

"I get that. And I get what's coming if I start yelling *conspiracy* after what happened with *Harrison*." He sees genuine fear in her eyes. "And if *you* say anything, with me on the case, you'll be the paralegal who tried to throw our top client under the bus to save the washed-up alcoholic lawyer you were having an affair with."

"I'm glad we're clear that's past tense."

They both drink. Jake was right—the 120 proof is growing on Grace. Bringing out the emotion she's been fighting all day. It also gives her the nerve to ask what she's wanted to since she first saw Jake this morning. "He was sitting right next to you? Rich?"

"Yeah. Yeah, he was."

"I'm sorry. I'm really sorry."

Her sympathy breaks through his wall of alcohol; Jake feels the image

of Rich's head flooding back and takes a huge swallow of bourbon to fight it. And there, at the bottom of his second glass, he gets his answer. He knows, with full clarity, what he has to do. He slams the empty glass on the table to punctuate that resolve, reigniting Grace's worry.

"Jake, we don't know the firm has anything to do with—" She stops herself. She can't finish the lie she's telling.

"Rich found something—something big, something having to do with a client at our firm—and he was shot hours later." Jake delivers it like he would in court. Definitively.

"Maybe it's not connected." She's grasping at straws.

"I'll tell you what else bothers me," Jake continues, on a roll now. "How did the case come to Rich in the first place? No money, no prestige. He's a contract lawyer, for God's sake, I bet he hasn't done criminal work since . . . maybe not ever." He's looking to her for support. Encouragement. Agreement.

"Settle the case, Jake. Let it go. That's the smart thing to do here."

"When have you ever known me to do the smart thing?"

Meeting him here was a terrible idea. She can't be party to this; she has to go before she makes anything worse. She gets up, but he puts his hand on top of hers. She could easily pull away, but his touch sends a bolt of electricity through her entire body. She sits back down, takes a deep breath, then one more slow sip of the drink.

"He took the case because Daria Barati 'suggested' it."

Jake takes that information in, his mind spinning on how one of the other partners at the firm fits into this.

"We're in a fuckin' snake pit, Jake. You jump into this, you're gonna get bit."

"I love it when your Southern comes out."

He's being flip, but she's right to be scared. *He* should be scared. He *is*—which is why he signals for another round.

6

At roughly the same time Jake is lubricating his fears about taking on his father's firm, Sioban McFadden is in the belly of the beast. She stands in the conference room of Thompson & West, looking out from the thirty-seventh floor at a panoramic view of downtown Los Angeles in the distance. Placing the conference room here is an interesting choice—the other side of the building would have provided a view of the ocean, but clearly West or Thompson or whoever signed off on the office design wanted guests to look out at the city proper. Demonstrating the firm was part of it. At a remove, above it, certainly, but unquestionably part of it. It was an impressive move, Sioban thinks. This is the world their clients want to control.

After Norman West barged in on her interview with Jake, and she willingly conceded that no charges would be filed "at this time," she spent three hours reading everything she could find about her prime suspect and the firm both he and the victim worked for. Knowing she would have to be sharp, that she was going up against people who like to twist the rule of law into pretzels, she went home, showered, slept for four hours, showered again, had three cups of coffee, and dug back in. And the clear starting point was here.

"You can't have Mr. Kaplan's files, Detective."

Sioban turns to see Daria Barati, standing in the doorway as a sentinel.

"It would violate the rights of every client in them. If you want to try and get a warrant—"

Sioban holds up a hand to stanch the flow of argument. "I'm well aware the court won't grant me access. I was just hoping the murder of one of your partners might induce some cooperation." She smiles, attempting congeniality.

Daria isn't falling for it. "Why come to me? I'm not the managing partner. My name's not on the door."

"I wasn't in the mood to be condescended to or dicked around by either West senior or Stephen Gibson. Word is, you're the reasonable one here."

Daria is fairly sure this is a lie, and what she sees as the detective's real agenda pisses her off. "No. I think you figured, woman-to-woman, I'd give you a little leeway. A tactic I find offensive."

While Daria is dead right, Sioban doesn't acknowledge it. She sharpens her knife. "I'm not trying to play you, I just figured you might want some answers. Since one of your colleagues may have killed another one." If Sioban was hoping for a tell, a reaction, it doesn't come. She presses forward. "So—what do you think of Jake West?"

"I think he's an irresponsible drunk."

"You think he did it?"

"Maybe. But Richard Kaplan was a lawyer. That means plenty of people hated him."

"Did *you*?"

"Am I a suspect now?"

"Should you be? You have a motive you want to share?"

Daria takes a moment to regroup. The detective's ability to press her points quickly is laudable. Daria can usually manhandle the police, but she's coming to see this woman is not to be underestimated.

"I get it. You come in here and think 'I'm twice as smart as these lawyers, why do they deserve nice offices and nice houses and nice cars?' I'll tell you why, Detective. We work for it. If you want to succeed doing *your* job, you'll have to work for it too."

"Okay, fine—you want to play it that way, I'll do my job." Sioban shifts to a more formal tone. "Ms. Barati, without revealing privileged information, are you aware of any client that had issues with Mr. Kaplan?"

"I have nothing I can offer you."

"Are you aware of any attorneys who had issues with Mr. Kaplan?"

"I have nothing I can offer you."

Sioban studies her—Daria doesn't blink. One more try.

"Just to be clear—you're really broken up about Richard Kaplan's death and you'll do anything to help? That's what you're saying here?"

"Would you expect the male lawyers to be all broken up?"

"If one of my colleagues was killed, yeah—I think the guys *and* the girls and everyone in between would be, I don't know, a little *emotional* about it?"

"I've got clients and cases, I don't have time for emotion."

Daria goes to the door and holds it open for Sioban. She's done playing along.

Sioban takes a moment. This last comment confirms everything she feels about the legal profession. She's done, but she can't resist a parting shot.

"And people say lawyers get a bad rap."

Sioban leaves without files, but that was expected. She's accomplished what she came to do. Rattle the cage to see how the lions react.

Jake takes two plates, each holding three overstuffed soft tacos *al pastor*—the pork marinated in serrano chiles and achiote, sliced thin, gooped up with salsa, and topped with pineapple—and turns to walk away from the long line. Javi Alvarez stares at the concoction Jake hands him, his face filled with cultural disdain.

"This is not Mexican food."

"I don't care what you call it, it's"—Jake stuffs a bite into his mouth but keeps talking—"delicious."

They're at Leo's Tacos Truck, its flashing neon letters advertising a wide array of Mexican food and, oddly, french fries. The truck is parked unceremoniously in a parking lot in front of a WSS shoe outlet on the busy corner of Sunset and Western, where buses go in every direction, workers coming in and going out of the area. It's got the run-down feel of being two blocks from the freeway, and yet it's only three blocks from the Netflix complex, so

Leo's serves a wide and diverse clientele. Jake's appetizer of alcohol had indeed made him hungry, so when he asked Javi to meet, his old friend's desire to talk over food served Jake's purpose well.

Javi's Mexican. Not Hispanic, not Latinx. He has nothing against those other designations, it's just a point of cultural pride with him. It speaks more specifically to who he is. He's a year younger than Jake, but the gray is intruding in his thick hair at a far greater rate than with Jake. Maybe it's genetic, but the truth is, life has made Javi weary. Even so, he's still got a spark. Buried a bit, but it's in there. Jake's counting on it.

"Just try it, Javi. Trust me. These are the best tacos in the city. Think of it as a fitting send-off for Richie."

Javi takes the messy tortilla in hand, squinches up his face as if he's about to ingest the prune he was forced to eat at camp breakfast when he was eight, and takes a bite. Jake is expecting some demonstration of culinary nirvana.

"They're okay, but they aren't tacos. What my mother made—*those* were tacos. And as you may recall, Richie never liked food that dripped, so I'm not sure about your send-off argument."

"Yeah, that *was* kinda weird." Jake ponders the quirk, then shrugs, bites into his own taco again with gusto. Javi cringes as Jake continues talking with his mouth full. "You're the one who wanted to meet over lunch."

"It's just . . . I've got a little problem with my office," Javi confesses.

Javi's unintended second career is as a private investigator. Jake's been to his office, which is below second-rate, but Javi's work as a PI is first-rate, which is what Jake needs. Jake squints a question mark, still chewing, and Javi reluctantly explains: "It was demolished."

Jake stops chewing. "You wanna elaborate?"

"Place was red-tagged a year ago. I pulled the sign off the door and they seemed to forget about it. Until last week."

"I believe they call that squatting, my friend. Might be a Class Three misdemeanor."

"I kept up the place; I even paid back taxes. I'd argue adverse possession."

"The judge would laugh you out of the courtroom. *After* finding you guilty."

"You think they have the time for that? Besides, when you've been disbarred, you don't have to worry about laws so much. The ethical lines for investigators are a little more . . . fungible."

"See, that's what I love about you—a PI who uses the word 'fungible.'"

"You want to know what I love about *you*? In the last year—honestly, very little."

"Ouch."

"I could only watch your downfall for so long."

"I would've thought it would make you feel comparatively better."

"No, Jake. I don't wish for my friends to tank their lives. Which is why I tried to help. But you stopped returning my calls, stopped answering the door, and God forbid you ever reached out to ask how *I* was doing."

"Wow. I feel like I'm on *Dr. Phil*."

"You think you're amusing. I'd like to disabuse you of that notion."

"I'm sorry. Really. I'm having a bad year."

"I'm having a bad life—I didn't blow *you* off."

Jake has often wondered how Javi's career would have gone if he'd been Norman West's son. Or how Jake's would have gone if he was in Javi's shoes. Back at Berkeley, one thing was clear: Javi was the smartest law student in their year. Rich probably worked the hardest—he wasn't as naturally gifted as Javi but fought his way into the top ten. Jake might've been in the top half. Maybe. But everyone liked him, and not just because he bought most of the pitchers at Kip's or planned excursions to out-of-the-way clubs in the farthest reaches of Oakland and across the Bay. Jake was simply fun to be around back then. And the people he chose to be around the most were Javi and Rich.

When they graduated, Jake and Javi both had plans to do the right thing. Jake gave up on that when he got married and took his father's employment offer. Javi didn't—he kept trying the right cases for the right people, working the system. But over time, he began to see there was a problem with his plan—the system was broken. And instead of doing the right things for the right people, he did a few wrong things to help the right people. Then a few more wrong things, knowing that in the grander scheme—in the view of God, if you believe in such things, which Javi does—his wrong things were right. He told himself that. He made convincing legal arguments and chose to believe them.

But here's what Javi forgot along the way: enough wrong things would, of course, catch up with you. Once they did, once he got disbarred, he couldn't even do the right things anymore. And while Jake tried to throw him a little PI work, Norman didn't like it. Maybe because he could read that Javi instinctively knew Norman was one of the wrong people. So Jake couldn't bring his friend into the firm more than sporadically, and once Jake got into his own trouble, he just stopped trying. He stopped trying to do the right thing for the one person who would have done right by him. Who would have done anything for him.

"I've been an asshole the last year," Jake admits.

"You've always been an asshole."

"I thought that was part of my charm, but let's concede you're correct. Let me make it up to you now. I have some work for you."

"I'm listening."

"You and me—we gotta find out who killed Richie."

Javi stares at Jake a long time. Jake doesn't like how it makes him feel.

"Don't we owe it to him?" Jake asks. Javi's response is to force himself to eat the tacos, trying to ignore this plea. "Really? Don't we, Javi?"

"Don't give me that crap. You're not doing this out of any kind of friendship. You're trying to clear your name."

"Can't it be both?"

"It could be, but we both know you're more self-serving than that."

Jake is stung. "Do you mean that? Or are you just paying me back?"

"Can't it be both?" Touché. But then Javi turns serious. "On a related note, I gotta ask—did you do it?"

Jake is waiting for the punch line. The *I'm just kidding.* It doesn't come.

"You don't really think I killed him." Jake says it as a statement, but it's a question.

"I don't *think* you did it, but is it beyond the realm of possibility?"

Jake sees no hostility in Javi's question. Shit. "Look, here's what I know. Richie was about to blow a case wide-open—by digging into the firm's top client." Javi is beyond skeptical. Jake tries to overcome this with the next piece of evidence. "Reagan Hearst." Jake delivers the name like a verdict. A condemnation.

Javi just shakes his head, and Jake can see this is going south fast. "I get what you're thinking, but this isn't *Harrison* again. Daria Barati sent Richie after a low-level criminal case. Why Richie, it doesn't make any sense—he's a numbers guy. A check-the-fine-print guy."

"Here's an idea—ask Daria."

"Really? You find that's effective? She's a hostile witness, Javi."

"What does your father say?"

"He wants me to keep my mouth shut, that much is clear. And now I know why—Reagan is his client." Javi takes a beat to process all this information. Jake decides to give him space. "While you digest that, I'm going to digest the rest of my lunch."

Jake digs into his tacos while Javi broods—over the ask, over the state of his life, and over the fact that an old friend is dead and quite possibly he could help do something about it, but it would require putting his faith in Jake. A dubious proposition.

"Christ, Jake, don't you have a better way to work out your daddy issues?"

Jake hears it in Javi's dig—he's coming around. He tries to close the deal. "Maybe I'll be wrong. Maybe I'll realize Dad has my best interests at heart—"

"This only ends badly."

"Javi—where's the challenge if it's not a losing battle?"

"You're gonna throw my own words in my face?"

"Someone just did that to me. Turns out it works pretty well." Jake can see Javi's still not completely swayed, so he reaches into his breast pocket and pulls out a check. "It's blank. Fill in a number—I really could use a friend right now."

It's a prop he had at the ready, and an effective one. Javi waits less than ten seconds before taking the check. He hates himself for doing it.

"What's the number?" Jake asks, not really caring.

"How much you think it's worth to get myself killed?"

7

One thing that makes renting an apartment in Los Angeles tough on newcomers to the city is that a building's exterior isn't a clear tell as to what you'll find inside. Sure, you can be pretty confident of what you're getting in Beverly Hills or Brentwood, but the exterior of an apartment in East Hollywood or Panorama City or South Central might have the same nice palm trees and grass and it doesn't mean you won't get shot out front some night. You don't get the real story until you're inside the gates. Part of it is the level of decay. Does the swimming pool have water, or is it an empty cement pit? Do the units have just wooden doors, or are there cast-iron outer doors necessitated by rampant internal crime?

Then there's the segregation. Some of that divide is by neighborhood, but even within neighborhoods there's internal segregation. There are Black apartments, Korean apartments, Vietnamese, Guatemalan, Salvadoran, and just plain dirt-poor white. A city of four million partitioned by race; a pattern followed the world over.

And it's why, standing outside the luxurious-sounding Kingsley Arms on the edges of Koreatown, Javi isn't sure what they'll find. Jake grabs the thick metal security door as two teens exit. From Jake's point of view—Hispanic. From Javi's—he's guessing Guatemalan. Either way, it represents an anomaly. Tiana is Black, and as they move farther into the property, there are no Black residents to be found.

Inside, the courtyard is LA run-down: once nice, but now there's rust everywhere, and the pool is indeed empty, the bottom blanketed with a thick layer of leaves and garbage. It's late afternoon, probably most residents are still at work, but some older Latinx women sit in plastic chairs by the pool, talking.

Off in another area, a few Latinx men smoke and drink beer. Jake and Javi get some sideways glances. Jake's race isn't as much the issue as his suit. Their concern about him is mitigated by Javi's presence, but only a little.

"Let me ask you a question," Javi says. "If I was white, you wouldn't have come to me, would you? It wasn't about avenging Richie—it was about the color of my skin."

"I am offended by your implication of my racism. But you do have amazing skin."

"Whatever. Your blank check pays for forgiveness."

"And it is weird, right?" Jake knows Javi will have made the same observation he did when he came by after the bar. The observation that made him think of calling Javi. "What was Tiana Walker doing living here?"

"Just stand here and try not to look like you're from Immigration."

Jake dutifully tries to appear nonthreatening as Javi speaks to the residents in Spanish—what he sees isn't encouraging. The women shake their heads. The men turn away without answering. Finally, one nods to an alcove, above which a fading sign reads M NAG R.

Javi walks over and knocks on the door. Nothing. Rings a bell. Rings again. Finally, an overweight man in his forties comes out—he looks to have been fast asleep. He eyes Javi distrustfully. Javi smiles, which often works for him, but not this time. Javi gestures toward Jake across the courtyard, who continues to try his best to appear harmless. It doesn't seem to work—the manager just shakes his head too, a firm no. They've hit a dead end.

When Javi was twelve, his father disappeared. Not as in it was a mystery or foul play, he'd just had enough and he was done. After he was gone two days, his mother took down any photos of him. They didn't talk about it, they just moved on to a cheaper apartment, followed by an even cheaper one. Over the years, there were ones like Tiana's—and many much worse.

Javi once tried to ask his mother what happened, but the moment he uttered the word "father," she slapped him. He was stunned—he'd never been hit before. His mother was equally stunned, and she broke down. Cried like he'd never heard before. He apologized, he was really, really sorry, it was all his fault. After that, they never spoke of the man again.

Following law school, when Javi had connections, he thought about searching for his father. But he ultimately decided that he didn't want to know what had become of him. His father had made a choice, and Javi did the same: he had no intention of allowing Roberto Alvarez to see that his son had made something of himself. He thought about it again briefly when he became a private investigator, when he realized how easy it would be to track him down, but at that point, Javi didn't want his father to see how far his son had fallen.

Being in this apartment complex brings back all he and his mother endured because that asshole walked away. It also dredges up how he feels about where he is in life now. This job—being the muscle, being the interpreter—is not how Javi saw his career going. He thought he'd be trying cases before the Supreme Court by now, or at the very least, state Supreme Court. He and Jake had dreamed of working with each other at one point, but not like this. He wishes he could've given Jake a flat no, but a blank-check retainer speaks volumes when you can barely pay the rent.

And Jake isn't entirely wrong about Rich. About owing their friend some sort of closure. It's also not lost on Javi why Jake needs this. Clearing his name to stay out of jail for a good chunk of his life, of course, but on a more personal note, Jake witnessed the horrific scene up close, their friend's blood and remains splattered all over him. Javi's seen enough murder scenes to know how gruesome it would've been. In truth, it's good that Jake was drinking at the time. Probably dulled his senses.

All of this tells Javi one thing: For Jake, for Rich, and for his own peace of mind—this can't be a dead end.

Javi's plan to plow through the dead end requires that fungibility with the law he'd championed earlier. So they wait until it's dark, until the courtyard of the

Kingsley Arms is empty, then move quickly and quietly toward the door of a ground-floor unit. Despite the fact that this is Javi's idea, he has misgivings, which is why he made sure Jake came along. If he goes down, Jake has to have a vested interest in fixing the problem.

"To be clear, if I get busted for picking this lock, you are repping me pro bono."

"Represent yourself. You always said you were a better lawyer than I am."

"I always was."

As Jake keeps watch, bullshit story at the ready, Javi digs in to take care of the lock. It's a cheap one, meaning easy entry.

The apartment is empty. According to the manager, it's unrentable, even six months after the fire. Word that two kids died in this place makes it *mala suerte*—bad luck. New rugs have been installed and the place has been repainted—both necessitated by the fire—but the carpeting is probably thirdhand and the paint job is sloppy. The whole apartment feels rickety and cheap, but Jake can't help but feel the waste of its emptiness.

He moves into the main room, trying to digest the geography of the apartment, to assess Tiana's story, see how it lines up with the arson report and whether he can find anything buried beneath the new layers of paint and carpet that could help validate her claims of innocence.

Jake hears a *whoosh* of air just soon enough to turn as a baseball bat is swung full speed at his head. He half blocks it but goes down hard, his hand throbbing from the glancing blow. He stares up at the angry eyes of an athletic Guatemalan man, maybe around thirty, who is breathing hard and spitting mad.

It's amazing how quickly Jake's halting Spanish comes out to fend off the next blow. "*¡Soy amigo de Tiana, ella solía vivir aquí!*"

The attacker pauses, evaluating Jake's claim.

"Look at you with your Spanish," Javi says, stepping out of the darkness, trying to show his presence and lighten the moment for whoever this angry man is.

"I'm a defense attorney in LA. It's required," Jake quips from the floor, also trying to keep the attacker from swinging again.

The man doesn't put the bat down. "Why are you asking questions about Tiana?" he says in clear English.

"I'm her lawyer." Jake tries to sound both authoritative and sympathetic, but it's hard to do that from a prone position.

The man glances to Javi, who nods reassuringly. "He's on the level, my friend. We're just trying to help her." Javi seems genuine, so the man lowers the bat.

"You got a pretty mean swing there. Who are you?" Javi asks.

"David." The stranger pronounces it as "Da-veed," followed by the explanation: "Jacinta's brother."

Jake starts to pull himself up. "Who's Jacinta?"

David slams the bat down right next to Jake, who flinches and falls back to the floor.

"You are *not* Tiana's lawyer!"

As David glares at Jake with suspicion, Javi makes his move. He grabs the bat and in a split second is behind David with the makeshift weapon pulled tight against his throat. Jake picks himself up again, then nods to Javi, who releases the attacker.

"I get your distrust," Jake says, trying to calm the man. "And I can see you care about Tiana. But let me ask you this: Is anyone else coming around to help?" The lack of response is all Jake needs to confirm his suspicion. "So talk to me. I get you think I should know who your sister is, but I've only met Tiana once. And I'll be honest, I don't think she's a fan. Yet. But at this point, I'm all she's got."

All the fight gone out of him, David plops on the floor in defeat, where Jake and Javi now see he's been sitting with a Solo cup and a bottle of something wrapped in a brown paper bag. Perhaps this is his private mausoleum.

"This was Jacinta's place. She let Tiana stay here."

Jake crouches down to work the situation. "David. I need to talk to anyone who was around the night of the fire. Where can I find your sister now?"

David meets Jake's eyes—for a fraction of an alcohol-infused moment, he had allowed himself to feel hope that these two strangers might actually do something about his sister. About Tiana. That someone other than him might still care. But asking to talk to his sister speaks volumes—they *know* nothing, which means they can *do* nothing.

"You really are a shit lawyer, aren't you? Do you know *anything* about this case?"

Javi tries to mediate once again. "Maybe we'll know more if we talk to your sister."

"That'll be hard. My sister was murdered. Just before the fire."

Javi looks to Jake—shouldn't he have known this? Yes, he should have, Jake thinks. *Why the fuck isn't this in the file?!*

8

There are two great things about Starbucks, aside from the coffee. The first is that wherever you are, there's a location just minutes away—at least that's true in Los Angeles. Jake remembers a trip to Boston with his kids, back when he had a family. They were a mere twenty minutes outside the city when Chloe had to have a Pumpkin Spice Latte. Had to have, meaning if they didn't get it, she was going to become unbearable, so Cara pulled out her phone and typed *Starbucks* into the search bar, and the closest one to come up was 16.7 miles away. Chloe was horrified. "I could never live here," she'd declared.

The second thing that's great about Starbucks is the reliable and free Wi-Fi. Which is why Jake finds himself sipping a Caffè Americano and watching Javi type on his laptop. It's the next best thing to an office for Javi since the whole red-tag problem.

Before they left the Kingsley Arms, they'd managed to glean some key details from David, last name Castillo. His sister, Jacinta, was killed less than two weeks before the fire that killed Tiana Walker's children. She was stabbed to death while walking to Paris Baguette to get slices of cake for Tiana's three kids—slices because they each had a favorite flavor and they couldn't agree on one cake.

She was found in an alley behind the chain bakery's strip mall. No one had seen anything. No suspects and no leads, and as far as David knew, no ongoing investigation. Her purse was stolen, but there wouldn't have been much in it, and anyone in their right mind would have known that. But Jake knew there were far too many people not in their right minds for one reason or another, so acts like this were all too common around LA. This wasn't unusual—just another random, senseless crime.

Unless it wasn't. That's what Jake and Javi are digging into as they lubricate their systems with corporate but damn fine java, looking for anything that might link the murder of Jacinta Castillo to the arson that killed two of Tiana Walker's kids. It may be a wild-goose chase, but the fact that there's nothing in the Tiana Walker file about her dead friend with whom she and her kids lived is a waving red flag. One friend murdered, the other nearly dies in a suspicious fire? It might be coincidence, but it's something any investigation should have covered. At least considered and dismissed. Its absence raises the question—did someone not want a connection made between them?

Jake is enjoying his coffee, enjoying being on the hunt, and enjoying watching Javi work. While Javi likes to bemoan his fall from grace, Jake has spent the last twenty minutes witnessing something impressive: his friend has become damn good at his new vocation. He's got the case number of the murder, the investigating officer, forensics on the knife wounds. None of which, at first glance, will help Jake build a case. But before Javi finishes his venti dark roast—they're brewing Gaia, which is always a bonus—he finds something that makes him stop typing, questioning the bounty his search just produced.

Jake watches him stare. "Is this a performance meant to provoke me to ask a leading question, or did you just find the map to the Holy Grail?" he asks.

"I might want to give back that retainer," is Javi's cryptic answer.

He spins the computer around to show Jake what he's found. It's an electronic image of a check made out to Jacinta Castillo for $880. Nothing all that odd about that, until Jake sees who the check is from: the personal account of Thompson & West's top client, the inimitable Reagan Hearst.

"What the fuck is it for?" Jake asks.

"Eight hundred and eighty dollars. Every week." Javi's in Jacinta's bank records, and he's showing Jake the deposits column. "My math suggests that's twenty-two dollars an hour, forty hours a week."

"For doing what?"

"Best guess?" Javi hits a few keys, then spins the screen back to Jake again.

It's a photo of what seems like a perfect family. Reagan Hearst—dark hair, no gray, expensive casual clothes, serious expression. Stephanie Hearst—blond, was probably gorgeous before going for the Beverly Hills special: overly botoxed lips and makeup in such excess that it makes you look like an AI-created avatar. Standing between them, eight-year-old Jane. A cute kid dressed too sophisticated for her age, with a lost look behind her eyes. The three are clad not in matching outfits, but in complementary colors, as if the photo had a costume designer. It probably did.

"The daughter," Jake notes. "Reagan's wife died about a year ago—Jacinta was probably the kid's nanny or caregiver, or whatever they might call it."

"David said she loved kids."

"This is it, Javi. This is the connection. This must be what Richie found."

Jake is excited. He feels alive. He feels alive and sober, which isn't a combination he's been all too familiar with in recent months.

"Slow your roll, Junior," Javi cautions. "It's a tenuous connection, it isn't evidence."

"It's enough," Jake argues. "All I need is one end of the thread. If I pull in the right direction, the whole tapestry will crumble."

"Okay, Mr. Mixed Metaphor, where are you gonna pull?"

"You cut the snake off at the head," Jake suggests. "I pay Norman West a visit. If he hasn't changed the keypad code."

Javi stares back without making any facial expression. He's sure Jake will get his point without him actually having to say a word.

"You're right, we don't want to tip him off that we're sniffing around Hearst's connection to two murder cases."

"Jake. You're overstating what we have here."

"Whatever. I'd love to pin Gibson to the wall, but it's the same problem."

"Yeah, I don't think the managing partner who told you not to take the case is likely to give us anything useful."

Jake ponders the best game plan a moment longer. His eyes fall on the chalk menu board where they write the daily special coffees. At the top, a slogan: START YOUR DAY HERE! It gives him an idea. Go back to where the case started.

It's almost ten p.m., but Daria Barati is diligently banking client hours at her desk when Jake barges in, furious.

"I just have one question: Was Richie supposed to win—or make it all go away?"

She takes a moment before responding, a moment that gives her clarity—lying will only forestall things. So she makes a rash decision to try the truth.

"Why don't you sit down, Jake?"

He doesn't. So Daria comes around her desk and moves to the plush armchair. She likes this chair—she picked it out herself. It has the perfect combination of soft fabric and firm backing, but that's not why she chooses it now. She chooses it to leave Jake two options: either take the upholstered Art Deco couch with the diamond tufting, usually reserved for clients, or continue to stand. She thinks he'll be forced to the couch, which is a good three inches lower than the chair, and that should improve the power dynamics for what follows.

Jake goes for door number three. He sits on the edge of her mahogany desk. Waiting her out. Okay, then.

"I was trying a case in front of Merrin," she begins. "My case was next up, so I was in the room when Tiana Walker's public defender no-showed. Merrin asked me to sub in, but I was booked. That should have been that. But there was something . . ."

"Something like *what*?" Jake pushes, annoyed by her meandering tone.

"Something about *her*. The idea of her killing her own kids, it didn't seem right. She was gonna end up with some shit overworked public defender, so I mentioned it to Rich—"

"Yeah. Because pro bono was really his forte."

"Jake—"

"Your story is either bullshit or merely obfuscating the truth."

"I know you're angry. And you have a right to be. But you don't have to treat me like a hostile witness—we're on the same team."

"No. You're on Reagan Hearst's team."

Like any good lawyer in the courtroom, Jake knows the most telling reactions come when you take a left turn in the conversation and spring an unexpected question on a witness. Here, Daria seems truly confused—whether it's real or performance, Jake's not sure.

"You really want me to believe you didn't know one of our biggest clients is involved in Tiana Walker's case?"

"What are you talking about?"

"Tiana Walker—her roommate, one Jacinta Castillo, worked for Reagan Hearst. Until she was murdered."

Daria is not a good enough actress to fake the level of bewilderment registering on her face now. "I don't understand what you're getting at. More to the point, what does that have to do with anything?"

That, for Jake, is the question he needs answered. That answer is what could save Tiana Walker. Maybe himself as well. But Daria isn't answering questions, she's asking them, so he tries again.

"This case you say you wanted Richie to help on. Tiana Walker and her kids lived with a woman named Jacinta Castillo. Jacinta was murdered—a crime that's still unsolved—two weeks before the fire."

"Doesn't that go to Tiana's state of mind? Why she was drunk out of her head and set that fire? I think you're putting together evidence to convict, not help her."

Jake takes a moment to digest that. He is, indeed, treading on dangerous ground.

"You have a point, I concede that. But here's the thing, Daria. I don't believe in coincidence. I'm pretty sure you don't either."

Daria studies Jake, wondering if he's been drinking. That would certainly explain this sudden paranoia. He doesn't seem drunk, but she's not sure how often a functional alcoholic can pass for sober. Lord knows Jake's tolerance must be astronomical if all the stories about him are true. Either way, he's making extraordinary leaps.

"One day in and you're back to paranoia and conspiracy theories? You really want to replay the *Harrison* case?"

Jake doesn't answer. He's come to the conclusion that all of this is news to her, that pulling the thread here won't pay dividends. That said, his gut says she's hiding *something.*

"You know the definition of paranoia, Daria? Excessive suspicion and mistrust of others. I have that. No doubt. But it doesn't mean I'm wrong."

Jake feels that line is a good punctuation, so he starts to leave. But like all good lawyers, Daria wants to get in the final word.

"You were wrong the last time, Jake. Maybe you want to learn from your mistakes."

While Jake would like to dismiss her parting shot, there are more similarities between what's going on here and the *Harrison* case than Jake would like to admit.

The case of *Guadalupe v. Harrison* was Jake's crucible. It could just as easily have been called *David v. Goliath.* And the particular problem it created in Jake's world was that Harrison Foods was one of Norman West's top clients. But when Jake met Ramon Guadalupe—whose wife was one of seventeen illegal immigrants who died in a fire at a corporate packing plant—he couldn't resist. Admittedly, the fact that he'd be taking on his father's client was half the attraction when the case started, but then he began to truly believe in the cause. The firm didn't want the case, of course, but Jake wouldn't budge. He'd made a commitment, and he argued it would look bad for Harrison not to allow the families of their dead employees proper representation. And since Harrison claimed it was a tragic accident and they were willing to pay out damages, where was the harm?

So they set up a Chinese Wall. Jake understood that by today's cultural standards, they should generically call it an "ethical wall," but he didn't feel the term was racist. He thought it an apt metaphor—like Chinese silk screen walls that weren't solid structures but created distinct separation. A way to ensure that no information on either side of the case was accessible by the other, though they were both on the firm's servers.

With those guardrails in place, Jake took the case and began to dig. What started to emerge was something almost unthinkable. Harrison Foods was in financial trouble. And it turned out their packing plant was vastly over-insured. Then "tragedy" struck; there was an employee bar stocked with alcohol that somehow ignited. Their experts' best guess was a spark from a faulty heater jumped to some spilled alcohol; it ignited and the flames carried to the bar, where bottle after bottle was consumed in a conflagration that became uncontainable. Tragic accident—maybe. But as more revelations came to light, Jake became convinced the fire wasn't an accident. It was arson, set exactly where it would connect with the alcohol and cover the intent: to collect on that big insurance policy and keep the company afloat.

It was a good plan. Rather—it would have been a good plan, but somehow the fact that the plant was behind schedule and crews were working through the night was lost on whoever's job it was to set that fire. So along with the overinsured structure, seventeen lives went up in flames. Countless other lives were destroyed. Most notably to Jake—Ramon Guadalupe's.

Filled with the bravado of alcohol and the fervent belief that his firm was perpetrating a cover-up, Jake did the unthinkable—he breached the Chinese Wall. He was going to find the smoking gun; he couldn't let the murder of seventeen people go unpunished. It particularly irked him that Harrison seemed to think they could get away with this because the victims were "illegals." As if that made their value intrinsically less.

Climbing over that wall, Jake was rewarded. His deep dive into his firm's vast trove of Harrison documents paid incredibly large dividends. The hunt turned up buried treasure—a smoking gun document literally too good to be true. But Jake was so obsessed he didn't see that. What he saw was a confidential memo from the head of the company to his right-hand man. *Out of the ashes will rise a better company.* Its implication was clear: set the fire. But when he sprung it on CEO Edgar Harrison himself in open court, Jake was so blind with outrage that he didn't see he'd walked into a trap.

Norman let him have it—the document was fake. A shiny object it turned out Stephen Gibson had concocted to test the efficacy of the Chinese Wall. A sidebar was called, the parties brought to chambers. Jake argued that the fake memo itself was a breach of faith, but the judge wasn't buying that. It was a document buried in files that were not part of discovery, and it would have been immaterial had there been no breach. But there *was* a breach, a serious one, and there were to be consequences. Jake could have lost his license if his father hadn't intervened. Instead, Jake was censured, and his clients had to settle the case. They were paid generously for the "accident," but not the true value of their loss.

It wasn't the censure that drove Jake deeper into the abyss. It wasn't losing. It was having failed Ramon Guadalupe. Because despite having fallen into the trap, Jake remained convinced that Harrison—and his own father's firm—had covered up murder. But when he raged on that point in a subsequent staff meeting, having consumed more Uncle Nearest 1856 Premium Aged Whiskey than he could keep track of, he sounded batshit paranoid like Mel Gibson in *Conspiracy Theory* crazy. Never mind that Mel had been right.

When he was sober again and could see his mistake, Jake still couldn't shake the feeling that his firm had dark secrets. Why else would they go to such lengths to conceal them? It can't have been just to set Jake up—horrible as his father is, he wouldn't have sanctioned that without a strong motive.

Now Jake finds himself in the middle of another case that casts an unwelcome spotlight on Thompson & West. Every pore of his body is screaming that there is a smoking gun to be found. But he has to give a competing thought its due: Is his hatred of his father skewing his view? Is he searching for a connection not to help Tiana but to redeem himself? In the eyes of Cara, or Rich, or Ramon Guadalupe, or his children? Is he fighting the good fight, or just trying to prove to the Irish detective she's wrong about him?

Richard Allen Kaplan—Partner. Jake can't take his eyes off the frosted vinyl lettering that marks the office he's been in hundreds of times, the office he drank in hundreds of times, the office he's *been* drunk in hundreds of times.

It's a place he went to vent and celebrate and mourn and hide. And Rich, for all of his faults, would listen. He would drop whatever he was doing and be there for Jake.

Jake wills himself to step inside the darkened office. He flips on the lights—not bright white, but the more amber bulbs Norman feels convey weight and importance. The fact that it also keeps things from coming to light is an apt metaphor not lost on Jake.

The first thing that hits him now is the overpowering fragrance of the condolence bouquets. Just three, which makes it sad, though what makes it more so is that the firm has placed the flowers in the one space where no one will see them. Likely to be tossed in the garbage tomorrow.

On the walls are framed photos. Rich staring back at Jake from different life milestones. Jake goes to his favorite: in black robes with purple sashes and mortarboards, there stand Javi, Rich, and Jake—exuberant, goofy, happy. Better times. Now—one disbarred, one murdered, and the third the prime suspect in said murder, hanging on to his career and personal life by a tiny thread. Jake feels a deep sense of grief. Of loss. Then another thought hits him—he's standing in the office of the person who his wife cheated with. The office of the friend who watched him fall and then stepped into the void, whatever the excuses were. But Jake finds it hard to sustain anger for a dead man. A dead friend. And he's sure, if he thinks on it hard enough, he'll come to realize what they did was really his own fault.

Jake turns his attention to the black onyx desk, wondering if it holds some clue to what Rich found. But if he'd been so worried that he wanted Grace to meet him *outside* the office, if Tiana's file had already been stripped of any mention of Jacinta Castillo or Reagan Hearst in an attempt to bury what he'd found, Rich wouldn't have left a telltale clue here, either. He was too careful. Though as Jake thinks about it, if he'd *really* been careful, he might not be dead.

So how can Jake find what Rich discovered? If he wanted Reagan Hearst's billing information, and information on attorney/client privilege, Jake can think of only one reason. Whatever he found that would exonerate Tiana had to do with the firm's top client. And if he was going to expose it, he had to know exactly what it would cost the firm. Jake is aware this is circumstantial evidence, that him wanting it to be a smoking gun doesn't make it so. But deep down, a very sober, reasonable part of him feels the truth of it. Now, he just has to prove it. Prove what he has come to believe: that Rich Kaplan knew he was starting a war. He just didn't realize he was outflanked.

As his eyes scan the neat desk offering no clues, Jake can't help but smile at the clock. It's an old-fashioned job, with numbers and two hands, only the numbers are all in the wrong places. On the bottom it simply says: *Time Becomes Meaningless in the Face of Creativity.* It was something Richie said once, drunk or stoned off his ass, and it was so anti-everything that Thompson & West stood for that Jake couldn't resist this as a gift. And Rich, out of character, kept it here. A small act of defiance. But taking it in, Jake has a belated epiphany. While the hands point to a four and a seven, the positions indicate it's 10:15. Shit.

He grabs for his cell phone—the ringer is off and there are a string of missed calls and texts. From "Wife," a designation he has no current intention of changing. But the messages are an escalating stream of anger: *You coming? You at a bar? Where the fuck are you? Nice job with this whole co-parenting thing.* He's forgotten his time with the kids. Again. He's lied to Aaron. Again. Which makes no sense—he wants to reconcile, he loves Cara, he loves his kids, so what the fuck is his problem that he can't do the bare minimum to prove that? Something to talk about with his therapist. Not that he ever intends to go back to his therapist, his weekly chance to speak out loud all he knows is wrong with himself. He doesn't need a sounding board to decipher how and why he is broken. He knows. He just can't seem to fix himself.

He also knows with absolute certainty he has to go to what used to be his home. Immediately. He has to face the wrath for his transgressions, and try, somehow, to make things right.

9

The dimly lit parking garage still has enough cars in it to show that Thompson & West lawyers aren't full of shit when they bill eighteen to twenty hours a day. Why doctors and lawyers have to prove their mettle working themselves near to death, and why both professions remain coveted, is a mystery to Jake. At least law clients won't die if your sleep-deprived brain makes a mistake. You might lose everything, but probably not your life—death penalty cases aside.

Jake heads for his car, pondering that as he tosses his keys in the air. Distracted, he misses, and the keys clank on the slick pavement. He stops . . . and hears the echo of a footstep. Not his own—someone else is here. Someone who stopped one step after Jake did.

He looks around—sees nothing. He shrugs it off, grabs the keys, and resumes walking. Alert now, he thinks he hears the footsteps again, so he stops on a dime. Again, the echo of another footstep a moment after he stops. Shit. Mel Gibson paranoia be damned, there's someone following him.

His Genesis G80 is just up ahead. He hits his key fob—*beep beep*. It unlocks as he turns and sprints in the other direction toward a green glowing EXIT sign. But he doesn't run straight for it, he works his way between parked cars and cement barriers, ridiculous behavior if he's wrong, but all he can think of are Tubi reruns of *The Rockford Files,* where Jim Rockford had to dodge trouble he's walked himself into.

Not ridiculous—Jake hears those footsteps now giving chase. He sees a shadow on the far wall, but he was never good enough at physics to make the quick calculation of light and angle to figure out where his pursuer actually is.

Ducking behind a wall some twenty feet from the exit, Jake looks back, but he sees nothing, no movement—until a flashlight beam sweeps the garage. An eerie visual echo of the flashlight at the car window when Rich was killed. The light settles on the exit door Jake wants to use. He thinks for a few seconds, then hurls the car keys in the opposite direction. As they clatter to the ground, the beam tries to place them, at which point Jake bolts, hits the exit door at full speed, and plows into a stairwell.

Jake sprints up the stairs, two and three at a time. He reaches a landing, glances down. Below there's a shadow . . . and that flashlight beam again. He runs, not looking back.

He sees a door at the top, bursts through, and feels the cool night air of Constellation Boulevard. Nicely landscaped, but very quiet since construction across the street has rendered the block impassable to cars. Breathing hard, Jake scans right and left—which way is safest? Fuck it—he chooses dead ahead and sprints into the morass of construction. As he hits the fencing, he looks back across the street, and sees a figure in the shadows. Just standing there, but facing his direction. He's too far to make out who it is, and he has no intention of getting a closer look. Jake ducks through a break in the fencing and disappears into the construction site.

Jake's intent to face his family's wrath hits a second roadblock a half hour later. Going back for his car seemed a bad idea, but it had occurred to him that Century City's only a twenty-minute walk from his old house. As that classic eighties song declared, nobody walks in LA, but extraordinary circumstances call for extraordinary measures. He actually makes it to the house in sixteen minutes, which, added to the ten minutes of hiding and panic in the construction site, means he made good time. But now he's been standing out front for another five. Brooding. Not about the fact that someone wants to kill him, not about the dual travesty of Rich's murder and Jake being labeled a suspect, not even about Tiana Walker and the fact that it's becoming increasingly clear she may be sitting in jail for something she didn't do. Instead, he's brooding about the FOR SALE sign on the front lawn. Because more than Cara kicking him out, more than having to schedule time to see his own kids, this—the wooden cross hammered into the edge of the flowerbed they spent hours planning with the landscape architect—is the thing that makes him realize how deeply he's screwed up.

He remembers the first time he saw the two-story house. He and Cara were in Santa Barbara, a weekend away at Bacara, something they'd planned forever but kept putting off. They were both in thick white waffle terry cloth robes, sipping coffee, debating whether to go out to the pool or take the robes off and climb back in bed, when her phone dinged. A text. A photo of the front of this very house—minus the current landscaping—with a note from Cara's best friend. It was going on the market tomorrow; if they wanted to make a preemptive offer, they had to see it today.

Jake's first instinct had been to say forget it. Getting this time away had taken too long. Then Cara showed him the photo. Window boxes with flowers. Dark green painted faux shutters offsetting the windows. A flower bed in front. But more than all of that, it was the look on Cara's face. Through her eyes, he saw it was everything they wanted.

They made the drive back to LA in eighty-four minutes; the old couple who'd lived there for forty years showed them around and Jake had made the offer by four-thirty. Never mind the chimney work they discovered would cost a fortune, or the roof that needed replacing, or the outdated electrical wiring. It was perfect.

At least, it *had* been perfect. It had been perfect when they moved in, when he ceremoniously carried Cara over the threshold. Perfect when he carried Chloe into the house in her car seat for the first time. It was a perfect place to toss a baseball with Chloe, then with Aaron, working to get them to cock the arm at the elbow, to break the wrist on release. All the things his father never did for him, he was gonna do. Things he *did*—for a while.

Now all that's gone, and it's his fault. He was consulted about the house going on the market, he's even seen the sign. But tonight, with everything that's happened, it hits him anew. It makes him crave a drink to help him ignore the pain, and to withstand the earned rebuke he's sure is coming. But taking his medicine sober is what he deserves.

A pissed-off teenager opens the door. Chloe, who once leaped into his arms when he got home, stares daggers at him. Daggers with serrated edges to cause maximum pain.

"I screwed up," is Jake's opening.

"What else is new." She's her mother's daughter, that's for sure.

"I wanted to be here, Chloe—"

"Were you drinking or working?"

Wow. That stings, coming from your kid. He's got to change the playing field here.

"Chloe, let me—"

"What? You gonna buy me a puppy again? You think I'm five and that's gonna make up for you not being here?" She's blocking his entry and has no intention of ceding the high ground. "You're too late. I'm going to bed—I have school tomorrow. Some of us try to keep to our commitments."

Having delivered her strong closing, she walks away. Jake starts to follow, but Cara intercepts him. "Let her go."

Jake watches his firstborn disappear up the stairs. "She's right to be mad," he acknowledges.

"Aaron wouldn't even say good night to me. He was so pissed at you that he wouldn't say good night to me."

Jake sees her searching his face, trying to locate the man she once loved. He doesn't think she's finding him.

"Someone tried to kill me."

Her eyes wrinkle at the corners, trying to process that. There's a momentary flash of concern before her eyes become hardened and set. "Is that the new 'the dog ate my homework'?"

Hard to blame her for that. Jake doesn't argue or attempt to defend himself further. But she sees something in his face. And she can't help herself; she softens. "Seriously? Did that really happen?"

"I don't know," he sighs, opting for honesty. He slumps against the entry wall. "I went back to work. To find out who killed Rich. I started asking questions—"

"Questions about what?"

"It's . . . complicated."

He lost her with that one. He scrambles to get back to some semblance of sympathy. "Someone followed me, chased me. And no, that's not me being paranoid—it happened. I think they don't want me digging into what happened to Richie."

Cara is trying to parse how much is real, how much is Jake going down a rabbit hole.

"I realize how it sounds—"

"Then don't." She sees he's confused about her meaning. She clarifies, emphatically. "Don't dig into it."

That surprises Jake. "You don't want to know why he got killed?"

"You think it helps me or the kids if *you* get killed?"

He's almost touched by that, by her concern. Until he realizes she's probably just being practical. God, he wants to hold her. To be held by her. To go back in time.

"I think it helps everyone if they believe it wasn't me," he says softly.

She must see the truth in that, because she doesn't pursue the point. They just stand there, a mile apart. Jake hates this feeling. "You really want to sell? You loved this house."

"I loved you. I figure if I can get over that . . ."

He wonders if she truly is over that. Over him. He wants to figure out how to bridge the gulf, but she cuts off anything further. "Good night, Jake. Be careful."

She closes the door slowly, but without hesitation.

As Jake starts the long walk back to find his keys and collect his car, he wonders how much of the sting of her words some Clase Azul Reposado will dissipate. Truthfully, he'll probably have to settle for Jose Cuervo. He isn't as flush with cash as he once was.

An hour later, Jake's still thinking about that drink, because he didn't get to a bar. He didn't get to his car, either. Instead, he's sitting on a swing set at Holmby Park, a place he once took his kids. During the day it's filled with people and dogs and nannies and their charges and old men lawn bowling—or playing bocce? Jake has never figured out how to tell which is which. But now he's cold and alone, trying to train his mind not to fixate on alcohol.

"Why am I here?"

Grace stands over him, and seeing that she came, that he's no longer alone, Jake feels better. He tries a playful answer to her question.

"Because you wouldn't meet me at a bar."

She's unamused, so he changes tacks, tries a drop of honesty—at least as far as he's aware it's honest. "I need someone who believes in me."

Grace finds this both heartening and maddening. "I'm not the thing to tide you over 'til your wife takes you back."

"She's not taking me back."

That's not the response Grace was hoping for. "So I'm the backup plan? Fuck you."

Her eyes don't leave his, and this time it's him who looks away. She's right to be angry. She's been right about their relationship from the get-go.

He'd like to blame it all on the *Harrison* case, but it would be too easy to tell himself the story that everything was fine until that pivotal moment in his life. The truth is, his dissatisfaction with his work, with his firm, and even with his marriage had already started to creep in. A more evolved person who gave himself over to therapy might have made the leap that if he was finding fault with so many parts of his life, perhaps he should look at the common denominator—himself. But Jake wasn't one for deep introspection, so he buried his growing malaise with alcohol and work. And sure enough, *Harrison* came along, and suddenly he was inspired again. Maybe even happy again.

It should have been a good thing, but for Cara it certainly wasn't. Jake was gone more, he was obsessed—she might say self-obsessed. And he started drinking all the time, which he thought made him a better version of himself, but that's not the way she saw it. In her eyes, he saw not just judgment, but unhappiness. Maybe it wasn't all about him, but it felt that way.

On the other hand, Grace saw what he saw in the case, and was willing to put in as many hours as needed. She did everything Jake asked, found things he would never have thought to look for. She dug into other cases involving Harrison—using only outside sources, nothing that breached the Chinese Wall—and found patterns and hints of patterns that were gold. Edgar Harrison had wanted to take his company public but decided at the last minute not to. Why? Because beneath the surface there were financial woes. If that were to be uncovered, it would hurt their brand.

Jake and Grace worked late, they planned, they strategized, they drank. And one night, in the heat of a case breakthrough, he doesn't remember which one, Jake blurted out, "I could kiss you." And they both froze. And maybe if he hadn't had close to half a bottle by then he would have laughed it off, made a joke, and let it go. But the alcohol lowered his inhibitions, and he kissed her. And it shook him. He hadn't felt something like that in years.

Despite the fact that she felt it too, she stopped it cold. He knew it was wrong, apologized—profusely—and offered to report himself to HR. He owned up to the fact that he was her supervisor and it violated so many tenets: company policy as well as California employment law and federal civil rights law. She just laughed at him. Said that made her want to kiss him again. She in turn admitted that she'd wanted it in the moment, and she wasn't sorry, but that was it. It was one and done. Not because he was her boss, but because he was married. That meant something to her.

"I shouldn't have called. But I know you care about what happened to Richie."

Grace takes a seat on the swing next to his. Kicks her feet for a little sway; the back-and-forth motion soothes her like it did when she was six and her father left her waiting all day when he was supposed to pick her up and take her to the park. Jake lets her settle in, waits for her to be ready. Finally, her feet brake her swinging and she voices her fear.

"Maybe I just got scared. Maybe his murder has nothing to do with the firm. Sometimes bad shit just happens."

"If you're gonna be a good lawyer, you're gonna have to do a better job selling facts that you don't believe. You have to lie with conviction."

Watching her react to the truth she doesn't want to admit, Jake feels bad. She's young—the swing set they're on makes that all the more apparent—and this has nothing to do with her. He should keep her out of it. He's putting Grace in jeopardy by relying on her, but here she is. And he needs her, so he forges ahead with the thing he shouldn't say.

"I found a connection. To Reagan Hearst." She closes her eyes. The train has left the station. Jake's next words confirm that. "I realize you're scared. Rightly so. But I can't settle the *Walker* case. I can't let this go."

She sees there's no changing his mind. "I get that. I do. But I can't help you."

He doesn't argue. He just asks: "So why *did* you come?"

She takes a moment to really think about that. A moment of self-reflection. She knows the answer, but offers only a half-truth. "Because I have a blind spot when it comes to you. Because I hoped you were going to tell me you'd figured it out and it's all over."

Jake sees through her obfuscation. And while he should just accept it and let her go, he doesn't. "No. You came because you know I'm right. You know what has to be done. And you know I'll do it better if I have your help."

"Maybe you're right about all of that. But even if you *are*—I'm not gonna help you dig your own grave. I can't."

She gets off the swing, eyes him for a sad moment, and leaves without another word. This time he lets her go. It's what she needs to do. Now he can do what he needs to do without condemnation.

Which is how Jake finds himself holding a glass filled with clear Patrón Silver. He lost his last test of sobriety with the Knob Creek, so he doesn't want to repeat that. Seeing as tequila has been on his mind, he figured that was the better test, but he realized it wouldn't really be a test with Cuervo. No, if he intends to tempt his impulse control, Patrón is the way to go.

He takes in his apartment and wonders how a place can be both sleek and depressing. The high-rise on Century Park East had seemed like a good idea when Jake moved out—close to the office if he ever decided to go back, a pool and a gym, making it feel almost like he was on vacation, not kicked out of his home. And it came with a modicum of furniture. But all of it is fake. Nice enough, but not like real life. The worst part is what it says about him. It says he's a middle-aged cliché, thrown out of his own house and trying to look cool when he's really just pathetic.

There are still unpacked boxes in the corner. Not much but takeout and IPA in the fridge. Jake absorbs it all and it depresses him, which brings his focus back to the Patrón Silver. It's not long before he loses the battle of wills and drinks. And even though he's alone, he feels judged. By Cara. By Grace. By Javi. And much as he hates to admit it, by his father.

Which is why he pours himself another healthy round, finishing off the bottle.

10

"You were drinking that night. A lot."

Jake's back in the holding room at the Foltz courthouse, what used to be called the CCB, or Criminal Courts Building. He's sitting across from Tiana Walker. She's his client, for now at least, but he's cross-examining her. If he's going to counsel her to pass on the deal Austin Bell has offered, he needs more information and, more importantly, he has to know what he has to work with. Which is why he's being a bit of an asshole right now. That and the fact that he feels like crap after a long night of his own drinking. The entire Patrón Silver logic had been a bust. After finishing the bottle, he'd found he had one more.

"Yes. I was," Tiana says, daring him to judge her for that.

"You were angry."

"Yes. I was."

"Because your friend was dead and no one gave a shit?"

"I gave a shit."

"I don't think you did. I think you'd given up, and you figured you'd just go to sleep and your kids would go to sleep and you wouldn't have to deal with it anymore—"

"You know what it's like to have kids?! To love them more than anything in the world?!"

Of course he does, but if he digresses to that thought, he'll be done. He puts on his lawyer armor, which wards off all emotion. "I'm asking the questions—"

"No, you're telling me what I was feeling to make a point. Well, let me save you some time. Yeah, I drank." She eyes him with an unwavering gaze. "But I. Didn't. Do it."

Jake's impressed. He thinks her performance could play well on the stand, but he doesn't give her the satisfaction of saying so—it's much too soon.

"Tell me about Jacinta Castillo."

The name fills Tiana with warmth and sadness. In Tiana's dark world, where not much went the way she wanted it to, Jacinta was the one fucking light. Aside from her kids, Jacinta was her lifeline. "She was my friend. And you're right—no one gave a shit when she was murdered."

"Did Reagan Hearst give a shit?"

Tiana is genuinely thrown off by the question, and Jake can see that. She takes a minute to place the name. "The guy she worked for?"

"The rich prick she worked for."

She screws up her face a bit—she doesn't understand the point of the question. But she can see he wants an answer. "Yeah, I knew he was a prick, but his wife died, and Jacinta loved his little girl, so whatever."

"He ever try anything with her?"

Tiana is lost in this line of questioning. "What does this have to do with me?"

"That's what I'm trying to find out."

Jake's armor slips a bit here. Because he's not just an attorney pressing for information, he's a man desperate to find something that may be out of reach. He's excited and frustrated and hungover and impatient. And his client, or the woman who may be his client, is looking right through him. Can she see all his failings?

Tiana's thinking something quite different. As much as she doesn't trust this man, and as much as he looks like shit—maybe *because* he looks like shit—Tiana begins to think from this line of questioning that maybe he's actually here to help. So she gives him something. "*He* never tried anything. One time, a friend of his asked Jacinta out. But he just wanted to get laid. And he didn't like it when she said no."

"Didn't like it how?"

"He didn't do anything, if that's what you mean. But Jacinta felt . . . uneasy."

"You know who this guy was?"

"No. I saw him once; I helped at a party." He seems to come alive at this information, but she doesn't understand how this helps or how this has anything to do with her. "I told the police all this, after what happened. They said they looked into it."

Jake makes a mental note—he has to check this. He has to get Jacinta's murder file, because he's beginning to see this one case may actually be two. And if it really is what led to Rich's murder, three cases. He starts outlining on the yellow legal pad in his mind:

- *Jacinta murdered*
- *Tiana points finger at friend or colleague of Reagan Hearst*
- *Someone tries to kill Tiana - to shut her up? Instead kills two of her kids*
- *Tiana charged with murder*
- *Daria Barati asked to take case*
- *She says no - points Rich at Tiana*
- *Rich finds connection between the murders - and/or to R. Hearst*
- *Someone murders Rich to keep connection secret*

Jake is almost breathless at the thought. Three cases and four murders connected in some mysterious way, having to do with a client at his own law firm. A fucking conspiracy. Except no one will believe him. They'd be 100 percent correct to doubt him.

He sees Tiana watching his brain spin—he's got to hold it together. Focus.

"You think this guy had something to do with what happened to me?" she asks.

Jake does think so. But can he prove it in court beyond a reasonable doubt? That is the lawyer's constant question.

She presses him. "You actually gonna help me now?"

For the first time, Jake sees a glimmer of hope creep into her eyes. And it scares him. Hope is dangerous.

Jake has offered hope before. Exhibit A: Ramon Guadalupe. A man who'd lost his wife, lost everything. And Jake's fervent belief in himself gave the man the aforementioned hope.

The night Ramon played Jake home videos, the night he watched Ramon's wedding to Estelle and the birth of their son, Manny, Jake felt a deep need to drink with Ramon. He could see the pain in his eyes as he watched what he'd lost, a pain Jake desperately wanted to salve. And so, three drinks in, Jake promised that he'd make Harrison pay. Ramon had nodded, moved. He was salved. By hope.

When Jake had been called up to the bench for a sidebar, right after he'd introduced the smoking gun memo, and the judge ordered them all into chambers, Jake had felt the noose of the trap cinch around his neck. In that moment, he wasn't worried about losing the case or losing his career, he was thinking about the promise. He was thinking that he had failed Ramon.

Now here he is again. Seeing a wrong that needs righting, but knowing the odds are he'll fail. And if he gives false hope once more, chances are he'll have to watch it destroy Tiana Walker at some point down the line.

Tiana's brain is on its own tangent. She is thinking about Reggie. Does he think she walked away from him? That leaving him now was her choice? Or worse—are people telling him his mother killed his sister and brother? Tried to kill him? At seven years old, how can he make sense of that?

This man before her is different than he was yesterday. She sees that he may actually want to help. And that terrifies her. Because she doesn't know if it's too late for Reggie. Maybe it's better if he just forgets her, if he can just block it all out, forget he had a mom, that he had a sister and brother. He's probably too old for that, but it would be better. It would spare him a world of pain. It's what she wishes for herself sometimes. Maybe instead of prison, they can put her in some mental ward where they shoot electricity into her head and make her forget who she was and what happened. Better than what they're calling her. More than that, better than *being* what they're calling her. Because despite what this man is getting at, that there's a different answer to what happened that night, a good 10 percent of her brain worries that she really did it. Tiana's pretty sure she didn't, but she did drink more than she ever had. She blacked out, cold. Could she have done what they said and not remembered?

The only thing she knows right now is that the man sitting here is scaring her. Because deep down, she's not sure the truth matters. As far as the system goes, it doesn't matter if she's guilty. This is a lesson spanning her whole life, growing up on the poorest streets of LA. You're always judged as guilty, regardless of the truth. Why should now, today, be any different?

"You're not answering," Tiana says, coming out of her trance and breaking Jake's own mental diversion. "Can you help me or not?"

Jake really thinks about it. Is he going to open this door that offers salvation . . . or damnation? Maybe for both of them. Is he going to risk her future to prove what he wants to be true? Who is he doing this for anyway?

After a long moment, Jake realizes what he has to do. And Grace will be pleased.

"The best way I can help you is this: take the deal."

Tiana's confused now. And fucking angry. All this buildup to tell her to give up?

"I thought you believed me!" She spits the words at him.

Jake tells her the hard truth he's been slow to learn. "What I believe . . . and what I can prove are two totally different things."

Tiana is trying to figure this man out. He goes from complete asshole to white savior (*that* part's certainly not been lost on her) to looking like he's going to cry. She feels her throat tighten, the tears coming, the emotional whiplash of anger and hope and fear and grief consuming her. Jake finds it hard to watch, but he can't turn away.

"So you want me to give up? Lose my son, let him think I killed his brother and sister? You think he'll ever forgive me?"

"I know kids don't forgive easily," Jake says, a truth he's learning the hard way.

Tiana studies him, and suddenly something is very clear to her. "Is that why *you* were drinking last night?"

Her question catches him off guard. He takes just a moment to gather himself. *Never let the client get the upper hand.* He remembers Norman hounding him on that. But then he decides to ignore his father. She deserves the truth.

"It's one of the many reasons I was drinking last night." They are both surprised by the honesty of that. Jake tries to adopt his kindest tone. "I'm sorry, Tiana, but here's the problem. I don't know what Mr. Kaplan found, I don't know what happened to your friend, and this deal is off the table after today. So yes, what I'm recommending is that you take the deal. I'm sorry, but if I'm going to represent you, that's my best legal advice."

For a brief moment this man had given her hope, only to show his true colors, that he's like every other part of the system. And the system doesn't work. At least not for people like her.

"You sleep okay at night? Telling people the best you can do is make them lose everything?"

Jake doesn't sleep well at all, but he knows better than to make promises he can't keep.

Ten minutes later, Jake sits at the defense table. What drink would make the spinning in his head stop? What extraordinarily strong liquor would ease the pressure to do the right thing, which is the wrong thing? Maybe absinthe. He hates licorice, so probably not, but how much would it take to kill him? Or is that just a myth?

His phone rings. He shouldn't have his phone on in the courtroom, but they haven't brought Tiana in and the judge isn't here yet, so it won't cost him.

He's about to silence it when he sees it's his son, Aaron. A quick glance at the side door—still no Tiana—tells him he's got a minute. He's disappointed his son so many times he doesn't want to fail him again. So he answers, speaking quietly.

"Hey, champ. What's up?"

"Where were you last night?"

Jake hears disappointment but not anger, which is a good start.

"I am so sorry. There was a work thing, and I lost track of time. Which is no excuse, but that's the truth." Well, it's part of the truth, anyway.

"Come tonight."

"It's not my night, kiddo."

"Mom'll say it's okay."

Jake wants to say sure. He wants to make it all better. But again, making promises you can't keep only forestalls the pain.

"I'll see you on the weekend, okay?"

"I want to see you now. Not later, not Saturday. Now."

"I want to see you too."

"You could make it happen, Dad. You know you could."

Jake could probably call Cara and make an argument that would sway her. It's what he does best. "I'll see, kiddo. I'm in court right now, so I gotta go. Love you."

Jake hangs up. The bailiff is bringing Tiana into the room now, her eyes cast down at the floor tiles. Jake opens her file. At the top—the offer from Austin Bell, the one Jake's told her to accept, the one she *should* accept, is written in black and white. He reads it again.

"What's it gonna be, Jake? Ticktock."

Austin Bell's words don't penetrate Jake's concentration. Nor does Judge Merrin, coming in through the door from chambers. The clerk intones, "All rise for the Honorable Eleanor Merrin," and Jake stands, but he doesn't let go of the file. The judge takes her seat and aims her gaze at Jake, but he's seemingly in a trance.

"Mr. West. The court gave you a day to confer with your client. Where are we?"

Jake shifts his attention to Merrin, her impatience to get this over with all too clear. He turns to Austin Bell, whose expression says, *Come on, let's stop playing games.* At least, that's Jake's interpretation. And it probably is the responsible thing to do, but then he glances at his client and finds Tiana's eyes boring deep into his soul, as if she sees every competing thought running through his brain.

"Mr. West!" Merrin says sharply.

Jake turns to her. "My client is passing on the deal, Your Honor."

Jake is almost as surprised by his words as everyone else in the courtroom.

Austin Bell can only shake his head at the waste of time he has in store. "You are out of your mind," he murmurs.

Jake shrugs. "Probably."

Judge Merrin isn't sure what to think. She's not sure if Jake is even fit to go to trial. "Ms. Walker. Do you understand the deal that was presented to you? Did Mr. West make clear what your options were?"

Tiana looks to Jake to make sure she doesn't misstep here, and he nods encouragement. "Go ahead. You can answer."

Tiana doesn't understand what's changed, and she's not 100 percent sure this is the right thing to do—Jake told her it wasn't—but the feeling coursing through her is one of excitement. She feels alive.

"I understand what the offer is. The offer is I plead guilty. To something I didn't do."

Jake couldn't have coached her to a better answer.

At the prosecution table, Austin Bell takes a breath. Regrouping. He should be happy; the deal was too good. So be it—time for plan B, and plan B comes to him in the form of a woman with vibrant red hair in the back of the gallery. Bell has done his homework on his opponent and what transpired two nights ago, so he can guess why Detective Sioban McFadden is here.

"Your Honor, before we move forward, the State has a motion. We move to have the defense attorney replaced."

"You've gotta be kidding—" Jake can't constrain the involuntary outburst.

"He's a suspect in a murder case. He could be arrested, then we have a mistrial—"

"This is bullshit!" Jake says, directing it not to the court, but directly to Bell.

"Gentlemen! Approach!"

This is not how Eleanor Merrin wanted today to go. She feels a stress migraine coming on. Why is it that Jake West triggers her so?

Jake tries to squeeze out an argument. "Your Honor, this is completely—"

"Say another word, you're in contempt." She turns to the deputy DA, whose smug expression she's in no mood for. "Mr. Bell? Really?"

"Your Honor, you want to waste your time starting a trial we can't finish? He's been on this case five minutes, it's not a hardship—"

"He's just pissed because I passed on his deal. You can't move to replace the other side so they'll accept your deal."

Judge Merrin isn't sure who's infuriating her more. Before she can decide, Jake has an inspiration.

"You know what, I'll make *you* a deal. I'll recuse myself if that's what the court wants. But here's what follows: I will subpoena Mr. Bell's campaign finance records—"

"I'm not running for anything—"

"The DA is stepping down, you have an exploratory committee, and I want to know which of your donors is pressuring you to settle this case."

This avenue has just occurred to Jake in the moment, but hearing it out loud, and watching Bell's reaction? He thinks he may have stumbled onto something useful. Bell is watching the judge, expecting outrage. Instead, she seems to be taking it seriously.

"Your Honor, you can't honestly be considering this?" Bell is good at keeping his outrage sounding neutral, respectful.

"Mr. West is offering to step down. I find that offer quite compelling."

Just thinking about the offer has eased the pounding of her migraine.

"It's not an offer to step down," Bell argues. "It's a way to attack me. This'll set me on fire. I've done nothing wrong, but I see where this is going."

"Tell you what, Austin," says Jake. "You drop your motion, and I'll agree to put that sword back in the stone."

He likes that analogy, it makes him feel like King Arthur. He can see Bell wants to kill him right now. Bell's good at covering, but in the corners of his eyes, Jake sees the growing hate. He loves it when he has that effect on people. At least in court.

"Fine. Motion withdrawn," Bell says.

Jake has barely a second to savor his win.

"Done. Trial starts at nine a.m. Tomorrow," Judge Merrin clarifies.

Austin Bell seems to like that. Jake, not so much. "Your Honor—"

"No more games, and no more delays, Mr. West."

"Absolutely not. It's just . . . I have a funeral to attend tomorrow."

That defuses her. She doesn't like to concede, but she liked Rich Kaplan. A good, solid attorney. Mediocre, but a good man.

"Nine a.m., the day *after* tomorrow. And Mr. West—come Friday morning, there's no turning back. I hope you know what you're doing."

He nods with confidence, then looks back at Tiana. Shit, he hopes so too.

11

As Jake walks down the steps, not sure whether to feel he just won a round of the fight or got sucker punched, Detective Sioban McFadden falls into step with him.

"Was that fun for you, Counselor?"

"I wasn't doing it to amuse myself."

"Well, it was ballsy. Are you itching to get back to trial, or do you really have a case?"

"You wanna ask me questions, I love Irish pubs. You can get me drunk, maybe I'll confess."

"You might think about easing up on the drinking if you're going to trial."

"Gee thanks, Mom."

"I will buy you a coffee, though."

Jake stops walking. Friendliness is not a tactic he expects from a police detective, and he has to assess her intent. Befriending the cop trying to charge him with murder is a dangerous move, but the upside is she's smart, good at repartee, and he *is* innocent after all. And despite the conflict presented by the adversarial nature of their relationship, he would like nothing more than for her to find Rich's real killer. Even though the son of a bitch slept with his wife.

Also, he's suddenly feeling ravenous.

"Let's compromise. Dave's Hot Chicken. But you're still buying."

It's LA's latest food craze—various Nashville chicken places popping up from Koreatown to Pacoima. It's nothing like old-fashioned fried chicken. You marinate strips of white meat chicken in a signature blend of seasonings loaded with cayenne pepper to make it fiery red, then offer various heat levels to let patrons test their tolerance for their mouth being on fire. Dave's Hot Chicken—started by four friends in an East Hollywood parking lot—has become the gold standard.

Jake and Sioban walk the six blocks from the courthouse to a tiny storefront at the edge of Little Tokyo and sit across from each other on red metal chairs under the neon-colored mural. Jake goes with "extra hot" for the Nashville chicken tenders and is impressed that Sioban—she said he could call her that, another tactic no doubt—went with "Reaper." Jake tried that once and never again, the heat level making his brain explode, and not in a good way. Probably why Dave's literally has you sign a waiver acknowledging that it "can cause you harm, including, but not limited to, bodily injury, property damage, emotional distress, or even death." Jake's never been clear if it's a marketing gimmick or a real legal necessity.

As they wait for their order, Sioban turns their small talk to business. "So—was this morning in court bullshit, or did Rich Kaplan really find something on the *Walker* case?"

"If that were true, it would mean someone else had motive to kill him."

"Don't get me wrong, I'm not saying I buy it. But I do like to cover my bases."

"So my A-plus charm hasn't convinced you of my innocence yet?"

"God, no. Your charm is offset by the fact you have motive, opportunity, state of mind. What's bigger than a trifecta? You're the pick-six of suspects."

"Horse racing, is it? You like to hang out at Leopardstown? Your dad an inveterate gambler?"

The Leopardstown reference impresses Sioban. She sees he's done his homework on her, a fact that makes her more suspicious of his guilt, but not damningly so.

"Does your know-it-all thing usually work for you?"

"Usually. Speaking of which—why no *h*?" She's confused. "Your name. Doesn't Sioban usually have an *h*?"

He's showing off, and she's not impressed. "My father wasn't a good speller. And my mother thought it made me different. Like Caitlin with a *K*, or Lisa with a *y*."

"So you're trendy. Interesting."

"Can we move on from you proving you did your homework on me?"

"Sure. What do you know about Tiana Walker?"

"She was drunk, depressed, the cops gave up on solving the murder of her friend, so she herself gave up. They found *her* matches, booze she'd bought was open and spilled, her blood alcohol was .32. You know how much liquor that is? Maybe just another night for you, but for most people, it's nearly fatal."

"You do your homework."

"Irish public education is good training."

"So let me ask you this—all of that is true, so why did Bell offer such a good deal?"

It's a good question, admittedly. But again, not particularly exculpatory.

"DAs offer deals all the time."

"Bell doesn't want a trial. Maybe it's because he's hiding something. Could be something about Tiana, could be something about the murder of Jacinta Castillo."

"Who?"

"Tiana's roommate was also murdered. That's Castillo with two *l*'s. First name Jacinta."

"Wow. You're tossing out alternate theories like you're Oprah at one of her giveaways. Which does not say to me I should listen, it says to me my number-one suspect fears more and more is going to point to him, so he's grasping at straws."

Jake is about to argue when he realizes that is an extremely viable interpretation, one he would make if he were on the other side. Combined with the six blocks of conversation and her interrogation the other night, one thing is becoming crystal clear. She's smart. But that could work in his favor—he can actually use her to prove his innocence. He just has to get her on board.

"I meant what I said the other night before my father barged in. I want you to find Rich's killer. I'm having lunch with you because I think the more you investigate, the more you'll see this case isn't what it seems. All you have to do is look in the right places."

Sioban is intrigued by Jake. Not because she believes him, but because his casual nature makes her wonder if he could be an actual sociopath. Or maybe he's just a drunk who's reaching. That's the likelier of the two, because the more she's dug into Jake West, the more she has reason to doubt him.

"Isn't this what got you into trouble on your last case? Seeing shadows?"

Their order number is called, and Jake dodges the question by going to retrieve the chicken combos. He skips the signature Dave's sauce, while she likes to dunk. A waste as far as he's concerned, burying the flavor in mayonnaise-based goopy muck, but he does enjoy the fact that she's not shy about eating with her fingers. And maybe it explains why she can tolerate the Reaper—she cuts the heat with the sauce. Makes him feel better about himself. As does savoring the sharp bite of his own spicy chicken strips. Which would go down so much better with a hazy IPA, or maybe a double hazy, but alas, that's not an option here.

After a few bites, Jake decides it's time to move the conversation in a new direction. "Here's the thing," he tells her confidentially. "Someone came at me in the Thompson and West parking garage last night." He pauses for effect before delivering the kicker. "Carrying a flashlight identical to the one that shined in the car window before the gunshot that killed Rich." He waits for a reaction. She keeps eating. Maybe the Reaper is dulling her other senses. "Seriously. I had to run for it."

He's exaggerating about the flashlight, but he *could* be right.

Sioban stops eating. Wipes her fingers. Takes a sip of her Coke. Only then does she say: "You want me to believe you can identify a specific beam of light from a flashlight? Is this some forensic expertise I haven't heard of?"

"I meant it was the same that they *had* a flashlight," Jake explains, kicking himself that he overreached.

"No, I think you were overstating the point for effect. Or just making up details."

"It happened."

"You report this . . . attack, chase, whatever you want to call it?"

"Tell me how that would go over."

Sioban considers that scenario. It's a fair point. They'd take the report, find nothing, and conclude Jake was so guilty he had to invent a mystery suspect for them to chase down.

"So instead you float the idea to me to work on *my* reasonable doubt?"

"I'm not working on anything. You're the one who followed me after court, not the other way around."

She slowly takes two more bites as she plays it out in her head. "Sorry, I'm not buying it. The attack, the two old cases. I think all of this—including whatever your gambit is with Tiana Walker—is a game. You're using this case to make it appear there's someone with a motive to do what *you* actually did. You're gambling her life to save your own."

Jake puts up his hands in surrender. "That would be a reasonable strategy, I admit. But I don't think you believe that. I think you think you're *supposed* to believe that. But I think your instincts are better."

"What do you know about my instincts?"

Jake has his mouth full, and he chews slowly. "Why did you leave Ireland, Detective?" She may be good, but he sees the flinch. "Word has it a boy went missing? They caught the guy . . . but he got off. I'd say someone screwed up."

She stops eating. She doesn't like this turn. He really has done his homework.

"Like you said—I pride myself on being a know-it-all."

Callum Duncan was twelve, but he looked far younger. Some would say he was very independent. Others would say his mother was negligent. Either way, he was walking home along the edge of River Liffey the last time he was seen. Some thought he'd fallen in, some thought he'd run away. Inspector

Sioban McFadden talked to everyone who knew the boy, and she knew he didn't leave of his own accord. He had a dog, Seamus. He would not have left Seamus behind.

A security camera from a local pub she'd been to one too many times showed Callum being followed by a young man. That was her clear interpretation. Brin Maloney, nineteen. The kid was trouble—he'd been kicked out of two schools, picked up and sentenced for a half dozen things, and was currently floating around with no apparent source of income. And unsubstantiated rumor had it that Brin liked young boys. Whether it was for sex or the fact that they looked up to him wasn't fully clear. Either way, Sioban knew the minute she looked in Brin's eyes and asked her first question that Callum was dead. And that Brin Maloney was responsible.

The problem was, she couldn't prove it, and her superintendent had a thing for the mother. Meaning that he had mother issues—his own must've been a piece of work—and he wanted to blame Callum's mother and boyfriend, who'd clearly never liked the kid at all. He felt the boy was too soft, too small, too quiet. And probably, too smart.

There was no question that breaking the padlock on Brin Maloney's shed was a bad idea. But deep in her mind, Sioban weighed the consequences of that against the possibility—remote as it was—that Callum was still alive somewhere. And she decided the boy's life was far more important than her career. So she broke in. And found Callum's pocketknife. Which she would have found some way of entering into evidence as the probable murder weapon if Brin's father hadn't appeared at the door of the shed.

The knife went away, her career went away, and Callum Duncan was never found.

"It's almost as if your eyes just rolled back in your head."

Sioban emerges from her grim reverie. This is no time to be mired in her own shit. *Shake it off, McFadden. Don't let this guy get to you.*

"This isn't about me."

"No. I'm just pointing out things aren't always how they appear."

She takes a minute to decide how to respond. "Things aren't *always* how they appear, but more often than not, they are. Odds are, Tiana Walker is a mother who either wanted her kids dead, or was so fucked up that she accidentally killed them. Either way, her case is irrelevant to yours, which still leaves you as our number one suspect in the murder of Richard Allen Kaplan."

He registers her overcompensation in this speech, which pleases him. "Just so long as I'm not the one and only. Just so long as you keep an open mind."

"I do have an open mind. That's why we're here. I'm exploring alternatives, but you have to give me more than wild speculation."

"You want me to do your job for you?"

"I would if I were you."

She has a point. Jake pops a couple of seasoned fries in his mouth as he ponders how to answer. "In law school, they give us hypos. Hypotheticals. Let me give you one."

"Meaning you want to tell me something you can't tell me?"

He neither nods nor shakes his head. Either could be problematic, so he simply continues: "Let's say an attorney is defending a client. He discovers evidence that could help exonerate said client. But bringing forth that evidence would require violating the attorney/client privilege of *another* client. What are the attorney's options?"

Sioban takes a deep breath. Lawyers and their verbal games are so tiresome. A part of her longs for the days of police working with impunity, trampling over the rights of suspects in the name of justice. If only so many of her kind weren't so inherently vile and corrupt that such actions would render said justice unjust.

"In this hypothetical, are you the attorney, or are you the client?"

"Interesting question, which I cannot answer. But for hypothetical purposes, let's apply that question to both."

"Both. So you want me to believe there is evidence that the fire that killed

Tiana Walker's children and the murder of your 'friend' are both wrapped up in some conspiracy having to do with another case at your firm? Or a client?"

Jake is treading a thin line, but he shrugs and pushes ahead. She's a quick study. "I don't want you to believe anything. I want you to find the truth."

He tries fixing her with an earnest gaze, but it doesn't seem to have the intended effect, so he decides to try a different path to sway her to his side. "Hey—you ever find the woman I was with that night? Camila? She back up my story that I wasn't angry at Rich?"

"We found her."

"And?"

"I don't think she's pining for a second date, if that's what you're asking. Not after she found out what happened."

"But did she back my story?"

"Well, you're not locked up."

"You should be a lawyer yourself, the way you duck questions."

"Sure. Choose the one profession that's more hated than cops."

"Fair point. I wish I'd had a talent for anything else. You're probably no different—I'd imagine you have a talent for investigating things. That's why I think you'll come to the inevitable conclusion that I'm *not* your guy. Because whatever else you've heard, Richard Kaplan *was* my friend, for many years. And I really do want you to find the truth because until you do, until I'm cleared, I can't fall apart the way I should."

She's almost moved—whether by the real emotion Jake's showing, or the words, or just by the performance, she isn't sure. But it's enough for her to grant him a tiny crumb.

"Okay, Counselor. I'll keep digging. But to be clear—I'm gonna keep digging into *you* as well."

Jake nods. That's fair. He digs back into his chicken. He'll take this lunch as a win.

12

A maintenance man scrapes the frosted lettering from the glass marking the office that only three days ago was occupied by Richard Kaplan. The flowers are gone. Bankers Boxes sit on a dolly waiting for transport to God knows where. The walls have been stripped bare. Daria stands just down the hall, marveling at how easily one can be erased. If she'd been the one shot dead, how long until all traces of Daria Barati would have been wiped from these offices? Would she be mourned? Would people just angle for her cases and her office and her connections?

Seeing the frosted lettering come down almost hits her harder than when she first heard Rich had been murdered. That had seemed unreal. This is all too real.

"I'm worried about Jake."

Daria startles and turns to find Norman West standing behind her. Always a ghoulish presence, in this moment he feels more so. He scares her, always has, but what she's feeling is a different kind of fear. It's irrational—he's the one who hired her. She figured he initially had ulterior motives—she was a twofer, a check mark for both gender and racial diversity—but she has earned everything that's come her way, and Norman has seemingly recognized that. Even championed her at times, which has allowed her to rise within the firm. Despite that, in person he's always had a chilling effect on her, but she can't let him see that. One can never let their guard down around Norman West.

"Worried how?" she says evenly.

He holds out a hand, inviting her to step into Rich's office. It feels like an intrusion, like entering a morgue, but there's no saying no. Norman follows her in and closes the door. He can feel her apprehension. It's by design.

"Jake has taken on a case he can't win. I'd like *you* to get him to reconsider."

Red flags and alarm bells wave and clang in Daria's mind. She imagines he can sense her fear, so she goes on the offensive—she turns it back on him.

"Maybe he *can* win."

Norman watches her. In normal times, he likes her fire, her strength. Today, though, it's an obstacle. Not a difficult one, but his reserves are drained. The past week has been grueling. He hardens himself. "You don't have kids, do you?"

Men. Fucking high-level corporate men never see what it costs someone like Daria to be where she is. "No. No I don't. Kind of hard to fit them in with my hours."

Her anger isn't lost on him, but he's not sympathetic. "We all make choices. But my point is, Jake is my son. I'm looking out for his best interests. Children can't always see that, appreciate that, but that's what we do. When we love our children."

She watches him try to paint himself as someone who possesses even a modicum of empathy. He's not a very good artist. More like one of those journeymen who learn to mimic the great masters—their work may appear similar, but there's something missing, a depth of feeling in the strokes that can't be copied.

She cuts through his bullshit. "You want him to settle."

"You saw what happened to Rich."

She can't believe he's going there. Saying that out loud. "You think that was about the *case*?" she asks cautiously.

He takes a step toward her. Reaches out and takes her hand. Like a grandfather. Or the Godfather, maybe. He's not gripping hard, but she couldn't pull away if she tried.

"Something tells me *you* can get my son to listen. He always had a weakness for a pretty girl."

He lets that disgusting attack-disguised-as-a-compliment sink in. Then he releases her hand and starts to go, to leave her to ponder her options. But Daria can't think about her options—she is seething. Her boss just told her quite plainly to whore herself out.

There is an apocryphal story about Norman West. How back in the day, when he was younger and attractive, at least to those who find a hunger for power attractive, he set out to seduce a judge. She was married, unhappily, to a man most thought was gay, whether he knew it or acknowledged it or not. This was back in the day when such things were viewed as a career impediment, where one could actually be terminated from their employment for being out. So they stayed married, and she stayed unhappy, and for a brief moment, Norman West made her forget all that.

Then the other shoe dropped. A case came before her where the defendant was represented by Norman's partner, Archie Thompson. It was a case Archie couldn't possibly win. Until Norman let it slip that if Archie didn't prevail, the judge's husband would be exposed. Which would hurt everyone involved. The judge wanted to recuse, but Norman made it clear that wasn't an option. Nor was resigning from the bench. There was only one choice: steer the verdict for Thompson & West. Which is exactly what she did.

Norman loves to tell that story. True or not, the fact that he prides himself on it speaks volumes about the lengths he will go to get what he wants.

"I don't like to sabotage colleagues," Daria says before Norman reaches the door.

Norman turns back, surprised she's not acquiescing. But of course, if she did, he would have thought less of her.

"Nor do I. I can do it, mind you. I can bring anyone down . . ." He pauses for effect. "But sometimes a soft touch is better. Especially when doing what's best is also doing what's right. And I know you know what's right. After all, this is really your fault, Daria."

"Excuse me?"

"You think I'm not aware this case started with you? This case I said no to?" There's an underlying, vicious anger that is unmistakable.

Daria is totally caught off guard by the accusation, true as it is. "I—"

"Just make him settle. And I'll let bygones be bygones."

He holds her gaze for a brief moment, then goes, leaving Daria shaken to the core.

The pastries are from Clementine just across Santa Monica Boulevard. The bagels and lox from Gjusta, which is not nearby, and which is not a Jewish deli, but is viewed as the best at everything they do. And the coffee is Peet's. It's all part of the ambience. The plentiful spread that is vastly more than is needed. The leftovers are donated to a food bank so the firm can feel like it's doing something progressive, when really what it's doing is ridiculously wasteful. But excess is the point. It sets a tone and declares that this law firm spares no expense and has only the best. God help the poor assistant who fucks up the order for the weekly partners and associates meeting.

Jake stands in the doorway, the smells so familiar, even if he hasn't been here in almost a year. He steels himself and enters the lion's den. Fourteen ergonomic chairs around the long, beveled glass table, another fourteen lining the walls for those who have yet to earn a place at the grown-ups' table.

Heads turn as Jake heads for a silver urn, pulls down the black knob and fills his mug with straight Peet's. Probably the Arabian Mocha Sanani, their darkest and most expensive roast. He downs it like it's hard liquor, willing it to calm his system the way booze would.

Daria moves in close. "You sure you know what you're doing?" she whispers.

"Drinking coffee, I think."

"That's not what I mean. Rich negotiated a huge win. You don't have to prove anything to anyone here." She's trying empathy. Jake isn't buying it.

"It's what you wanted—someone to fight for her. As long as it wasn't you."

She ignores the sting of that remark. "Please. Can we at least talk about it?"

"Nope," Jake says simply, and he moves to take a seat.

Norman West enters the conference room with a phalanx of attorneys in tow, his latest batch of sycophants. He searches out Daria, who shakes her head. It's subtle, but the silent communication isn't lost on Jake.

Annoyed, Norman takes his seat as Stephen Gibson begins to address the room. Jake wonders if he's going to start with some dig about the prodigal son returning, and from the faces glancing furtively in his direction and then away, he sees that others are thinking the same thing.

"All right, let's get started. First order of business—of course—is Richard Kaplan. We are shocked, and saddened, of course. If anyone here, any of your support staff require grief counseling, we continue to have a team available all week. Just coordinate with Nancy."

Gibson gives this somber thought a fraction of a second, then moves on.

"Okay, McClintock—"

"Really, that's it?" All eyes turn to Jake at the interruption. This is simply not done.

Gibson works to regain his composure, then says: "You've been gone awhile, Jake, but we have rules of order—"

"And we have a dead colleague. Don't we owe him more than a perfunctory announcement and sterilizing his office for the next in line?"

Gibson is ready to lay into Jake, but a sampling of glances makes him realize that despite his checkered history, the guy has supporters. But Gibson can't—won't—let him have the victory. "What would you like, Jake? A hymn?"

"Maybe a moment of silence? Maybe something more than performative grief? Some reflection, perhaps—there but for the grace of God go I? Or maybe—here's an idea—maybe a reminder about the service this afternoon, an encouragement to show up and pay respect to one of our own?"

Gibson is having a sense memory of how he felt most every week at these meetings when Jake was still here. The past year has been a respite so sweet he'd forgotten this feeling that can be likened to indigestion. But he handled Jake then, and he intends to do so now.

"I'm sure everyone is aware of the service, and also of their obligations to clients. But, sure. Let's have a moment. And if you can be there for Richard later, by all means." Translation: take time off at your own fucking peril. Gibson lets the silence go maybe another six seconds before he can't help himself: "Anything else, Jake? Maybe you want to take this opportunity to confess?"

"Stephen!" Norman's rebuke comes harsh and fast.

"I'm just saying, if it's weighing on his mind—"

"Actually, I have a case weighing on my mind. I start a trial tomorrow." Jake sits back. Bomb dropped. He takes a bite of a blueberry sour cream coffee cake muffin.

Most of the attorneys are wise enough to sit back and watch this play out like the tennis match it is. Gibson looks to Norman. *Do with this as you will,* Norman nods.

"I'm glad you brought that up, Jake. Because I have to ask—what the *fuck* are you doing? Rich had a win."

"Don't worry, I have a strategy. A *move.*" Jake is pleased with his mocking tone—Gibson uses that expression ad nauseam.

Gibson understands the dig is meant for him. "You want to share what that is?"

"I do. Because it involves you." *Here we go.* "You're going to have to drop Reagan Hearst as a client."

No one says a word. Gibson actually takes a beat to digest the absurdity before laughing. Or forcing himself to do so—Jake isn't sure which.

"It's no joke. He's potentially involved in a cover-up. We can't protect his interests—"

Gibson explodes. "Enough!" Then immediately calms himself. "While I'm sure we were all entertained by your last crusade, I'm afraid we're not dropping a billion-dollar client to save a welfare child killer."

"Yes, Stephen, we are. Because my client's friend worked for your client, that friend was murdered, and when my client started asking questions—"

Norman can't take it. "Good God, Jake, stop. Now."

Jake turns his eyes to his father. The room is dead quiet, which is exactly what Jake wants in order to platform the accusation: "Rich Kaplan found a connection between his case and Reagan Hearst. Damning enough that he was researching precedent for breaking attorney/client privilege."

Norman doesn't flinch. The two just stare at each other across the room. The entire room waits for an explosion. Instead, Gibson inserts himself into the showdown. "You know this how?" he scoffs.

"Because I'm good at what I do. Finding the truth. And I intend to protect this firm from any client or lawyer perpetrating a fraud. As my oath requires of me."

Norman digests this, then sighs. Weary. At least that's the emotion he's performing. "Enough, Jake. If you want to work for me—"

"I don't work *for* you. I work *with* you. I work *for* my client."

"Your client for the last fifteen minutes. Reagan Hearst is developing a major downtown plaza, and this firm has put together the entire package—"

"This is America, Dad. Everyone gets equal representation."

Norman finds no humor in this. He stands up to his full six foot one. For a moment he says nothing. Just letting his power, his authority, radiate over the disciples and any who would dare take a different side. "This is *my* firm, and if you want to bring Reagan Hearst into a nothing pro bono case, then there is a conflict. A conflict that means you have to recuse. So you have two options—settle this case or let it go."

"I don't accept that."

"There's a third option," Gibson offers. "Stay on the case and be fired."

Gibson just made a bold move against the son of a name partner. Jake can't help but glance around to see if he has any support, but if he has any allies right now, they're keeping silent. He presses on.

"You can't fire me. I'm an equity partner."

"And we have bylaws. If you choose to pursue this case, we will dredge up the *Harrison* mess, and you will be terminated for cause under article 7, subsection B, by a vote that I'm sure will be close to unanimous." It's not lost on anyone in the room that this is not the first time Gibson has raised this exact point. This conversation was had a year ago and shot down by Norman himself. But this time, Norman doesn't weigh in. "Have I rephrased your options to your liking?" Gibson finishes with a flourish.

Jake was prepared for this. This was not a battle he could win—instead, it was a setup for what follows. The move he's already thought out. "God, lawyers are annoying, but your point is well-taken. Let me rephrase now. I quit. Or rather, I will divest my equity shares so that I can represent Tiana Walker outside the firm."

He gets up from the table for effect. Gibson lets him get a few steps toward the door. "You can't. You have a noncompete."

"Which SB 699 renders moot."

"There are pending legal challenges to that bill. Your agreement was signed prior to that, and while I accept you will argue it's void, the litigation to verify that will take so much time, this case will be long over. But knock yourself out, Jake—you can divest and quit or whatever. But you can't help this woman. Pick up and leave, or sit back down and shut the hell up."

Jake needs a drink. He hadn't thought this through well enough. He goes to take a sip of his coffee instead, but the mug is empty. He decides to fake it to save face. And in that moment of fake drinking a beverage that isn't what his body is screaming for, before he has to sit down and eat humble pie, he gets a new idea.

"You mentioned a vote of the partners. That applies to disagreements and conflicts of all kinds. I don't remember the specific article and subsection, but I'm sure you do. So let's put *this* to a vote." He turns to Gibson. "As you said, we have rules."

Gibson is seething, but is well aware of what is written in article 11, subsection F.

Jake scans the room, trying to do some quick math. It's a long shot, but maybe today is the breaking point. Maybe Rich's death will tip the scales; maybe this is the opportunity those who are not in Norman's inner circle have been waiting for. At least half of these assholes have to hate both Gibson and Norman and would relish a win for the underdog. Or maybe, just maybe, there are some who believe in the truth. He thinks about *Jerry Maguire*. No, that moral stand didn't work out too well. He thinks about *Dead Poets Society*, all of Robin Williams's students standing on their desks in support—*O Captain! my Captain!* Shit, now that he thinks about it, that didn't end too well either. But he has to take a shot.

"Let me frame this for you," Jake begins, playing to the top candidates for defection. "One of our own, Richard Kaplan, a man you likely ate lunch with, had drinks with, asked for financial advice—his head was blown off right in front of me. And what I'm telling you is his murder is linked to one of our clients." Now he turns to Gibson. "Maybe to one of our lawyers—"

"Fuck you, Jake," Gibson seethes.

"He found dirt, and it likely got him killed, and it could have been any one of you."

Jake shifts his gaze from one attendee to another. He can see he won't win, but he's laying groundwork. For what, he's not sure yet.

"Is this what we wanted our lives to be? Protecting the rich and screwing over everyone else? We're lawyers—that doesn't mean we have to sell our souls because Stephen Gibson says so. You went to law school to fight the good fight, and you came here, and maybe you *do* fight the good fight, but can you really stand by and watch a colleague die and hide the facts—"

"Enough!" Norman pounds the table. "You want a vote, let's vote!"

"All right," Jake allows. "All in favor of dropping Reagan Hearst as a client so that we can pursue the truth?"

Jake tries hard to project strength and sober confidence. But there are no takers. Not a single flinch. That stings—he thought he was better liked than this. But his moment has fallen entirely flat. He wonders if it would've gone any better with tequila instead of coffee.

"Grow up, Jake," Norman says with annoyance. "No one's sold their soul. We have many clients and many responsibilities. The rest of us understand that. So don't make this into something it's not. Just take the great fucking deal your client has been offered and move on. No one wants you to leave."

Gibson barely suppresses a smirk of doubt on that point, but all eyes move to Jake.

He feels like he's eight again, and he's been caught cheating on his math test and called before the whole class. Only this time he didn't cheat. He may not be legally right, but morally right.

"Let it go, Jake. I know you don't believe this, but I'm trying to protect you." Norman tries for a paternal smile, but it doesn't work.

"You said it. I don't believe you." Jake holds his father's gaze for a long moment before laying down his sword. "But I can see when I'm beaten."

"Good. You'll drop the case."

"No, that would be unethical. I will, however, refrain from any conflict. We'll just keep the charming Reagan Hearst out of it."

Jake sits down without another word. He may have lost, but he's stirred the pot. Which was really the best he could have hoped for.

13

Sioban is still getting used to Los Angeles. It may be the second-largest city in the U.S. and three-and-a-half times bigger than Dublin, but in her view, it isn't really a city at all. Dublin has a feel to it. A flavor, a smell, that makes it a singular thing. Los Angeles isn't that at all—it's a borderless conglomeration of disparate districts.

Westwood has its college vibe, influenced by UCLA at its center, but when you get to the eastern and northern edges—to Holmby Hills, or to the area just below Sunset on the east side of the university—it's all "old money," a term that makes her laugh. "Old" in Los Angeles means from the mid-twentieth century; while in Dublin, "old" means from the 1700s, at the very least—the city dates to 841, a mere 940 years before the founding of LA. The term "history" here is almost laughable.

The property that people hold here is laughable too. Not the *land*—go to Iowa or Georgia or outside a big city in California, and properties have a vast expanse. But as for interior space, space to live in, Westwood has so much space for so few people. It's the exact opposite in countless other neighborhoods. Sioban was at a crime scene last week in Pico Rivera where eight people were sharing a one-bedroom apartment. No wonder someone got shot. Maybe the situation isn't that unusual; the world isn't fair anywhere. Certainly not in Dublin.

The traditional Cape Cod architecture of Jake West's house, the perfect lawn, the perfect landscaping—they make her wonder why everyone in this city needs to strive for perfection. Still, from what she knows of Jake, the exterior hides more imperfections than one can count. The FOR SALE sign also shouts failure. She knows it isn't just the house that will go, but the promise of the life he'd had here.

When Cara walks out the front door headed for the Audi Q5, Sioban isn't surprised to see that she's attractive—of course she is—but the way she carries herself is different. She seems somehow more substantial than the caricature Sioban dreamed up. The detective moves quickly to catch her before she gets in the car.

"Ms. West? Or is it Ms. Bishop now?"

Cara stops and turns, and something makes her instantly wary of this redheaded woman coming toward her.

"It's West. For now."

"I'm Detective McFadden." Sioban shows her badge to make it official and remove any chance of some future legal argument to invalidate anything that comes from this conversation. "Do you have a minute?"

Cara could tell she was a cop. She knew this was coming. Dreaded it, but it's not unexpected.

"I'm picking up my son." But Cara doesn't move. She knows she can't avoid this entirely. "This is about Jake? I don't see him much, I don't see how I can really help you."

"Why did you split up?"

This is not the question Cara was expecting. And the answer to that would take a lot longer than the time she has. There are so many reasons, she can't say what the breaking point was. The drinking? The wallowing in self-pity? Failing the children? The lack of sex? That one isn't entirely fair—it wasn't the sex she missed. It was *him*. Having him there. She had loved Jake. Still did. But he'd been gone long before she told him it was time to leave.

"Why does anyone split up?"

Sioban's ready with options. "Infidelity, drugs, drinking, you fall out of love, realize they're not who you thought they were . . ."

Can I check all of the above? Cara wonders, but she doesn't answer. It's a trap, of course. Sioban tries another approach.

"Is your husband capable of hurting someone? If he's angry enough?"

Cara tries to fix her expression. She knows it's the reaction, not the answer, this woman is looking for.

"Did he hurt *you*? Did he hurt you and you decided not to report it?"

How on earth does this woman know so much so fast? "Who told you that?"

"So it's true?"

Cara knows what her sister would say: that it's never the victim's fault. And Cara agrees. But if she ignores political correctness, she's also clear she didn't report what happened because she knew she played a role in it. She was angry about a hundred things, and the one she picked that night was just an excuse to vent at Jake about all that was making her unhappy. Eighty percent of which was about him, but there was that other 20 percent, the part that resented the dreams she'd given up to raise their kids. She'd made the choice willingly, but that didn't mean it came without a cost.

That night, Jake had come home around three a.m. And while it was possible he'd fallen asleep working on a brief as he'd said, she was pretty damn sure the smell of liquor was mixed with perfume. A perfume she was pretty damn sure she'd smelled before, attached to a very attractive paralegal who often seemed to end up working on Jake's cases.

Cara didn't lead with that, though. She'd built her case against him like any good attorney worth their salt. She'd learned a lot watching Jake in court over the years. When she used to watch him—when watching him used to be tinged with pride instead of resentment. So she built her case, got him to commit to his story, and then hit him with the evidence that made it all a lie.

But it was their bedroom, not a courtroom, and when he tried to leave, she blocked the door. She wasn't done, hadn't exacted the confession, and she wanted to keep sticking in the knife repeatedly, make him own his failings, and when he tried to move her aside, she hit him—hard. A right hand across his left cheek. It stung her hand, but it felt good; it released her anger, and she reached to do it again, grabbing his arm with her other hand, but when he struggled to pull loose, he ended up backhanding her in the jaw. Difficult to say how much him hitting her was intentional and how much was reflexive.

They both froze. And she thinks they both knew in that moment it was over.

Her jawline showed a brownish-purple bruise, and her sister wanted her to press charges. She didn't care that Jake could be disbarred, lose the career that supported their family. She wouldn't allow Cara one iota of shared responsibility. This was *his* fault, and he had to pay. But in the end, Jake moving out of the house had to be payment enough.

Sioban is still waiting for an answer. Cara won't give her one.

"I know you have to go. Just one more question," Sioban says softly. Then, just as Cara eases up with the relief of this being over, the detective hits her with the thing she most wants to know: "How angry was Jake that you slept with Richard Kaplan?"

Now Cara wishes she'd answered the first question. Because this one, if she responds honestly, will not help Jake's case. The affair with Rich Kaplan reeks of motive, something that's been nagging at Cara since Jake told her Rich was dead.

It started innocently enough. They'd run into each other at Gelson's. Shopping at the overpriced food market in the basement of the overpriced mall was perhaps extravagant, but Cara loved the feeling of overstocked shelves lined and organized to perfection. Going there for groceries didn't feel like a 1950s domestic housewife activity, it felt decadent. It was the expensive bins of fresh nuts, the fish selection that rivaled Santa Monica Seafood, the hot-food counter where you could take a real dinner home and feel like you'd cooked it yourself. It was like another world—a brightly lit, colorful other world where you could have anything you wanted. She knew it was a luxury, but she didn't allow herself many of those, so it felt okay to stroll the wide aisles and fill her cart.

Rich's cart was sad. A single T-bone, some russet potatoes, some sour cream, and a bottle of Bordeaux. By contrast, Cara's cart was packed more than enough to feed three people for the next week. Rich was clearly uncomfortable, not knowing if Cara's fury at Jake would spill over to him, but it had been a few months, and she wasn't one to misplace blame. She knew Rich was a good guy, and the sad dinner in his cart reinforced that notion.

He asked how she was and how the kids were holding up, and truly seemed to want to know. And something about that simple kindness made her impulsively suggest he get a second steak and some more potatoes and bring it to her house and join them for dinner. Her only company for weeks had been the kids and her overbearing sister, and having some adult conversation not polluted by smoldering fury seemed like a good idea.

The steaks he seared on the grill were good, but it was the Bordeaux that turned the evening. They both loosened up and talked. Really talked as they never had. And the Bordeaux led to the Guatemalan rum, which continued after the kids went to bed, and she put some music on to mask their conversation, and the liquor and the music and the pent-up anger and her feeling for Rich—which in all honesty could most accurately be labeled as pity—led to a kiss. And it went from zero to sixty incredibly quickly.

It felt foreign. Sex with someone who wasn't Jake. It wasn't bad, but it wasn't good, either. There was so much guilt—on both sides, she guessed, from the struggle Rich had to complete the act—that the sensual feelings, welcome though they were, took a back seat. They didn't talk about it after, except awkward excuses and mutual assurances that it was all fine.

The thing she wonders now is: Who did Rich tell? He wasn't the type to brag about the conquest. In fact, he would have been deathly afraid of Jake finding out, because deep down, he still cared about Jake. So who did he tell that let it slip? And is it possible that those mistakes in judgment—first hers in sleeping with him, then his in confiding in someone about it—created enough motive to make Jake do something in a drunken rage? Something like what happened that night when her marriage ended?

"Do *you* think he did it?" Cara asks.

Sioban sees that beneath her flip *answer a question with a question* thing, she really wants an answer. And she's afraid of what that answer will be. Interesting.

"He was there. He had gunshot residue on his hands. He was drunk, angry, he had motive, and now I'm hearing he has a history of violence when he's been drinking."

"Whoever told you that—you consider they might have an agenda?"

"Everyone has an agenda. Even you. I mean, he's the father of your children. He supports you. Him going down—that wouldn't be good for you."

Sioban sees that Cara is not as good at hiding her thoughts as her estranged husband, because the truth of these words clearly pierces her armor. And that gives her an opportunity to try one more push to get answers.

"Ms. West. I do understand you're in a terrible predicament, one not of your own making. But whatever the truth is about you and Richard Kaplan—doesn't Richie deserve justice?"

14

What Richard Allen Kaplan gets instead of justice—at least for the moment—is his body lowered into the ground, witnessed by depressingly few people. Rich was an only child born to older parents who have long since passed. The extended family was filled with acrimony and warring factions, and Rich had left them behind. Apparently there is a distant cousin mentioned in his will, but despite that fact, she chose not to fly out, making excuses about her kids and the expense. He obviously had plenty of colleagues but few friends, which means Jake ends up front and center at the graveside service. Javi's here, of course, as well as Grace. The people who clearly cared the most.

Daria and Gibson are here representing the firm, along with a small contingent of others, those secure enough in their standing not to care about Gibson's subtle exhortation to stay away, nor sweat the fact that he decided to show up himself—probably to see who had the audacity to ignore his warning. Kendall made the hard decision not to come because she needs the income, and with Jake now on shaky ground—or so the rumors suggest after that epic meeting—she decided to mourn privately.

As for the firm's partners, Archie Thompson couldn't be bothered to show, but that isn't surprising since he can't be bothered to come to the office at all most days. He's become a de facto "Of Counsel" without actually declaring himself so. Probably a means to keep his name on the door. Norman is here, though, and Jake wonders why. Is it for Rich, whom he watched graduate, who dined at his table, who made him a sizable profit? Is it for Jake, in solidarity? Or is there some other reason? Jake is clear there's an agenda, he's just not sure what it is. Regardless, the attendance is lower than Rich deserves. Even Cara has stayed away. No surprise there, given everything.

Jake cranes his head to find Sioban. It's SOP for her to be at this kind of affair, to read what she can from who's present and who isn't, but he doesn't see her. He tries to focus on the nondenominational words said by a man who clearly never met Richie. The officiant did his job, clearly asked some questions of "loved ones," got some information, and he seamlessly mixes it with his standard died-too-young speech in a way that feels both appropriate and nowhere near enough. Jake's mind wanders to what his own funeral would be like, to what his kids might feel. He knows they'd be sad, but would there be relief that he couldn't disappoint them any longer? And what would Cara feel?

A nudge from Grace brings him back to the moment. The casket—dark wood, sleek, mahogany maybe—is six feet down. The officiant is holding a small hand trowel, inviting guests to toss dirt on top of his ex–best friend. In truth, Jake finds the tradition awful. He wants no part in burying his friend. But since Jake is probably the closest one here to Richie, regardless of the fact that he's the prime suspect in his murder, he steps forward.

Jake takes the trowel, scoops it full of dirt. He catches sight of his father, standing stock-still, not moving to join them but watching Jake intently. Does he think Jake actually did this? Does he think his coldhearted son is scooping soil on the grave of his victim to throw off suspicion? Does he know what forces are moving behind the scenes to cause all this chaos? Does he have any feelings at all?

But today isn't about him. Jake tosses the dirt on his dead friend. Javi then takes the trowel and does the same. The two of them stand together, looming over their college third. Jake can't help flashing to the last moment he saw Rich, face exploded. He shakes the image loose—it makes him angry. His thirst for vengeance in this moment might be fueled by his father's unmoving face, but this isn't the time or place.

Grace is next to join them. She takes the trowel from Javi, but she sees Jake's hand is shaking as he stares down at the casket. She grasps his hand in hers, and it steadies under her warm touch.

Jake is moved but whispers, "Probably not a great career move. They're gonna think you're with me."

In this moment, she doesn't care. Grace digs the trowel into the dirt, aware that with this small act of kindness she may have just dug her own grave at the firm. But shouldn't decency matter? She tosses soil on the casket. She's made her bed—for better or worse.

Two hours later, Grace and Jake eat dripping tacos as they pore over the discovery from Tiana's case that Austin Bell has just dumped on them. If Jake had the support of the firm, a crack team of associates would be farmed out to some secure location to divvy up boxes and make short work of this. Jake has a feeling Bell is well aware that is not the case, that Jake's on his own, and this info dump is meant to give him no time to prepare for tomorrow's proceedings. So the three of them are camped out in Javi's brand-new, makeshift office space in a tacky, mostly vacant strip mall, one he's been able to secure thanks to Jake's blank-check retainer. It's better than Jimmy McGill's office behind the nail salon in *Better Call Saul,* but only because there's no smell of nail polish remover.

Javi can barely stomach his co-conspirators masticating. "How can you eat that crap?"

"It's not crap, it's al pastor."

Javi remains unswayed.

"Cut us some slack, we're in mourning," Jake says with a mouthful.

"I'm in mourning for my career," Grace ventures.

Javi has to wonder about Grace's motives for endangering her job and following Jake down this treacherous road. "What's with that, anyway? He pull out his Jerry Maguire mission statement and you went all Renée Zellweger?"

"I actually did that," Jake admits. "Earlier today, in front of the whole partners meeting, I tried to turn the troops against Gibson and Dad. Fell a little flat, though I'd say my speech was equal to anything Cameron Crowe wrote."

"Not how I heard it," Grace says. "Regardless, I'm not using my 'bereavement time' for Jake. I'm here for Rich."

"Yeah, well, I hope you get just how hazardous choosing sides with Jake can be," Javi replies. "See what it did for my career?" He points to a sign: DO NOT ASK FOR SEXUAL SERVICES. "This used to be a massage place."

Jake considers the sign. "You think they mean that, or is that a hint that you *can* ask, they're just covering their legal asses?"

"This is what you're thinking about right now? Hand jobs?"

Actually, what Jake is thinking about once again is just how far Javi has fallen from being first in his class. The plastic blinds are closed, blocking out the parking lot, but the string woven through them is kinked in a dozen places, making them distractingly uneven. There is a bamboo room divider, cheap but with a lovely print, clearly left behind by the former tenant. There is one secondhand desk, a thirdhand couch, and a coffee table that was probably picked up on the street before the garbage men could haul it away.

Grace slams her file shut, but her anger isn't at the sexual innuendo. "There's nothing here. The police actually did a good job. They connected Tiana's grief to Jacinta's murder. They weren't lying to her—they *did* talk to Reagan Hearst about his friend who came on to Jacinta. He claimed if one of his friends did that, it was a joke, nothing more. In these interview notes, he comes off as wanting to find Jacinta's killer. Like he really cared about her." She sees Jake's mind whirring. "Read it for yourself, Jake, but they did their job. There was nothing there, they moved on."

"Then it isn't nothing," Jake says, arriving at a conclusion that is far from conclusive. "The evidence of what they're up to is the *absence* of evidence." Javi and Grace are equally baffled.

"Have you been drinking?" Javi asks? "I mean, more than usual?"

"Why wasn't all this in Richie's case files? If it was all aboveboard?"

Javi tries to talk Jake off his conspiracy ledge. "Maybe—and just go with me on this—he didn't *have* Bell's discovery. Because hello, we just got it."

"Or maybe," Jake counters, "Richie was as good an attorney as you and I know he had the potential to be, and he went down that route, found the connection, found something . . . and then either he took it out of the file to avoid anyone else seeing it or someone at the firm took it out after they killed him. To cover their tracks."

Jake alone seems to follow this winding and convoluted path.

"Jake," Grace says gently. "We all want to find something. But much as I respected Rich, much as you two did, I think this was his first criminal case. He was watching old episodes of *The Practice* to study up on how to be dramatic in the courtroom."

Jake winces at that. "Really?"

She nods. They're all embarrassed for him.

"But still . . ." Jake starts to make another argument, but he doesn't have one. He looks to Javi for something, anything.

"It's a great story for a screenplay, Jake. Maybe that can be your fallback career when you finish imploding. But you have no evidence of anything you just argued. I get you're a little rusty, but most lawyers would actually have evidence before they went out on a limb against their own firm."

"I'm not most lawyers."

He's pleased with himself over his clever comeback, only to be met with two sets of deadpan eyes.

"You're really okay getting fired over this?" Javi asks. "Because you told them you *weren't* going down this path, toward Reagan Hearst. It's how you kept your job."

"I kept my job to keep my access," Jake explains. "And when push comes to shove, I don't think the great Norman West has the balls to fire his own son."

Jake sees that both Grace and Javi are completely convinced he's wrong. Which gives him some doubts, but he affects bravado. "I'm fine being fired. I will honestly feel a weight lifted," he says, convincing no one.

"You don't want to hear this," Grace says, "but maybe the best thing for Tiana Walker is for you to do what the firm wants. Drop the case." She sees his glare and rushes to clarify. "I'm not saying tell her to take the deal. If she wants to fight, someone should fight for her. But *you* have one hand tied behind your back. You can't bring up Reagan Hearst in court without it being a conflict and you getting fired. And nothing in the discovery overrides that. So maybe you give what we have to someone else."

"Sure. Judge Merrin will love that, me bowing out after passing on the deal. I'm sure that will go over well with the bar association, too."

He's hoping Javi will be the voice of reason, but he just throws up his hands.

"We don't need Reagan Hearst to win this," Jake argues. "We go after Bell. He flinched when I threatened to go for his campaign finance records."

This is a whole new path of conspiracy, and Javi's not having it. "*Jake*. Do you *hear* yourself? This isn't a treasure hunt where you keep diving in different spots. You talked yourself into a *trial*. You can't plan trial strategy on hope and a prayer."

"I've won with less."

Jake sees he's getting nowhere with Javi, and Grace doesn't even seem to be listening. She's intently comparing two documents from two separate folders.

"Grace?"

Her voice is halting, stunned: "I hate to say it, but maybe Jake's onto something. Maybe we *do* go after Bell."

They both give her the moment, waiting for her explanation. Finally, she gathers her argument.

"What if Bell's offer was so good because he thinks if you go to trial, you're going to find a hole?" She shows them a page. "This says one hundred and fifty-one interviews turned over in discovery."

Jake is disappointed—he thought she found something good. "I already went through all of them; there's nothing."

"So did I. But right here: *their* summary page says there are one hundred and fifty-two."

Jake goes wide-eyed, like she's found the Ark of the Covenant.

Javi's not sold yet; he takes the summary document from the DA's office, then starts flipping through pages in Rich's file, comparing.

But Jake seizes the straw. "Bullshit. One hundred and fifty-two was the guy. I'll bet a month's salary they found Reagan's friend." He sees they're wary of his baseless certainty, so he dials it back. "Or at least someone who saw something."

"A month of whose salary?" Grace asks, still not convinced.

But Javi is chewing on this. Slowly coming around. "Even if you're right, how the hell do we find someone if they're not here?"

Jake has a shit-eating grin on his face, which gives Javi a queasy feeling in the pit of his stomach. "Something tells me you have an idea—and I'm not going to like it."

15

Detective Sioban McFadden had indeed been at Richard Kaplan's funeral, watching from a vantage point where she could see who was there and how they acted, but also from where she wouldn't draw attention to herself. She was surprised at the meager turnout. In Dublin, death is far more sacred. Doesn't matter who you are in life, people mark the end of it, if not out of genuine affection, then for the booze that is sure to follow.

Jake put on a good performance, remaining stoic amid glances that blamed him, not letting himself be intimidated or baited. If he is indeed Kaplan's killer, he played it well. She's clear on only one thing in the burial's aftermath—her suspect isn't going to slip up easily.

Which is why she's surprised when the phone on her desk buzzes and the desk sergeant tells her that her suspect just walked in the door. She's intrigued. "Bring him back."

Moments later, Jake is escorted into the bullpen. As soon as the sergeant goes, she can't resist: "You come to confess, Counselor? Or just to dig up some more of my past?"

"You went to my wife."

"You told me things aren't always how they look—I was looking harder."

Jake takes a moment to evaluate how much bullshit is coming his way. But she doesn't seem put off by his arrival, which is a good sign. "Are you really open to suspects who aren't me?"

"I know it's not popular these days, but I do want the truth."

"What if other people in this building don't want that?"

While she could easily dismiss this as typical lawyer overreach, what he's saying isn't inconceivable. She hasn't seen it on this case, but she's seen other cases take turns because someone on some floor with some degree of power is protecting someone. On the other hand, she's dealing with a potential murderer who has a history of barking up conspiracy trees.

"More hypotheticals?" she shoots back. "Because intimating corruption in the police force is really the Hail Mary play of the accused. And before you ask, yes, I do like American football, so I understand the metaphor."

"Do you also like following the news? Because if you do, here in LA or in any city really, police corruption is not only real but pervasive."

He's tapping a file folder in his hands. A prop or evidence? Or both? "You have something you want to tell me?"

"I want to tell you a lot of things. But as we discussed, some of what I know, I can't share without being disbarred."

"So don't tell me what. Tell me who."

"I can't, same problem. But . . ." He holds out the folder. "I can give you this."

She takes it, her eyes on him the whole time. But he gestures to the folder. She relents and opens it, does a quick scan to see where this is going.

"Witness statements on Tiana Walker. I already have these."

"Compare this—what we were given in discovery—to what you have. Then tell me what I'm missing."

She hands back the paper. "If you think something's missing, file a motion."

But Jake doesn't take the folder. "You want me to give them fair warning? You think that's a good plan if I want the truth?"

She's irritated because she's being played, but he has a point. She glances around to see who's watching them. A few looky-loos, but Captain Gantley isn't in. Which means she has options.

Jake can see she's on the fence. "Someone knew something about the night of the fire in Tiana's apartment. Maybe when you figure out what, you'll have an idea of who really killed Richard Kaplan." He waits. She's not arguing. One more push. "You did tell me you thought I should work harder to save myself. This is it. Me, working harder."

Jake walks away—without the folder. Sioban watches him go, hating herself for keeping it and hating herself for not having a rejoinder, but mostly hating herself because she's beginning to like him. She sits back down at her desk and reopens the folder.

Consuela Estrada looks older than she is. Which is old. She has fake teeth of some kind, and they don't fit very well, so she keeps running her tongue over them, sticking a finger in and adjusting them, pulling them out occasionally and putting them back in, with no apologies. Makes it hard for Sioban to focus.

"After the fire, you talked to the police. Can you tell me what you told them?"

Mrs. Estrada scrunches up her face in confusion. Sioban waits for her question to register and process through the language translation and decaying synapses of Mrs. Estrada. "Didn't they write that all down?"

"I can't seem to locate your statement."

That was the biggest red flag Sioban found after perusing Jake's file. It wasn't just the omission of the witness—Mrs. Estrada—from the documents turned over to Jake. It was that when Sioban went to the original files, Consuela was listed on the summary, but her statement itself had ceased to exist.

Mrs. Estrada seems to really think back to what she said, then she shrugs. "That was . . . a long time ago."

Sioban studies the missing witness. Sitting here in a once-white plastic chair by the once-refreshing swimming pool, outside these once-nice apartments, her assessment is that the woman isn't lying. Even so, something tells Sioban that this is worth a little extra effort.

"Forget about what you told them. Do you remember what you saw? Can you tell me that?"

Again, the delay for translation and processing, like accessing the internet on an old dial-up modem line. But, as in those old days, eventually a connection is made.

"I saw Tiana out here drinking. She was angry. Drinking a lot, I think. Poor thing could barely get her kids to school after Jacinta was killed. We tried to help, some of us, but . . . she was sad. So sad."

Basically, a confirmation of everything in the case against Tiana. Which works against Jake—there's nothing in this missing witness statement to help. Just a clerical error.

"So that's all? Anything else?"

Mrs. Estrada shrugs apologetically.

"Well, sorry to have bothered you." Sioban gets up, ready to close the book on this and stop feeding into Jake's paranoia. But she decides on one more push, one step further.

"Mrs. Estrada. Let me ask you this: Is there something you might've told the police that wasn't about the night of the fire? Something about Jacinta Castillo, maybe?"

Again the processing delay, again the scrunched face. "No. Nothing about Jacinta . . ."

"But something else?"

Mrs. Estrada can't see the relevance of what she's remembering, but she's certainly one to do her civic duty. "I did tell them about the white boy."

Sioban wills herself not to show her true level of interest in this pivot. "Which white boy was that?"

"I saw a white boy hanging around, around then. A few times. It felt . . . wrong." She gestures to the courtyard filled with non-white people. "You know what I mean? What'd he be doing here? I asked the police to keep an eye out, long as they were here. But I can't guess how that helps you."

"Can you tell me what this white boy looked like? How old, how tall, hair color, that kind of thing?"

Something in Mrs. Estrada's teeth bothers her, so she yanks them out again. Then she refocuses on Sioban. She really seems to want to help, but she gives a sheepish toothless grin. "Sorry. White people all kind of look alike to me."

Austin Bell takes in the impeccably decorated office. Say what you will about Bob Forrester, he may not be the best boss, or the best DA, or even a very good lawyer, but he has taste. The desk is a Mahogany Serpentine from Scully & Scully. The couch—an Eleanor Rigby Gaga from Perigold. He knows this because he looked up both before deciding he couldn't afford them. Yet. As for the art, it's probably worth more than Bell's house.

Taking in a photo of Forrester and his third—or is it fourth?—wife, he takes solace in the fact that the taste is all hers. Forrester is an embarrassment, and his forthcoming "retirement"—an attempt to dodge fallout from a host of ways he's used the office of DA for personal gain—is overdue and greatly welcome.

Having been summoned to a meeting, one that Forrester himself seems to have forgotten, Bell takes a moment to size up the office that should soon be his. Energized, he starts to leave when he sees a full head of red hair coming his way. Detective Sioban McFadden has found her way past the gatekeepers and is heading right for him. This could be interesting. Maybe she's ready to nail Jake West? Then his problem goes away.

"Measuring for redecoration?"

She's making a joke, but also signaling that she understands he's likely to be a power to be reckoned with in the near future. He's not about to play along, and instead replies with: "Shouldn't you be out catching killers for me to prosecute?"

"That is exactly what I'm doing." She nods to the ostentatious and currently vacant office. "Can I have a private word, Mr. Bell?"

"Sounds ominous."

He says it lightly, but he senses it *is* ominous. And not in a good way. They step back into Forrester's office. Sioban takes it in: American excess at its finest.

"So?" Bell says.

"Tiana Walker. There's an . . . anomaly. The witness list you turned over in discovery omitted a witness."

Thank goodness. Not a big problem, just a nuisance. "A witness who saw the real killer? We should call the *LA Times*."

"I don't think you want that. Because even if the witness saw nothing, even if it was a clerical oversight, it's not a good look."

Bell can't argue that, and he doesn't have to, because they shouldn't be talking about Tiana Walker at all. "I'm confused, Detective. As the prosecutor on the case, I am well versed in just which officers on the LAPD worked that case. You are not one of them. Unless Mackenzie has been reassigned."

"Let's call my involvement a possible tangent."

"Yes, you're working on the murder of Richard Kaplan. So let me guess—this is what Jake West is selling as his defense? He found a clerical error in an unrelated case, and he's now managed to co-opt the LAPD as his private investigative team? I knew he could be persuasive, but this is above and beyond."

"I am merely doing my job, as you'd want me to do if you end up prosecuting that case."

"I'm all for due diligence. But for the love of God, don't tell me you're buying into his insanity." He watches her screw up her face, assessing him. "What?"

"I was just thinking about all those words you threw back at me. I don't think it was—how do you lawyers say it?—responsive to my question."

"You didn't ask a question, Detective. You made a baseless implication of impropriety. But let's put the verbal gameplay aside. I will certainly look into this matter, and I will certainly find out what kind of oversight it may have been, and I will certainly rectify said oversight. But what I can assure you of is this: On Tiana Walker? We have the right person. And we have nothing—nothing—to hide." She's trying to read him, and he doesn't like it. "You see a lie in my eyes? An evasive quiver in my voice? Did my eyes dart to the side to indicate obfuscation? Sorry, not sure if that translates, it means—"

"I'm quite versed in the English language, thanks."

"I meant no offense."

"I think you did, but we Irish have thick skins."

Austin Bell is coming to the same conclusion Jake West did a few days earlier: this detective is not to be underestimated.

"Well, I do appreciate you bringing this to my attention, Detective."

His tone is light, but Sioban's not sure if it hides something darker. Regardless, she has been dismissed. She takes in the office once more. "I'll be interested to see how you redecorate. My two cents—less opulence. You can smell the corruption in here."

She leaves the office, giving Bell a moment to scan his future surroundings a final time. How right she is about the stench. He will make it so much better. But if he wants this office to be his, he realizes he has a real problem. One that he needs to go away. ASAP.

Jake feels like he's just won the lottery. He wants to plant a kiss on Sioban, which is insane since her stated goal is to either put him behind bars for the rest of his life or have him executed, if they find there are special circumstances. Though maybe, with what she's found, that's no longer an option.

"Get that look off your face," Sioban orders.

"What look?"

"The one that says you think I broke the case wide open and you're in the clear."

"Didn't you, though?"

Jake takes a bite of the triangular scone on which he's slathered a little real butter. He'd suggested Canyon Coffee in Echo Park when Sioban called, as a good halfway point between Javi's Hollywood strip mall office and downtown, mostly because he wanted the scone. Though the quad shot latte with the foam shaped into a leaf is doing the best it can to make him forget his craving for a different kind of liquid. He got there first, scored two chairs at a green metal table on the sidewalk, and got Sioban exactly what he's having. She's only sampled the coffee—the day is gray, and coffee cuts the cold.

"One unreliable witness saw a random white person hanging around Tiana Walker's apartment complex days before the fire. It doesn't clear her, and it sure as hell doesn't clear you. Losing that statement was likely a clerical error."

"That's what Bell said?"

"He said he'd investigate. And for what it's worth, I didn't smell a lie or any fear."

"And yet you came to fill me in."

"I owed you the truth. They'll have to give it to you anyway."

"No—my read of the situation is: you know they hid it. A witness who saw someone at the apartment? If it really meant nothing, why hide it?"

Sioban wonders exactly that. It's an anomaly, a puzzle piece that doesn't fit. She could jam it into the empty space of the puzzle and make it almost fit, but she'd know something was off. "Let's say for the sake of argument they did hide it. Am I convinced the reason for that is that one of your firm's clients killed Jacinta Castillo—then got Tiana Walker to stop asking questions by setting her up for the murder of her children—then killed Richard Kaplan because he found out? That's not only far-fetched, it's really a bad plan."

"Killers make mistakes."

"What killer, Jake? Give me a name. A place to start. Anything."

"All I can say is—I'd start with our firm."

"I tried that. I was told it's all privileged. I mean, you think they'd want to help your defense, but then, I get the sense you're not very popular at your place of business."

"It's jealousy."

"Of what? That your life is falling apart?"

"I figure you're going to fix all that for me."

"Maybe I could if you used some of your legal gymnastics to help in your own defense."

"I've skirted enough edges. If I even tiptoe across the line, I only make things worse. Anything you found based on what I told you would become inadmissible. I'd be hurting your case, not helping it."

She throws some money on the table. "Well, all I can tell you is—my case is the murder of Richard Kaplan. And right now, aside from an unidentifiable white guy in Los Angeles, what I have is you." She gets up from the booth.

"You know I already paid," Jake tells her.

"That would constitute a gift—your lawyer could use it in court to impeach my impartiality."

"Only a sleazy lawyer would do that," Jake says, though she's not wrong.

"Eat up while you can, Jake. I hear the food's not so great at Corcoran."

She leaves, but Jake has taken another stride forward. If Dave's Hot Chicken broke the ice, Canyon Coffee has increased the speed of the thaw. He can tell that she's no longer sure he's her guy.

16

When people picture Los Angeles, they usually think of palm trees, endless beaches, boardwalk Rollerblading, the Hollywood sign, the Walk of Fame, the arching gates of the Paramount Studios lot. Maybe add in Rodeo Drive (not actually in Los Angeles) or the Ferris wheel at the Santa Monica Pier (also not in Los Angeles). The point is, they think of sunshine and glitz, of swimming pools and movie stars, as the song says. What they don't think about is downtown.

But that's changing. Starting with the building of the Staples Center—now the Crypto.com Arena—followed by the adjacent LA Live venues, and the opening of Metro lines heading west, the downtown area is becoming a destination. Not just a corporate district, but a vibrant live-and-work environment. At least that's the vision of developers like Philip Anschutz, Donald Sterling, and Reagan Hearst.

If the era of Donald Trump has proved anything, it's that real estate is a ticket to wealth—real or imagined. Valuations are so fungible that you win when you hit it big, and you also win when you lose.

All of that is in the air as Jake and Javi stand at a deep pit behind a fenced-off construction site a quarter mile from the court buildings. It's six p.m., the workers have been gone for a few hours now, but one can't mistake what's being built because a large sign proclaims it as Hearst Plaza, complete with an artist's rendering of a glossy, glowing place you'd want to move to, work in, walk your dog around, and go to the theatre (they'll use the more sophisticated spelling of the word, no doubt).

"I should just give Reagan Hearst to the Irish cop," Jake ventures as he stares into the pit that will fill said Hearst's pockets with money.

"Give her what? We've got nothing," Javi insists, not for the first time. "Let's say Hearst is involved in what happened with Tiana. He wouldn't have done it himself. He wasn't lurking outside that apartment. He would've hired someone, through an intermediary, who would never give him up. On top of that, you just can't go there, Jake. He's a major client of the firm where you are a soon-to-be-former partner. If you dig into it and actually find something, you still can't reveal what you learn. If you really think that's where this case goes, Grace is right, you have to quit and give this all to someone else."

"I won't give them the satisfaction."

"You really never learned to see when you've lost. It's almost pathological."

"Sorry, I don't have much experience with losing. Regardless, while I still have access, I'll have Grace go through all the client files—"

Javi immediately objects. "You can't—"

"Not Reagan's files, those are out-of-bounds, but all the other ones. I want her to get every name of every white male who has some connection to Hearst—clients, sons, cousins. Then we get their pictures—"

"Jake. Look around you. The man is developing two blocks of prime downtown real estate—half of Thompson and West's clients probably have a piece of this. And, if in the course of this fishing expedition Grace finds anything useful? You have the exact same problem. You *can't* use it. Not to mention what happens if she gets caught."

"But if Tiana can ID the guy who tried to sleep with Jacinta, and if it's the *same* guy Mrs. Estrada saw—"

"And if reindeer can fly . . ."

"Okay, fine. It's a bad plan. Give me a better one."

Javi hates to indulge in Jake's conspiracy theory, but it's the only way he might actually get him to acknowledge the obstacles they're up against. "We recanvass at the apartment. Maybe someone else saw this generic white guy? It wasn't what the police were asking about, so maybe it didn't come up. Not to mention half the building is probably undocumented and they don't want to tell the police anything."

Jake is energized now. "That's good. You do that—you'll get more without me as white baggage. I'm gonna go see Reagan."

"That's a bad idea."

"I want him to know I'm coming for him."

"It's a bad idea, Jake."

"He doesn't know I have nothing. I'll make him nervous, maybe he'll make a mistake."

"And Merry Christmas—we're back to flying reindeer."

"I'm a believer. Team Rudolph."

Javi shakes his head—there never was any use trying to talk Jake out of a bad idea.

LA is home to some of the finest country clubs in the world, and each has its own personality. Riviera is showy, it's a stone's throw from the ocean, and it hosts an annual PGA tournament that draws huge galleries. The fact that its initiation fee is in excess of three hundred thousand dollars is no obstacle for the Hollywood talent and agents who thrive on such status. Bel-Air Country Club is nestled in the elite hills that once served as home to people like Ronald Reagan and Michael Jackson and Elizabeth Taylor. Its clientele is older, preferring privacy and seclusion—it's less a place to see and be seen, and more a place to be away from it all. But possibly the most exclusive of the "Big Three" is the Los Angeles Country Club—the very place that wouldn't give Groucho Marx membership, prompting his famous line: "Why would I want to join any club that would have me as a member?" While it wasn't a stated policy, Jews in general were not permitted, nor were other "undesirables." Hugh Hefner, whose Playboy Mansion sits a half-block from the course, and whose famous "zoo" full of wildlife can still be heard from the tee box on the fourteenth hole of the North Course, couldn't get a membership. The list of rejections was long, and in spite that, or more likely because of it, this is the club where Reagan Hearst spends most of his time.

Jake has enough connections to get past the guard gate. It won't get him a round of golf, but that doesn't matter as he doesn't play. He often thinks he should pick up the game; he needs a hobby that doesn't require alcohol, but the problem is his father loves the sport. It's quite possibly the only thing he truly loves. So Jake has decided to hate it on principle—to find any common ground with Norman West would be morally reprehensible.

The driving range sits in the bottom corner of Holmby Hills, where golfers hone their game hitting shots in the direction of what once was known as "Candyland," Aaron and Candy Spelling's showpiece mansion where you were greeted at the door by maids in full uniform, who would let you know "The Mister will see you now." Now called "The Manor," the property has been sold at least twice since the Spelling days, at one point for $119,750,000, the priciest purchase in Los Angeles at the time. So there is no doubt of the obscene property value of this little strip of land being used to hone ball-striking skills.

Reagan Hearst has a good swing. Jake knows enough to recognize that as Reagan cracks a crisp five-iron at least two hundred yards. He's dressed in his Payne Stewart best, complete with chapeau—he's not just rich, he's an asshole, exuding that out of every pore.

Jake slips, unnoticed, into the slot behind Reagan. Waits until he has a ball lined up and ready to go before saying loudly, "Let's talk about Jacinta Castillo."

Reagan pauses his swing, takes a centering breath, and pounds the ball, but it arcs way to the right.

"Nice try. You were trying to show that question didn't bother you. But the slice—it's a tell, Reagan."

Reagan turns to take in Jake. "Wow, look at you. Are you actually sober, Jake? Last time I saw you, you spilled a drink on me."

"Last time I saw you, you were hitting on my wife. A few months after *your* wife died."

"Really sorry to hear you two split. Cara is so . . . delectable. You do have good taste in women, I'll give you that."

"Was Jacinta delectable?"

Reagan's response is to scoop another ball with the face of his club, line it up, and swing—this one is crisp and straight. "What happened to her was a terrible thing," he says without turning to Jake.

"Being murdered often is."

Reagan turns back to Jake, his legendary temper flaring. "She worked for my family for two years, and I liked her, okay," he spits angrily. Then a bit softer he says, "My daughter loved her."

"She was dating a friend of yours. I'd like to know who that was."

Reagan just laughs. "Sorry. My friends wouldn't 'date' Jacinta."

"Okay, what friend was fucking her? Or trying to?"

Reagan bites back anger. "The police already went down this road."

"Yeah—and after they asked you about it, the person who gave them your name ended up as the prime suspect in a murder case. So the question I have for your friend is: When he tried to kill Tiana Walker, was he aware there were little kids in the house?"

Reagan is tired of letting Jake have the run of a place he doesn't belong. He waves over an attendant.

"It's good to see you, Jake. I really should give Cara a call. See how she is. That would be the neighborly thing to do, don't you think?"

The attendant arrives, and Reagan motions for him to take his clubs. "I'm done here." Reagan starts to walk away.

Jake lets him get a few paces before saying: "I don't know if you're involved, or just covering. Either way, I'm gonna make sure you lose Hearst Plaza."

Reagan slows just a fraction, then continues on his way. Jake turns and does the same, each of them feeling unnatural hate for the other. The moment is interrupted as Jake's cell phone rings, evoking glares from those on the range.

"Phones not allowed, sir," the attendant announces. Jake sees from the various dirty looks that he's committed a faux pas nearly equal to the charge of murdering Rich Kaplan. He glances at the phone—it's Grace—but he lets it go to voicemail.

Grace is in the cavernous parking garage beneath Thompson & West when Jake calls back. The signal is good—she's heard the legend of how much Norman spent to make sure there'd be reception even five floors beneath ground level. Thompson & West lawyers were never to be unreachable. She walks fast, eyes darting, nervous.

"Meet me. Now."

"You okay?" Jake asks, hearing what sounds like fear.

"No."

"I can be at the office in five."

"Not here." She looks around, trusting nothing. "You remember the place where we first . . ."

Jake remembers. He has a tactile memory of the smoothness of her skin. "I remember."

Grace hangs up and starts for her car, but she hears an echo of footsteps and stops cold. Are they hers, or is someone else here? Is this whoever came after Jake? Is this whoever murdered Rich Kaplan? Her heart is pounding but she starts toward her car again. She beeps the alarm, half expecting the car to explode. It doesn't.

She gets in, fast; locks the door, fast; then peels out.

17

The interesting thing about houses in the Hollywood Hills is that from the front, most appear to be small, one-story buildings. Which is the antithesis of places like Beverly Hills, where the façade is meant to overwhelm and impress. Here, the topography lends itself to mystery. Accordingly, Jake parks on a twisting road in front of what seems like a bungalow. But after the elaborate bolt lock slides and the door opens, Jake finds himself staring at Grace, framed by a huge house-length window that looks out—past a deck up on stilts to maximize the feeling of floating over the trees—to a 240-degree vista of the city below.

Jake remembers that deck. He remembers what they did on the lounge chairs of that deck. She didn't invite him back here to go down memory lane, but he can't help himself.

"I thought you didn't want to sleep with me."

It's intended as a joke, an icebreaker, not a come-on. Unamused, she yanks him inside and rebolts the door. Jake takes in the place. It's still a spectacular showpiece. There's an indoor pool kept at eighty-seven degrees. Towels draped over the edge of deck chairs like it's a hotel. Every item in the kitchen is in place. The fridge will be stocked with anything he could want, regardless of the fact that no one lives here.

It's like a safe house. Thompson & West paid a cool six million for the place back in the real estate dip of the early nineties, and it turned out to be a steal. It'd probably go in the mid-teens today, but it wasn't intended as an investment. It was to be used for various kinds of secret rendezvous—off-the-books meetings, out-of-bounds recruiting of clients and lawyers, a place for clients to do dirty shit even their partners and colleagues couldn't know about. And, occasionally, for "in-house" use—which is how Jake and Grace's "meeting" more than a year ago would have been categorized.

All of those thoughts percolate in Jake's head in a flash as he waits for Grace to tell him why he's here. She's scared, pacing. He lets her take her time, until he realizes he needs to help calm her, get her through whatever this is.

"Grace—"

"Someone followed me. In the parking garage. Just like with you."

Jake wants to make her fear go away, to normalize this. "We knew we were starting World War Three—"

"I don't want to end up like Rich—a bullet in my head and you accused of killing me."

It's not an implausible scenario. "You're safe here, though," Jake says as calmly as he can. "We can work the files from here, it's almost always vacant—"

"We can't get any files. They locked us out of the system. I tried my ID. I tried yours."

That's bad. They have crossed the Rubicon.

"Okay. Well, the good news is, they haven't fired either of us yet. So we find another way in—"

"Jake—"

"I'll figure it out. We have to put together photos of the clients, their contacts, some way for Tiana to ID this friend of Reagan's."

"It's too late for that."

"No, we can—"

"Bell made a better offer."

Jake stops in his tracks. That doesn't compute. "How? How is that possible if he hasn't talked to her attorney? Me."

"You were gone. He talked to Daria, and she took it to Tiana."

Jake feels the fury of being railroaded. "No, it doesn't work that way. Daria doesn't have the authority."

"Gibson does, and he delegated her."

Again, outmaneuvered.

"Doesn't matter, he can offer what he wants, it's a pass—"

"Tiana took the deal. Five years, she'll be out in two."

"No—"

"It's a good deal, Jake."

"It's too good."

"And you're willing to risk Tiana's life on that?"

Is he? Because him being right doesn't mean he can win.

"It's over, Jake. Let it go and maybe they'll leave us alone. Tell your father it's done."

He sees her futile hope that it can all be taken back, waved away with a magic wand. If he were a better person, at least a more reasonable person, he'd do as she suggests. It'd be the best thing for Grace, that's for sure. And for Tiana, most likely. Probably even for himself. It wouldn't solve Rich Kaplan's murder, but he's put enough reasonable doubt in Detective McFadden's mind that he hopes that problem may solve itself.

But Jake can't do what Grace is asking. He heads for the bedroom.

Grace misreads the move. "If you think we're gonna fool around to celebrate . . ."

She can tell that's not what he's thinking when he emerges from the bedroom holding a gun.

"Lock the door." Grace stands there, mute. "Say yes," Jake commands. "Say that when I walk out that door, you will lock it and bolt it and not open it for anyone but me."

"You're gonna give them more reason to think you killed Rich."

"You want to know something? Right now? That's what I want them to think. I want them to think I could kill anyone."

Daria Barati stands in the office she once loved and wonders, not for the first time, what would have happened if she'd taken that job at Skadden in New York. It was a good offer, at a more powerful firm. But something during the interview told her she was a diversity hire, which didn't mean the job wouldn't be good, but the whole place felt more corporate. And the competition down the line would have had many more players. She certainly saw Norman West for who he was, but Archie Thompson had charmed the hell out of her. So she did the math—fewer attorneys, fewer women, fewer spots later on, but weaker competition—which suggested her odds of rising to the top were better at Thompson & West. And let's face it, there was one more key factor: she hates the cold. Seven years at Harvard made that abundantly clear.

Fuck it, she thinks. No time to second-guess her life. She did what needed to be done coming to LA, just as she did what needed to be done today. It was a good deal for Tiana Walker, and maybe it means life can finally get back to normal. For her, for the firm. It obviously won't bring Rich back, but it'll bring some closure. She grabs her Prada bag and shuts off the lights . . . then flicks them back on. It isn't beyond Gibson to check office lights to see who's still working. Daria's leaving earlier than usual, but she's entitled.

In the parking garage, she listens as her heels clack and echo as she heads toward her Mercedes, a car she bought more for the prestige than because she actually liked driving it. Hector washes it twice a week whether it needs it or not, a perk of Thompson & West employment she doesn't mind at all, so it both looks good and is perfectly functional.

She beeps the car unlocked as she's walking, so when she gets there she just pulls the door open—and is jolted to find Jake sitting in the passenger seat. The metal plating of the gun he's holding glistens on the console between them.

"Are you crazy?!"

"Yes."

Daria knows he wants her to be unsettled, and she's trying to hide that it's working. She calls up her favorite trick—false bravado.

"Are you gonna shoot me like you shot Rich?"

"I don't think you actually believe I did it. So get in. Talk me down, Counselor. Show me why Dad hired you."

She weighs the odds—get in or run? The heels make fleeing a bad proposition. She climbs in. "How did you get in here?"

"You unlocked from five cars away. I was waiting on the other side of the car."

"You're a regular Houdini."

"I think he broke out, not in."

"What do you want, Jake?"

"Someone connected to this firm set a fire that killed two children. I want to know what you know."

"I don't know anything—"

"Bullshit. This all started with you."

She says nothing. Jake reaches for the gun and examines it in an intentionally threatening manner. If it's an act, it's a good one. Daria's scared—she has to give him at least something.

"I told you I was in court the day Tiana Walker was arraigned. That was just chance—that *is* how it started." He waits her out, knowing this is a half-truth at best. "I'm not lying to you. But I couldn't get it out of my head, what happened to her kids, her wailing that she didn't do it. The twenty-five-year-old public defender, who had to stand in when her first guy didn't show, she didn't give a shit and didn't know what to do even if she did."

Jake just waits for more. She knows one of his things in court, one of the things that made him great at trial, is his ability to hold the gaze of a suspect or the jury.

"I mentioned the case to your father. I knew I owed some pro bono hours, and maybe Walker really didn't do it. And he said, 'Doesn't matter if she did it, the question is whether they can prove it. And they can. So I'm not taking on a loss.'"

Now she's really got Jake's attention. "You think he *knew* she didn't do it?"

"I think he knew something."

This is exactly what Jake feared. But even when you suspect your father's evil, you don't root for proof of that to roll in.

Daria sees she's making headway and decides to pull a few more wires out of the bomb.

"I had drinks with Rich that night. I probably had too many. I was going on about injustice, someone should step in for this woman—"

"So long as it wasn't you—"

"You know how hard it is to go against your father. But Rich . . . he wanted to impress me."

Jake shakes his head, disgusted. "I tried to talk him out of it."

Now Daria's confused. "Wait—you knew?"

"I knew Rich had a thing for you. I warned him it would end badly."

That pisses her off. Except it did end badly. She didn't intend for any of this to happen, but it did.

Jake presses on the guilt he can see all over her face. "You didn't tell him he was going against Norman? Against the firm?"

"He was just gonna get her a good deal, the best he could make. But then . . ."

"But then what? What did Rich find?"

"I honestly don't know. But he called me that last night. Excited. Said he was gonna change what everyone thought about him."

This rings true to Jake. As much as he loved Rich, as much as he valued his friendship, and as much as he knew his financial value to the firm, the intricate work he did with contract language and profit definitions and esoteric legalese was utterly boring to Jake. Maybe Rich was a real lawyer, at least more so than Jake, but standing in the firm was based on style as much as anything, and Rich practiced law exactingly, not with style. The turnout at his funeral, while largely a by-product of Gibson's heavy hand, was also indicative of what people thought of Rich. They weren't compelled to give him the send-off he deserved.

"You didn't ask him to explain? What it was he found?"

"I did. But he was so . . . happy. You know Rich, he was never great in court, but he thought he finally had his Perry Mason moment. The truth is—he wanted to be you."

The truth of that stings. "You're making this my fault?"

"No. It's my fault. You said it—I got him killed. And you don't know how sorry I am."

He watches her; she's clearly wrecked. Maybe for the first time in their decade of working together he understands she's actually a human being.

"You really cared about Richie."

She hasn't confessed this to anyone. "I did. This is a tough place. He made it easier."

It surprises him, but it shouldn't. He loved Rich, why shouldn't someone else?

"So why did you do it? Make Tiana Walker take this new deal to send her away?"

"Because I'm a good lawyer, and I know that what I believe and what I can prove are two different things."

"You want me to believe you think it was the right thing? Not what you were told?"

"I want you to see it was both."

"If that's true, help me fix it instead of working to make it go away."

"I understand the biblical nature of father/son dynamics, but you can't beat him, Jake." She reaches out a hand and puts it on the gun. "And all this is gonna do is make you just like him."

She picks up the gun and he lets her. Daria's fascinated by it, but it doesn't change what she has to make him understand.

"Some cases, you just can't win. Haven't you learned that by now?"

18

All that remains for Tiana Walker is for Judge Eleanor Merrin to sign off on yesterday's agreed-upon deal. She should feel relief that this is over, that in as little as two years she'll be free to see just what's left of her life, what's left of her family. But the man sitting next to her at the defense table is tying her stomach in knots.

Jake continues to fight a losing battle with his client. A battle waged in whispers.

"You can't do this. I believe you. I believe you're innocent."

"But you can't prove it," she reminds him.

"I want to try." Tiana doesn't budge. "I want to be able to sleep at night."

"So this is about you?"

Despite her anger, he can tell she wants to say yes.

"I'll be out in two years," she says instead. "I'll try and explain to my son, my last child—"

"Tiana. Don't do this."

"The world isn't fair, I've known that all along. I'm taking the deal, Mr. West. It's better than the one you told me to take a few days ago."

She sees over his shoulder that Deputy DA Austin Bell is walking in. He smiles over at them, warmly, pleased that this case is about to be over. She's ready.

"Excuse me a moment," Jake says to her, then heads over to intercept Bell.

What is he doing? She just wants this over.

"You are a generous man, Mr. Future DA."

Bell eyes Jake warily as they both reach the prosecutor's table.

"We can both call this a win, Jake. Doesn't always work out so nicely."

Bell offers his hand to shake. Jake doesn't take it.

"I'm going to ask you to do one more thing for me," Jake says evenly.

Alarms start going off for Bell, but he's sure he has the upper hand, so he's not really sweating it. "Seriously, Jake—you have to know when it's over."

"It will be over. Just as soon as you file a motion to dismiss all charges."

Bell takes a beat. Then actually, genuinely laughs. "I'm gonna hate myself for asking, but I can't help it. Why am I going to do that?"

"Because if you don't, I'm going to destroy you for willfully withholding evidence from discovery."

"Consuela Estrada? A one-hundred-and-twelve-year-old woman whose statement clearly didn't feed correctly through the copier?"

"Yes, Consuela Estrada. The one witness who places another suspect at the scene. The one witness whose statement your office—I'm giving you the benefit of the doubt that it wasn't you personally, though frankly I'm not convinced of that—whose statement your office buried."

"It was an oversight. That's all."

"She saw the killer, Austin. That wasn't an oversight."

"Contrary to popular belief, we actually like to find the real killers. But no one else saw her phantom white guy. It wasn't on the night in question. And last I checked, it isn't a crime for a white man to be walking in a Hispanic neighborhood. Even to enter a public area of a building." Jake just stares back, and it annoys Bell. "You want to put her on the stand, be my guest. You think they'll believe a half-crazy, toothless woman?"

"She's lost her teeth, not her mind. So yes—I will put Mrs. Estrada on the stand. I'll ask questions in Spanish, let the jury see that I care about the people of the city I live in. And there's your problem, Austin. You may not have announced, but we both know you're gonna run to replace Bob Forrester. And while you may be the front-runner now, what percentage of Los Angeles is Hispanic? Forty percent? Something like thirty-four percent of likely voters? You attack her—not great optics."

Bell sees very clearly what Jake is proposing. It's nothing more than a Hail Mary, but he also knows how the press is. The city council was rocked a few years back by a leaked tape in which Hispanic council members were trashing Blacks. The city council president was forced to resign, and other members were hounded mercilessly for months.

Bell contemplates the imaginary headline that destroys his career. It pisses him off.

"Nice try. I'm not dismissing the case."

"Then I'll file a motion to dismiss."

"Go ahead. Merrin hates you. She'll never rule in your favor."

"Probably not. But it will lead to an investigation, and then to charges. Want me to quote PC 141? 'A prosecuting attorney who intentionally and in bad faith alters, modifies, or withholds any physical matter, digital image, or relevant exculpatory material' blah blah blah 'is guilty of a felony punishable by imprisonment pursuant to subdivision' something or other 'for sixteen months, or two or three years.' "

"Is the 'blah blah blah' the exact language?"

"I bet you could quote it better than I can. In fact, I bet you looked it up. Because you have to see, regardless of your culpability, how this plays. So when I'm done—in court, in the press, however this little dance ends—even if it was a clerical error? You'll look guilty. I may lose the case, but you'll lose more."

As Bell walks himself through the hypothetical attack and its hypothetical damage, Judge Merrin comes in. Everyone rises. He's out of time. This case should have been an afterthought, but now Bell realizes he has to recalculate. Quickly.

Austin Bell was fourteen when the LA riots brought the divisions of Los Angeles to the fore. A group of white cops beat the living hell out of a Black man—on camera—then were acquitted by an all-white jury. The city exploded, a collective rage expelled across every swath of Los Angeles. Bell remembers watching the looting. Some of his friends said he was lame for not going into the stores, that he wouldn't "repatriate" his due. He took a lot of shit for that. But he knew, deep down, crossing that line would mean something. He wasn't afraid of getting caught, he was afraid of deciding it was justified.

He wrote about that on his college entrance exams. It got him a full ride to USC for undergrad, then the same four years later at UCLA Law. That had been his goal—he wanted to stay local because he knew, from Rodney King forward, he wanted to be here. To make things better here. And he had. A stint as a public defender, then working his way up in the DA's office to become the heir apparent. Now he's going to have the backing of the mayor and more than half of the city council. He'd even have Bob Forrester, the outgoing DA, on his side if Austin hadn't told the man he thought he should withhold his endorsement. That hadn't gone over well, but he can't afford to be seen as Forrester's guy. Bell wants to be seen as the solution. Bob swallowed that pill at the time, but Bell has heard he's considering putting his endorsement elsewhere as punishment. He hopes that comes to pass—it would be a seal of approval for Bell to have Forrester endorse his opponent.

Bell contemplates the mess that is Jake West standing before him. An alcoholic, washed-up murder suspect threatening legal moves that probably won't win him this case, but could easily cost Bell his future.

"There's another option," Jake whispers, bringing Bell back to the moment. "We could work together. Tell me who's pressuring you to make this go away."

"No one is pressuring me. There's no conspiracy here, Jake."

"No reason the first attorney on this case was executed in front of me? No reason people are coming after me now that it's my case? No reason my own firm went behind my back to have you make this offer?" There's a small pause that Jake observes. An opening. "What have *you* been offered, Austin? And is it worth becoming just like the man you say you want to replace?"

Jake sees Bell struggling. And that is great progress. But he hasn't sold it.

"Whatever happened to Rich Kaplan—this case has no connection," Bell insists. "And if people are coming after you, look in the mirror, Jake. You have a way of pissing people off."

Either Bell believes what he's saying or he's a good actor. Doesn't matter. Jake sees Merrin reach her throne—he's out of time, because he doesn't have his client's blessing to do what he wants. He gives Bell one last whispering prod. "Ticktock, Austin. That's the clock on your political career ticking away."

"Be seated," the bailiff intones.

Jake slides back into his chair, purposely not meeting Tiana's probing eyes; he's not about to tell her he just ignored her wishes, that he's gambling her life. Merrin, meanwhile, seems pleased. She's clearly ready to be done with this.

"Gentlemen. Are we ready to go? Make this official?"

Jake concentrates on appearing resolute. But Bell isn't saying anything. He's looking at Jake's client, one he's certain is guilty, and who he's already cutting way too much slack. Jake needs to push him over the edge. "Your Honor—" Jake begins, but Bell interrupts.

"Your Honor, at this time the prosecution moves to dismiss all charges against Ms. Walker."

Bell is stunned to hear himself say this. Jake even more so—his bluff actually worked. But he's not so far gone he doesn't think to add: "With prejudice."

Which means Bell can't refile charges later.

Bell grits his teeth. "With prejudice."

"I move for immediate release and reunification of my client with her son," Jake says, trying to keep his astonishment and glee and sudden craving for celebratory alcohol in check.

Tiana appears equal parts elated and confused. She stares at Jake like he just pulled a rhinoceros out of a hat.

Judge Merrin might be the most perplexed of all, in a way that might better be described as livid. "Both of you. Approach. Now."

Jake enjoys his walk to the bench. Bell, less so.

"Someone want to tell me what the hell just happened?"

Jake indicates Bell can go ahead. "Whatever culpability Ms. Walker bears, Your Honor, the district attorney's office has come to the conclusion she's been punished enough by losing two of her children."

Merrin studies the two men and reaches the only logical conclusion. "Is he blackmailing you, Mr. Bell? Because this court won't be hijacked by that kind of criminal behavior."

"I resent that implication, Your Honor," Jake says, but he doesn't really. He's enjoying being a lawyer for the first time in a long while.

"I don't give a damn what you resent. You play dirty, Mr. West, and I don't like it."

"All due respect, Your Honor, you wanted to make sure my client had proper representation. Given this outcome, wouldn't you say I delivered on that?"

As far as the client goes, he's indeed served her well. But right now, Eleanor Merrin has one thought: she wants Jake West out of her face. While she worries about what's gone on behind the scenes, she knows Austin Bell to be an excellent advocate for the people. So despite her misgivings, it's clear what she must do.

"Step back, gentlemen."

They do. Awaiting her blessing. Or the next bombshell.

"Ms. Walker . . ." Tiana practically holds her breath, awaiting the ruling. "This case is dismissed. You are free to go."

And with the pound of a gavel, it's over. The judge rises and quickly leaves the room.

Jake turns to Tiana, who is not crying, not joyous—she is frozen in disbelief. Jake gently touches her hand.

"It's real, Tiana. Time to go home to Reggie."

And those words bring on her tears—such deep relief Jake can barely fathom it. But he knows one thing for sure. This is why it's good to be a lawyer.

19

Jake watches a female deputy process Tiana out. She looks almost reborn in clothes Jake had Grace pick out, which she did very quickly and tastefully. It's a black-and-white print dress, not showy, not fancy, but classy. Jake knows it's a great moment, but also knows the hardest part for his client lies ahead. Which is why Tiana's face is tense.

"You ready?"

It's a stupid question. He knows that the minute he says it. She doesn't bother to answer. He guides her to the door.

They emerge from the Century Regional Detention Facility—referred to more commonly as the Lynwood Jail—into bright light. It makes Tiana squint, and at first she doesn't see anyone. Then she spies Jacinta's brother, David, holding up a hand to get her attention. Standing nervously in front of him is Tiana's seven-year-old son, Reggie.

Tiana stops, terrified, her heart swelling and breaking at the same time. She wants so deeply, and fears more so. Jake nudges her forward. "Go."

She slowly walks toward her son. To meet her fate. Her real judgment. She stops in front of him, not wanting to force herself on him—God knows what he thinks or feels. The moment just hangs there, no one saying anything. And then Reggie literally flings himself at his mother, arms clutching on to her for dear life.

Jake feels something he hasn't experienced in a long time, a swell of emotion so deep that his first instinct is it needs to be drowned in alcohol. He's not sure if he wants celebratory alcohol or just something to numb an emotion he's not ready for. Either way, that feeling is trampled upon by a voice.

"Your client's got her life back."

Jake doesn't turn. His father has to take even this moment from him.

"Well done, Jake. You pulled off a miracle."

Jake turns to take in his father and wait for whatever's coming to ruin this triumph.

"So—what's she gonna do now?" Norman asks as casually as he can manage.

"She's going to Disneyland."

"Funny."

"No. No it's not. It was her kids' favorite place. The happiest place on earth. Don't you think she deserves that?"

"Yes. But you know that wasn't what I meant."

"Oh, you mean literally. What's she gonna do? Why? Are you still in danger from what she knows?"

"Jake—"

"She's going someplace no one can find her. Not even you."

Norman sees the depth of Jake's anger, and despite it all—it hurts. This isn't how a son should look at his father. "You really think I had something to do with all this?" Stupid question, but he had to ask. "I'm not a bad man, Jake. A tough father perhaps, maybe not a good one. But I want the best for you. Always."

Jake wonders if his father actually believes this. He knows it's bullshit, but does his father?

"The case is over. You got your win. Let's move past this." Norman's words almost sound genuine. He holds out his hand. A peace offering.

Jake was nervous. He was eleven and about to start his first game on the mound. His Sidewinders were playing the Mud Hens, and Coach Chris was trusting the big game to Jake. He'd thrown an inning in late relief in lost cause games twice, with mixed results, but this was going to be different. He'd been throwing every day, working to get his curveball to break, but more often than not, it just dove into the dirt. So today was gonna be fastballs. Which in

Jake's case were like medium-speed balls, but they were accurate—Jake could hit his spots. And since half the kids closed their eyes and swung at anything, accuracy was worth a great deal.

Jake pulled on his teal hat with the snake looped into an S. He rode his bike to the baseball field, since his dad worked and never came to an afternoon game. Or any game, for that matter. But it was okay—this wasn't about pleasing his father. This was Jake's sport, his world, his thing.

When he got to the field for warm-ups, he had a sense his teammates were looking at him funny. He assumed they were worried about him starting the game, worried he would fail them and they'd lose big. He intended to prove them wrong and Coach Chris right to put his faith in Jake. But as game time got closer, it became clear it was more than nerves. The other players seemed angry? There were definitely some death glares.

Jake went to the drinking fountain to calm himself, which is when Caitlin came over. The one girl on the team, which meant she wasn't as prone to groupthink. Seeing that they were alone, and she wasn't avoiding him, he was compelled to ask for clarification. "Are they all so that sure I'm gonna screw this up?"

She turned to see if anyone was watching, then told him the harsh truth. "No. They just heard why Coach Chris is starting you."

Jake stared at her blankly. Confused.

"You don't know?" she asked, surprised.

"Know what?"

"Your dad threatened him."

The bottom of Jake's stomach fell out. He wanted to argue. To say that never happened, no way, but of course it did, it made too much sense.

He rode home before the game ever started.

He didn't say anything to his father that night, but a few days later—in which time he hadn't spoken to his dad, not that he seemed to notice—Norman sat him down. And it turned out he understood the silence. But all he said by way of explanation was "I was trying to do something nice for you."

Eleven-year-old Jake studied his father, trying to decipher if he believed that. Norman was uncomfortable with the scrutiny.

"Jake. Let it go. Let's move past this."

Norman put on his face something Jake could only assume was meant to be a smile. Jake walked away. He never answered him and never played baseball again, not until Aaron begged him decades later. His dad had taken that from him. Something he dearly loved.

Here it is again. No matter how awful a thing he's done, Norman just wants to move past it. It's sociopathic. Jake looks over to Tiana and her son. The kid still hasn't let go of her.

"Some kids can forgive. Some can't."

And Jake walks away once more, this time toward his client. Forgiveness isn't in his nature.

"I'm your father, I'm supposed to be the one you can rely on. And I haven't been."

Jake stands outside Chloe's locked bedroom door and the irony of his words is not lost on him. He has become what he hated most. But seeing Reggie forgive a mother who was supposed to have done far worse things than he has, Jake decided it was time to act: to go to his daughter and make things right. Or at least start on that path.

She's letting him twist in the wind. He loves her with every ounce of his being, and the feeling in his heart makes him understand what it means when someone says their heart is broken. It is literally, viscerally, painful. The silence. The chasm.

It wasn't supposed to be this way. He remembers the excitement of the day Chloe was born, the sunshine and clear sky as he and Cara drove down Wilshire Boulevard toward the hospital. As if the world was going to deliver all the promises it had withheld. Now—he's a stranger in his own house, a house that is no longer his, distant to his own daughter. And the question he's asking himself is: Is it too late? He just won an unwinnable case, so isn't there some way to pull off a miracle here as well? He summons all his skill in making the unassailable closing argument.

"I've messed some things up. A *lot* of things. And I could stand out here and promise up and down, but we both know me well enough to realize that somewhere, sometime, I'll mess something up again."

He takes a breath. Not happy with his opening salvo.

"But I've loved you since the day I first saw you, Chloe. Since the day I first held you. And I wish I could take back all the things I've messed up. But I can't. And I can't just buy you a puppy, you're right about that. All I can do is stand here and tell you . . . I'm gonna try and be a better person."

Still nothing. He sees Cara at the bottom of the stairs, watching him with pity.

"Don't think you swayed the jury on that one," she says gently.

Jake makes a final try anyway. He takes out a tiny stuffed puppy from inside his jacket. He lays it outside the door. A small gesture of atonement. He looks to Cara, expecting to see derision. But she's gone.

Aaron runs out from his room. Eager as ever, his disappointment and anger from the phone call the other day forgotten. "If she's not coming, I get to pick, right?"

"Anything you want, champ."

"The Pier. There's this cool new arcade game, you actually get to hunt people."

"Sounds like a good life skill."

Aaron high-fives him, then flies downstairs. Jake trudges after his son—at least someone still loves him. At the bottom of the stairs, Cara reappears.

"I'm glad you won the case. You're a good lawyer, Jake. You always were. When you're sober."

He silently accepts the praise tinged with judgment. He starts to go, but she grabs his arm. Her face says there's something else she has to say, and he isn't going to like it.

"That detective—she asked if you were capable of violence. If I'd seen it. I said no."

That surprises him. Not that the detective asked, but that Cara had lied. She hates lying—the fact that she had to do it for him kills him. "You know I never meant to . . ."

He stops himself. Hates how cliché it sounds. He wants to find the perfect thing to say, something that might pave the way back to her. But nothing comes. He's not sure that's a winnable case.

"Tell me you didn't kill him."

Jake is startled by that. How is it possible she really believes he could've done this? He feels a pang of anger, then realizes something that should've been clear from the moment the police homed in on him as a suspect. It's a fair question.

"I didn't kill him." His voice is soft, his eyes unflinching. After a long pause with no response, Jake presses her. "Tell me you believe me."

She nods, but all she says is "Have him back by nine thirty, okay? He gets tired."

Jake feels the pain that she can't unequivocally answer his question. But the moment is interrupted by his cell phone. He checks it and answers.

"Javi? I can't—" He stops. Listens. Closes his eyes. This is bad. "I'll be right there."

Cara can read just how awful the call is. But before she can ask, Aaron is back. "You'll be right where?"

Shit. His son is looking up at him the way Jake once looked at Norman—filled with dread. Aaron knows he's going to be disappointed. Again.

20

TV shows get one thing wrong about crime scenes. They're usually shot bathed in blue and red light from the police cruisers on scene, which makes them appear almost pretty. They're not pretty—they're incredibly grim. You can feel death in the air.

Also, there's nowhere to park. Jake has to park three blocks away from Mrs. Estrada's apartment, not just because of the police activity, but because there are so many apartments in this area without adequate parking that the street spots are filled 24/7. So he's a little winded when he finally reaches the uniformed police officers blocking the security gate. He flashes a business card at one of them.

"My client's in there."

They size him up, figure there's no other logical reason a person dressed like Jake would be here, and wave him into the courtyard.

A few scattered residents are still milling around, wanting to be part of the chaos, but most have vanished as a forensic team stands over a body on the ground. No hurry here. No one to save. A bank of portable lights casts large shadows of the surrounding investigators, which adds a sense of horror to the already macabre scene. Jake can't get a good look at Consuela Estrada, but sees her limbs splayed at odd angles. And he can see blood, a dark, purplish-black ooze that seems to emanate from her head.

Javi's already seen it all; he's smoking a cigarette off to the side. Jake heads over.

"Those things'll kill you."

"Odds are, being your friend gets me first."

"What the hell happened?"

"They say she took a fall. Calling it an accident."

Jake frowns in disbelief, takes another look. As a crime scene tech snaps photos, he notices Mrs. Estrada's fake teeth have fallen out and are lying next to the body. A final indignity.

"No. Someone didn't want her to ID that phantom white guy." Javi doesn't respond. He, too, is looking at Mrs. Estrada's body, and purposefully not at Jake. "You're thinking it's somehow my fault. That I did this. I made Reagan Hearst nervous and—"

"I'm thinking you made *someone* nervous."

The two men soak in the awfulness as they think about what their investigation may have wrought. Both making lists—of who might have been freaked out enough to kill an old woman.

The speakeasy is bathed in red-orange tinted light. Dark wood surrounds booths with fancy upholstery, sitting areas have Victorian-era plush couches and an abundance of throw pillows, and an ornate chandelier sticks out from the mirror behind the bar itself. Jake ignores all of it as he sits on a stool at R Bar's counter. He gazes at the amber liquid in front of him, as if daring the drink to fuck up his life more. And it in turn dares him to pass up what he so desperately wants. Needs, even. Jake picked this place because it's dark and quiet and no one he knows would come here. Not trendy enough for the Thompson & West crowd, which really means not pretentious enough. Also, it was close. For the drink, he went with the middle ground—a Bushmills single malt. He's enjoying the aroma. That's it. So far.

Sioban slides onto the stool next to him. "Whiskey and cranberry," she tells the bartender. Then she takes in Jake—he looks like shit. "What round is this?"

"First."

"Sure. If you say so."

They sit in silence until she gets her beverage. She takes a big sip. She's impressed. A solid pour.

"You've been tailing me, Detective?"

"I had people watching the crime scene. They picked you up there. Called me."

"This place has a code. How'd you get the password?"

"I have a badge."

"That kinda takes the fun out of the whole speakeasy vibe, doesn't it?"

"I'm not here for fun."

"Oh? I thought you were hoping to get lucky."

"I am. I'm hoping you're gonna give me a name. Off-the-record, between friends."

"We're friends now?"

"I think we share certain goals."

"What you're saying is: you need me to do your job."

"No. My job is to prove you killed Richard Kaplan. Mrs. Estrada, Jacinta Castillo, Tiana Walker—those aren't my cases. You are."

"I gave you a name. You interviewed her, and a day later she's dead. You really believe these four cases aren't connected?"

Sioban just sips her drink.

"You can't still think I'm guilty."

"I'm really hoping you are. Because if whoever killed Jacinta Castillo and Tiana's kids and Consuela Estrada *also* killed your friend Richie Kaplan because he was about to blow the whole thing wide open, then logic dictates that Tiana's not safe. Neither are you, for that matter. Maybe not even me."

Jake finally gives in to the whispering of his drink. He swallows half the glass.

"Does that help?" she asks.

"My wife left me, my kids hate me, my best friend is dead, and you, my supposed friend, are still trying to prove I killed him. Me—I have a pretty good idea who's behind it all, but if I tell you, I lose my career." He downs the rest of the drink. He loves the sting in his throat. And hates himself for it. "Yeah, it helps. Because if I thought about all that . . . it'd be too much."

Sioban is still not sure if she buys all this conspiracy. She's growing sympathetic, but that doesn't equate to belief.

"Save us both some time, Jake. Just tell me if you *are* guilty. Because if you are, I *will* find proof."

Jake takes a long time to think about it. "We're all guilty. Of something."

Their eyes are connected by that. Both feeling their own guilt about their own things. But a phone alert on Jake's end kills the moment. He checks his phone. A text from Grace: COME—NOW.

Sioban sees the worry hit his face. "You gonna tell me what that was?"

Jake gets up, pulls out a wad of bills, tosses it on the bar.

"What I'm gonna tell you . . . No, what I'm gonna *ask* you, is to keep digging. But do it carefully. I can't imagine you ending up dead will be good for either of us."

Sioban watches him go. She downs her own drink to try and dull the thought of what'll happen when she does keep digging.

Jake turns a key, undoes the bolt, then opens the door of the Hollywood Hills loft, gun in hand as a precaution—ready for anything. The place is dark. Quiet.

"Grace . . . ?"

A knot of panic wells deep in his core, but then he sees a light shimmer on the wall, and there she is, sitting by the indoor pool overlooking the city. Drinking. A bottle of something is there, half-full, and an empty glass waits for Jake. He takes it as an invitation, comes over, and sits. It's a Japanese Whisky in a stunningly designed bottle. Hibiki—it promises Japanese Harmony, which sounds awfully good right now. Jake pours. And waits. Grace is not talking, and that's worse than her panic. Finally, he breaks the silence.

"You scared me. I thought you were in trouble."

"Aren't we? Another dead body tonight?"

"That what this is about?"

"No. What this is about—you're gonna need to do more than hold that glass."

He downs it all at once. Only then does she slide across to him a tiny black flash drive. He waits for the explanation. She takes her own glass, drinks the rest in one shot.

"I think what happened to Rich wasn't really about Tiana Walker. Or Jacinta Castillo."

"What are you talking about? Someone just killed a witness because we were getting close—"

"On *that* case, maybe. But it's bigger than that." She taps the flash drive.

"You gonna tell me what that is?" he asks. "Did we get our access back?"

"No."

"You have some Deep Throat source?"

"I don't know what that is."

"Watergate? Nixon?" No recognition. "Never mind. Keep talking."

"It kept bothering me," she says. "If Rich found some smoking gun he was going to use in Tiana Walker's case, why wasn't it in the file?"

"We've covered that. Either he hid it or someone at the firm got to the files before we did."

"I checked with someone I trust in IT. No one got in and deleted anything. The information about Jacinta Castillo—Rich must've pulled that out himself."

"And you found it?"

"This morning, after you won the case, I thought, okay, things might get back to normal now. I may no longer have server access, but I do have an office full of material I'm supposed to be working on. Let's see if I can prove my worth and save my job. I was going to work from this place until the dust settled, so I grabbed everything on my desk—and everything in my inbox. Where I found that flash drive in an interoffice envelope."

"From who?"

"From the dead, Jake. From *Rich*. He didn't trust anyone and he was scared—that's why he told me to meet him outside the office—but he wanted a backup plan."

Jake lifts the flash drive, imagining his old friend, hands shaking, trying to be a hero, putting it in the envelope. And then sending it, not to Jake, not to the friend who would've done anything for him. No, Rich knew Jake was useless to him. Instead, he sent it to Grace. But it was too late.

Grace pours them each more liquor. Jake takes a long pull to steady himself.

"So what did he send you?"

"Reagan Hearst's files. Every piece of business. Lawsuits, trust funds, charities, criminal cases, business ventures. And there was a sticky note attached."

She shows him a crumpled-up yellow square of paper. In black Sharpie ink, circled a half-dozen times, is: **USE RE: TIANA WALKER**.

Jake's mind starts to swirl, and it's not just the booze.

"Rich pulled out everything having to do with Jacinta Castillo from Tiana's case file, because Jacinta led him to Reagan, and Reagan led to something else. Something in these files. Something that is worth killing, at a bare minimum, five people."

It's a good closing, Jake muses. She's linking the murders of Jacinta Castillo, Mariella and Quinton Walker, Richard Kaplan, and Consuela Estrada. It's circumstantial at this point, but closings are about argument, not fact.

"So Richie *was* killed over a case—we just didn't have the right one," Jake says, both vindicated and kicking himself.

"That's why the body count keeps rising. And why we're probably next if we open that file. You, me, and Javi."

Jake finishes the second glass she poured. She does the same, then holds out her glass for more. He refills for them both, and they both slam down the third round. They're going to need them.

21

The fourth cup of coffee is finally beginning to put a dent in the hangover migraine. Sioban prides herself on her culturally ingrained alcohol tolerance, but last night's drink count is lost in a haze. She hasn't gone on a bender like that since . . . Callum Duncan.

But the caffeine is fueling her research, and one thing stands out like a red flag waving before a bull in Valdemorillo. Detective John Mackenzie. Johnny Mack, as he irritatingly likes to be called, ran the investigation of the apartment fire in the *Tiana Walker* case. And lo and behold, he's just been assigned to the murder of Consuela Estrada.

It's true she could find a way to justify the coincidence—the crimes occurred at the same location. Furthermore, it could mean the powers that be *are* looking for a connection. But she happens to know Mack's caseload is overfull—he's an inveterate and loud complainer—so it's odd he's been given this new case. Then there's the fact that Austin Bell mentioned Mackenzie by name. Sure—he'd know Mackenzie was the cop on the *Walker* case, but Bell has a lot of cases, and that name was at the ready.

She takes a sip of the mediocre brew to ponder this when she becomes aware of a looming presence. Captain Ryne Gantley, out of cop central casting—fifties, thick mustache, thick in the middle, old-school—is giving her the once-over.

"Can I help you, Captain?"

"You were wearing that outfit yesterday."

"I didn't realize you were keeping track. You like it?"

"I'd like to know why you never went home."

"Because I work so hard in pursuit of the truth that I didn't have time to go home and change. But here I am on a Saturday morning, doing the job. What brings *you* in?"

Gantley ignores her question. "You know, those lines in your eyes match your hair this morning. Something tells me it's not just from lack of sleep."

"If you're implying there was alcohol involved, you are correct. And if you're concerned, color me touched. But if drinking after hours is somehow a problem, I'll just advise you you're gonna have a lot of desks to fill in here."

"If you think being a smart-ass is gonna get you out of answering my questions, think again."

"I hate to be a stickler, but I don't think you really asked a question."

"My office."

He walks away. Sioban knew she wasn't getting out of this conversation, but at least the preamble was entertaining.

She takes time to get a fresh cup of coffee, both to drown out the headache and to stall. By the time she closes the door to Gantley's office, she's figured out how to play this.

"You want to know why I'm accessing cases that aren't mine." He neither confirms nor denies her assumption, but she takes that as a go-ahead. "The Richard Kaplan murder seems to have tentacles."

"Tell me Jake West hasn't gotten in your head."

"Jake West can spin whatever bullshit he wants. But when his bullshit ends up dead, I have to at least consider that his bullshit isn't bullshit."

"I think you're getting lost in your analogy."

"I'm not lost, and I think it's a metaphor."

"I don't care."

"It's always good to be precise with language—"

"Cut the shit."

"Okay. I'll get to the point. I'm not falling for a line of metaphorical *shite,* if that's what you're worried about. I'm just doing my job. Thoroughly."

"Let me give you a piece of advice, Detective. I don't know how things worked back in Dublin, but here? You start digging in someone else's 'shite'? 'Shite' tends to blow back in your face."

"Are you telling me to back off? Is this some edict from above? From Austin Bell, maybe?"

That hits a nerve—she watches his effort to restrain himself. "No, Detective. This is not a conspiracy. It's a paternal warning."

"Thanks, Dad. Is that all?"

The way she's treating him may not be fair. He wants to throttle her, but she has to see if poking the bear is going to bring the weight of the department down on her. If it does, if the reaction is disproportionate, she'll be more inclined to think Jake is onto something.

But Gantley manages to center his breathing and offer one last caution. "If your digging goes south, don't come running to me to complain."

Gantley's look says *go now*. So she heads out, thinking he played that well. It'd be hard to prove that little talk wasn't anything but managerial advice.

Stephen Gibson didn't sleep well last night. He hates the Breathe Right strips that Anne makes him wear. They make his nose itch and they keep springing loose, but she swears he snores without them. Not only do they impinge on his sleep, they impinge on his sex life. Who the hell feels amorous either wearing one or looking at someone wearing one? He wonders, not for the first time, if that's part of her goal.

But the Breathe Right isn't the only thing disturbing his rest. What should be a great time for him, basking in the marvel that is the breaking of ground on Hearst Plaza, has become a nightmare. He's set up the biggest construction project currently going in the city, involving multiple clients, and the firm will reap the financial benefits for years to come. It should be his crowning achievement, a prelude to his name on the wall. Thompson, West & Gibson. Or Thompson West Gibson without the ampersand. Probably a better way to go.

But that advancement is not on the table because things are spiraling out of control, and Jake West is driving the spiral. That man he can handle. The real problem is Reagan Hearst, who's livid over Jake's meddling, and the target of his wrath is Gibson. He refuses to trust that Gibson is handling things, and the fact that he doesn't trust that makes Norman not trust that, and he's already on thin ice with Norman. It was so much better when Archie Thompson was in charge. Gibson had Archie's implicit trust. But now that Archie's stepped back from the day-to-day at the firm, it's Norman he needs to keep in his pocket.

All of these thoughts were provoked by the irritating itch of the Breathe Right, which made the night interminable, and the morning hasn't gone any better. Starting with Reagan Hearst whining about Jake West's campaign of annoyance. Gibson misses the past year of Jake's alcoholic indifference. This new version is way too much like the pre-*Harrison* days, sucking the oxygen out of any room he's in. And Gibson has real business, important business, to attend to. He doesn't need this headache, nor does he need Reagan badgering him—he's been yammering away on this call from the point Gibson's Porsche crossed the 405, all the way to the parking garage and up the elevator to the office. Norman's whole 360-degree cell-coverage thing is sometimes counterproductive. Being unreachable can be a virtue.

Gibson moves the phone from his mouth as he curtly orders Kendall—"Messages"—and holds out his hand as he resumes pacifying his client. Gibson is one of those people whose true colors show in how he treats people he views as beneath him, though in fairness, he views everyone except Norman West and Archie Thompson as beneath him. Truthfully, maybe even them.

Kendall holds out the messages, and he snatches them up without meeting her eyes. He turns to go but finds Jake West blocking his path.

"Is that Reagan? Tell him I send my regards."

Gibson is momentarily stymied. "I need to call you back, Reagan . . . thanks," he manages in a measured tone.

He hangs up. Jake continues to block his way. Gibson wants to hold the upper hand but can't figure out how. Kendall watches all this, barely covering her amusement. Finally, Gibson buckles.

"Something you wanted, Jake?"

"Yes, Stephen. Clarification."

Gibson knows what he means and decides he doesn't want to play this out in full view of anyone coming in, nor in front of the receptionist he thinks can't stand him.

"My office." He sidesteps Jake to head for cover.

Jake winks at Kendall. "And good morning, Kendall. Putting in Saturday hours—I hope we pay double time," Jake says loudly, for Gibson's benefit.

It has the desired effect. Jake's ability to be liked is one of the many things Gibson hates about him.

Once in the confines of his office, Gibson feels good again, like he has regained home-court advantage. He sits at his desk to appear superior, but instantly regrets the choice as Jake comes in and stands over him.

"Have a seat, Jake."

"No thanks. I don't want to get comfortable if I've been terminated."

"Terminated?"

"Yes. See, one of two things happened yesterday, Stevie. Either A: there was a vote to terminate my partnership—or in layman's terms, I was fired, as was Grace Jamison—and no one had the balls to say so. Or B: there was an inadvertent server error that just happened to lock both of us out of the firm's system. Which would be . . . kinda weird, right?"

"Wow. Locked out. This is news to me."

The performance isn't good, nor is it intended to be. It's a pro forma denial.

"You have two options. You can have me here on the inside, or out there somewhere you have no control or power over. But you have to choose."

"Do I?"

"You do. You see, I've read the firm's bylaws. You once suggested I do just that, when your point was about something else. And though it may shock you, I listened. I read. And now I consider myself an expert on what you can and can't do around here."

Gibson's facial muscles don't really move, but his eyes give away his anger. A flash, then it's gone. "I think we should—"

"Go see Norman? Because managing partner or not, you don't have the balls to decide this on your own?"

There's a moment when Jake thinks he's won. When he thinks he's called Gibson's bluff. But it's very short-lived.

"Actually, Jake, I do have the balls. Which is why, under article 4, subsections 6 and 7 of the Thompson and West bylaws, you are hereby terminated from employment for cause. That is within my power as managing partner. You will leave the building immediately. Any personal items will be delivered to you at . . . where is it you live now? The Oakwoods or some other cliché?"

Jake really didn't think Gibson would have the guts. And the move against him is sound—the bylaws are clear on that point.

"And before you say it," Gibson continues, "yes, your equity shares will have to be bought out. As you are aware, since you claim to have read said bylaws, there is an independent mechanism that will arrive at a fair price. But from my point of view, *any* price is worth having you gone."

Jake wanted clarity, and now he has it. He thought he'd feel relieved. He doesn't.

"I hope you're prepared for my father's wrath."

Now Gibson laughs. "Jake. Do you always miscalculate this much? This was his idea."

22

The strip mall office that was meant to be a temporary stopgap for Javi has now become the base of operations for proving Jake West is innocent of murder, and uncovering who was actually behind Rich Kaplan's killing . . . and why. Grace is hard at work on her laptop, having set up camp in the former massage spa lobby at a second table Javi bought at Staples this morning. Watching her work, Javi realizes that while he appreciates her commitment to the venture, what he feels for her is pity. He knows what it's like to put faith in Jake, but at least he was never in love with him. Or whatever it is she feels for his mess of a friend.

"Stop watching me," she says without looking up.

"I'm not." Javi should have just let it go at that, but instead he says: "Can I give you a piece of advice?"

"If you wanna give me career advice, you might wanna wait until you've moved out of the massage parlor."

"Be nice."

"I know what I'm doing, Javi."

"And what are you doing?"

The look on his face says everything Grace is afraid he's thinking. "I'm not in love with him."

"Did I ask?"

"You think I don't know what people think?"

"I'm not one to judge. Even after everything, I'd probably lay down my life for the guy. But that's because I don't have much left. You, you could have . . . anything."

"Really? What could I have, Javi?"

"You're smart, you're . . ." He stops himself. He's aware he's stepping very close to a misogynistic land mine.

"Finish that sentence, I may cut your balls off with a letter opener."

"I don't think we have a letter opener."

"Lucky for you."

"It's just . . . you have potential. And throwing your lot in with Jake? It's *potentially* career suicide."

She really seems to take that in, then shrugs it off and digs back into her files. *It's truly a marvel,* Javi thinks, *how Jake engenders loyalty.* He considers himself Exhibit A.

It was Christmas break of their first year at Berkeley. Jake didn't want to go home, so he organized a trip to Cabo San Lucas. Rich Kaplan hated his family, so he was an easy yes. Three or four others followed suit, either for the fun, the drinks, the girls, or just to go along with their de facto ringleader. Javi begged off—he said he was going to spend the holidays with his mother; it was important to her.

That was a lie.

Jake didn't call him on the lie, nor did he try to talk Javi into coming. But a day after turning down the invite, Javi found an airplane ticket in his dorm room—to San José del Cabo. Jake never mentioned it, but Javi knew he'd done it, and he accepted it without questioning its provenance.

The trip started out well. There were drinks, and girls, and loud clubs, and more girls, and a lot more drinks. Many of which had been consumed when they took their party out to the beach late one night. They were on the Pacific side, where what looked like calm waters hid a violent undertow. That's why there were red PELIGRO—RESACA signs all along the beach, and during the day it was patrolled by hotel staff with whistles, trying to prevent the stupid gringos from drowning themselves. For those who wouldn't listen, they made you sign a waiver, holding them blameless if you were swept out to sea.

But at night the guards weren't there, and Jake always loved the idea of flaunting rules, so he goaded the whole group to swim from their little stretch of beach just a few hundred yards south to the famous El Arco, the arching rocks of Lover's Beach where the Pacific Ocean meets the calmer waters of the Sea of Cortez.

The water was cold, but the alcohol consumption dulled its sting. And at first, the swim was easy. It really wasn't very far—if you climbed the rocks from the hotel, you could walk there in ten or fifteen minutes.

But then, without warning, a huge wave came up, breaking over the top of Javi, and then the undertow grabbed him, knocking him below the surface and mercilessly dragging him out to sea. Javi couldn't see, couldn't yell; he was at the back of the pack, so the others wouldn't know he was gone. They'd get to the beach, laughing, drunk, and think he chickened out and swam back. In all likelihood they'd never find his body.

He worried about his mother, that'd she fly down here and spend the rest of her life searching, coming up with explanations for his disappearance to keep hope alive, even in the face of what would be the likely truth. He wondered where his body would end up. He wondered how long it would hurt his lungs—he'd read drowning was an awful way to go.

Then he felt a hand pulling him up. Jake. Javi coughed out water, then his body sagged. He was too tired to swim back to shore, so Jake towed him gently, talking to him the whole way about how his beloved Raiders were going to turn things around next year.

When they got to Lover's Beach, the others hadn't realized the two had been gone. Jake said nothing, letting Javi take the lead. Javi decided that it was best not to say anything, so he laughed, and drank more, and climbed the rocks back to the hotel, and the two friends never spoke of it again. Jake was like that—he didn't need credit for the small things. Only the big things.

Jake walks in the door, ending Javi's reminiscence. He's holding a tray of coffees and a box of Noah's Bagels, affecting good cheer. "Gooooooood morning, Vietnam."

"This is Thai Town," Javi points out.

"Not aiming for geographical accuracy." Jake hands out coffees and starts laying out the spread. "We needed to celebrate our big win, so I got lattes, I got bagels—everything, sesame, and salt. I also got lox and low-fat cream cheese and onions and capers and—"

"We're fired, aren't we?" Grace asks point-blank.

How did she see through his gambit? "Well, yes. But I see it as a positive development."

Grace is stunned. She knew what she was risking, that this was a likely outcome, and she'd made the informed decision to go forward anyway. But she's never been fired before, not even from a babysitting job she wasn't very good at, and it stings. All that time put in, and now no job, no plan. What was she thinking?

"You don't have to worry about money, I will continue to pay you—"

"You can't."

Jake waves off what he thinks is her concern. "I'm not broke or anything."

"That's not the point. You paying me . . ." She glances at Javi. She assumes he knows about their affair, but she doesn't want to acknowledge it out loud. "You get what that would look like?" she manages.

Jake hadn't thought about that. Javi is tactful enough not to comment or inject himself into this in any way. Jake tries again. "We'll figure something out, but the upside is Thompson and West is now on record as thwarting our investigation."

"They are well within their rights," Grace replies. "They had cause for you—the whole *Harrison* mess—and me? I don't have your contract. I'm an at-will employee; they don't need cause. So there's no positive value in our dismissal."

"You're missing the *key* value—we are free of the evil empire."

"And who's going to hire *you* now?" she asks.

"I'm setting up my own shop. This place, right here, is the ground floor of a burgeoning legal practice."

Jake's sweeping gesture to make his point causes him to notice a ceiling tile that looks like it could fall at any moment. It's covered in splotches of black that are probably mold.

"Well, not here, physically, Javi only took a three-month lease, but I mean *us*." Jake is hoping he has rallied the troops.

Javi grabs a bagel. "How about you stop selling bad as good and I'll fill you in on what you've missed."

Jake grudgingly takes a salt bagel and digs in as Javi brings him up to speed.

"So—Tiana and Reggie are safe. They're up in—"

"Don't tell me. I don't want to know."

"What, you think someone's gonna torture you for information?"

"Maybe. Or maybe this place is bugged."

The place is a shithole—it's not bugged. Jake waves him off.

"Fine. Point is, they're safe. For now. But given your new employment status, Amex won't keep them there forever. So the question of the morning is—what's next? After this positive development of you getting fired."

A half hour later, Jake has the four-by-six rolling whiteboard set up, with a rainbow of colored dry-erase markers in the tray below it. He writes away, switching greens and blues and reds and blacks, making arrows and question marks and exclamation marks to try to link the cases and not get overwhelmed by the dry-erase fumes.

"I like the whole serial killer vibe you're going for," Javi comments.

Jake steps back to take in the board. It does look insane. But Grace is studying the chaos carefully.

"It may *look* crazy, but . . . he's got the facts right."

"Thank you."

"It's all over the place," Javi complains. "We need to bring order. Pretend it's Criminal Procedure. Pretend you're laying it out for Highsmith."

"Shit. Haven't thought about him in years. What a dick."

"I got an A."

"For the same project that got me a C. Clear bias."

"You remember what you did to him?"

Yeah, Jake remembers. Grace is very interested to hear what he did, but Jake's not telling that story. It's not a story in which he comes across very well, but it was funny as hell at the time.

"Fine, I will lay it out for you. Like you're Daniel Fuckin' Highsmith." He draws more lines and arrows as he attempts to connect all the dots. "Let's start with what we know. Our first relevant fact point is that our mystery white guy—let's call him Mr. X—"

"Let's not." Javi plays Highsmith quite well.

"Fine. We'll call him Mr. White."

"Now we're playing Clue? Mr. White, in the courtyard, with a match?"

Jake ignores his friend. "Okay. Mr. White sees Jacinta Castillo at Reagan Hearst's rather opulent home. He likes what he sees, he asks her out, thinks he's doing her a favor. But she shoots him down, which likely did *not* go over well. He's stewing on that, no doubt, when sometime after, he's at a party at Reagan's. Tiana Walker is there this time, helping out. He sees *her* looking at him funny and he can only imagine what's been said between the two. Which pisses him off, he starts spiraling—"

"Objection—speculation," Javi chastises.

"Yes, it's speculation. We're trying out theories."

"You said you were laying out facts."

"And I will. But at this point, speculation is appropriate." Jake plows ahead. "The question is—what set him off? Embarrassment?"

"No. It wasn't about that," Grace says with clarity. "Think about the flash drive. The key is Reagan Hearst, not Mr. White."

"Again, how does that all connect to Jacinta and the party?" Javi asks. They all ponder that. No answers. Javi steps back in. "For now, let's put that aside. Stick with what we *do* know. Since the police really did grill Reagan, and some of them are actually good at their job, let's assume for a moment that Reagan was on the level—he had nothing to do with Jacinta's death."

"I don't concede that point," Jake says, "but for now, fine. We stay with Mr. White, who now has two things gnawing at him. First—this bitch had no right to refuse him. Not my words, I'm playing him here. Second—maybe he thinks she talked about it to her friend. And he will not be made the butt of a joke. So he intercepts her on the way home from Reagan's a few nights later. That's important, the time frame provides at least a small connection to Reagan."

Jake scrunches up his face. Something about saying that aloud bothers him.

"Yeah, it's not enough," Grace agrees with his face. "In this version, Reagan's a bystander. He's not really gonna be party to killing his daughter's nanny, and it doesn't explain why Rich said to look in his files."

They all think on that a minute. Javi studies the board carefully. "Okay, for the moment, let's run with it and keep going. His daughter's nanny is dead. Reagan Hearst wants to show his daughter what a big man he is—he'll make sure something is done about it. But when he starts asking questions, he finds out that some friend of Jacinta's has given the police a suspect—that friend of his who tried to ask her out."

Grace joins in. "Now he gets worried, so he deflects to the police. 'That story isn't possible.' But it rings true to *him*. Let's face it—we all have a stupid friend."

"Amen to that," Javi says pointedly.

"Point for humor," Grace allows, "but let's stick with Reagan. The police now have him thinking. Maybe he remembers some comment Mr. White made, somewhere along the way, about Jacinta? Fuck, he thinks. Could Mr. White be this stupid?"

Jake jumps back in. "Yeah, Mr. White *is* that stupid. Reagan knows this and he confronts him—'What the fuck did you do?' Mr. White probably denies it, but now he's sweating. He remembers Jacinta wasn't alone at that party. There was another woman with her, eyeing him in a way he didn't like. She's probably the one who told the story, which means she can ID him and connect him to Jacinta. She knows about him hitting on her."

Jake is hoping Javi will jump back in. Whatever Jake might say out loud, he knows Javi is fractionally smarter than he is, and he needs him to validate this theory. Javi just keeps studying the whiteboard, seeing this scenario in his mind's eye. Finally, he gives an involuntary nod and picks up the thread.

"It doesn't take much to figure out who Tiana is. I mean, she was living with Jacinta. Which is what takes Mr. White to the apartment complex, scouting it out. And that is when Mrs. Estrada sees him."

Jake's too excited to listen—he has to talk. "So Mr. White gets the lay of the land, then sets the fire. Means to kill Tiana, ends up killing the kids instead, but it's all good, because this means she's going away for their murders. Which would have been a great solution if Richie hadn't wanted to impress Daria Barati."

This last thought takes the steam out of Jake. Beginning to see his friend's inexorable march toward his own death because he was trying to impress someone. He can't help it, the exploded head and blood-soaked car flash to mind and he turns away. Grace doesn't know what he's thinking but decides that what he needs is for her to press forward, gently.

"And that brings us back to the firm. Someone at Thompson and West figures out what Rich was onto. That someone tipped off Mr. White, or Reagan—"

"Or decided to fix this themself," Jake says, and he has a certain someone in mind when he says it. A certain someone with whom he shares a last name.

Javi chimes in: "They take action to shut Richie down to bury what he found. They come after you in the parking garage for the same reason. They think you know something."

"Which we do," Jake replies. "We finally see the sequence."

There's a minute of breathless wonder at how they've put the puzzle together. The amazing satisfaction seeing tiny pieces begin to form into a clear picture.

"Except we're missing the bigger picture," Grace says hesitantly.

She looks up from her laptop and realizes she has a rapt audience. Whatever their failings, these two men, these two lawyers, at least lawyers by training, view her as an equal right now. And in the clarity of this moment, Grace realizes that she knows what she wants to do with her life. Whatever fears she has about the LSATs or her ability to succeed as a lawyer or whether she can actually be a force for good—this is her calling. When this case is over, she's going at it, full tilt. Fuck. She realizes they're waiting for her to explain.

"What if it's *not* about Mr. White and Jacinta at all? What if that party had a point? What if it was a way to close some backroom deal, or celebrate some backroom deal, and what Mr. White was angry about wasn't being rejected, it wasn't about two women gossiping about him, it was about two women who saw him *doing* something. Or *talking* to someone. *Connecting* two people who should not be connected."

Jake and Javi take a moment to contemplate her hypothesis.

"It's a lovely theory," Javi says, "but what-ifs don't help. We can't just guess."

"It's not a guess. Jacinta's murder?" She points to what she just found on her laptop. "It happened a week after they announced groundbreaking on Hearst Plaza. Which means the party was just before or just after. It was a party about Hearst Plaza. And that connects us to Reagan Hearst."

Javi equivocates: "It's good, but it's not enough."

"Come on, Dr. Highsmith," Jake argues. "There were people there sealing some major deal, maybe a dark deal, maybe with the wrong people. There was something dirty going on, and Mr. White—he thinks Jacinta could ruin everything. Or . . . *Reagan* realizes she could ruin everything, and *he's* behind it."

"Slow down, Perry Mason," Javi cautions. "Do I think it's plausible? Maybe even likely? Yes. But what do we do with this *theory*? The date of the party isn't enough."

"But we have more than that," Grace insists. "We know Rich wanted precedent on attorney/client privilege. Gotta be about Reagan, because he gave us Reagan's file, and he wanted Reagan's billing numbers. He did all of that because he knew that pursuing the truth would cost the firm. And the thing that would cost the firm the most, that might make someone want to kill Jacinta and Tiana and Rich and Mrs. Estrada? It's Hearst Plaza. That's the goose that laid the golden egg. For Reagan. For the firm. For the entire city."

Javi sighs. The bigger the theory, the worse he feels. "Again," he presses, "what do we do with that?"

"It's simple," Jake says. "It's basic algebra. *X* plus *Y* equals *Z*. *X* is *who*. Whodunnit. Likely Mr. White, but we don't know who he is. *Y* is *why*—why did he do this, what did Jacinta see? We don't have that yet either. *Z* is what. The five murders. We have *that*. We just need to plug in some more variables to solve for *X* and *Y*."

"As usual, math is mind-bogglingly unhelpful," says Javi, who always hated math.

"It's not. That party is the key. It can give us both *X* and *Y*. We figure out who was there, and we show photos to Tiana. I know we can't get into the firm's files, but between the three of us, we can piece together a pretty good list of clients—"

"It's a needle in a haystack, Jake," Javi says, growing frustrated.

"We also have the flash drive. We comb through it, find whatever Richie found. Something shady with that development or—"

He stops. Because a new idea hits him. A better idea. "Or—we take a shortcut. We get Reagan Hearst to talk."

"You really do like to dream big," is all Javi manages.

"He'll never talk," Grace agrees. "Especially not to you."

"No. Not unless we compel him to. So we *subpoena* him. A deposition."

"A deposition on what case?"

"Leave that to me. Meanwhile, there are now five murders we're trying to connect, so we don't have to just solve this using the party. There's also the parking garage at Thompson and West—someone came after me there, someone came after Grace there. Another piece of evidence that someone at Thompson and West is connected. So who are the suspects? Gibson? My father? I mean, as horrible as both of them are, are we ready to say they could be accomplices to murder? That they're trying to kill us?"

Grace looks around at their shithole workspace. One that's extremely vulnerable. "All I know is—I think we need to improve security."

23

"You need to find out what they know."

It's Monday morning and Stephen Gibson is beginning to think this week will be as bad as the last. Which, given the murder of a colleague and the ongoing war with Jake West, says a lot. Reagan Hearst arrived at the office at nine a.m. sharp and has been monologuing about what Gibson needs to do. And Gibson hates being told what to do, especially by an arrogant, rich prick. That's what got them into this mess in the first place.

"I'll tell you what they *don't* know, Reagan. They don't know shit. Because we've locked them out of the system. They're gone. Don't work here anymore."

Reagan's never liked Gibson, he's a necessary evil, but this news pleases him. "You fired him? You actually fired Norman West's asshole kid?"

"I did."

Maybe there's more to Gibson than he's given him credit for. Or maybe this is yet another mistake.

"Wouldn't it have been better keeping him close, to monitor what he's doing?"

"No, it would not have been better or that's what I would have done. I'm not going to tell you how to build your Taj Mahal, please don't tell me how to run my firm."

Reagan is not used to being spoken to this way. It irritates him, but probably less than if Gibson groveled and begged.

"And the woman?" Gibson's obtuse; he's not following. "The witness, the woman with the kid?"

"They're gone. Off the grid. Not coming back."

"I feel so relieved," Reagan seethes, making it clear he feels anything but, and all but implying Gibson needs to do something about it.

"I'm not a bounty hunter," Gibson points out. Reagan doesn't react at all, and the silence does its trick. "But let me see what I can find out."

"How about you say *I'll find out.* How about you say *I'll get it done,* not *I'll try.*"

"How about I say I'm your lawyer. And that's it." Gibson's words are strong, but a telling bead of perspiration begins to form on his brow.

"You do realize that my business is forty percent of your book."

"It's actually thirty-four percent."

"And I can make it zero. Today. Other firms come poaching all the time. Regaling me with tales about how Norman West's lost a step, how Stevie Gibson is a functionary without any real power."

"I'm a functionary who could make your life very difficult. You talk about keeping someone close—you need to keep *me* close, Reagan. Keep us close."

Reagan could eviscerate the man here and now. But despite the threat, he sees second and third beads of sweat forming. He's made his point successfully.

"Just find them."

Tiana Walker can feel the central coast wind biting into her face and she loves it. Reggie doesn't care, he's just riveted by the ground squirrels darting in and out of the ice plant on the edge of the rocky cliff. In all her dreams of what her life would be like, there wasn't a dream like this. How could there be? She didn't know places like this existed. Even its name, Cambria, sounds like a fairy tale.

Reggie's joy is a soothing balm, but it doesn't remove the deep pain or loss. Mariella would have loved this. Quinton would have said he hated it—he would've wanted to be on an asphalt court shooting baskets, which he could do by the time he was five—but this would have been good for him, nonetheless. To see that the world is so much bigger than what she'd been able to show him.

Reggie makes a futile attempt to coax one of the squirrels to his hand, but it runs off down the path. Tiana wonders what Reggie's path will be. Will he be able to live a life better than hers? Will this small, out-of-the-way seaside town become home?

"I wish I could fly." He's now diverted his attention to a seagull flying low over the Pacific, searching for prey.

"Me too, baby."

She puts her arms around him from behind, a little bit for the warmth, more for the connection she cherishes—one she'd just about given up on.

"Can we stay here forever?" he asks from the warmth of her embrace.

She's joyous that he feels this level of contentment here, but she knows the answer. The real answer isn't what he wants to hear.

"Sure, baby. You, me, the ocean, and the squirrels. Forever."

It's a good lie. There can be such a thing as a good lie.

Kendall is nervous. Powerful people come and go through the offices of Thompson & West all the time. She's seen princes and billionaires and rock stars and even one former president. And she prides herself on her calm, her professionalism. But today is different. What she's about to do will likely change everything, which both excites her and freaks her the fuck out. But it's time to decide her life is going to be more than all this.

Stephen Gibson is walking Reagan Hearst out, and Kendall isn't sure which one she likes less. She knows Gibson better, which means there is more to dislike, but Reagan's open leering is offensive. He hit on her coming in the door, and she's fairly certain he doesn't remember that he's tried that before and was rebuffed. Because it isn't a real attempt to ask her out, it's just how he believes he should present himself to the world. As someone who's entitled to whatever and whoever—or is it whomever?—he wants. In some ways, she feels sad for him, what his life must be like, getting everything. She has to laugh at herself. Really? That's what's pitiable? Getting everything?

Reagan reaches the desk and holds out his parking ticket. But he doesn't put it down—he wants her to touch his hand to take it. She's seen this gambit before.

"Would you like me to take that?" Her tone is flirty.

"I would love you to take that."

"Well, how about I take it and give it back with a little something extra."

She reaches over, slides her hand over Reagan's as she takes the ticket. Then she carefully puts three validation stickers on it but doesn't give it back. She's deciding if she can really go through with her task.

"Some of us have work to attend to," Gibson snaps, annoyed. "Maybe you can send Mr. Hearst on his way, Kendall."

Her eyes flit to Gibson, and she finds a hatred welling up that finalizes her decision. She reaches under the counter, then puts Reagan's parking ticket on top of a manila envelope. She slides both to Reagan.

"What's this?" he asks, intrigued. When she doesn't answer, an idea occurs to him. "Are there photos in here?"

"Why don't you see for yourself," she says neutrally, though he interprets it as coy.

Reagan slides open the envelope, pulls out a document. As he scans it, his face turns red.

"Oh—I think I'm supposed to say this," she says innocently. "You've been served."

The string of expletives that follows is so loud and profane, Reagan so on the verge of violence, that Kendall doesn't notice the unassuming young man trying to slide past them and leave the office unnoticed. But Roger Whitby keeps his head down and escapes. He has an appointment.

24

Walking into the bar, Roger begins to think there's been a mistake. Since Grace Jamison suggested meeting here, he assumes it's a place she frequents. He is well aware West Hollywood bars are generally gay bars, but he isn't a native-born Angeleno, so he reasons there are likely exceptions. But seeing the shirtless, six-packed bartenders and the neon colors behind the bar, he realizes Trunks isn't an exception. He starts to get the feeling Grace might have the wrong impression about him, which is disappointing because her call made him think she could be interested. Yes, she's probably out of his league, but *she* called *him*, right?

His eyes take a minute to adjust to the contrast of bright lights behind the bar and the dark leather booths, not to mention the fact that the pulsating bass of the house music is disorienting. He doesn't see her, so he moves toward the back room, bathed in smoky orange light. His eyes scan the room.

"Roger."

Sure enough, there she is, sitting toward the back at a dimly lit table under a Tiffany lamp. He's confused as to why he's here and what she wants, and that confusion must be visible on his face as he reaches her table.

"I won't bite," she teases. He slides onto the chair opposite her. She continues to read the thoughts in his head. "You're wondering why we're here."

"I'm hoping you don't have the wrong idea about me," he says tentatively.

"I'm hoping I have the *right* idea about you. I've just been fired, Roger. I wanted a place no one from the office would see us. I don't want you tainted by association."

"I heard. And I'm sorry. But what I didn't hear is—what'd you do?"

"That's a rude assumption," she says playfully. "That I'm at fault."

"I just mean . . ." His face goes beet red to match the siren light that's casting beams across his face.

"Relax. Order a drink." She nods to the shirtless waiter who's walking by. "Hey. He'll have a . . . ?"

"Bourbon," Roger says decisively. "Maker's Mark. Neat." Roger sizes up her drink. "Rum and Coke?"

"Hold the rum."

"You invited me to a bar, but you're not drinking?"

"I invited you to an out-of-the-way place to ask you to put your job and maybe your life on the line to do the right thing."

He laughs, assuming it's a joke, but he sees she's not laughing. He also sees that her eyes are a very deep green that he finds so distracting, he almost forgets what they're talking about. This time, she misinterprets his expression.

"I know. I feel the same way," Grace says.

He's puzzled by that. "You feel the same way as what?"

"Like someone just asked me to jump off a cliff. Only, let me reframe it for you. I *am* asking you to jump off a cliff, but I'm also asking you to trust me that there's water at the bottom, and that you'll not only survive the jump, but you'll feel . . . exhilarated. Alive."

Those eyes are so damn distracting. Is she using that? Does he care? Thank God his drink arrives. He takes a good-sized swallow.

"I don't have any idea what you're asking of me. Or why? Why me?"

"Because you actually seem like you care. IT guys, they mostly talk like the rest of us are idiots. But every time I ask you anything, you answer like I'm an intelligent human being. I sense you took the job not just because it pays well and you're good at it, but because you like the idea of helping people. You said that to me once, and I didn't think you were full of shit, and I didn't think you were trying to get somewhere with me. I felt like you meant it. Only I'm not sure if you've realized what I have—that what we're mostly helping people do at Thompson and West *isn't* good. And it *shouldn't* be done."

Grace takes in Roger's earnestness, his sad, involuntary nod at that truth.

"Yeah, I think you've realized that," she ventures.

Grace is aware she's using his attraction to her in order to get what she wants, which makes her almost as bad as the people they're trying to stop. But her little mini law firm needs his help. And she tells herself that *this* bad thing she's doing isn't in the same league as what they're trying to stop, or expose. But her guilt makes her flag the bartender again.

"With rum this time around."

He winks his acknowledgment. Then her gaze falls back on Roger. He's holding his drink, trying to decide. Suddenly, he downs the rest of it in one gulp.

"Okay. Tell me what you want."

In another dark bar with a distinctly different vibe, Sioban McFadden is trying to ignore the fact that Detective John Mackenzie is leering at her. She liked the vibe at R Bar the other night when she followed Jake here. She also liked the drinks, but more importantly, she calculated that Johnny Mack seeing her on the plush couch with the red-orange lighting would have the desired effect. She calculated correctly, but that doesn't make the leer on her colleague's face any less nauseating.

Mack, with a beer—domestic, no doubt—already in hand, slides into the booth on the same side as her. He's probably five foot ten and a half but tells people he's six feet. One of those guys who works out so much his muscles don't fit his body. He wants to be something he's not. She's betting he was an awkward kid who got beat up on, and who now has a badge and wants to exact his revenge on the world. He thinks he's hot shit. He isn't.

He picks up her glass and sniffs it. "Smells interesting."

"Me or the drink?"

That gets a grin out of him. "So. This was a long time coming."

"Was it?"

"You been here, what, a couple of years now?"

"Four."

"And I had the impression that you . . ."

"Didn't like you?"

"I would have called it 'disdain.' I wasn't sure if it was me personally, or the department, or LA, or . . . what. But you asking me for drinks was not on my bingo card."

His leering is almost too much for her to continue the pretense, but she forces herself to play. "Bingo."

He likes that. He downs the rest of his beer and signals for another.

"So . . ." He wants to get right to it.

She does as well, but what she wants is not what he's expecting. "How's your caseload these days, Johnny?"

"Okay, I see how it's gonna be. Sure, I can slow play this if you like. Small talk. I get it. The caseload's fine. Pretty full, actually."

"I figured, which was why it seemed so odd you got this new one. Estrada. How's that going?"

She's speaking casually. But an alarm goes off in Mack's head.

"You know, I work all day. When I'm off, relaxing, getting to know someone, I figure business should stay where it belongs. At the office."

"Sorry, not trying to talk shop. Frankly, if I can be honest, I'm looking for advice."

That surprises him. Flatters him. "Okay."

"I'm just thinking, as an outsider, maybe I'm not working the system the way I should. I mean, you get *so* many cases, the good ones—why is that? Is it Gantley? I mean, do I need him in my debt to get my share? Or is it something else?"

Her question is friendly, but alarm bells are going off louder now. This whole evening begins to smell all wrong. His second beer arrives, and he sips.

"Why are we here, Red? No bullshit."

She nods. Takes a sip of her own drink. "We are here, Detective Mackenzie, because I want to hear you tell me that you got the Estrada case because you were next man up. I want to hear you tell me that no one asked for you personally, no one wanted you to bury anything or overlook anything. And I wanted to do it here, in public, so that if you don't like my question and you report it, and drop a hint that I'm not playing ball the way I should, that I will be able to say that you came here because you wanted to get laid and got pissed off that is *not* happening, ever, not in a million years, and you reporting me is retaliation. Which could be cause for suspension or even dismissal, depending on the union's current appetite for culling out bad cops, and the current political climate. Neither of which is likely to work in your favor."

Her gaze is unflinching. He's fighting a thousand impulses, trying not to take the bait.

"I see that you're calculating," Sioban says. "So let me provide some added information to help your math. See that guy over there?"

She gestures to a man sitting alone at the bar. Six two, dark hair, serious as fuck. He salutes a greeting at her.

"He's a friend. Internal Affairs. Truth is, he's had his eye on you for some time, and he'll back me up on my version of the story."

Through gritted teeth, Mack asks what he can only guess. "And what would that version be?"

"That I came here with reservations. I wanted to talk to a colleague who was working a case adjacent to mine, but I feared how he would react to my questions, so I came with backup. And while you may be thinking to yourself, you have friends in the department who outrank mine—you know that's true, I know that's true, it's why you're on that case—I also have friends *not* in the department. Like, at the *LA Times*, for example. And as watered down as the paper is these days, they do love to expose rings of bad cops. I think they have a couple of Pulitzers for doing just that."

Mack had a girlfriend once who made him try meditation. He hated it then, but draws on it now, focusing his breathing. He doesn't want to lose his shit in front of IA, if that's who the guy really is. Which he doubts, but it can't be risked. So instead, he finishes his second drink and gets up.

"It's been a pleasure, Irish. Enlightening. See you around."

Sioban watches as he walks out, trying hard to project that this was nothing. She is aware she just made a formidable enemy and put a bigger target on her back, but she got what she came for. Confirmation that Detective John Mackenzie is being used by someone, for something.

She gets up, slips the fake Internal Affairs officer the prearranged twenty bucks, and heads out. She has to keep pushing. Consequences be damned.

25

Roger Whitby pulls into the strip mall parking lot and thinks he must have the wrong address. He's trying to find Jake West's new law office, and this mostly vacant, run-down fire hazard can't be it. But then he sees Grace's smiling face holding four cups of Starbucks in front of a storefront with no signage whatsoever. He parks and gets out.

"Don't worry, it's worse than it looks," she assures him.

She hands him a coffee and points to the newly installed security camera over the door. "On the positive side, we've just upgraded security, so we'll know if someone comes in to kill us all." The joke doesn't help. "I'm kidding, Roger. No one's coming here to kill us. We haven't done anything." She holds the door open. "Yet."

Inside one of the back offices, Javi and Jake are plotting the deposition of Reagan Hearst, pursuant to the wrongful death lawsuit just filed on behalf of David Castillo, claiming that Hearst, alone or through intermediaries, was directly responsible for the death of his sister, Jacinta Castillo.

In order to get around Jake's conflicts, the suit has been filed not by Jake West, but by Javier Alvarez. Acting not in his capacity as an attorney—because he isn't one any longer—but as an advisor to David Castillo himself, because the law says every person has a right to file a lawsuit, and to represent themself in the matter. Convincing David to go along with this wasn't hard. He'd do anything to find his sister's killer and make them pay.

The hard truth is, they'll lose in court. But winning isn't the end goal. What they're going after will come in discovery: the guest list of the party at Hearst's, including any photos, security camera footage, invitations, and/or correspondence related to said party. They're well aware that getting these things is a reach, but the deposition will be the first building block to get there. And it will allow them to put Hearst himself in their gun sights.

"Gentlemen—the cavalry has arrived," Grace announces as she enters with Roger.

Jake and Javi take in their visitor and his wide, frightened eyes. He's in his twenties, wearing khakis and a short-sleeve designer button-up that likely comes from Nordstrom Rack or Marshalls, has a Supercuts hairstyle, and it's clear he doesn't get much sunlight. His appearance does not engender confidence, but they see Grace willing them to play along.

"What do you think—Conference Room A?" she suggests. Knowing full well there is no Conference Room A.

In the small room newly christened Conference Room A, Roger has a hard time not focusing on the whiteboard. The colors, names, and arrows are straight out of a movie. And every time he glances at it, he fears he's been called in to be the "red shirt," the expendable *Star Trek* character who winds up dead, and the audience won't really care. He realizes he's not the lead of this movie—he wouldn't want to be—but he prefers that someone have a rooting interest in his survival.

"Explain the keystrokes."

Roger is shaken out of his reverie by Grace's gentle prodding.

"Okay. So remember a couple years back, when we upgraded computer security? Well, we did that, that part's true. But the specific program I was directed to install did more than that. We adapted software that companies use to root out corporate espionage. It . . . captures keystrokes."

Jake is livid. "You're telling me a law firm with protected attorney/client information is violating that privilege themselves?"

"I was told it was legal, that it was only viewable by those inside the firm who were bound by the same privilege."

Javi shakes his head. "You were told a lie, but I'm guessing you knew that."

"It was touted as a way to protect the clients. And I don't have a law degree, but . . ." Roger sees that Jake and Javi aren't buying his justification. "But yes. I knew it was a lie."

"Who else knew about this?"

"In IT—just me. I did the final checks, and we added it in last. As to who knows, and who has access? I only created three admins. Mr. West—your father. Mr. Thompson."

"And Stephen Gibson, correct?"

Roger nods his confirmation, and just like that, it's clear to them how someone at the firm knew what Rich Kaplan was up to. The question remains: Which one of the three was it? It's a question Roger can't answer. He explains that he can't use the program to track the principals. But Jake has another idea.

"Can you track what Rich Kaplan was working on the night he was killed?"

"I figured you would ask that. So I took a careful stroll through the files and I hate to tell you—he's gone from the system."

"Shit." Jake actually bangs the table as he says it. "They've covered their tracks."

"Hang on." Javi is up on his feet, pacing now; he thinks best this way. "You said you can't use the software to track the principals. I get that it was set up that way. But—theoretically—could you alter it?"

Roger doesn't like the sound of that. "You just told me that the program itself is against the law if the users don't know it exists. Before today, I could argue I didn't know that. And I could argue that whatever I did was at the behest of my employer. After today, if I did what you're asking, I have no defense."

Jake laughs. "There's always a defense. That's how we make a living, Roger. That said, you make some fine points, so let's tackle your conundrum in parts. As to the employer issue, I would argue that you still work for me. While I've been asked to leave, there are bylaws that lay out a process for dismissal, and until the details of that termination are finalized, I am still a partner at Thompson and West, and thus, effectively still your boss."

Javi sees Roger is still dubious, so he jumps in. "I'd like to argue a different way. Breaking the law is not always against the law."

"That sounds like an oxymoron," Roger ventures.

"I don't know, let's put it to the test. You're in the mountains. Alone, freezing to death. There's a deserted cabin, so you break in to save your life. Illegal?"

Roger isn't sold. "Isn't it illegal but defensible?"

"Perhaps," Javi says, really leaning into law professor mode. "But there are whole courses in law school devoted to the philosophy behind the law. Legal moralism, the harm theory. I won't bore you with details."

"Too late," Jake interjects.

"Then let me just say this," Javi continues. "What we're discussing is a case of *malum prohibitum*, not of *malum in se*."

"That's so much better," Jake deadpans.

"Some of us studied Latin, moron. *Malum prohibitum* translates roughly as: conduct that constitutes an unlawful act only by virtue of statute. As opposed to conduct that is evil in and of itself—*malum in se*."

"I get your point, I do," Roger says. "But isn't that just bullshit legal justification?"

Javi laughs. "You say bullshit legal justification, I say *malum prohibitum*. Either way, I'll always argue that when adhering to the law leads to greater harm than breaking it, then logically it follows that to break that law is not only acceptable, you are impelled to do so."

Maybe it's the Latin, but Roger doesn't appear to be buying it.

"Let me put it this way, Roger," Jake says, working to win him over. "If someone at the firm used the system that you put in place to get information that led to a murder—maybe as many as five murders—then if you allow that system to remain, doesn't that make you part of the cover-up?"

That sounds bad, Roger thinks. And he doesn't want Grace to think badly of him. But he's uncomfortable with what they're asking.

Grace brought Roger in, and she feels perhaps it's up to her to push him over the top. "We get your hesitation, Roger. It's natural. But I think what

Mr. Alvarez and Mr. West are saying is that the greater harm is covering up murder. Both legally *and* morally."

Roger looks at her green eyes. Then walks over to the board and takes in the names. Consuela Estrada. Jacinta Castillo. Mariella and Quinton Walker. And finally, Richard Kaplan. He liked Mr. Kaplan. He was always kind, which stood out in the den of vipers. He turns to face the others.

"I'll set up access for you, but only to those three. Thompson. West. And Gibson."

Jake claps him on the back. "Excellent. And, out of curiosity—which argument made you say yes?"

None of them. He's doing it for Grace. To impress her. He wants her to see him as something he's not sure he is. But maybe he could be, so he goes with the answer that will play best to her. "Because I want to help people. And . . . it's the right thing to do."

Jake's mind is spinning from the legal maneuverings of the morning, trying to craft the strongest questions to get what they want from the forthcoming deposition of Reagan Hearst. Which is why he's no longer working, instead he's fixated on his screen saver. A photo of Cara, Chloe, Aaron . . . and him. A slightly younger, distinctly happier version of himself. They're at the beach. He thinks it's Santa Barbara, but it might have been Laguna. Both close, weekend getaways that he didn't partake of enough. The photo is maybe five years old, and he wonders if it was the last time he was there. In recent years, even before the split, Cara had taken to booking weekends and taking the kids herself. She told him, invited him, but she knew he'd likely stay behind.

None of that is visible in the screen saver photo. It's like the front of a Hallmark card, or a Target ad, or one of those photos they put in a frame in the store to sell you what it'll look like when you substitute in your own family. Only Jake knows what those picture can't show—that the perfect family, dressed in complementary colors, all smiling, all beautiful, all happy, may not be happy at all.

Jake wonders, staring at Cara and Chloe and Aaron—were *they* happy in this photo? Was he? He thinks they all were. But it's getting hard to remember that feeling.

"You should go home."

He didn't notice Grace come in, catching him in his reverie.

"It's not my home anymore."

"No, but the way you're looking at it, you want it to be."

He doesn't agree with that or deny it. Instead, he sidesteps.

"What I want is to figure out how to get my daughter to stop hating me."

"She doesn't hate you."

"You don't hear her. I go to see her, and she pushes me away. She levels me with disdain I'm all too aware I deserve. But none of it, none of what happened, has anything to do with her. With my love for her."

"So as I said—you should go home."

"She says she doesn't want me there."

Grace wonders, *Is he stupid, or is this just a male thing? This level of obtuseness.*

"What she wants, and what she needs? They're not the same thing."

He's not so obtuse that he doesn't get the double layer of meaning there, but her basic point is well-taken. He lost his family because he didn't put them first. It was work first, work second, alcohol third. And it makes no sense, because he loves them. When things started getting hard, Cara tried to get him to go to therapy to work it out. Usually he liked talking about himself, but he hated therapy—probably because it brought up things he'd rather bury in alcohol. Which thinking about his family makes him want to do now.

But the expression on his daughter's face in that photo, that look of . . . adoration? It tells him that in this moment, alcohol isn't the answer. At least not the right answer.

26

At 3:10 p.m., having resisted the urge to drink, Jake finds himself in the long middle school pickup line. Tucked away at the foot of a hill, the Brentwood School is a Westside enclave for the rich, the connected, and also a good sampling of normal but high-achieving kids. The cars are the giveaway as to what category you fall in. The pickup line is a litmus test. There are the Range Rovers and Bentleys, the BMWs and Mercedes and Teslas, and the Hondas and Toyotas. Make no mistake—the kids know who's who.

He watches young people bound out and sulk out of the school. He watches warmth exuding from parents being mostly accepted by their offspring. No physical manifestations of said warmth—God no, these kids are too old for that—but he senses a reasonable amount of happiness here in this protected little pocket. Sure, there are some disconnected parents on their phones or connecting with each other and not their kids, but even they seem happy.

His daughter, Chloe, is talking animatedly with two friends: one he knows is Kelsey; the other he thinks he's met but can't recall. He's encouraged to see Chloe seeming happy, but when her eyes fall on his Genesis, that evaporates. He's not who she was expecting. She exchanges dark words with her friends, then walks to the passenger window and leans in.

"Where's Mom?" she says with a challenging tone.

"She had a thing. I said I was happy to step in since technically it's my day anyway," he says, brightly lying.

"Bullshit. It's not your day, it's your *night*, which you already canceled. No, you have an agenda, you asked her, and she caved."

"Either way—get in."

"I'm not going anywhere with you."

"No? Gonna walk home? Across the 405?" He says it lightly but pointedly.

"I'll Uber," she throws in his face, then backs away from the window.

Jake's had enough. He gets out of the car. A few honks let him know this is totally unacceptable, but he doesn't care. He reaches her fast, and she's horrified.

"What are you doing?"

"I am giving you a choice. You can get in the car and go with me, or I will make a scene that, this place being what it is, will make you a social pariah. Or at least an item of gossip that will mortify you until graduation."

She wants to argue but she realizes her father has a point—people are beginning to throw glances in her direction. Middle schoolers have a great radar for drama.

"Word of warning, Chloe. You stomp into that car and slam the door, you'll be the one making a scene. And middle school kids have *long* memories."

Time to recalibrate. She puts on a fake smile and turns to Kelsey.

"Bye, Kelse!" And with a fake happy wave, she gets in the car.

Jake climbs back into the driver's seat. He's won, but it's only round one. "Thank you."

There's one blissful moment of peace, and then she levels him. "Am I okay to drive with you? I mean, you haven't been drinking, have you? I know that's your thing these days."

It's like a dagger. He puts the car in gear, and they drive for a while in silence, Chloe feeling her Pyrrhic victory until she realizes they're not headed home.

"Where are we going?"

"On an educational outing."

"What kind of bullshit is this?"

"The truth? It's probably a bad idea. But you think you know me—I want you to understand that what you know, or rather, what you *think* you know, is . . ." Jake stumbles over what he wants to say. "I don't believe you understand as much as you think you do."

"How could I? You're never honest about anything."

He wonders if that's really true. He hopes it's not.

"Fair enough. But today—we'll try for total honesty."

He pulls into a parking space in front of O'Brien's Irish Pub.

Chloe takes a seat that Jake has pointed her to, a green leather-topped stool at the end of the bar. From her vantage point there, she takes in the full wall of colorful booze. How can there be so many different variations? Her father is in a hushed conversation with the bartender, who glances her way for a moment. It makes her feel odd. Like a spectacle. Not so much being in the pub—it has a sports bar vibe and serves food, so it's not that different from her old favorite birthday dinner venue Rush Street, sadly gone now—but being in a bar midafternoon is strange. There are just a smattering of people—an older couple, two biker-looking dudes, and a grizzled man sitting alone—and Chloe wonders if they're drunks. Like her father.

Jake comes back and takes the stool next to her. He seems actually happy to be here with her, which she finds confusing.

"What are we doing?" she asks earnestly.

"I want to demystify this for you."

"I've seen a bar before."

"Yeah? Been out drinking with friends?"

She gets that it's a joke, but also wonders if he worries about that. And that idea pleases her—that he should worry about her. Turnabout is fair play.

The bartender comes over with two drinks in hand. "One Patrón Silver. One Coke."

"I don't drink Coke," she tells her father, annoyed because he should know that.

"The Coke is for me. The Patrón Silver is for you."

She's confused. He doesn't seem to be kidding.

"It's tequila," he explains.

"You trying to get this place in trouble? I'm thirteen."

"They have deniability. I said it was for me. They can't control my bad parenting."

He slides the shot glass toward her. She eyes it suspiciously. "You think I drink? Is that what this is about?"

"Do you?"

"I've had the Manischewitz at Jordan's Passover thing."

"Glorified grape juice. This—four to five times stronger. Eighty proof."

She looks at it. Her bravado is dissipating.

"Smell it," he encourages.

She does, and reels back from the fumes. "You actually drink this shit?"

"That shit, as you so eloquently call it, is my vice of choice. I have a bad day, a bad week, lose a case, disappoint your mother, or you? A sip of that takes the sting out."

She searches his eyes, still feeling like there's a catch to all this.

"It's a coping device. A dysfunctional coping device, to be sure, but it becomes . . . a pull. When things get overwhelming, when I feel like I don't know how to deal with something, it pulls at me. Like—remember when you used to say you'd die if we didn't go to Sweet Rose Creamery? You had to have the salted caramel? It's like that. Your body starts to crave it, your *mind* starts to crave it. Eventually, you can't help yourself."

She picks up the drink. Studies the clear liquid through the thick beveled glass. It doesn't look like much.

"Take a tiny sip, that's how you drink it. Unless you're on the beach in Cabo."

She takes a moment to make sure this is really what he wants, not some test, then sips. She doesn't flinch, doesn't spit it out. Just experiences it.

"*Shit*. You like it."

"It's strong."

"Wouldn't work if it wasn't."

She takes another sip. He watches her. She sets it down. "I don't think I do like it. I don't hate it, but I don't like how it makes me feel." She slides it toward him. "You want it?"

"Yes, but I'm not going to have it." He sips his Coke instead.

"You know that's probably worse for you than the . . . Patrón Silver."

Jake laughs. And suddenly Chloe feels like laughing too.

"You're right about the liquor. It does make you feel different. And I hope for you that your life—with your mother, your brother, maybe even with me—isn't so awful that any feeling that's different feels better. But for me, at your age . . . You know I didn't have a good relationship with my father."

"I know."

"He wasn't much of a father to me. And now, with what's going on with me and your mother, my biggest fear isn't what happens to us. Me and Mom. It's what happens to me and you, and me and Aaron. Because I don't want to be like my father. I want to be there. I want to be someone you want to be around, not someone you hate or are angry with all the time. I want be a good father. Whatever that takes."

"And you think getting your thirteen-year-old daughter drunk in a bar makes you a good father?" she says, deadpan.

She'd do a mean cross-examination, Jake thinks. "Fair point, Counselor. But it was the honesty I was going for. If you want to be disappointed in me, or furious with me for drinking, you should know what it really is and *why* I do it. Not as an excuse, but as a way to understand how someone who loves you can fuck things up so badly."

She starts to tear up at this. To drown whatever the feeling is, she reaches for the drink and takes one more sip.

"Does that help?" Jake asks gently.

"No."

"Good."

She decides to offer her own honesty in exchange for his. "I don't hate you. I miss you. I miss you . . . being there."

He puts his hand on hers. "I miss being there."

She looks down at their hands, then withdraws hers and hardens again. "Then do something about it."

27

Javi always has mixed feelings walking into the lobby of Thompson & West. His first thought is that this is everything he hates about the law. The pretense of the glass and dark wood and moody lighting, all to impress a clientele that uses the law only to break it. His second thought is—damn, he should be working someplace like this, a firm that says to the world: *I am one of the best attorneys ever to graduate Berkeley Law.*

Thompson & West and its ilk are certainly what he dreamed about when he was at Berkeley. While his notions of service have always been strong, he didn't dream of using the degree to sit in a public aide law firm with cubicles and files piled everywhere. *This* was the dream, the visual manifestation of the goal, celebrated in movies from *The Firm* to *Presumed Innocent* to *Michael Clayton*. Never mind the fact that all of those movies dramatize lawyers abusing the profession, the offices were goal-worthy.

He turns his eyes from the décor to the receptionist. Kendall's always been friendly, but he can see she's out of sorts this morning. As he approaches, her eyes dart sideways to see who's watching.

"I take it serving papers on the firm's biggest client didn't go over well."

"It did not, thank you very much. I think they would have fired me if they didn't see the potential liability in doing that."

"Jake was fairly certain they'd see that was folly."

"Well, I got an official reprimand, which as I understand it, paves the way to getting rid of me later. So until I line up my next gig, if you and Jake need something else, I'm gonna have to pass."

"Worry not, I'm not here to cause trouble. I've been summoned."

"By whom?"

"I love a woman who knows her relative pronouns."

"You should have seen the job interview process. You'd think they wanted us to have a law degree to sit at reception." Kendall leans in and speaks quietly: "I don't mean to be rude, Mr. Alvarez, but me talking to you is dangerous. Who are you here to see?"

"Norman West." Her concern for him is apparent. "Yeah—I feel the same way."

Ten minutes later, Javi is sitting in a posh conference room with sweeping views of the city. It's way too big a room for this meeting—the overt opulence is intended as intimidation. Making him wait is also part of their game, whatever that may be, but Javi's here because whatever Norman West wants, it's worth hearing.

Jake would have told him to reject the meeting outright, but Jake operates on emotion too much of the time. There is no question they're in over their heads, and while the goal hasn't changed—justice for Rich—if there's a way to do that that doesn't fuck someone over and ruin Javi's life more than he's done to himself already, it's worth considering. At the very least, whatever the meeting's about will give them insight into how scared Norman is about what they're digging up. So he justifies the move to come and the lie to his friend as necessary reconnaissance.

Javi decides to avail himself of the silver tray of coffee. No sense in wasting a good cup. It's not being traitorous, it's almost like pillaging from the other side. He takes his time getting it just perfect, then sips. An excellent brew. He's in no hurry. He'll wait them out. This is on their dime.

Just down the hall, Norman West sits in the near dark, redlining a document with zeal, the sharp pen strikes on paper manifesting his general anger at the world. His spacious corner office is a showpiece—it looks like an exclusive British men's club. Dark ziricote wood, hunter-green wallpaper, lit only by muted lamps and deeply recessed lighting. There's a small painting on the wall with its own showcase lighting. An original Caravaggio. That the artist is known for keeping most things hidden in darkness is an intentional metaphor, Norman's little joke.

He has achieved everything he ever expected in life, so why does he feel perpetually empty? Perpetually angry? These feelings drive him, they may be the cause of all his success, yet he's come to learn that getting what you want isn't all it's cracked up to be. He wanted to be more than his father—check. He wanted to be more than the people who told him he'd never amount to much—check. He wanted to prove to his bosses and colleagues that he was better, smarter, more devious—check.

He met a beautiful girl who came from money, who never would have given twenty-year-old Norman West the time of day. But he decided he wanted Evelyn Price and he set out to get her. Succeeded in convincing her, over her mother's objections, to marry him. And like everything else in his life, attaining that goal left him empty. It certainly left *her* empty. Evelyn stayed—they had a son, she loved her son and she loved her life and she loved her friends—but she wasn't really there. Norman could have made a change, cut ties, found someone new. But he felt that would have signaled defeat. And Norman West refuses to lose.

"Alvarez is in the conference room."

Norman looks up at Stephen Gibson with the same gut feeling of disdain he's always had. A feeling that's been magnified in recent days. He needs someone like Gibson, but his current managing partner is not to his taste. Nor was the last, for that matter. Perhaps the problem with them all is they're not Jake, at least not as Norman would have him. But he's never been one for such introspection.

Gibson is clearly eager to get to business. Norman understands that making Javier Alvarez wait, allowing him to soak up all he doesn't have, is a necessary preamble. He's aware Javi will reject what he has to offer. But the idea is to sow seeds of doubt. The idea is to slowly, gradually peel away everyone Jake relies on. Make him feel like he's on an island. Alone. Because there's something he knows about his son—it's been true since he was three: The boy loves an audience. Needs an audience. Craves it like a drug. Right now, he's got Javi Alvarez and that blond paralegal—the one little voices told him Jake was banging for a while, Grace something or other—to witness him playing out this grand rebellion. Without witnesses, the rebellion won't be any fun. He'll get no satisfaction.

"Before we go, may I venture a thought?" Gibson prods Norman out of his musing. "I wonder if this is something you need not get your hands dirty on. If I handle things, you remain above the fray."

"If you handle things? Haven't you *been* handling things, Stephen?"

"Well, yes—"

"And how is that going? How is that going for us?"

"It's under control."

"No. It isn't. Which is why it *does* require me to handle this. Personally." Norman lets the rebuke land, then dismisses Gibson with: "Give him five more minutes, then bring him here. And by all means, join us—never too old to learn."

Six minutes later, Gibson ushers Javi into the inner sanctum. Javi's never been in here, and rather than head toward the couch, he goes to the power wall, taking in the photos of Norman with various dignitaries and billionaires. On the desk, he notes a photo of Chloe and Aaron. He sees it for the prop that it is, selling the image of a loving grandfather.

"Nice. You're a family man. What are their names again?"

He wouldn't be surprised if Norman couldn't remember.

"I'm guessing you're feeling quite pleased with yourself today," is Norman's nonanswer.

"The lawsuit?" Javi feigns confusion. "That's not me, that's David Castillo. Exercising his constitutional right to be heard in a court of law. And if he's wrong, if he's totally off base, then I'd think your client would welcome that deposition as a chance to vindicate himself."

"David Castillo is not why I asked you here."

"I assumed not, given that it's not my case and I'm not a lawyer at all. But I am curious what it is you think we have to discuss."

Norman takes a moment. He likes to build anticipation. " 'The State Must Provide,' " he finally says, pronouncing the phrase like a title.

Javi gets the reference, it *is* a title, but he's not going to help Norman along.

"It was a good paper," Norman offers.

"It was a *great* paper."

"Yes. Announced the heralding of a superior legal mind."

"The Federalists didn't like it much."

"The Federalists saw a future opponent in the making. They didn't care about the legal precedent as much as slapping down someone who, if he had the right tools, might fight them for years to come."

"I might still. It's not like the work of affirmative action is done."

"True enough. But as you note, you're not a lawyer anymore, Javier."

"There are other ways to fight."

"Yes. And if you thought they were equally effective, you probably would have gone down a different path in the first place, rather than spend three years in law school."

"Is that why I'm here? To discuss my checkered career path? I'm touched, Mr. West. I wasn't aware you cared."

"I hate to see talent wasted. You might know this—I have a son with some pretty spectacular legal talent that *he's* wasted. And you—well, I'll deny I ever said this, but you're twice the lawyer Jake is. Sorry—you *once* were."

Javi allows himself a moment to revel in the compliment. He knows Norman has some agenda that negates the value of the words, but it's validating nonetheless. Only for a moment. He grows tired of playing along. "Since I assume your time is worth somewhere on the scale of twenty-five hundred an hour between the two of you . . ." Javi's eyes fall on Stephen Gibson, still mute, and he digresses. "Or are *you* not billing since you're just a spectator?" Before Gibson can respond, Javi continues, "Regardless, I'm merely suggesting that you get to the point. 'Time is money' is certainly an apt metaphor here."

"That it is. Everything is about money, isn't it?" Norman says. "Which is why I want to offer you a job. As our in-house investigator."

Javi is irritated. This seems a seriously weak move. "I'm not interested in corporate."

"No, I imagine half of what I'd have you do you'd find morally objectionable. Legal, certainly, but objectionable, nonetheless. However, there's an end goal in what I'm proposing. You put in six months as Thompson and West's in-house investigator, and on the first day of month seven, I go to the California Bar Association and use your time of service to have your law license restored."

There is a point in every negotiation where the balance of power shifts, where one side offers up something the other didn't see coming. Either something so bad that the offering party loses sway or something so good that the receiver has to rethink whatever lines in the sand have been drawn.

Javi hates that he feels the lines shifting. More like the tide has come in and washed them away. In this moment, hearing this offer from a man he loathes—but a man fully capable of delivering on his promise—reawakens something in Javi. His mind goes to the things he could do with his law license back, the people he could help. Some of those old arguments like "The State Must Provide" might actually be things he could strive for.

On the other hand, the offer comes from the Devil himself. And it would mean selling out a friend. Admittedly a friend who's been not much of a friend, but that has more to do with Jake's own demons than his lack of devotion to Javi.

All of this plays out in microseconds, and Javi has long trained his face to belie what goes on inside his mind. Which is why he doesn't respond to the offer. But it seems Gibson has realized he must contribute something to this meeting, because the next words are his.

"It's a good offer, Mr. Alvarez. A one-day-only, once-in-a-lifetime offer."

Javi looks past him to Norman. There's only one man with power in this room.

"And the catch?" Javi demands.

"No catch," Norman replies. "Beyond the obvious. If you work for me, you can't simultaneously work for Jake. Which might sound cruel, but the truth is, you'd honestly be doing him a favor. Without your support, he may come to his senses and stop throwing his career away. In time, he could even come back here. You could be colleagues again, without having to resort to a strip-mall sex shop for your offices."

Norman lets that sit just a moment, then rises.

"You chew on that, Javier. Sit here in my office, soak it up, think about this being something you'd experience every day. Then go home and take stock of your life now. And call me with the answer we both know serves you best."

Norman slips him a sealed envelope on the way out. Javi doesn't mean to take it. But he does.

28

Javi pulls his 2018 Toyota Camry into the strip mall parking lot. The lot seems different to him today. Seedier. More pathetic. Also, he has started to notice a slight rattle in the Camry's engine, and as he parks, the car lurches. Then he gets out and notices how badly it needs to be washed. So do the windows of the so-called office. Not that it'll help it be what it is not. And what it is not is Thompson & West.

Javi comes into the office carrying a pink box of donuts from Trejo's. He was inspired to stop by the iconic pink building on the corner of Santa Monica and Highland, with actor/former convict Danny Trejo's face etched in the glass of the front window. "Good morning. I come bearing gifts." Jake and Grace are already hard at work, and he ceremoniously sets down the box as if he's delivering manna from heaven. "You know why people don't eat donuts? They're embarrassed to buy them. So I've done us all the service of picking up Danny's best."

Javi waits for appreciation. Instead, Jake eyes him appraisingly.

"What?" Javi asks.

Jake decides to let it go. He turns his attention to Danny Trejo's snarling face staring at him from the top of the pink box. Jake opens the box, picks a white-frosted creation with flecks of something green.

"You would pick that one. The Margarita. Lime and salt. But no real alcohol, so no danger you start spiraling."

Jake takes a bite. Nods appreciation. Grace takes a red one.

"Da Berry Bomb, excellent choice," Javi commends her.

That cheerfulness is too much. "You've got bad news," Jake says warily. "What did my father want? He have some dark move on the David Castillo front?"

Javi sighs—Kendall must've tipped Jake off. He wasn't ready for this conversation, but so be it. He takes a donut of his own—the Abuelita, raised chocolate with chocolate crumble. He bites into it, then casually goes to the coffeepot and pours himself a cup. Smells it—it's no Peet's. He turns back. They're waiting him out.

"It wasn't about Castillo. Or Hearst." He pauses for effect. "He offered me a job."

Grace is stunned, but Jake knows there's more. "What was the offer?"

"Thompson and West's exclusive in-house investigator. Six months at thirty thousand a month. My own office, name on the door in frosted letters, assurances no laws will be broken. And after six months—he goes to the bar association. I get my law license back."

"Fuck." The word involuntarily escapes Grace's mouth. It's a good offer.

"And?" Jake presses his soon to be ex-friend. At least that's his fear.

"I'm open to a counteroffer."

It's unclear how serious Javi is. Jake takes the Margarita donut and tosses it into the trash. "Here's my counteroffer. You don't want to work for the Devil. So don't."

"You make a fair point," Javi acknowledges. "But it turns out the Devil pays really well. Not to mention the fact that some could argue that you—not *you* Grace, just Jake—that you're closer to the Devil than he is, tempting people into breaking laws with promises of eternal salvation. Which I'm not really sure you can deliver."

"What about friendship?"

"Friendship means wanting the best for each other, regardless of how it affects you."

"You get that from a fortune cookie?"

Javi sees the pain on Jake's face. The edges of anger. Perhaps he's pushed this as far as he needs to. "Okay, it's true I don't want to work for that asshole. But his offer, it *reawakened* me. To what I can do. So. Here's the deal. I stay. I match your earnings on whatever we do, dollar for dollar, regardless of your hourly versus mine. We fight him, we win, and when we do, you're going to call in every fucking favor with everyone you know until you find someone to go to the bar on my behalf. Someone with the proper weight. So that next time I draft a lawsuit, I put my own damn name on it."

Jake takes only a moment, then says: "I'll go to a bar on your behalf right now."

The joke falls flat.

"Jake—just say yes and take the deal," Grace urges. Then she has another thought. "Actually, Javi, I think you forgot an important term. While we work this case, no booze."

"Come on—" Jake complains.

"That is a great point," Javi says. "We need to be at full strength. Because when you're sober, you're almost as good as I am."

Jake wants to argue. Both about the terms and Javi's denigration of his talent. But right now, he needs to short-circuit his father's end-around.

"Fine. I will not get drunk."

"You will not *drink*. At all," Grace clarifies the exact wording of the deal.

Jake is pinned in a corner. "Fine. We have a deal. Can we get back to work now?"

But Javi has another thought. "Actually, there's one more thing."

"No backsies."

"Backsies? Really?"

"It's a legal term. The deal was done, you can't go back on it."

"Oh, I'm fine with the terms as negotiated. On *my* deal," says Javi. "But there's a third member of this team whose deal needs to be ironed out. Since you're the one who cost her her job."

"We talked about this. We're matching her salary, and you're the one paying her so there's no appearance of impropriety."

"That's a start, but she's risking a lot. I want to make sure she's as vested in the outcome as we are. Incentivized, if you will."

"I thought we were doing it for Richie," Jake argues.

"Can't it be both?" Javi counters.

"Fine. Grace. Pray tell—what else do you want?"

"The salary is fine," she says. "But if we win, the firm—the new firm—pays for law school."

It's a big ask, but Jake isn't annoyed, he feels deeply proud of her.

"Fuck—this is long overdue. I'm thrilled to make that deal. The hypothetical firm may not be able to afford it, and Cara will very likely kill me if she finds out, but I think we can draft language that legitimizes it as a job perk. So what the hell—we gamble on success. Let's toast and be done."

He can tell by the lack of enthusiasm that his alcohol end-around was not missed. "Fine. We'll toast with donuts." He grabs an odd rainbow-colored donut—it's covered in Fruity Pebbles. "I feel like I'm six, but . . . booyah, we have a deal."

They simultaneously bite into their donuts. The Three Musketeers. Sure, like Dumas's heroes, someone may want to kill them all, but in this moment, Jake can't help but feel good about their odds.

29

Grace knows enough to be skeptical, but she's excited nonetheless. Not only did Reagan Hearst agree to be deposed, in person, but he agreed to do it on an expedited basis. "A chance to clear his name" was the quote. Standard bullshit, but it's a chance for her to see him in person, assess for herself if he's really the archvillain they're making him out to be. It isn't just the answers they're after in the depo—odds are he won't give them anything useful—it's how he comes off. Beyond that, if they can tie him to a story they can later prove in court was a lie, that would be like her beloved Atlanta Braves winning the World Series.

The most exciting part is the team has decided that Grace will function as lead attorney. No, she's not an attorney, but Jake can't be here—his departure from the firm is not signed and sealed, and they want no appearance of a conflict. Javi has been disbarred, and the attorneys at Thompson & West know enough of how that came about to use his past against him. Grace, however, is a blank slate. She can operate as David Castillo's advocate. He has filed this claim *pro per*—meaning he's representing himself—and she is technically there to assist him. There is a big upside to this move: seeing a non-lawyer as their opponent will make Gibson and Norman and Reagan Hearst overconfident. Grace is aware that part of Jake asking her to do this is playing on their perception that she's not up to the job, but she knows Jake doesn't believe that, and she refuses to disappoint. And if she can get Hearst to crack—a remote long shot—that would be a real high.

Javi is with her, but only to run the videotape, a quiet observer. No doubt they will assume he's the real power in the room, but that will be used to their team's advantage. Grace is nervous, but ready. Everything's in place and they just need David Castillo. Javi catches her checking her phone for the third time.

"He'll be here. Probably being hassled at security," he reassures her.

"We should have met him downstairs."

"He'll be fine. He's been through it a hundred times. You get used to it."

"Do you?" she asks, really wanting to know.

"You don't ever accept it, if that's what you mean. But if being hassled for the color of your skin scared you? You'd always be scared."

Grace is reassured about David's lateness, but depressed about the world. Then a very smug Stephen Gibson appears in the doorway.

"Wow. This really is the B Team, isn't it?"

"I guess both sides sent in the B Team," Grace answers back without missing a beat.

She's surprised that came out of her mouth. So is Javi, and he likes it.

"As you can see, we're using the small conference room. What you saw the other day, Mr. Alvarez? You won't be going back there. On either side of the table."

"I can live with that."

"Anyway, it's all moot. You can pack up now. Great to see you both, though."

Gibson starts out of the office. It's an act, but Javi plays along.

"Mr. Gibson," he says with enough semblance of respect to get Gibson to stop. "Is your client backing out?"

"My client will not be sitting for your Hail Mary deposition, if that's what you mean."

Grace won't let that go easily. "You do realize a judge signed that subpoena. If you want to fight it you can, but you'll lose."

"No, I won't. The subpoena is invalid."

Javi takes this one. "It's not. I checked it myself."

"Who are you kidding—you *wrote* it yourself. Which is fine, your work was adequate. However, it is a subpoena in reference to the case of *Castillo v. Hearst*. That case has been settled."

"You bought him off?!" Grace says with shock. "For how much?"

"I'm afraid the terms of the settlement are confidential. And don't ask

Mr. Castillo; he signed an NDA to that effect, and I wouldn't want him to risk violating that."

"You ambushed him downstairs," Grace practically spits out. Javi holds up a hand—she's not used to being in the middle of these legal games; her fury won't help. The move, while despicable, is a smart one. And a legal one.

"Ambushed?" Gibson replies affably. "That usually has a negative connotation. When you offer someone more money than they ever thought they'd see in their lifetime, it doesn't matter how much they loved their sister. And slugging it out with you and yours wasn't going to do anything but stir up Mr. Castillo's anger. So—good day, my friends."

Gibson heads out again. Javi moves to cut Grace off from following him out to continue the back-and-forth. She wants to kill the man.

"No good will come of it, Grace."

"I know, I just . . . I fucking hate lawyers," she complains.

In the corridor outside the conference room, Roger Whitby is working hard to appear like he's doing something important. He's got his head in a stack of papers, which is meant to cover his slow walk to suss out how the deposition went. As he crosses the doorframe, he catches Grace's eye and it's clear it went badly, but someone is coming up behind him. He has to move on.

Walking away, seeing all the lawyers working on cases where they're probably doing things he would never condone, Roger feels a sense of resolve. Yes, part of it is that he wants to fix this for Grace and prove to her just who he is. But part of it is wanting to be a different person. He wants to be someone who fixes things, and not just computer programs.

He picks up his pace, walking with purpose. His heart is beating fast because he's about to do something he's never done before. He's about to break a law.

David Castillo won't answer their calls. Jake is apoplectic—he wants to break down the door of his apartment and yell that he's selling out his dead sister, but Javi takes David's side. This wasn't his battle. What did he have to gain by holding out? Jake doesn't want to hear that, nor the gentle voice of Grace when she knocks on the door to what he's co-opted as his office—a small, rectangular room about the size of a massage table.

"Jake? Have a minute?"

He sees she's grinning from ear to ear. "What is it?"

"I don't actually know. But whatever it is, I think it's good."

Two minutes later, they're in Conference Room A, where Roger Whitby is slow to get to the point. "First—you now have access," he tells them. "I set it up so you can track any time any one of the three principals accesses the keystroke program. But it turns out that once I changed the access codes, there was a side benefit. It allowed me to check their access going back."

"You found who was tracking Rich?" Grace blurts out.

"No. Rich Kaplan is gone from the system, so that chain is lost. But you got me feeling badly about setting it up in the first place, so I did a little digging into how they *have* used it, and one thing stood out." He pauses for effect. "*Guadalupe v. Harrison.*"

An elevator drops forty stories in Jake's stomach. He feels like he might throw up. "You're saying . . ."

"They were watching everything you were doing."

How is it possible to experience vindication and utter and complete loathing in the same moment? Jake feels the corners of his mouth hardening, his fists involuntarily clenching. "Now I *am* gonna kill someone."

"I get how you feel, Jake, that it's validating and awful and you want to lash out," Javi says in the best therapist voice he can muster. "And I promise you can go back through that door at some later date and do what you will—short of murder. But you are going to have to let that go. Pursuing this now doesn't help us."

"Actually, it does," Roger says, trying to be helpful. "There's a connection between what's happening now and what they did then."

No one moves a muscle. Everyone hanging on Roger's next words: "Harrison Foods is gonna have new corporate offices soon. Want to guess where?"

Jake's head explodes with the possibilities of what this implies, but he answers in a low, steady, deadly voice. "Hearst Plaza."

While others argue that Mozza or Quarter Sheets is the best pizza in Los Angeles, Jake sides with the perfect, slightly sweet crusts made in the imported Italian ovens at DeSano Pizzeria Napoletana. Jake has ordered two large pies and a round of focaccia to fuel the afternoon's deep dive into the shadow workings of Thompson & West, and what possible connection there may be between Harrison Foods and Reagan Hearst. They're in the front lobby, the only place with viable seating for all of them. Jake's eating a slice of the Hot Honey Doppio while he scans documents, but he's barely tasting anything. His adrenaline's running on overdrive, his mind replaying his downfall—what the firm knew, who knew it, and how they used it to beat him. To destroy him.

"You know what would go really well with this pizza? Beer." Jake floats the idea not so subtly.

"Hard yes to that," Roger says, thinking he's one of the guys, not realizing he's being used as a pawn. Javi and Grace don't dignify the pathetic move with any response.

"One beer. Come on, guys," Jake pleads. The truth is, the deal he made not to drink has been killing him. He's honored it—barely—but it's troubling how hard it's been.

"I just need a jump start," he argues, "something to help me start filling in the variables in our equation. I'm digging through *Harrison* and, beyond office space, I don't see anything that connects to Reagan Hearst or Tiana—" Jake stops mid-sentence, which draws everyone's attention to his next thought. "We're not going to find it. It's *not* here. Of course it's not here."

"Try making your inside voice an outside voice," Javi suggests.

"On *Harrison* they were watching me because they expected me to breach the wall. But if there was nothing to find, it wouldn't have hurt them and they wouldn't have cared. Which tells us there *was* something to hide. They knew I'd find a smoking gun, so they planted a decoy. But what they were really afraid of, it's not here. They wouldn't have let it be here." He turns to Roger, urgent. "Can you see if they deleted anything back then? The way they deleted Rich from the system?"

Roger takes his laptop and starts running over the keys. After a few minutes, he stops. "One file. They deleted one file. *This* file."

He slides his laptop over to Jake, who finds himself looking at a police file. An interview with a person of interest in the fire at the Harrison Foods plant. An interview with a known arsonist named Milo Stapp.

Arson. This is the connecting factor. In the *Harrison* case, it burned a factory and killed seventeen people. In the current situation, two small children. Two arsons, both using alcohol as an accelerant. Can't be coincidence.

Jake studies the weaselly face of Milo Stapp on the police report. "Long list of priors, interviewed as a suspect a week after the Harrison Foods fire, then cut loose. But later he's erased from the files altogether. Totally unnecessary—unless he did it. Any idea how to find where this guy was the night of the fire that killed Tiana's kids?"

Javi starts typing. A lot of typing.

"What are you doing?" Jake asks.

"*Malum prohibitum*. Something you can't have prior knowledge of, so shut up and let me break the law."

It's quiet. Just the sound of typing, scrolling. Then Javi takes a deep breath. "Milo Stapp was out on parole the night of the fire at Tiana's apartment. Had a meeting with his officer that very day."

"A meeting where?"

"North Hollywood. He was here, Jake. Milo Stapp—he's our guy. Tiana didn't start that fire—*he* did."

30

Jake started the day with a run on the beach at Will Rogers. He hadn't exercised like that in months, and his body rebelled. Or maybe it was rebelling against the lack of alcohol in the last few days. But two quad shots of espresso later, he was energized for the big drive he had ahead. He just had one stop to make first. Along with his quad shots, he had picked up a Pumpkin Spice Latte for Chloe, a White Hot Chocolate for Aaron, and a Honey Almondmilk Flat White for Cara. He wisely left the gifts by the front door and texted news of the delivery to the various parties so it would feel like Santa Claus had come.

Then he hit the road, and it struck him that his drive to Corcoran revealed the breadth of what California has to offer. He'd started at the beach, then through the mountains of the Grapevine, through Grapevine itself, with its vineyards at the foot of the mountain range, and now through the barren, flat farmland, past Bakersfield and into nothingness. This isn't what people think of when they picture California, but then, prisons aren't meant to capitalize on the best real estate. They're meant to be remote, dreary, certainly not-in-my-backyard. No one *chooses* to come here, but Jake is excited about it.

Milo Stapp is being held at California State Prison, Corcoran, in Level IV housing, a level so secure it was good enough for Charles Manson and Sirhan Sirhan. Today, it houses less famous murderers and serial killers and kidnappers and rapists. And select arsonists.

Taking in the barbed wire and gun towers, Jake is reminded, not for the first time, of the consequences should he fail his clients. Even when they're guilty, it's hard to feel good about the outcome. They're housed not unlike the herds of cattle he's just driven past. And the stench here isn't the same, but it still stinks. It stinks of antiseptic strong enough to make him nearly gag.

Jake shows his ID—it's checked, he moves through a metal detector, and he's then allowed in through multiple secure doors courtesy of the assigned deputy. He's been here before, but he feels a hole in his stomach every time. What all this says about humanity.

They hit a T in the hallway and turn left.

"Isn't the visiting room the other way?"

"Yes. But we're not going there." The deputy sees the confusion on his face. "Don't worry, not locking you up, just waiting for your colleague to meet you before you go in."

Jake tries to keep his face impassive. He currently has two colleagues, and neither Javi nor Grace is coming. Of that he's sure. Suddenly he feels like he's walking to his doom. Dead Man Walking.

They reach the door to a small meeting room Jake knows is sometimes used for low-risk prisoners to meet with their lawyers. *What the hell is this,* he wonders as he sits for five minutes . . . ten minutes . . . Something is very, very wrong.

Then he sees Sioban McFadden's red hair through the small window in the door. As she walks in, he's not sure if he should feel relief—or if things just got a hell of a lot worse.

Since her run-in with Johnny Mack, Sioban McFadden has been going down the rabbit hole of an insane hypothetical: What if Jake West is telling the truth? The mountain she'd have to climb to prove that has made her want to drink. Her mind keeps circling back to the soothing, calming, balming effect of the drinks at R Bar, conveniently forgetting about the hangover that inevitably follows, only remembering the tingling feeling that starts to distort reality and make her feel like she could do anything. Or that anything could happen and she wouldn't care. It's like the world blurs a bit, sounds get louder, her visual field becomes hazy, and she doesn't give a shit about things she should probably give a shit about.

But in her sober moments of the past few days, she has focused on one simple fact: if West is right, then it follows that someone else set the fire that was blamed on Tiana Walker. That's not her case, and Tiana is now in the clear, but going with the hypothetical that all the cases are connected, she needs to assume that Tiana is innocent and Rich could've proved it. Which makes the answer to who set the fire well within the scope of her case. So the entry point to solving *her* case is to figure out who started that fire.

While it's certainly possible that some bigwig client of Thompson & West is the culprit, these aren't people who get their hands dirty. Which means she's looking for an arsonist for hire. That narrows the search considerably, but it's still a long list. A list so long, it led her to another round of drinks at R Bar.

But two boulevardiers loosened her mind enough to realize something. Jake West, if he's innocent, is trying to find the same thing she is. Only he has an advantage—he knows who he thinks is behind this. So, armed with a bag of Irish truffle butter chips and some Diet Coke she bought at a market across the street from the bar, she decided to follow her top suspect and see if he might lead her to something good.

Watching him run on the beach this morning was depressing—it's never fun to sit in your car and watch other people enjoy the beach—but then he showered, changed into a suit, dropped coffee off for his family (she's betting the gesture of atonement won't help), and started a drive north out of the city. When he left the county via the Grapevine, she began to wonder if her suspect was making a run for it, if the coffee drop-off was some kind of parting gift. But when he made the turn off the 99 onto the Central Valley Highway, she figured exactly where he was headed—Corcoran.

Sioban called ahead with a bullshit story to stall him, then while he parked, she used her Wi-Fi hotspot to go back over the list of known arsonists she pulled up the other day. Narrowed to those now at Corcoran, the list yielded a huge dividend. Milo Stapp not only fits the profile, but he was in LA the night of the arson. She's sure of this because his parole officer's report in his file makes it undeniable. And her access to Stapp's police jacket gives her another gem—he was a suspect in another corporate arson, though the investigation clearly hit a dead end. But the burning of the factory at Harrison Foods catches her eye because her deep dive into Jake's background brought up plenty of information about his lawsuit against them. Which means she may have just found the mysterious Thompson & West client Jake thinks is behind all this.

Edgar Harrison. CEO of Harrison Foods.

"Hi, colleague," is Jake's opening. He's both keeping up the ruse for the guard who lets the detective in and calling her out on her bullshit.

"Hi yourself," Sioban offers, playing along until the guard leaves them to discuss their case. When the door closes, the jig is up. "Are you out of your mind?"

"Can you be more specific?" Jake asks amiably.

"You claimed to be Milo Stapp's attorney. Are you? Did you magically sign him as your client last night?"

"By the end of the meeting, I very well *could* be his lawyer."

"You are *not* meeting with him," Sioban spits, leaving no room for doubt.

"Afraid of what I'll find?"

"Afraid you will muddy my investigation." Sioban is pissed to be arguing with this man who may have committed murder last week. "How did you find Stapp anyway?" she demands.

"How did *you*?" Jake throws back at her. Neither intends to divulge their methods. "Come on, I'll get more out of him than you will. You're a cop."

"No."

"You're not a cop?"

"No, I am a cop, and you're my suspect, and I'm not letting you get to Stapp."

"Okay. We can do it together."

"Absolutely not."

"I get this is out of the ordinary. But I'm going to go out on a limb and say you're not here in an official capacity either. Milo Stapp setting fires is not your case."

"It has probative value," she argues.

"Look at you with your big legal dictionary."

"I'm gonna make you a deal, Jake. Leave now and I don't put your visit in my report."

"Who are you kidding? You're not filing a report. Because if you do, you'll be directing traffic at Wilshire and Westwood for all the construction. I mean seriously, how long does it take to build a subway?"

It's true, she's not going to file a report, but the idea of working with a civilian, with a suspect, is antithetical to . . . everything.

"If we do it together, we both have deniability," Jake suggests.

She decides this is the moment to test her new theory of the case. "I have a question. Edgar Harrison."

She watches him for a reaction. Nothing. He just says, "That's not a question."

"It is. Is he who you can't point me to?"

Jake takes a moment to evaluate what he can and can't say. He does the best he can. "I think there's a connection. But no, he's not the one."

Sioban is confused by this. "There's more? Your conspiracy is bigger?"

"Let's talk to Milo Stapp and see if he can help us connect some dots."

Jake clearly knows more than he's saying, which means he may ask questions she won't think to ask. Sioban weighs what she needs against what's right. And she weighs all the obstacles in her way: Johnny Mack, Gantley, the legal power of Thompson & West.

"I take the lead."

"A team. I love it. But one more suggestion. If I say you're *my* colleague, which is arguably not a lie, then you can ask questions without him realizing you're a cop."

"We'll never be able to use what he says against him."

"He's already locked up. We just need to find out who he was working for." Jake sees her wrestle with his genius and her rules. "Don't worry, when you get fired, I'll hire you as an investigator. You found Stapp, you're not half-bad." Then he puts it together. "Or did you just follow me here?"

Sioban's expression gives Jake no information. They are a team, but clearly neither trusts the other.

Milo Stapp sits at a table picking at his fingernails as Jake and Sioban are brought in. Whether he's disinterested in them or feigning disinterest is hard to say. Stapp is not shackled—he's not a physical threat. Gaunt, a small head coming off a long, skinny neck, whiskers, beady eyes, he's a weaselly little man—but a weasel can be deadly. Once they are seated, he sighs loudly, as if he's bored, but the truth is, whatever this bullshit meeting is, he'll let them do their song and dance. At least it's a break from the monotony. But the song and dance doesn't come. They're waiting him out.

"You guys just bulking up the billable hours? 'Cause I got all day."

The redhead gives him nothing. Not a smile, not a snarl. He decides to push Jake.

"I know who *you* are."

"That because my firm hired you to set a fire at Harrison Foods?"

He laughs. "Is that it? You're here for some kind of confession? A chance to clear my conscience, save my soul?"

Now Sioban steps in. "I don't think you have a conscience or a soul. I've read your rap sheet."

Stapp shifts his eyes back to her. "So?"

"So where were you on August seventeenth of last year?"

"Something tells me you already know the answer to that question."

"And yet she's asking," Jake says.

Stapp is familiar with Jake's tone. With people playing tough with him, undoubtedly feeling superior. It doesn't bother Milo—he's enjoying this meeting. The day is already better than most in here.

"Let me ask *you* a question. What's in it for me, playing ball with you and your Irish friend. Or is it Scottish? I can never tell the difference with those accents."

Sioban replies: "What's in it for you is that if you play ball, we get you immunity on what we're asking about. It's clear you don't set fires for kicks."

"No, the kicks are just a side benefit—"

Jake slams both hands on the table. Milo doesn't flinch.

"I thought this only happened in the movies," Milo says calmly. "Good cop, bad cop. Don't you know we're all onto that by now?" He sees Jake fighting the urge to come at him. "Is this where you throw me against the wall? Make me feel like you're a loose cannon?"

Milo sees that the good cop, the redhead, decides it time to get back to business. "You do this for the money, Milo. We get that. What we care about is who paid you for that thing you did on August seventeenth of last year. So the offer is—you give us that, we make sure no one comes after you for it. If you don't, you're what we have. So we give you to the cops, and given that your current sentence says you could be out of here in twenty-three months, I'd think that has value. Because if you're tried and convicted on that thing from August seventeenth, that's probably life."

The bad cop wants the last word. "I'd vote for death, but the current governor has other thoughts. So life it will be."

Stapp takes time to think about his response. Sitting here, it's easy to think that making a deal is the way to go. But if he's learned one thing, it's that talking to anyone about anything is more than likely to backfire. And the visit of these two strangers gives him the idea that he may have a new hand to play. If they're here, they probably know who paid him, they just can't prove it. Which means that person is in seriously deep shit. So maybe he should roll the dice and try and make a better deal elsewhere.

"Sorry. August seventeenth? That's like a lifetime ago. And being in here, everything before just blends together. Like a fire, when it burns, what was there before . . . ceases to exist. It's nature. Kind of beautiful when you think about it."

Stapp is excited. There's a path that some way, somehow will lead him out of here early. There's almost a spring in his step as he's taken back to the cell block. The guard releases him inside a secure door. On the way back to his cell, he makes a stop in the open doorway to another cell where a Mexican lifer is sitting on his bed, an open book in front of him.

"Whatcha reading, Carlos?"

Carlos, who is six four, two hundred forty, and covered head to toe in tats, shows him the book cover: *Harry Potter and the Prisoner of Azkaban.*

Stapp laughs. "A kid's book?"

"It's another world, man. Don't being in here make you want to go to another world?"

"It does. And I think I got a way, which is why I'm here."

Stapp offers a pack of cigarettes. Carlos puts Harry Potter down, reaches for another book on his shelf. An old hardcover edition of *The Man in the Iron Mask.* Maybe Carlos is a fan of Dumas, or of irony, because the book about an imprisoned man isn't a book at all—the insides are cut out, and in the cutout is a cell phone.

"Half hour."

"Don't need it that long."

Stapp takes the phone, hides it in his waistband, and heads back to his cell. Alone again, he dials a number from memory.

In his office at Thompson & West, Stephen Gibson answers his cell phone. He doesn't give the number to a lot of people, and the kind of people he gives it to might call from anywhere, so the fact that the number isn't a known one isn't surprising.

"Yes."

"Mr. Gibson," says a voice that rings a vague bell. "I'm about to do you a favor. And I can't wait to hear what you're gonna do for me in return."

In a much less glamorous office, Javi's computer pings. While he convinced Roger Whitby they're operating under the principal of *malum prohibitum*, he's used the access Roger created for the keystroke capture program to remotely turn on a recording function via Stephen Gibson's computer. This is definitely illegal, and he knows Roger would never have condoned it. Nor Grace. Maybe not even Jake, though he puts that at fifty-fifty. Regardless, he has spent the last day skimming the voice-activated recordings, and he could have used most of what he's heard as a sleep aid. Gibson is a numbers and clauses guy, so Javi has little expectation when he clicks on the newest audio file.

"Yes."

Gibson's voice comes through loud and clear. What follows is distant, but with some audio enhancements, Javi is able to hear it. *"Mr. Gibson. I'm about to do you a favor. And I can't wait to hear what you're gonna do for me in return."*

There is a pause on the line. More enhancements may or may not have helped Javi decipher what's next, but Gibson had put his cell phone on speaker.

"You're trying to place the voice. It's Milo. Milo Stapp."

"I'm not your lawyer, Mr. Stapp."

"I remember you telling me that. I remember because the guy I got stuck with instead was shit, and I ended up here in Corcoran."

"You're calling me from prison?"

"Relax—it's a secure line. We need to talk."

"*Not on the phone,*" Gibson says.

"Well, I'd drop by your office, but that might be a little difficult."

"I'm not coming anywhere near where you are."

"So you're passing? Because I can get back the lawyer who was just here. You might know him. Since his name's on the wall of your firm. And he made me a very interesting offer."

"Jake West came to you?"

"Yup. Him and that red-haired colleague."

There's a pause. Javi speculates that Gibson won't make the leap to Sioban McFadden. He probably thinks Grace dyed her hair. Regardless, Gibson finally breaks the silence. *"His name isn't on the wall of this firm. That's his father's name."*

"Yes, I remember his father. Norman West. And if you don't want that memory to spill out of my mouth to his son, you're going to find a way to continue this conversation."

"I'm hanging up now, Mr. Stapp."

The connection is cut, and Javi realizes he's been holding his breath in astonishment. Here it is—recorded confirmation. They can't use it in court, of course, but all of Jake's paranoia has been proven correct. *No wonder he drinks so much,* Javi thinks.

31

"I'm breaking my deal, I know I am, but I don't think even you will begrudge me."

To avoid Grace's pitying gaze across the table, Jake looks around at the dark bar. It's not atmospheric dark, it's more like hiding-the-dirt-and-grime dark. He knows they're somewhere in Hollywood, but he doesn't remember the name of the place. It was the closest place to the office he could find when Javi broke the news. He was going to go alone, but Grace opened the passenger door of his car and got in. She didn't try to talk him out of what she knew he was going to do next, and she doesn't now. As a show of solidarity, she downs her own drink, tacitly giving him permission to do the same. Hers is a skinny margarita. His is bourbon, straight. He took the house pour—it's cheap and it's bad, but he downs it like it's water, and it burns. The pain is part of the attraction.

"My own fuckin' father."

"You did suspect that was the case."

"But I held out hope, which is pathetic. Now I know—he's responsible for murder. Not for getting a murderer off—that's part of any criminal lawyer's gig—but soliciting."

"We don't know that for sure. Stapp just said he remembers him."

"That is a weak argument."

"I'm not saying it's not true," she clarifies, "just that we can't prove it yet. Gibson was careful on the phone. We have work to do. But if they *are* behind this, if *he* is—we're going to make him pay."

Jake waves at the bartender for another round. Grace is watching him.

"What?"

"I want you to promise me something," she says gently.

"That this is my last round? Sorry, can't do it."

"No. You drink as much as you need to. But then you go home, sleep it off, and we start in tomorrow to make things right. Don't go off and do anything stupid."

"Like what?"

"You think I'm going to suggest things to you in this state?"

Suddenly he's overwhelmed with feeling, that in his hour of need, she is here with him. "God, you're beautiful."

"Thanks, Jake, what every woman wants to hear. Declarations of passion when you're drunk out of your head."

"I'm not halfway to drunk out of my head."

The way he's looking at her makes her uncomfortable. Not like it's creepy—it stirs feelings she has worked hard to suppress.

"I get it. If you need to do this, do this, but hand me your keys. I can't watch, I'm taking your car. When you're done, call an Uber and go home. Do not pass Go, do not collect two hundred."

He starts to well up with tears. "I miss it."

"Miss what?"

"Monopoly." He sees she thinks he's lost it. "When things were simple. The rich get richer and fuck over everyone else for sport, but no one gets hurt. Unless you count the time I threw the metal shoe game piece and took a small chunk out of my cousin's skull."

The new round of drinks comes. She sips. He downs all of his at once.

"Promise you won't do anything stupid."

Jake sees she's really worried, which touches him. "The only stupid thing I can think of would be taking you home, only it doesn't seem that stupid to me."

"Jesus, you're an asshole when you're drunk."

"I know. Hard to understand why you'd want to work with me."

"Because I see what you're like when you're *not* an asshole. And when you're *not* drunk. And I've seen your father at work, so I accept that part of this is his fault."

"Wow. You should've been a shrink."

She wonders about the forgotten psychology degree, and what her path would have been like if she'd pursued it. Whether she would have helped more people that way. The answer, she's quite sure, is unquestionably yes, because she hasn't been helping people, she's been helping people get away with things. But that's why trying to find the truth about what happened to Rich Kaplan means so much. It's atonement for all of her sins. One of whom is sitting across the table from her right now.

Maybe if she finishes her drink and has another, she'll lose the inhibitions—or is it conscience?—that tell her going home with him is emotional suicide. Maybe she should embrace being the bad guy right along with him.

"Something's bothering you," he observes.

Yes, something is bothering her. What bothers her is that when she drinks she wants to go home with Jake. The choice to drink is a strong pull, and she doesn't want to believe that's why. That she *wants* to have an excuse. Then she sees the glassy sheen his eyes have taken on, and her moral side wins out.

"Like I said—I'm going home. Alone. You'll have to find something else stupid to do."

It doesn't take long for Jake to find something else stupid to do. Grace is actually the one who planted the seed of the idea—going home. Which is why he's standing in the dark on the sloped Bel Air street, staring up at the twenty-foot-high hedge that serves as a compound wall around his father's house. The gate is wrought iron, and there are cameras mounted over the top and at two other distinct places along the border of the property. It has, at first glance, the air of impenetrability. But Jake knows it's a façade. Like much of Norman's life, he wants it to appear a certain way, but he doesn't care how it really *is*.

Jake knows the half dozen points of access where the hedge is penetrable and cameras don't cover ingress or egress. He laughs to himself, using tenth-grade vocab words he argued would never have real-life applications. But it was back then when he started using said ingress and egress, sneaking out to meet friends and drink and smoke and just once to snort cocaine, which made his brain explode. In a bad way, thank God, because if he'd liked that, he'd surely be dead by now.

He finds his favorite spot, where it's easy to climb the fence and the landing inside is soft. There's another spot he'll use to get out, but that's supposing he doesn't decide to just shoot his father and wait for the police to arrive. That would be ironic. Accused of a murder he didn't commit, but it leads to one he does.

He keeps out of range of the motion sensors as he crosses the strip of lawn behind the hedge—where he first got to second base with Lisa Ackerman. He skirts the pool—where he passed out drunk and nearly drowned. If Paul Margolis hadn't jumped in and dragged him out, there's a high probability he would've been a footnote on the high school IN MEMORIAM page.

He finally reaches the plateau on which sits the house of his youth, an overbuilt monstrosity constructed in the style of a French chateau. Norman bought it not because it was tasteful, but because the previous owner had been a 1920s Hollywood star known for throwing outrageous parties, a fact he is sure to work into conversation for guests he wants to impress. Ignoring the multitude of legitimate ways into the house, Jake finds the two-by-two-foot utility door that leads to an unfinished basement. He knows full well it has no security.

Once inside, a little dirty and with cobwebs—or is it spiderwebs?—nestled in his hair, Jake quietly opens the door from the basement. Back in the day, Boris, his oversized Great Dane—which says a lot, because regular size is big enough—would have barked to wake the dead. Or in the case of Jake's house, the heavily lubricated and medicated. He understood that lubrication; what he never understood is why his mother stayed. But there's no dog now; Boris was his mother's dog, and when she died, Norman had Boris taken to a shelter. Jake would have taken care of him, but Norman expected Jake would fall down on the job eventually and he had no intention of doing anything about the dog himself. So he made the move preemptively.

Now—the house is still. Jake tiptoes down a wallpapered hall plastered with family photos and wonders how hard it was to find ones with people actually smiling. With photos of Cara and Chloe and Aaron, he knows there *were* times of happiness. With Jake and his father and mother, there were only photo opportunities.

He reaches the inner sanctum—Norman's office. Wall-to-wall shelves lined with books, like a Victorian library, but they're just for show. Jake would bet a hundred grand Norman's never read any of them. In fact, his guess is they were picked for the color scheme of the spines, a decorator's vision of a home legal office befitting a powerful partner at a prestigious firm.

But Jake isn't here for a trip down memory lane. He's here for the safe, hoping that Norman hasn't changed the code, because he assumes he alone knows it. What he doesn't know is that Jake and Javi, drunk one night during Christmas break of their second year at Berkeley, decided to settle a bet on what exactly Norman kept in there. They set up a camera that, depending on Norman's angle when he opened the safe, might yield a view to the code. Sure enough, Norman obliged.

Javi won the bet. They found tens of thousands in cash. Found files that Javi argued would be a breach of ethics for them to open, which would taint their fledgling law careers, never mind the fact they were already deep into illegal trespass. However, what won Javi the bet was the gun. Jake never knew his father had it, and the idea of him holding one was absurd. Only, was it?

Jake snaps out of his reminiscing. The code still works. He opens the safe, ready to break all kinds of laws.

"Can I get you a drink?"

Jake whips around to find his father impassively watching him. The movement makes his head spin, and he has to grab a chair to keep from falling over.

"Maybe coffee?"

Jake is calculating, but the fog in his head is making that task difficult. So he takes the easy way out. He goes to the side table filled with liquor and fixes himself a drink as suggested. He has to get the taste of the cheap well bourbon out of his mouth, so he chooses the Woodford Reserve. Stirs in a bit of sugar, some bitters, and adds some dried orange slices.

"Pour me one?"

Jake tries to figure out why his father is calm. Why he hasn't laid into him about this intrusion. He can't figure it out, so he pours the second drink. Then he walks away—if his father wants a drink, he can damn well get it himself.

"You're not going to ask why I'm here?"

"I'm sure I can guess. You want to find a smoking gun. As you can see, there *is* a gun in there, but it's not smoking. I used it on the range. Once. It was actually Archie's idea—he thought I'd like the power. But I have enough of that without needing to feel I could take a man's life with something in my hands."

"No, I imagine you have better ways of taking a man's life."

"What is it you imagine, Jake?"

"It's more than imagination. *I know.*"

Jake's accusation hangs in the air. Norman comes over and takes the drink, then settles in on the couch. "What is it you think you know?"

"Nice try. You're fishing for what we have against you."

"How can I refute your claims if I don't know what they are?"

"Did you kill Richard Allen Kaplan? Or have him killed?"

"I did not," the witness answers.

"Did one of your employees? Or clients?"

"Now look who's fishing." His father can't resist the jab.

"Let's talk about Milo Stapp."

Norman at least makes a show of trying to place the name, then eventually shrugs.

"Maybe you don't remember him. But he remembers you," Jake says pointedly.

"I tend to make an impression—"

"This isn't funny."

"No, Jake, my son breaking into my house and into my personal safe is not funny at all. I see you believe what you're spewing here, but I want you to listen to me. For two minutes. That's it. Two minutes. Then decide what you know."

Two minutes to listen and not talk is probably a good idea in Jake's current state, so he takes a seat in the oversized chair behind Norman's desk like he used to when he'd sneak in as a kid.

"I hate that it's come to this between us," Norman begins. "Despite what you think, I love you. And I want you at my firm. *Our* firm. I see the path you're on taking you further from that, further from being able to come back even if you wanted to. So I want to try, this one last time, to offer you something."

"You think I can be bought?"

"I'm not offering to buy you off. I'm just offering you a way back. A way to save face, put this all aside, and take your place in the firm that bears your name."

"The firm bears *your* name. Which taints it. Why would I want to come back?"

Maybe it's the bourbon, maybe Jake made the old-fashioned stronger than he would have, but hearing Jake voice his hatred, his disdain, makes Norman think about his son as a baby. He didn't really know what to do with a baby, but when his wife held the boy, Jake cooed and gazed up at her with a devotion that was beautiful. Norman thought he wouldn't mind that kind of adulation. So he'd take the baby in his arms. And Jake would start to wail and cry in a way that Norman understood as not just fear, but revulsion. Something about Norman revolted the baby. So he'd give the boy back to his mother. And he'd calm down.

Still, he tried. He tried when Jake was older, too. He'd take him to the park, or on drives, to meetings, figuring it would be good for the boy to see what his father's world was like. Past a certain age, Jake didn't cry anymore, but he didn't appear happy, either. Not like when he was with his mother.

The way Jake's looking at him now is nothing new. It's just a progression. But at its core, it's the same revulsion Norman has felt from his only son since he was born. God knows he's tried to forge a bond, getting Jake into the firm, handing him high-level cases, giving him every chance to succeed at no small personal cost. But now it would seem they're past all that. And Norman has to accept what comes next.

There's an expression on his father's face that Jake is unfamiliar with. It most resembles pain, as if Jake has really hurt him, which, if true, would be a first. Jake has never been able to get through his father's armor.

Jake remembers when his father used to take him places. Not often, but it happened. And Jake would feel a bigger gulf in those moments than he did when his father wasn't there. Norman didn't know how to talk to him, so he just carted him along, and Jake felt the chore of it. He imagined Dad had some late-night fight with Jake's mother about his lack of attentiveness to "the boy," and it had spurred whatever weak attempt at connection was being made. But Norman's heart was never in it. If he had a heart. Over time, Jake came to like it best when his father was gone.

A foreign thought hits Jake. What if he's wrong? What if his father isn't the mastermind behind whatever has gone on with Harrison Foods and Reagan Hearst and Tiana Walker and Rich Kaplan? What if he's empowered Gibson, and Gibson is behind it all?

No. That's the booze talking, lubricating his logic, bringing out the remnants of a little boy who wants to look up to his father. Or is it the opposite? Has the booze made him jump past circumstantial evidence to conviction? Does the good lawyer in Jake need to give this man a chance to put on his defense before ruling on his guilt or innocence?

Jake decides to let the little one-act play they're acting out go a little further.

"Maybe there is a way back. Maybe the things I think you've done . . . it's possible you don't know about them. Maybe it's all been taking place behind your back. But I'm telling you it *is* happening, it's being done at Thompson and West, and if you want me back, if you want me to take the mantle of the name, then help me. Help me root it out. You do that, maybe I can help you clean house. And then it'll be a place I could be proud of."

What utter bullshit, Norman thinks, watching his son closely. Watching him go from angry and hostile to needy, pathetic little shit. Or bad actor, it's hard to tell. Either way, he finds it depressing. Depressing that this is what he has. This will be the legacy of the West name. He had more respect for the purity of Jake's anger two minutes ago than this.

Out the window he sees something that tells him how to play the next minute.

"There's something you don't know, Jake. And you should before you try and take on the world." He pauses for effect, then lowers the quiet boom. "You don't know what I've had to do behind the scenes to prop up your cases. You're not half as good as you think you are."

Jake flushes with anger. First, he's angry that he let this charade of a conversation continue, that he dared entertain the idea that his father would offer up a defense. But he's also angry because the blatant attack of these words, the implication of Jake's weakness, actually bothers him. He finds himself running scenarios in his head, wondering if it could be true. Shit. He needs another drink.

But he's not going to get one, because red and blue lights cast their beams through the window. Jake sees them flicker on his father's expressionless face. Jake goes to the window and spots the two LAPD vehicles. He doesn't turn back to his father—his father, who has just turned him in to the police. He should feel something—pain certainly, but the alcohol is masking even that. What actually goes through him is a rush of clarity.

"You were stalling. You never wanted there to be a way back."

"Breaking and entering is a serious crime. It'll be hard to keep your law license with that on your record."

Now Jake turns back, and somehow, it's only the red light that's cast on his father's face.

"I always suspected it, but now I know. You *are* the Devil."

32

Jake sits in the back seat of the police cruiser like a common criminal, which in this case, he is. He knows he's guilty. According to California Penal Code Section 459, *every person who enters any house, room, apartment, tenement, shop, warehouse, store, mill, barn, stable, outhouse or other building, tent, vessel . . . with intent to commit grand or petit larceny or any felony is guilty of burglary.*

The fact that he took nothing is irrelevant—it's about intent. They'll also come after him for criminal trespass under section 602(c). There are certainly defenses to both charges. On intent, he can argue he was only gathering information, or that hidden in the safe he believed he would find his Luke Skywalker light saber, an original used in *The Empire Strikes Back,* that his father claimed was lost. For trespass he can argue this used to be his home and he was drunk and got lost. But he senses none of these would be winning arguments.

He's thinking about which lawyer to call to help him navigate these waters when the driver's door opens and Detective Sioban McFadden gets in. She buckles her seat belt and drives out the brick-paved driveway without saying a word. Jake takes a moment, trying to figure out the game.

"They demote you to beat cop?"

"I pulled a favor."

"You here to save me? We gonna make a run for the border?"

"I thought you might want to talk. You might want to confess like you were about to the night Rich Kaplan was killed, until your father showed up and rained on our parade."

He's beginning to think this night may end better than he'd hoped. "Sure. I'll talk. What would you like to talk about?"

"I'd like to talk about what took you from Milo Stapp to your father's house."

He'd love to tell her what he knows, but there's no way to do that without opening Javi up to criminal charges.

"This isn't a game, Jake. I'm still a cop and I have a job to do and I'm not throwing my career away over you."

"I don't want you to. I agree we should talk. But I have a different topic in mind."

She sighs. Some people just can't be helped. "We have about twenty minutes until we hit downtown and I book you. So the floor is yours."

"Okay. Let's talk about Callum Duncan."

She stops the car so fast he's thrown into the plexiglass divider. You can't brace yourself with cuffs on. "Oww!"

He clearly touched a nerve.

"You think this is gonna help you?" she asks.

"You tell me when I'm done talking."

She glances at him in the rearview mirror. He's not smug. He's willing her to listen.

"Clock's ticking." She puts the car in gear and starts making her way to the 405. Fastest way at this hour is to go north to go south. It's not a great freeway system.

Jake chooses his words carefully. The jolt against the divider partially sobered him up. "People think defense lawyers have a moral quandary. How do you represent clients who may be guilty of immoral acts? I can tell you all the justifications I've used over the years, treatises on the system and constitutional justice, but it's all justification. It is a morally suspect job."

"Refreshingly honest."

"I think you cops have a similar problem. How do you find justice for the guilty when you have to follow rules that may prohibit it? Rules that may be counterproductive to the whole notion of justice, that may actually serve to help bad people survive."

"I didn't realize I was getting a TED Talk on justice. This is so enlightening."

"Here's my point. Callum Duncan was your last case. An innocent boy who died. You didn't close the case, but you had a prime suspect. Brin Maloney."

She doesn't like where this is going, so she just keeps driving. Not playing along.

"After you left Ireland—I'm really not sure of the actual terminology, whether you quit or were fired or given a way out, that doesn't matter. What matters is the guy you knew did it got away with it. And what I want to know is, how is that to live with?"

Jake thinks he sees her hands gripping the wheel a little tighter. She's not talking, but he's getting to her. "He's still out there, you know that, right? Brin Maloney." Still nothing. "You wanna know how many boys have gone missing in the last four years?"

"No, Jake. I don't. I don't live there anymore, I don't work there anymore, it's not my case and there's nothing I can do about it."

"Exactly. Excruciating as it is, you are powerless. But on *this* case, on this case that's leaving a trail of bodies—not just your case, Rich Kaplan, but Mariella and Quinton Walker, Consuela Estrada, Jacinta Castillo, Estelle Guadalupe—on *this* case you have some agency."

"And where do you think that agency gets me, Jake? Where do you think it gets *you*? I don't have evidence that will hold up anywhere. And to back you is to get either marginalized or fired, and I'm not sure where I go to start over next time. New Zealand? I hear it's nice there. Not much crime, but maybe that's all for the best."

"All I'm suggesting is that I think you know what's right and what's wrong here."

"And what is right? Letting you go, losing my job?"

"No. I don't want you to let me go." That confuses her. "I want you to pull into the station, print me and book me and charge me."

"Well, that's just peachy, as some of you Americans like to say. Because that is exactly my intent."

"Good. I want my father to think he's won. To think he has the upper hand."

She catches up with his plan. "You *want* a case against you so you can go to court and get discovery. How much alcohol did you have to come up with that bullshit plan?"

"I may be technically drunk, but I am mentally sober."

"I hope that's not a legal argument you're gonna make."

"Let me ask you one question that helps me decide what pieces to move on the chess board." He pauses to make sure she's following along. He can see her eyes locked on his in the rearview mirror. "Have you been told, or pressured, or has it been alluded to you that you should back off your investigation of the fire that killed Tiana Walker's kids?"

She thinks about how to answer that. He sees her calculating.

"Don't be careful, you're not on the stand, I'm not taping this. Whatever you say, you can deny with full confidence no one will believe me."

He may be correct, but she doesn't want to make a mistake. She *should* be careful. Except she thinks about Brin Maloney and his smug face, and his complicit father, and a smoldering fury, always there, just below the surface, wells up inside her, the injustice of policing meaning no closure for Callum's family and loved ones, and more pain for whoever that loathsome kid has attacked since. Jake may be drunk, but he isn't wrong.

"Yes."

"And will you heed that warning?" She hesitates. "Before you respond, let me ask a second question. When has being told to back off ever served you before?"

Sioban's mind goes to something her father once said when she told him she was going to become a cop. *I'm gonna do good,* she'd promised him. And he said something that always stuck with her. *There's only one way to do good.*

It's to be *good. To be a good person.* She's tried to heed those words but hasn't always succeeded.

"I have a question for you now," she says. "Obviously you think your father is involved. And maybe he is. But I've done my homework about him *and* you. My question is—is this real? Or is this you working out your daddy issues in some insane way?"

Why is everyone suddenly a shrink? Jake thinks, wondering why dissecting other people's psychology has gone from being the ground of erudite experts to a common parlor trick. He blames Dr. Phil, spinning obvious bullshit into entertainment.

"Maybe I'm wrong about him," Jake says. "There's always that possibility. I accept that. All I'm doing is this—I'm looking for proof. One step at a time."

With all the trouble he's gotten in over the years, Jake's never been printed and booked. It occurs to him that this milestone is good for him. To really understand what clients go through, it should be part of basic legal training. Every potential lawyer should be arrested and processed, and not just as an exercise—it only works if there's some jeopardy, if you're not assured that you'll actually find a way out of it. He makes the first of several mental notes: the roughness of the hands forcing his fingers onto the ink pad; being lined up for a mug shot, that dreaded photo you don't want taken; the tightness of the handcuffs; how he's treated at every stage. All filed away for further consideration because this should be SOP at his new firm. West, Alvarez & Associates has a nice ring to it.

Even as he makes these notes, he knows—as a white man, a lawyer, and a connected one at that—what he feels is nothing compared to a powerless person who no one worries will be able to voice complaint. But it's at least a taste. It's more than he's had before.

Finally, the moment arrives: he's told he's allowed a phone call. And it brings up the question he's been turning over in his mind. Who is the one to call? Javi? He's not a lawyer. Norman? There might be an interesting argument to be had there. Cara? That wouldn't really be fair, and he doesn't want to put her in that position.

Weighing it all out, the choice seems clear. He gives an officer the number to dial.

Daria Barati stands on the balcony of Ten Thousand Santa Monica Boulevard having a glass of $135-a-bottle Brunello di Montalcino. And it's not calming her nerves. The view of the mountains isn't either. Maybe because the mountains are Beverly Hills and Bel Air, and they represent something much different from real mountains. They don't represent *escape,* but instead all the excess she works so hard to preserve and expand every day.

She should have thought of that when she bought the condo, but the real appeal was her ability to walk to the office. And to have a place that told the world how much she's achieved. That aspect was sad, needing her home to be anything other than a place she wants to live, but she'd worked so damn hard to get here, and needed that validation every night when she got home from another punishing day. Because the work itself doesn't feel validating any longer, but more like a survival course. And not a fun one.

There's a horrible story baked into the property's history of a man who jumped from his balcony here. He'd inherited $600 million and lost it all, by some accounts. There was drug use, by other accounts. Accusations of dark things by yet more accounts. Whatever the pressures were that were mounting, the world got to be too much for him. Who knows what he was really thinking, but when a cool wind blows across her body, Daria thinks she understands the desire to just jump and fly away from it all. She's not suicidal, but this isn't the life she'd planned. And at the moment, she doesn't see a way out.

Her cell phone rings. She sighs—always on call. Time to clock in once again and help yet another client do something meaningless, no doubt. But when she checks the phone, the caller ID says LAPD.

"Hello? Daria Barati speaking."

"Hey, Daria. It's your favorite ex-colleague, the one who pulled a gun on you. Hopefully that narrows it down."

"Jake? The caller ID says LAPD."

"Funny story about that. I've been arrested. They gave me one call. I'm calling you."

"And why would you do that?"

"I'd like you to represent me."

33

Daria's clientele doesn't generally drag her to the downtown office of the LAPD, and certainly not at two in the morning. She'd applied cream under her eyes to fight any bags and dark circles—not for Jake, but because her vision of who she is isn't a weary lawyer bailing out a criminal in the dead of the night. She put on a simple silk blouse and black pants, and she's wearing a thick wool coat because in the past few years, Los Angeles in late February has begun to feel arctic. If she wanted cold, she would've stayed back East.

"Who are you here for?" The desk sergeant can tell she's a lawyer.

"Jake West."

"Lucky you. Have a seat."

The place is dingy and depressing, and as Daria sits, she thinks she must've lost her mind. The proper thing to do, the *smart* thing, would have been to tell Jake she wasn't able to represent him, then hang up and immediately call Norman. Or at least call Gibson to report it, because there are procedures and protocols about conflicts of interest.

But a question nags at her: Why did Jake call *her*? Is he trying to sow division at the firm? He has to know she won't violate privilege, so he can't expect to *get* information from her. And he's unlikely to *give* information she could use against him. Besides, the outcome of the charges against him—trespass and burglary—seems clear-cut. Norman will likely want him to sleep it off and then he'll offer Jake a deal: drop what he's pursuing in exchange for Norman doing the same. And while Jake won't like it, it's a deal that Jake will need to make to keep his law license. The thing is, Jake will have gamed all this out himself. So what does he want from her?

Jake seems energized. Excited. Daria wonders what he's on, but he assures her drugs aren't his vice, and the alcohol has worn off by now. They've put him in the office reserved for meeting with attorneys and given him coffee. A lot of it. The rest is the result of clarity.

She hasn't agreed to represent him, just to hear him out and evaluate a course of action. Should she choose not to represent him, she'll gladly make a call on his behalf. With that clarified, she turns the floor over to Jake and asks him to tell her what happened.

"I broke into my father's house to find proof he is responsible for Rich's murder."

She takes a minute to let the wave of adrenaline pass, before she answers calmly, "And did you find it?" She knows the answer to the question.

"Didn't quite get the quiet time I was hoping for."

"It was a stupid move. And not just because you're wrong."

"You don't know that."

"Why did you call me, Jake?"

"I hear you're a good lawyer. I hear you're a sucker for lost causes."

"If you're not going to be serious, I'm going to leave."

"I called you because I think you making this move will be good for you at the firm, and I want to have someone I can half trust in a position of power."

"So this is you doing me a favor?"

"Pretty much."

"Goodbye, Jake. I didn't drive down here to play games with you."

"Let's *both* stop playing games. You did drive down here. You could have told me no, you could have called my father, maybe you did, but if you had, I think he would've stopped you. So I'd say you're flying solo on this. And I'm betting you came for the exact reason I called you. Because you think—at least you hope—this is the key to your advancement."

"You think your father would want me to do this."

"God, no. But you've learned that trying to please Norman West is a fool's errand. His respect is won at war, or by the unexpected. He may not like it, but the truth is, if you make the expected moves, you're proving he doesn't need you. No, if you want his attention, you need to do something out of the box that tells him you're a force to be reckoned with."

"And helping his recently fired son is the out of the box you think will do the trick?"

"Yes. I think he'll be furious, and you'll tell him that he's wrong. That you doing this is the best thing for the firm. You're demonstrating that it's not the firm or the power of Norman West punishing his son for pursuing a case they don't want him to go within five hundred feet of. Because if it's that, it'll blow back so hard it'll permanently damage the firm, and him, and you can't allow even the perception of that. Which is why he has to let you do this. Let you protect the firm by protecting me."

His plan is convoluted and audacious. And probably dead on the mark.

"What do you think?" he presses her.

"I think you are your father's son."

"That's just mean."

"I meant it as a compliment."

"I don't take it as one."

"Oh, I think you do. I think you want his approval every bit as much as I do. Which is why you're going after him. You know it's the only way. To be as ruthless as he is."

"Maybe you're right. Maybe therapy would get better results than accusing him of murder. But, for the sake of argument—what if I'm right? Don't you owe it to Richie to help?"

I should have this, Gibson thinks. He's sitting by the pool in Noman West's faux Tuscan backyard. It's nine a.m. and the sun has risen over the top of the huge hedge that Jake had to scale last night, putting the beveled glass table and the pool in direct sun. The hedge functions as a battlement, walling off this little oasis not just from enemies, but from the rest of the world. It's meant to feel like it could be in the South of France, or Lake Como. An escape from reality. Or a better reality. It does.

Biting into an everything bagel with lox cut as delicately as sushi, it's very apparent to Gibson that Norman West has won. Gibson deserves the same. When Hearst Plaza is done, he's going to find one of the real estate brokers from *Buying Beverly Hills* and go house hunting. Estate hunting. He wants what his boss has—this level of success. *But why,* he wonders, *with all the success, is Norman eating his lox and avocado on a rice cake, of all things?*

"That's a very virtuous choice."

Norman looks up from the unappetizing meal to the unappetizing attorney across the table. Stephen Gibson kills what little appetite he had.

"It's a shit choice. My doctor threatened he wouldn't see me anymore if I didn't cut down on the carbs."

"Is that ethical?"

"You think I want to argue ethics with him?"

Gibson laughs, but it's forced. He wants to convey that they're friends, equals. They are absolutely not.

"I want you to make a call," Norman tells his managing partner. "I don't care to whom. But I want it made clear that this prosecution of Jake goes forward. No deals. I want it dragged out, I want it slow-walked, and I want it played tough. Think about whoever Jake will call, then you call someone higher up the chain. Clear?"

Gibson can't stand the way Norman talks to him. He knows what the man thinks of him, and it's long past time for that opinion to change. That said, Thompson is gone, so he has to play the cards he's been dealt. And his hand is good. Because Norman may not think he needs him, but without him—or worse, with Gibson against him—Norman will be done.

"I will make sure that your son gets exactly what's coming to him."

Cara West was never able to enjoy the opulence of her father-in-law's home. Visits here were too fraught with Jake's childhood trauma, not that he'd call it that. But he got agitated anytime they were here, and she felt she had to manage him, buffer him, get him out in one emotional piece. Today she disdains the house for different reasons.

Getting in wasn't hard—Norman's house staff always liked her. Talking her way through to the yard was easier still. Zucchini bread and a lie. And while she's ready to do battle with her estranged husband's nemesis of a father, she wasn't expecting to find him with Stephen Gibson, a man who, in her experience, has no positive personality traits. Gibson is getting up to leave, but both men stop whatever conversation they're having when they see her coming. Norman rises, a small gesture of good manners.

"Cara—to what do I owe the pleasure?"

She places the homemade bread on the table. "I told Alvita that Chloe made it for Grandpa. She didn't, to be clear, but Alvita figured you might want to cheat with some carbs to counteract the rice cakes."

"You're upset," Norman says, stating the obvious.

"You had your own son arrested."

"For his own good. But I'm sorry for what this must be doing to you—"

"Yeah, I'm sure that's foremost on your mind."

Gibson tries to inject himself into the fray. "I'm sure things have been hard for you—"

"Spare me, Stephen. I know exactly what you think of Jake—*he* certainly does. I know what I think of him half the time, but he is father to my children, and I will not have them knowing he's in jail."

"That's not my call," Norman lies.

"I'm sure it's not. I'm sure you have no pull."

"You're angry."

"You can tell? I thought I was hiding it."

She can count on ten hands the number of times she's told Jake to not let his father get to him. But now she realizes something: she never understood how difficult that can be. It was always Jake's fight, not hers. But this is now her fight as well.

"I accept your anger, I do," Norman says condescendingly. "You having to come here, it's not fair to you. This whole last year, it's been *grossly* unfair to you. Frankly, I've wanted to reach out, but it's hard when your wayward husband is also my son."

The dig isn't lost on her. He's rubbing in her face that Jake has cheated on her, something she assumes but has never verified. And hearing it from Norman pisses her off because while he's being vindictive, he's being honest as well.

"Whatever you need, Cara—just tell me. And I'll do what I can."

It irks her, seeing the two of them no doubt conspiring about screwing over her husband. She sees what Jake is up against. He needs allies.

"I want to see that Jake is released with all charges dropped by the end of the day. Or you will *not* see your grandchildren again."

"Cara, please—"

"I don't care how you do it, but I know you can. And if you think I'm here being emotional, know this. I will divorce Jake, I will get full custody, and I will make sure you are off-limits for any visitation. So, no photo ops, which is mostly what you care about. You will cease to have a fictional family. You will be alone. A right you've earned."

She turns to go—this is the proper way to end this moment. But she doesn't get two steps before Norman chooses to have the last word.

"I don't understand."

She turns back. "I think I've been clear."

"Oh, you have. I just don't understand why. Why you would do this for him. He needs help. He needs intervention. You bailing him out—that isn't help."

She thinks about this for a moment. It's actually a fair question. But her hatred gives her the answer. "Why? Because most of his failings? I blame on you."

34

Javi and Grace enter the courthouse a half hour before Jake's arraignment. The activity of a busy court morning fills Javi with excitement and regret. This is where the wheels of justice turn. Most of it is boringly procedural, but if one steps back and takes it as a snapshot of humanity, of the human inability to keep oneself from doing what should not be done, it is breathtaking. And being a part of that system, trying to correct its mistakes, in a way it's like trying to reboot humanity. It's a grandiose thought, but Javi believes it. He misses it. And he hates that he misses it.

Once upon a time, this was his stage. He would come in here and maneuver through the minutiae and help people who were overmatched by the system. Now, he feels out of place. He feels small. Probably like most criminals, even more so the innocent. There's nothing like knowing the system has control over what you can and can't do. He could argue that maybe as a private investigator, he actually helps more people. That not being part of the system positions him better to fight against it, and not being bound by its rules is a blessing. But that's a lie, because it's precisely his skill set in using the system that made him what he was.

He looks over at Grace and worries she's reading his thoughts, and the last thing he wants is sympathy. "I know about your undergrad degree, so just a caution—if you were thinking of saying something? Don't."

Grace says nothing. Sometimes in psychology, that's the best tactic anyway.

Jake is surprised when the door to the small room opens and a bailiff lets Javi and Grace in.

"Who tipped you off?" he asks.

"Thompson and West rumor mill was in overdrive this morning," Grace explains. "I may be fired, but I still have friends."

"Well, nice to see friendly faces."

"You were supposed to *not* do anything stupid," Grace reminds him.

"Alas—I am who I am."

Javi isn't enjoying the banter. "Stop fucking around. We have a way to get you out. We think we can get the judge to go for alcohol diversion, which frankly, might do you a world of good."

"You want me to perjure myself?"

"How so?" Grace asks.

"I only get alcohol diversion if I have a problem with alcohol." Neither one is amused by his attitude. "Besides which—I have my own plan."

"A plan that calls for letting the enemy represent you? How much did you have to drink after Grace left?"

"I lost count, but regardless, yes. Though I confess I'm beginning to think Daria's not the enemy."

"It's a mistake," Javi says.

"Maybe. But it's the way I'm gonna play it."

There's a knock on the door, and the bailiff reappears. "It's time."

"Just stick around—it'll be fun," Jake promises.

At least it will be for him. It'll be so much better to have an audience.

Jake is seated in the back of the courtroom with a handful of defendants being arraigned. It's a different view of the process than he's had before, and he once again finds it fascinating, almost as if he's outside his body watching it. He begins to wonder if the alcohol is still in his system, but his rudimentary understanding of biology—or is it chemistry?—tells him that isn't possible.

Daria maneuvers her way to the seat next to him. "How are you?"

"I'm superb. Finding this an educational experience."

"You're an odd duck, Jake."

"Heard from Dad? He call to stomp his feet or offer a deal I won't take?"

"Not a word."

"And you haven't called him?"

"Felt like an in-person conversation. But I do have a plan that will keep you out of jail and still let there be the consequences you seem to desire."

"A plan. I'm excited."

"Alcohol diversion."

Jake finds it annoying that everyone thinks this is all about drinking. "Can't do it."

"It's a bullshit program, Jake. I don't care if you stop drinking."

"No, I could do the program. But to do the program I would have to admit to a problem with alcohol. Which would be a lie."

His line goes over no better the second time around, but before Daria can rebuke him, she's jostled by the guy next to her on the bench. Which annoys her, until she sees he's trying to get her attention. He gestures to Austin Bell standing in the aisle. Bell motions to Daria. She gets up to talk to him, but he then indicates to bring Jake along. Which she likes less, but complies.

"Let's step outside," Bell suggests when they reach him.

"I'm not sure I can do that," Jake says.

"You're with me. I think I can vouch for the fact you won't run."

"Isn't this highly irregular?" Daria asks.

"I think you'll both find this conversation fruitful."

When the three of them find a hard bench in the hallway that gives a modicum of privacy, Jake decides he'll start. "So—you're offering fruit?"

"The district attorney's office is dropping all charges."

Jake didn't see this coming. It makes him suspicious; he turns to Daria. "You pull some move I wasn't privy to?"

Daria's equally suspicious—of Austin Bell. "I wish I could take credit. So tell us, Austin—whom do we have to thank?"

"You're welcome," is all he says. And he gets up to leave.

"What's the catch?" Jake asks.

Bell turns back. "Not everything is a conspiracy, Jake." With that bumper-sticker–like comment, he leaves them. Daria and Jake both watch him, their minds spinning.

Jake states the obvious. "Something's not right about this."

"I'd tell you to count your blessings," Daria replies, "but, in the immortal words of your father, I'm fairly certain the other shoe hasn't dropped yet."

Jake has the same bad feeling. But mostly he's pissed. So much for getting discovery.

35

Forty-five minutes later, Daria arrives in the lobby of Thompson & West. She senses people giving her side glances, whispering. It's probably all in her mind; most probably have no idea what she's done, and yet the feeling is strong. That she may have dug her own grave here.

She goes to the front desk. At least Kendall gives a friendly greeting, but then a cloud washes over the receptionist's face. Daria's about to ask if the girl is okay, when the sound of a hard sole on marble flooring makes her turn to find Stephen Gibson walking toward her like the harbinger of death.

"Norman would like to see you," he says evenly. She senses an undercurrent of malice.

"And he sent you to fetch me? Isn't that beneath your station, Stephen?"

He's about to reply, but now *his* face takes on a pall. She wonders: Who is *his* harbinger of death? She turns to see that Reagan Hearst has arrived in the lobby. Gibson clearly fears him. Poetic.

"Something wrong, Stephen? I expected a witty retort."

"You know what, Daria? I think you're a problem that will solve itself."

He lets that hang for only a second, then peels off to intercept Reagan before he reaches the reception desk and has a fit that the bitch who served him papers is still working here. "Why don't you come back to my office?" Gibson says obsequiously as he steers Reagan away.

Daria watches them go, then turns back to Kendall, who looks almost as scared by Reagan Hearst as Gibson was.

"That man has no say over your employment," Daria reassures her.

"Thanks," Kendall says as she hands Daria her messages. "Have a good day."

"You know what? I think I will." Daria walks off more confidently than she has a right to. In the annoying words of one Stephen Gibson, she's about to make a *move*, but she has no idea how it's going to land.

Norman's door is open. He's scanning files on his twenty-seven-inch screen. He chose the large screen because he felt it made him appear more powerful, but it has also proved useful as a hedge against his weakening eyesight. There's a knock, but Daria Barati doesn't wait for an invitation; she comes in, closes the door, and takes a seat on the couch. Not across from his desk—on the couch. He recognizes the move. She expects him to get up and come to her. He decides to give her a little room to play. See what comes. He takes the large leather chair across from her. And waits her out.

"You want to know what the fuck I was doing representing your son. Your son whom you fired, your son who broke into your house."

"No. I can imagine the logic. I'm not sure if you came to it yourself or if Jake got you there, but that's not my concern. My concern is simple: Which side are you on?"

"I think my twelve years here have made that abundantly clear. My record of earnings and court victories and client signings have shown where my loyalties lie. Frankly, I resent the question, because what I did last night, what I did this morning, was a service to you. What you should have done is called me in here to thank me. Frankly, you should have come to *my* office, because you put something in motion that jeopardizes this firm. That jeopardizes *you*. And my fear is that the leadership you rely on now doesn't see that."

"You have a problem with Stephen Gibson?"

"No, *you* have a problem with Stephen Gibson. Under his watch, it's been one fiasco after another. *Harrison*—"

"We won that case."

"At what cost? Beating Jake just made us look clownish. Now Richard Kaplan's dead and Jake's accused of his murder? That too makes us look clownish. You having your own son arrested, then pulling strings to have him released? More circus."

He could argue, but he's interested to see where she's going with this.

"And while I understand your personal stake in it all, Stephen Gibson should be the clear-sighted voice of reason, not fueling the madness. He's gotten sloppy, and you've lost a step because you haven't seen it and stopped it."

Whatever he expected from this meeting, this wasn't it. This is a side of Daria he's never seen, suggesting a vast, untapped well of potential. "Continue," is all he says.

"As we sit here, Reagan Hearst, this firm's biggest client, is having to be talked off a ledge, and the one doing the talking is a man who's afraid of his own shadow. I saw him literally cower when Reagan came in. If anything, Reagan Hearst should fear this firm, fear leaving us, fear the damage to his own self-interest if he chooses to go. Instead, Gibson is the one terrified of him leaving and he's doing some pathetic tap dance to keep him. And as I read the room, Reagan Hearst is more like you. He may like to or want to make people cower, but what he needs is someone to stand up straight and keep him in line. He won't get that today. I give it a week, he'll be repped at Waxman Dunn or O'Melveny and Myers."

Norman never really considered Daria for any position of power at the firm. She'd been a diversity hire that panned out, but that was it. Now he believes he may have been wasting a resource. He gets up, walks to his bar, and pours two glasses of a Glenfiddich 23 Year Old Grand Cru. Gives her one. She simply takes it, keeping her eyes locked on his. This time waiting for him. The right move. More evidence in her favor.

"And what would you have me do instead?" Norman asks congenially.

She doesn't answer right away, taking a moment to savor the liquor. And the fact that her move has been played perfectly.

"It's being handled."

Reagan Hearst wants to grab Stephen Gibson and throw him through the window, then peer over the edge and watch his body explode in the grassy courtyard below. He wants to gaze down at the mess and feel his power. He literally has to turn away to fight the impulse.

"The police and lawyers are investigating things and people that may lead them back to us, Stephen."

"There are no viable links," Gibson dismissively responds.

"Yeah? Well, as you know, my guy is in a panic."

"Yes—I saw his sloppy work. We closed the door, and he reopened it."

"That's not how he saw it."

"Well, he's not very smart," Gibson says, his voice dripping with arrogance.

"Smart enough to see that you couldn't stop Jake West," Reagan fires back. "Tiana Walker was released, so he panicked, only proves my point. Instead of you handling things, *I'm* having to handle things. And I don't like it."

Gibson doesn't like the sound of this either. "You're handling them how, exactly? Never mind, I don't want to know."

"Well, you're going to know. There is one person who can make a visual ID of our mutual friend. Thanks to you—I've given him her whereabouts."

Gibson is horrified. Sort of. Relieved. Sort of. He can't decide.

"I can't know this."

"But now you do. I'm purposely removing your deniability. This was your plan, your intent, and if it comes to it, you will share the culpability. Because you *are* culpable."

"I haven't killed anyone."

Reagan fixes him with a glare. "Tell yourself whatever gets you up in the morning. You are not clean on this, Stephen. You gave me Javier Alvarez—the rest falls from that."

Gibson wants to argue, but it's true. Reagan must've tracked Tiana through Javi. And he tracked Javi because Eddie in the parking garage bugged his car when he was here to meet Norman. Only cost Gibson a hundred bucks.

"Whatever your guy is planning? I don't want to know. You shouldn't know either."

"I'm not stupid, I'm just a purveyor of information. But one who will gladly accept the benefits."

As will Gibson. But he hates seeing how far this has spiraled out of control.

Reggie doesn't understand. Why is there a castle in California if we don't have kings and queens? The fact that Tiana knows Hearst Castle wasn't really a place for kings and queens but rather the home of one ludicrously rich man doesn't make her confusion any less than his. How can people live this way? How is it possible someone with this kind of wealth doesn't spend it to help others? She doesn't know any more about William Randolph Hearst than what she's learned on the tour, but she knows places like this shouldn't exist. It's beautiful, but it makes her despair of the world. Of humankind.

Reggie likes it, though. He doesn't complain about the walking; he just runs from room to room and imagines living there. He *wants* to live there, and she supposes that kind of desire, or incentive, or at least awareness of the possible is good for him. Because before everything happened, what did he think was the best a person could do? Certainly not this.

She was drawn to the tour by the name. She doesn't know if Reagan Hearst is any relation, but from what she saw of his house, the night of that awful party, he's certainly descended from the type. People who think they're above it all, above consequence. *And they're probably right,* she thinks, as they ride the tram back down the hill from the castle. Literally above it all.

"Zebras!" Reggie's exclamation startles her.

She scans the hillside, thinking he must be mistaken, but she follows his gaze to two zebras grazing on the hillside. More evidence of misspent wealth, she supposes. Having your own private zoo. Ludicrous—but incredible. And it's equally incredible she's able to give her son this. This moment of escape. She'd give him anything.

Which is why when they arrive back in Cambria and he asks for ice cream, she says yes, though it will spoil his lunch. His joy is contagious. They're in a quaint small town, in a place safe enough that he can explore by himself. She gives him some money and watches him practically sprint to the ice cream "shoppe." It's spelled that way, just like in a fairy tale.

She sits on a bench and takes in the fairy-tale town. Sure, it's a vacation getaway for most, but there are shops, businesses, people must live and work here to keep the tourist economy thriving. She starts to think about what kind of job she could get to keep them here. As her mind wanders to the possibility, her eyes gloss over. Which may be why she doesn't see the man watching her. Noting her distraction. And moving to follow Reggie.

Two minutes later, Tiana's gazing at a photo of a two-story apartment building in the window of a small real estate office. The apartment is pretty rundown, but the advertised rent is only a little more than she was paying before her life took such a left turn. If she works enough hours, finds cheap-enough childcare for Reggie while she does, maybe they *can* stay here. Even after Jake and Javi track down whoever set out to destroy her life. Sure, she might be safe then, but going back will just be a constant reminder of all she's lost. And while some people who are grieving feel the need to do things like visit the grave of the person they've lost, Tiana feels she carries Mariella and Quinton with her. On a chain around her neck are two small gold charms: a basketball and a kitten. For Quinton, the choice was obvious. He had but one love. Mariella was harder, but Tiana had a tiny piece of guilt about her daughter. She'd always wanted a kitten, and Tiana had promised it for her next birthday. This is her making good. Tiana keeps these two representations of the children she loves so much that it hurts close to her heart.

She steers her mind away from the sadness and lets her gaze drift across the rental listings in the window. If Reggie can dream of living in a castle, can't she dream of this? Of giving him the life he deserves? He's a sweet boy, and the ocean and the squirrels and birds and butterflies amplify his sweetness. She knows exactly what will be amplified if she goes back, and he deserves better. Just like he deserves the double scoop she told him he could get.

A jolt of panic courses through her. Shouldn't he be back by now? She turns away from the window and searches in the direction he went. How long could the line have been? The town, though filled with tourists, is no hub of activity.

She moves quickly toward the ice cream shoppe. Not quite at a run—she's talking herself into the idea that she's just having an irrational moment of fear. Reggie is probably chasing a cat or a bird. But he's not in front of the store, and he's not inside, and that panic in her stomach starts to grow exponentially. Tiana spins around wildly, scanning the street for any sign of him, until her eyes come to rest on a man standing alone. Doing nothing but staring at her. There's something off about him. His dark hair's a bit unkempt, but that's not what's disturbing. It's his smile. More like a leer. He's giving her a big gap-toothed grin. Which is when she realizes all her fears are real.

36

They're in Jake's car because the Genesis is much faster than Javi's Camry. The specs say it can hit 149 mph, but Jake knows a ticket will slow them down, so he's keeping it under ninety and Javi's watching for Highway Patrol. They're on the open stretch of PCH that runs along the water, having cleared Ventura, now flying past Mussel Shoals. Jake grips the wheel so hard his hands are cramping, and Javi needs Jake calm and rational.

"It is possible her battery just died."

"Sure. Right after she texted 'I need h—' and hit send on a text that wasn't finished."

Javi tries to calm his own nerves, which have been jangling since Jake insisted on stopping to get the gun from the Thompson & West safe house. Much as Javi hates to think of using it, it may be necessary. He just hopes neither of them is the one who gets shot.

"We need a plan," Javi says. "For when we get there."

"We find them."

Okay. Jake isn't really in a talking mood. To distract himself, Javi focuses on the tracking app on his phone. A flashing dot on a map. A dock. Morro Bay.

"Signal's still coming from the same spot."

"You know if they push out to sea—"

"I know. Just keep driving."

Javi had told himself it was overkill when he put a GPS tile on Tiana's phone, but given the people they were up against, he wanted a way to track her even if her phone was off. It has been off for three hours now, in the middle of the day, which makes no sense.

"I'm a fuckin' plague," Jake says almost under his breath.

"You're not a plague."

Jake doesn't bother to argue. He's become dangerous to everyone he cares about. Every life he touches goes to shit. Richie's dead. Grace has been fired. Javi's being dragged into a life-and-death situation. Who knows if it'll spill over to Cara and the kids, but it could. He's become toxic. And the brunt of that has landed on Tiana and her son. His crusade to find out what happened to Rich and clear his own name has pulled Tiana and Reggie into the vortex, and he fears he'll find them dead. It will be his fault.

"I'm gonna say this now," Jake says, "so we don't argue when we get there. Once we figure out what boat they're on, we go in."

"I hear you. But both of us getting shot doesn't help anyone. I'm thinking one of us strolls past. The other goes in, sure, but at least there's backup."

"That's a shit plan. We only have the one gun."

Jake chews on Javi's point. They are walking into a setup, and whoever goes in will likely get shot. But they have no choice. Unless . . .

"Look in my wallet," Jake says.

Javi digs it out of the center console.

"There's a business card I stuffed in there somewhere."

Javi digs around, and in the flap underneath Jake's driver's license is an LAPD business card with contact information for Detective Sioban McFadden.

"Sure, Jake. Absolutely. She'll drop everything and come running to help. Not her case, out of her jurisdiction, she's gotta be dying to put her job and her career on the line to help the prime suspect in a murder she's trying to solve."

"Just dial the number."

Javi thinks about it. What's the worst that could happen? Shit, a lot of bad things: she could send local cops to intercept them, she could send CHP to pull them over. But they're in over their heads, so he dials the number. The car picks up the call, so it's on speaker. After four rings, Sioban answers.

"Yes, I'll take your confession."

Now that he's got her, Jake isn't sure what to say.

"Jake?"

Javi shoots Jake a look—*say something.*

"Can I interest you in the best clam chowder in the state of California?"

Tiana has never been on a boat and doesn't like it one bit. The circumstances are clearly part of it—she and her son both tied up—but the bobbing and rocking motion makes her want to throw up. Or maybe it's fear. Probably both.

What are they waiting for? Her sense of the leering, gap-toothed man watching over them is he's just hired help. He's waiting for someone with authority to give the order to kill them. That hasn't happened yet, and that gives Tiana a ray of hope. That and the half-text she sent to Javi before Gap Tooth took her phone.

Reggie hasn't said a word since they were brought onto the boat. She has no idea what Gap Tooth did to him. There's no obvious physical harm done, but for a kid who never stops talking to be this quiet, it must've been bad. She has the mother bear's instinct to strike, to do anything and everything to protect her remaining child. She will die trying, but doesn't see a move to be made now that won't make things worse. Still, she wants to find some way to keep Reggie calm. She's been watching him. He's almost frozen. His eyes are big with fear of the Gap Tooth monster.

She tries to get his attention, to convey a message. *You're okay. We're okay. I love you.* But it's just with her eyes. She doesn't want to talk or do anything to set Gap Tooth off. Reggie finally turns to her, and he seems to calm. He seems to understand.

Tiana's furious at herself. Even with fear coursing through her body, the fury is there. Jake and Javi had explained what they thought happened, why someone had burned her apartment, trying to kill her. They sold this escape as a way to keep her safe. Offered to pay for it while they sought to put an end to the threat. She not only chose to believe them, she allowed herself the dream of staying and giving Reggie a better life. But all this time, she should have been running. She should have trusted no one but herself.

She realizes Gap Tooth is now staring at her—looking through her, really—as if she's already dead. A chill runs down Tiana's spine. His cold expression shows no sign of humanity. No sign that anything she could say or do will move him.

But she'll have to find something. She'll have to *do* something.

The beauty of Morro Rock is lost on Jake. The dome-shaped remnant of a prehistoric volcano is visible across the water from the pier, and all Jake can think about is that if they don't hurry it up, it'll become a grave marker for Tiana and Reggie.

They made the three-hour drive from LA in under two-and-a-half hours, and Jake and Javi are at Rose's Bar and Grill. On another occasion, the view would be incredible. The sun hanging low over the Pacific, casting orange and pink colors into the expanse of sky. The bay dotted with sport fishing boats, seals twisting and splashing, pelicans diving at them to steal remnants of their dinner. The pier dotted with shops and restaurants. Tourists taking photos and laughing and enjoying life.

Javi and Jake are focused elsewhere, looking back and forth between the GPS blip on Javi's phone and the boats docked along the pier to determine which one Tiana—and likely Reggie—are on. They have pinpointed a midsize trawler with fading blue trim, aptly or ironically named *The Escape*. It's large enough to have an interior cabin and small enough that getting on board unnoticed is not much of an option.

"So tell me about this chowder," Sioban says, sliding into a chair next to Javi.

The cavalry has arrived. It's a small one, but it'll have to do.

Her badge, out of jurisdiction as it is, gets them aboard a boat called *Morro That*—a bad pun, but it's just across from *The Escape*. There is nobody on deck, but Javi pegs the movement of the boat in the slip as suggesting there is someone—or some people—inside the cabin. Jake studies it carefully, making plans and calculations in his head.

"No," says Sioban.

Jake is confused—he hasn't said anything. "No what?"

"No, you are not going in with me."

"Why not? You going in alone isn't safe. We've got a high-end team here—"

"We are *not* a team. Neither of you is law enforcement. You are not trained for this."

"They train *you* to walk into an ambush alone?" Javi asks.

"Or maybe you have backup you didn't mention?" Jake asks hopefully. "Maybe after I called you, you called in the rest of the cavalry."

"The problem is, I don't know who I can trust."

"I'm touched," Jake says. "You trust *us.* Does you showing up mean I'm officially off your suspect list?"

"You are *unofficially* off my list, but that doesn't mean we're doing this together. I'm choosing to risk my career right now. You being part of it only makes the chances of me losing that career exponentially higher. The two of you stay here and get ready to call 911."

"And if I decide to follow you in instead?" Jake floats as a possibility.

"That's fine. Just know I might shoot you."

Jake assumes she's kidding, but she's not wrong about the trouble ahead. So he nods.

"Okay. Be careful."

Before Sioban can do anything, they see a man walking toward *The Escape*. It's getting late, light is fading, and the setting sun is angling right at them, so it's hard to see him clearly. But this much is apparent—he's white, in his forties, he's dressed sharply, and he walks with the arrogance of someone who owns the world. Sure enough, he climbs aboard.

"That your guy? The client you won't name? Reagan Hearst?"

Though she's wrong about the newcomer's identity, Jake is pleased. She's followed his breadcrumbs. Maybe there's hope for them yet.

The thing that started Sioban on a new path wasn't that Jake got out of the charges for burglary and trespass. It was seeing Austin Bell himself come to deliver the news. She started to do the math. Tiana Walker was Bell's case—and he let that one go. Then he'd drawn Jake's break-in, and he let that go too. For a tough-on-crime candidate for DA, for a guy with a track record of getting the biggest sentences on his cases, it didn't make sense. That's why she started to dig.

Bell's political aspirations were no secret, and getting to the list of donors to his "exploratory committee" wasn't that hard. But since the Supreme Court had made it easier for corporations and political action committees to spend big dollars, and to hide those dollars, getting to who was really backing Austin Bell was more difficult. Because his biggest contributor, by far, was an organization known as CLAAC—Citizens of Los Angeles for Action and Change.

Still, there are limits on what any one corporation or individual can contribute. Ostensibly to prevent any one person or company from influencing policy, but CLAAC had a way around that: "chapters" in each of Los Angeles's eighteen congressional districts. With separate officers and separate boards.

But these chapters, while legally separate, do have something in common: contributors. Reagan Hearst, the Hearst Plaza Corporation, the Hearst Investment Group, and Hearst Construction, all separate legal entities, each have maxed out their contributions to each of the eighteen chapters of CLAAC. Which means that Austin Bell is being backed by Hearst—eighteen times over. Like it or not, he now owes Reagan Hearst a debt. Was dropping these cases payment for that?

There's no crime in what Hearst has done, not by the letter of the law. But it certainly sheds a new light on the connection between these cases, and on the reason Jake kept claiming privilege. Reagan Hearst is a client of

Thompson & West, and Jake, as a former partner now, is bound to keep secret all of their personal and corporate dirty deeds.

She knew Jake couldn't overtly confirm any of this. But it occurred to her that if she floated what she knew, using one of his hypotheticals, she might get somewhere. So she went to his new office, which depressed the hell out of her. Seeing how far he'd fallen. She was becoming increasingly convinced his fall was not of his own making.

It was a dead end—no one was there. And she'd been working pretty much around the clock and was tired, and her GPS told her that she was only 2.6 miles from R Bar. She was on her way there when the phone rang. And Jake made his plea for help.

She should have called it in. Called the locals in Morro Bay. Called Gantley. Instead, she got in her car, thinking that if all worked out, she might be able to nail Reagan Hearst. It wouldn't make up for Brin Maloney. But it was a start.

"That's not Reagan Hearst," Jake says, eyeing the man as he boards the trawler. "But it's nice to see your detective skills are as good as advertised."

"Someone he hired, then?"

"Maybe," Jake muses, "but not in the way you mean. That's no hired hand. I know guys like that, who have spent their lives surrounded by money. They walk around like they own the world."

"They do," Javi observes pointedly, eyes on Jake. But Sioban ignores him.

"So you recognize the type, but any idea who he is? And if you give any attorney/client crap right now, I'll shoot you."

"If I'm betting," Jake says, "that's Mr. White."

"What, are we playing Clue?"

"Exactly," Jake says.

"It's our nickname for the white guy who asked Jacinta out," Javi explains. "Tiana saw him at a party at Reagan Hearst's place. We think that's what this is all about. What she saw or heard that she shouldn't have seen or heard at that party."

"You think he's the guy who hired Milo Stapp?"

"It's as good a theory as any."

Sioban watches Mr. White disappear into the cabin of the boat—she's out of time.

"If they shoot me, it'll probably be Mr. White—in the boat cabin—with a gun. Hell of a way to go."

And she heads toward *The Escape*. She really hopes she doesn't die here.

37

Cameron Bancroft—aka Mr. White—is feeling good. The past week has been filled with anxiety that neither Xanax nor cocaine has helped. But now he smells the salty sea air, feels the refreshing cool breeze, and he's armed with the knowledge that here, on this boat, is potentially the last loose end.

He opens the cabin door and steps inside to find a gun pointed at his face.

"Put that thing down," Cameron orders his gap-toothed muscle.

Gap Tooth complies, and Cameron turns his attention to the problem at hand. Tiana Walker. She's looking at him, he thinks with recognition.

"What do you want?" she says, holding her voice as steady as she can.

He doesn't answer. Instead, he walks slowly toward the little boy. The kid doesn't scream, doesn't squirm, doesn't spit. Cameron kneels down to his level.

"Hello."

No response.

"Leave him alone," Tiana says. "He doesn't know anything. He has nothing to do with any of this."

He turns back to the woman.

"I take it you know who I am?"

"I don't know your name, if that's what you're asking."

"But you've *seen* me before."

She could lie, but she senses he wouldn't believe her. "Yes. But I left town, I'm not saying anything about anything to anyone."

Cameron wishes it was as simple as that. That he could let this go. But it would gnaw at him, the doubt about whether she'd resurface, have a change of heart, someone could make her an offer. He'd lose sleep. He hates losing sleep.

"That wasn't my question. But let me ask something more specific. Actually, even before I ask, let me just say this . . ."

He pulls a knife from a sheath on his ankle. It's got a serrated blade, maybe six or eight inches long. He examines it for effect.

"Let me say that if you lie to me, this will slice through a seven-year-old quite easily. His body will be dumped a couple of miles out. And you—well, you'll be alive to watch the whole thing."

Tiana strains at the ropes.

"Good. I have your attention. Excellent. So here's the question." He moves closer to Tiana now, still playing with the knife. "The night of Reagan Hearst's party. What did you see?"

She's puzzled by this. She saw *him*. She already *admitted* to seeing him. There must be a right answer, one that may not get them out of this, but maybe stalls things. It's so hard to think when the blade is so close to her face.

"I—I don't know what you mean."

He can smell her fear. Just what he needs. "Okay. I'll coach you a little. You saw me there?"

"Yes."

"With whom?"

"With Jacinta's boss."

"Okay. Good. And what did Jacinta tell you?"

"Nothing."

Suddenly, the blade is against her neck. She can feel his hot, bad breath as he spits: "*Bullshit.*"

"She told me . . . you asked her out. And she said no."

He holds the blade there for a moment, taking in her scared face.

"Leave her alone!"

Cameron finds the boy's fury endearing, and it suggests there's a better way to get what he wants. He approaches the kid. Kneels down again.

"Hey there. You want to save your mother?"

Reggie has no idea what to say. And he's tied up anyway. Which is why Cameron shows him the knife.

"Want to see this close-up?"

"Stop it!"

He sees Tiana's panic and seizes on it. "No more games. What did you hear and what did you see and who did you tell?"

She sees the knife and her kid and the heinous man she knows will use it, and she fights to clear her head. She's supposed to have heard something? She can't remember anything, but she has to buy more time, to drag this out. "Is that why you killed Jacinta? You thought she heard something?"

Cameron takes this in. He has his answer. He's satisfied that she's not lying, which suggests Jacinta knew nothing. Which means he *killed* her for nothing, but that's water under the bridge—it was a chance he simply couldn't take. Just like now. He believes this woman, but it doesn't matter. He needs to sleep at night. So whatever Tiana Walker does or doesn't know has to end here and now.

The party boat that's pulled into the bay is blasting Jimmy Buffett so loudly that it provides great cover as Sioban slips her legs over the side and onto the trawler. The problem is in what follows. There's a single door to the cabin and no alternate point of entry. She's going to have to go through the door, with no map of the layout inside, no idea of the number of people inside, and no backup. She's beginning to think having Jake and Javi behind her with a gun drawn might have been a better plan.

Sioban steers her focus to Tiana and Reggie Walker. A mother and son who need her. But the image that comes to the forefront of her mind is that of Alice and Harry Coyle.

Alice's husband, Sean, had taken them hostage. Sean was drunk and had a gun, neither of which was unusual, but Sioban's internal terror meter said this time it was bad. He'd lost his job. Alice was leaving him. He would never get custody of Harry, not with his criminal history. So she worried Sean felt there was nothing left to lose.

Liam O'Roarke was her superior at the time. Operationally, not intellectually, speaking. O'Roarke said they were going to wait for Sean's anger to burn itself out, like it always did, so he didn't call for backup. When Sioban argued, O'Roarke laughed in her face. Told her to grow the fuck up. She took the hint and stopped arguing.

Until three blasts from Sean Coyle's weapon made her stomach feel like retching.

She knew what she'd find. O'Roarke had yelled after her to wait, but she was done listening. She went in and saw Alice's head only half there. Little Harry looked like he was sleeping, except there was blood pooling from a hole in his stomach. And the top of Sean's head was gone. It was a strange sight—his mouth and nose and eyes were fine, but clearly the third shot was him putting the gun in his mouth and firing upward.

This horrific image comes to mind now because she can't bear for it to end that way again. So how does she make it different? She could go in guns blazing; shoot first, ask questions later. It goes against her training, but Lord knows there are plenty of cops—in both Dublin and LA—who operate this way, and they sleep just fine at night.

But she can't do that. It has less to do with the danger of firing a gun when two innocents may be inside and more to do with her internal moral code. It's an outdated notion perhaps, but she can't take a life so haphazardly.

There are two remaining options: edge the door open and hope they're in some anteroom below, or bang it open, gun drawn, showing force. There are clear pros and cons to each, but she lands on going big. At least they won't hear her approach, thanks to "Margaritaville."

She takes a deep breath, thinking it may be her last, and pushes open the door.

Reggie's the first one she sees, his eyes filled with hope. Just to his right, however, Tiana's eyes are filled with dread, despite the fact that Sioban has gotten the drop on the slick white guy holding a serrated knife. Mr. White—or whoever he is—has been outflanked.

A *click* disabuses Sioban of that notion. On her right, behind the door, a man with a gap-tooth grin has a gun pointed at her head.

38

The minute they see Sioban disappear into the cabin, Jake and Javi take off from their vantage point on *Morro That.*

"This is a bad idea!" Javi shouts over the sounds of the party boat as they sprint across the dock to the trawler.

"I know!" Jake yells, and he kicks it up a notch.

But neither of them stops until they get to *The Escape*. They don't hear gunshots, but also don't see anyone coming out. Jake can't bear the waiting. "I've got the gun—I'm going in. If I don't come out, call someone. And tell Cara I love her."

"You're so fucking melodramatic. Not to mention that's a bad plan."

"You got a better one?"

"I do. *I* go in. I go in like I'm drunk, like I'm on the wrong boat, which distracts them and lets you come in behind me."

"What is that? Some old *Nash Bridges* episode?"

"Are you kidding? *Miami Vice*. Michael Mann, baby."

"You know something? Maybe Michael Mann knew what he was doing—it sounds like a decent plan. And I'm sober, so I don't think I'm deluding myself."

"Just don't wait too long," Javi implores him, the daunting task he's just proposed sinking in.

They both slip over the edge and onto the trawler. The party boat has moved on to playing the Eagles' "Hotel California," so sound isn't an issue, but Jake covers Javi just in case, as he moves toward the cabin door. He knows how. From *Nash Bridges*.

"Javi," Jake whispers loudly over the music once Javi's at the door. "I'm sorry."

"For what?"

"For everything. I'll do better. When this is done."

"Sounds like a plan. Sounds like a bullshit plan, but I'll take it."

Arvin Drudge has turned out to be worth more than the fifteen thousand dollars Cameron paid him. Not only did the odd man with the odd gap in his teeth find the woman and her kid, but he disarmed the redheaded cop who failed to check her sides when she came in. Part of him thinks he should kill Arvin when this is over, but someone useful and reliable might come in handy again. He takes the gun from Arvin and turns his attention to the redhead.

"How did you find us?"

"I followed you from LA," Sioban lies.

"Bullshit."

"Not bullshit. Milo Stapp gave you up."

This sends a chill down Cameron's spine. If that's the case, he's in deep trouble. If it's not—how the hell *did* she find him?

"Also—when you killed the old woman you were afraid could ID you? Someone saw you. We got a sketch. Led right to you."

Sioban's stalling, but the stall is a big gamble. It only works if Mr. White is indeed the one who killed Consuela Estrada. If he is, then she'll have the added pleasure of solving one of the cases on Johnny Mack's plate. Though she doesn't think he'll thank her. She also doesn't think her tactic is going to hold for long, so she's hoping she knows Jake as well as she thinks she does by now—that he's going to ignore being told to stay back.

Cameron is making his own calculations, while willing his face to stay calm. "What old woman are you talking about?"

"Nice try."

"You think I'm buying this? Let's put it to the test. Who am I?"

Her best guess is Mr. White, which is not a real name, but perhaps she can use Jake's conjecture to stall.

"You think you're that hard to ID? You think Reagan Hearst has that many friends? Especially those with a penchant for going after the help, for reckless behavior?"

Cameron is a little unsettled by that. She's correct about Reagan, and clearly she's pieced together some damning details that *might* lead to him. But her vague answer tells Cameron two things. That she has no idea who he actually is. And that she will have to be disposed of. Carefully.

Gap-toothed Arvin Drudge interrupts his thoughts. "If we're doing all three, I'm due a raise."

Cameron is annoyed at this. "You'll be taken care of."

"That's what I'm afraid of."

Interesting. Arvin's not as stupid as he looks. "You'll be *financially* compensated. That was my point." That wasn't his point, but he'll go with it for now.

Arvin nods, as appeased as one can be when dealing with killers.

"I did an artist's rendering for my lawyer," Tiana blurts out. "They're already looking for you. If you kill us, you only make things worse."

Cameron knows she's desperate, that she's most likely lying. But if she's telling the truth and he has these three killed? He's done. Shit.

As he tries to figure out if there are any alternatives he hasn't considered, he's distracted by the sound of loud singing. It can be heard up on the deck, and he's pretty sure it's not coming from that party boat.

"Para bailar La Bamba
Para bailar La Bamba
Se necesita una poca de gracia
Una poca de gracia
Pa' mí, pa' ti, arriba, y arriba
Y arriba, y arriba
Por ti seré, por ti seré . . ."

With that, Javi bursts in and collapses onto the floor of the cabin, his body propping the door open.

Seeing Javi's ridiculous gambit of playing drunk, Sioban is both relieved and worried. She glances to the door—Jake has to be close behind—but she doesn't want to give anything away, so she wills herself to focus on Tiana. Is there a way to use this distraction to get Reggie out of here? They make eye contact, probably making the same calculation, but neither Cameron nor Arvin moves a muscle.

"Check him, now," Cameron commands.

"Let me have the knife," Arvin demands.

"You've got a gun."

"That isn't what I need for this."

Cameron is intrigued by the point and hands over the knife, then turns his attention back to Sioban. "Ritchie Valens with you?" he asks.

"Don't I wish," she says, hoping her bravado plays well.

Cameron isn't sure, but he turns to Tiana. "He with you?"

"Oh yeah. He's my knight in shining armor." Tiana sells her disdain pretty well.

Arvin, meanwhile, kneels beside Javi and slides the knife to his neck to see if he flinches, the cold of the blade running along the skin above his collar. Cutting him. With all eyes glued on the red line of blood spreading on Javi's neck—

Jake bursts through the door. Before Cameron or Arvin can react, he fires one shot directly at Cameron. It practically enters Cameron's mouth and explodes out the back. Jake's almost as shocked by the action and consequence as Cameron.

Arvin's eyes go wide, which is when Javi grabs his wrist and yanks it backward, hard. Arvin screams in pain but manages to get the knife hand free and take a swing at Javi. The knife never reaches its target because Jake puts a bullet through the side of Arvin's head, sending blood and brain matter spewing everywhere.

There's a frozen moment, then Tiana throws herself at Reggie, her hands still tied, to protect him from any more shooting. Sioban snaps up her service weapon from Cameron's limp hand and quickly makes sure both men are dead.

After a beat to catch his breath, Javi registers that Jake hasn't moved since he fired the second shot. He's squeezing a death grip on the hot weapon in his hand. He doesn't feel relief, he feels sick. Sioban registers the same thing, and it occurs to her that this is not the reaction of a man who just last week shot his best friend in similar fashion.

"Jake," Javi tries to break his trance.

Jake pulls his eyes from the carnage to his friend. His friend who is alive.

"I think I can forgive you now," Javi says gently. "For everything."

Tiana is reeling. They should be calling the police and getting her and Reggie to safety. Instead, she's still on the deck of the trawler, holding her disturbingly quiet son tight while the cop and the lawyer and the PI decide what to do to next. The sounds of the party boat seem to have masked the gunshots, but there are two men dead inside. If she was someone who believed in the system, she would have argued harder that 911 should be called. But what good has the system ever done for her?

Inside the cabin, Jake has a hard time taking his eyes off the two bodies and the bloody mess he's made. The scene is eerily like Rich's murder. That one was worse because he knew and loved the man. But the deaths of these men land hard in their own way, because this time Jake is the one who's done the killing, albeit in self-defense.

"You need to call this in," Javi quietly tells Sioban.

"I do. The question is, who do I call and what do I say."

Jake doesn't fully understand. "We all saw what happened. I'll get a good lawyer. This was justifiable."

Both Sioban and Javi are trying to figure out if he really believes this.

"What?" asks Jake.

"You want to take that question, or should I?" Javi asks Sioban.

"Go ahead. He's your friend."

"Okay. Think this through," Javi says. "If the truth comes out—we're all fucked. Tiana and the kid have nowhere to go, you're on trial for murder, Sioban's fired, maybe even charged. Frankly, I may be the only one who comes out of it unblemished, but there's an argument that by showing up with you and your gun, I'm an accessory."

"So what's your idea? We sail out to sea and dump the bodies? You know how that ends, Javi. We'll eventually get caught."

"And I won't do that," Sioban says. There has to be accountability of some kind.

"So we go with the truth," Jake argues.

"Yes," Sioban agrees. "And the truth is this: I shot them both." Sioban lets them digest that lie before expounding on her manufactured truth. "I was coming to interview Tiana about you. She was with you just hours after the killing, that's a valid lead for me to follow. Before I got to her, I watched dead guy number two kidnap her and Reggie. I followed them here, which is when dead guy number one showed up and took my gun. But I was able to get loose, I took *this* gun"—she holds up Jake's weapon—"from the kidnapper and was able to shoot them both to save Tiana and Reggie."

"And where do we fit in?" Jake asks.

"Is the gun traceable to you?"

"No."

"Then you don't fit in. You were never here."

She is quite sure this is the way it has to be, consequences be damned.

Jake sees Javi nodding, but Jake's not on board with this insanity.

"I can't let you take the fall for what I did."

Javi puts a calming hand on Jake. "If she's part of what we did, she's off the case. We need her on the case. This isn't over. Reagan and Gibson and your father—they still have their asses to cover, which means she's right. It lets us live to fight another day."

"I'm sorry, no," Jake insists.

"You don't like it, but it's how the world works. You lie if you have to if you want to keep going."

"My boss is already looking at me funny," Sioban says. "I'm not sure he's on the take, but I tell the truth, first thing he does is pull me off the Kaplan murder and he gives that case to John Mackenzie, who most definitely *is* on the take. You'll be locked up in twenty-four hours."

"I hear you, I do, but you taking the fall for what I did is still a terrible plan."

"Or is it the only plan?" Javi asks.

Jake takes a long time before he concedes he has nothing better. "Can't it be both?"

Sioban wishes they had been able to talk her out of it, because lying in a police report about shooting two men, lying about who was here, then forcing Tiana and her kid to lie? How can all of that be the right thing to do? But then again—they're all alive. And she needs to keep them that way.

She goes back to what Jake said. There's doing what's legal, and there's doing what's right. Maybe it's the same argument that cost her back in Dublin. She's just hoping this has a better outcome.

39

Sioban watches as Captain Ryne Gantley reads the report she gave to the Morro Bay Police Department yesterday. He keeps looking up at her, shaking his head, then going back to the report. He knows it's bullshit. Or rather, he *thinks* it is. But Sioban's been very careful—she believes the report will hold up, and she's decided the only way to play this is full tilt. She has to commit to the lie. In time, Gantley will come to see that the story is, if not true, at least impenetrable. So she tries to ease him in that direction with a little humor.

"You have such a great poker face, I bet you clean up at the monthly game."

Now he stops. He is not amused.

"Is there a problem?" she asks innocently. Or more accurately, feigning innocence.

"Oh, there are many problems, Detective. Problems of credibility, I'd say."

"It's *incredible* I got out of it alive. You would have preferred it ended differently?"

He doesn't appreciate her attitude. He practically snarls: "If I had security camera footage of what went down on that boat, on the docks—"

"Then you'd know it's the truth. But sadly for both of us, Arvin Drudge must've disabled any cameras before he brought Ms. Walker and her son on board."

His eyes narrow. He doesn't like being played. Gantley's not sure what to do about it, but he refuses to accept this report at face value. Her description—of where the bodies were, where the gunshots came from, where the woman and her kid were in all this—seems to defy the laws of physics. At the very least, the laws of probability. He wants to question the seven-year-old, but the mother refused, and the truth is, anything Gantley got wouldn't stand up in court. Not that he wants this to go to court. What he *really* wants is for this to go away—for *her* to go away.

He sets the report down on his desk, takes a moment to compose himself, then begins in a roundabout way. "Back in Dublin, when you left, there were . . . questions. Implications."

"You mean unsubstantiated rumors from ex-colleagues that went nowhere when you checked them out? Because you obviously vetted me, then put me on the team."

"I *accepted* you on the team. We had quotas to fill."

"Wow. Saying the quiet part out loud now."

"I liked you, Detective."

"Your use of the past tense is noted."

He ignores her jibe and continues. "I figured whatever had happened, you'd probably learned from it. But now I'm wondering—was it like this? Some situation went to shit, and they couldn't prove it was your fault, so they thought they'd push the problem across the pond?"

"People in America don't get to use that expression."

"You're very full of yourself."

"I'm very lucky to be alive. I killed two people. One who was a kidnapper. The other I understand is a Mr. Cameron Bancroft, who turns out to work for one of the richest men in the city. I'm sure we'll connect him to at least one murder, more likely four: Jacinta Castillo, Mariella Walker, Quinton Walker, Consuela Estrada—"

"Stop. We are not going down the road of conspiracy and speculation—"

"You really want to know about Dublin, Captain? Let me tell you about Dublin."

She leans forward, angry now, because this is not that different from how things played out there. And she's not about to have the same result.

"We had a department filled with people on the take, people who played it safe, and people who just didn't give a damn. I wasn't on the take, I didn't play it safe, and I *did* give a damn. And all those things cost me. So forgive me for being full of myself, but I see the same shit here and I don't like it."

She didn't intend to go this far, but the beauty of this performance is that, unlike her report from Morro Bay, everything she just said is true. From Gantley's expression, she's not sure if he's about to fire her or blow up or what. And she still needs him. Which is why she tries to defuse the bomb she just dropped.

"Look, you said you liked me when we met. I liked you too. You're no bullshit. I felt like you were an ally. So whatever comes of this investigation, whether it leads to Reagan Hearst or not, I'm hoping it proves my instinct was good. That it's other people creating roadblocks to letting this investigation go where it wants to go."

She watches him ruminate on her words. He has to know she's not wrong about the department. He may not be able to prove it, or want to prove it, but he must know there's corruption. Not pervasive, not beyond repair, but it's there. That said, he will also hear her compliment to him for what it is—a threat. He closes the file folder.

"Well, it's clear you've been through something, Detective. So—as required by department policy, you are hereby being placed on administrative leave. You'll need to schedule a generalized training update as mandated. You'll need to schedule an appointment with the psychologist, also as mandated. And perhaps you'll decide to open up, bare your soul about what really happened. Tell them what you might have left out in this lovely piece of fiction you wrote up in Morro Bay."

"The fact that I have a flair for writing reports doesn't make it fiction. There's nothing I've left out." Sioban tries to deliver the lie with the proper amount of indignation.

"Well—time will tell."

He stands up, signaling the end of the meeting. But she's not done. "So you're taking me off the Richard Kaplan murder case? Which I'm about to break?"

"I have to put you on the bench. You know that."

"Well, policy is policy, I suppose. But two things before I go." She can tell she's wearing his patience thin. "I want the ID on the kidnapper. I want to know who I've shot."

He nods. That's reasonable.

"And whoever you're gonna put on the case—it can't be Johnny Mack."

"You think you get a vote on this?"

"I have a harassment claim against Detective Mackenzie that I have yet to file. But it's ready to go. And if he comes anywhere near this case, or anywhere near Tiana Walker, I will file it. Which will put him on the sidelines for all of his cases."

"You talk like you have someone on your side." She shrugs—no confirmation, no denial. "I hope for your sake it's more than Jake West. Banking on that guy is a bad bet."

Stephen Gibson hates panic. It makes people stupid, and it makes stupid people even dumber. Which is why he has to rein in Reagan Hearst.

"You need to calm down." A piece of advice that has never helped anyone calm down. In fact, it's counterproductive, but Gibson's rattled. Reagan is freaking out that what happened in Morro Bay will lead back to him. Gibson shares that concern. Cameron Bancroft to Reagan Hearst is one simple step, and making the leap to Stephen Gibson isn't much harder. There are way too many loose ends on way too many cases that could lead there. But Reagan's need to pound his chest and toss blame around isn't useful.

"How do we handle the Irish cop?" Reagan pushes the issue.

"She's on leave," Gibson replies. "She killed two people."

"And you think that means she's letting this go?"

Gibson does not like the implication he hears in Reagan's tone. "I'm not sure you're clear on what we do here. We work within the system—"

"I'm clear on what you *need* to do. How you do it? I don't care."

"Why don't we look at this practically. Bancroft is dead. The police identified his body, so let's assume they know he worked for you. It's certainly possible some will have labeled him your fixer. Others will likely refer to him as your friend. Perhaps Tiana Walker will identify him as the person who hit on Jacinta Castillo before *she* was murdered. Maybe she'll tell some story about what he said at that party—"

"This isn't calming me down."

"Let me finish. Even if all that is true, even if Tiana Walker reports that he said anything about you before he met his untimely end—it's hearsay from a dead man. So unless there's something I'm missing, there's nothing to tie you or me or this firm to anything that happened other than knowing the man. And I'm assuming there's no financial trail beyond his regular compensation? No paper trail beyond his employment?"

"No."

"Good. He's dead, he can't testify against you. Congratulations, you can relax."

Reagan doesn't, though, and Gibson realizes he's been withholding something. "What aren't you saying?"

"There's nothing concrete, but if they get his phone records, they'll see we talked."

"You're friends. Friends talk. He works for you, there's business."

"It's the timing I'm concerned about. I call him. He calls this . . . intermediary. The intermediary goes to Cambria."

Gibson doesn't like how this intermediary fits in, but he's not letting Reagan in on that trepidation. Regardless, it's heavily circumstantial, that's what he's telling himself. Focus on keeping the asshole client happy. "In the past, you and Cameron talked a good amount? We can show multiple conversations are not out of the norm?"

"Sometimes yes, sometimes no. Of late—no, because he was out of control."

"Well, let's dig through your phone records then and find the sometimes yes. Let's find periods where you talked a lot. So that we're ready."

"That's it? We dig through phone records and wait? That's weak. I'd not only call that ineffectual, but it's unacceptable."

Gibson would be more pissed if Reagan didn't have a point. But before he can craft a reply, there's a knock at the door. Without waiting for a response, Norman opens it.

Reagan exhales. "Thank God, someone who can fix things."

Daria Barati appears behind Norman, and Gibson realizes his situation is worse than he imagined. But he can't let that show.

"Norman. Daria. Something you need?"

"Yes. We need to be brought up to speed," Norman says.

"We?" Gibson is unsettled by that turn of phrase. Daria's expression betrays nothing.

"Yes. I think it's time we looped Daria in."

Gibson is clear exactly what this means. Norman is preparing to let him be the fall guy. And he's already lined up a replacement.

40

Austin Bell likes to hold court, and this afternoon, court is being held at Johnny's, a West Adams neighborhood hangout that offers many things, but the fact that PASTRAMI is lit up in huge neon letters towering above the restaurant name is the clue as to what one should order. There's a cozy indoor room that has a bar, but the real Johnny's experience is standing in a long line, ordering at the counter, and sitting at tables on the outdoor patio. It's a neighborhood gathering place and it can be packed from noon to midnight.

As Bell waits with Jake for their order at the window, people come up to say hello, offer their two cents on what the city needs, where crime needs fixing, and how he'll have their vote because he's one of them. Austin eats it up—probably more fortifying than the French Dip Pastrami he's ordered. Jake takes in the scene as he inhales the intoxicating smell of barbecue meats and burgers and fries. He's impressed at how beloved Bell is, but his cynical side says that's not what's going to get him elected. He'll be elected because he's been bought and paid for. That's certainly what the evidence suggests.

The order is up. Two biodegradable containers are slid to Bell, who in turn slides a twenty into a tip jar and takes the two bags to a long wooden table with benches. He's not holding himself apart but sitting among the masses. His constituency. Bell slides one of the containers over to Jake. "I'm surprised you know this place."

"I know all the best places to eat. Lived in this city my whole life, just like you."

"I'm not sure if your life was just like mine, but I'm glad to see you made it out of the Westside and down to West Adams."

West Adams is a historic neighborhood that was once a vibrant home to the Black community, until powerful political forces decided to build two freeways through the middle of it. The Black homeowners in the 1950s didn't have the clout to stop it. Today, it's either on the upswing or being gentrified, depending on one's perspective.

Jake unwraps his thick-cut Pastrami Reuben on marble rye with mustard and coleslaw slathered on, and a coleslaw cup on the side. Jake savors a large bite, and as he chews, he watches the other patrons digging in, chatting happily, and occasionally glancing over to see who it is Bell's meeting with.

"It's gonna be your city, isn't it? You'll win in a landslide."

"I don't think you came to give me a pep talk. You gonna tell me what we're really here to talk about? I already dropped the charges against you."

"Yes. Very magnanimous."

"You wanted me to prosecute?"

"Actually—I did. I needed a way to get some information on the record."

"Well, I'm afraid the criminal justice system isn't for your personal benefit."

"And in my case, whose benefit was it being used for?"

Bell studies him for a second. "Are you suggesting that the grand conspiracy here is that I *didn't* come after you? Good luck selling that." Bell laughs.

"Laugh all you want, but let me connect some dots for you, Counselor. See where you think it goes."

"I always love a good story over a meal."

Bell dips his French Dip, takes a juicy bite, ready to hear Jake out.

"Let's go back a few months, then. Jacinta Castillo works for Reagan Hearst. This we know is a fact, so I'm not violating any privilege by saying this. Jacinta claims one of Reagan Hearst's friends hit on her. This we know from Tiana Walker's statement. Jacinta is murdered soon thereafter. This we know from the police record. Tiana tells the police about this friend who hit on Jacinta. They investigate. This, too, is indisputable fact."

"I'm on the edge of my seat waiting for the rest. Such a riveting tale."

"The next part you know really, *really* well. After Jacinta's murder, after

Tiana's report to the police, and importantly, after the police question Reagan about this friend, there is a fire at Tiana's home that kills two of her children."

"Can I interject? Sequence does not make causation."

"I concede that fact," Jake replies, "but let me continue. In the days prior to said fire, a white man is seen casing the place."

"I'd object to the word 'casing,' but go on."

"The witness who saw this man makes a statement that mysteriously disappears from discovery. I get that you want to call that an oversight, but let's consider what's transpired since. You agree to drop the charges against Tiana Walker. Thank you, by the way, I'm not quibbling on that one, but what it does is this—it creates the potential for that case to be reopened. Lo and behold, that very night, the witness who saw that suspect is murdered."

"Consuela Estrada's death has been deemed an *accident,* for now at least—"

"Just stay with me, Austin. Because now our story starts to get even better. Tiana leaves town with her one living son, but she's subsequently kidnapped. And who's behind that kidnapping? A man who just happens to be a friend and employee of Reagan Hearst."

"I agree, that's a good avenue of investigation. An investigation that's proceeding, and I can't share the details with you."

"I would expect not. But I wanted to lay the groundwork for what we're really here to talk about."

"You mean it wasn't just story time? That's rather disappointing."

"Let's return to where our little talk started," Jake suggests through a mouthful of Reuben. "To your campaign to represent the good people of Los Angeles." Jake uses a sweeping gesture to all the other patrons to make his point. He can't resist a little performance when he's building a case. "And my question is, how do you serve their interests when you have obligations to others?"

"I don't like playing games, Jake. Obligations to whom?"

"Well, as I see it, you really have a constituency of one."

He's waiting to see Bell's response. Bell seems genuinely confused, but he may be a good actor. "Get to the point. I'm losing my appetite."

Jake takes another big bite and continues talking with his mouth full. "That's a shame, mine is so good. Their coleslaw is perfection."

He finishes the bite with Bell watching. Waiting. Finally, Jake comes clean. "Reagan Hearst."

He was hoping the name-drop would provoke a reaction. Bell's good—there's nothing visible.

"What's your point? You think I give two shits about Reagan Hearst?" Bell responds.

"Yes, I think you do. Since he's your campaign's single biggest donor."

Bell's face squinches up, trying to make sense of this. Or trying to pretend he's trying to make sense of it.

"Turns out I didn't need a subpoena," Jake goes on. "Just a reporter friend filing a Freedom of Information Act request and I got to see *all* the contributions to your campaign. Or exploratory committee, if we're going to quibble over semantics."

Jake, of course, got the information from Sioban, but this is a plausible cover. He watches as Bell works to keep his face impassive while simultaneously running through a hundred things in his head.

"I have nothing to hide. I don't track each individual donor."

"I'm not talking about individual donors. Ever heard of CLAAC?"

"Sure. I've met them, I shook some hands. It's a political action committee wanting a better Los Angeles. But what does Reagan Hearst have to do with CLAAC?"

"Essentially—he *is* CLAAC. He's skirted campaign finance rules by donating to each chapter. One in every district. His company has done the same. His charity, his foundation—them too. And if you dig deeper, I bet there are others on his payroll who have followed suit."

Bell dips the pastrami again.

"Are you stalling, or is this really news to you?" Jake presses him.

"It's news to me."

"You're telling me you've promised nothing to Hearst in exchange for his support?"

"I am absolutely telling you that. I've met the man in passing, we've exchanged inane pleasantries. But I don't know him, and I don't owe the guy a thing. Whatever grand conspiracy you're imagining—I'm not a part of it."

While Bell speaks those words, he's running back the past, homing in on the day Bob Forrester told him he was stepping down. Bell had tried to hide his excitement, but Forrester wasn't stupid. He told Bell it was okay to be happy, that he had a little parachute that would see him safely down from his perch. But he did want to make sure the city was left in capable hands.

Bell played it close to the vest—he knew it would be folly to become Forrester's heir apparent. Forrester saw that hesitation but pushed past it, encouraged Bell to take a meeting, no obligations, with an organization called Citizens of Los Angeles for Action and Change. They had expressed interest in his candidacy.

For a guy who wanted an office you had to run for, Bell had a problem. He hated politicians. He could *be* one, but in general, he despised the game. And that meeting he had with CLAAC was clearly a game with rules he wasn't privy to. They said all the right things and had all the right goals—but in a generic, noncommittal kind of way. And that failure to put on paper what they really wanted from him should have been a red flag, but he saw the numbers they'd raised in previous campaigns. And the thought of that amount of money being used to campaign against him was daunting.

So he shook hands. He smiled. He took their money. And they promised to help make him DA.

There's a second memory firing in his brain. One of Forrester actually encouraging him to offer a deal on the *Tiana Walker* case. It wasn't overt, it was played well, as if he was moved by her story, her loss, perhaps because he was on his way out and was more susceptible to seeing the humanity in the case.

Bell wasn't pushed to do anything, but looking at that moment now, he sees it—he was definitely encouraged.

"I hear you. And I want to believe you," Jake tells him as he digs back into his Reuben.

"I don't care what you want," Bell practically spits back. He doesn't mean to lose his temper, but he's agitated.

"I agree my wants are irrelevant. But here's the problem. When I hold a press conference about what's happened to my client, I'll be laying the groundwork for a lawsuit against Reagan Hearst and the law firm of Thompson and West. And part of my case will involve outing their connection to you."

"I am *not* in their pocket—"

"Why did you drop the charges against me?"

"Because my office felt that you and your father going at each other would be a circus. I know who he is. I know the stories. And frankly, I felt that if I prosecuted you, I would have been doing his bidding. And I don't play that way."

"That's a well-reasoned argument. And I'd accept it, I would. Except for this—I happened to be speaking to my estranged wife last night. To let her know I was well on my way to proving my innocence in that other case, you know the one where I'm a suspect in a murder? Sorry—that's a digression. But she told me something I didn't know. That I had *her* to thank for my release. You see, she threatened my father. If he didn't intervene and have the charges dropped, he'd never see his grandchildren again. His grandchildren, who he uses to project an image he cares about. So while I hear your version of events, what I know is that Norman West reached out to *someone*. And hours later, you dropped those charges. You do the math."

Jake sees just a flicker cross Bell's face. Maybe he's rethinking something. Remembering something. Jake presses ahead.

"See, I was pretty good at algebra in high school, and I know that *X* plus *Y* equals *Z*."

Sadly for Bell, he sees the truth of the equation as a third memory rears its ugly head. A more recent conversation with Forrester. Again, it was casual. Paternal even, which in and of itself should have been a red flag, but Bell had chalked it up to a man who no longer had to fight for the next election. Jake had been arrested for burglary, and Forrester had come in with some sage advice. Bell going after Jake West days after facing off with him in court wouldn't play well. And frankly, Forrester had pointed out, it was probably Jake's old man using their office's time and manpower for some family grudge, which fit with everything Bell had learned about the fucked-up West family. So if Bell went after Jake, it might seem as if he had been used by Norman West. Bell wanted no part of that, so he'd heeded the advice and dropped the case. On his own. Or so he thought.

Either way, Bell has to defuse this bomb.

"You don't have all the variables, Jake. Maybe neither do I, but I promise you—I did *not* sell out on this."

Jake thinks he means it. He almost feels bad for Austin. "You should go ahead and finish that French Dip while the juice is still hot. Dipping it in cold liquid kills the taste."

Jake takes another bite of his own amazing sandwich. Chews long and hard, not because the pastrami is tough, but to give Bell a chance to mull over all that's been said. Finally he swallows and returns to his performance. "Here's the thing. It really doesn't matter if any of what I'm hypothesizing is true. Because I have an obligation to my client, I will hold that press conference, I will lay out the equation, and *other* people will do the math. Your campaign won't be able to sustain the damage."

"You don't care if it's true, you just want me out of the running."

"Actually, no. I don't mind you winning. But your campaign may be collateral damage." Jake gives him a minute to ponder that before adding, "I do, however, have an alternative course of action to suggest."

"Of course you do. You want me indebted to *you*."

"No. You owe me nothing. Whatever you do, I'm going full bore at Reagan

Hearst and my father's firm. But you don't have to be caught up in it. Not if *you're* the one to expose it."

Bell stops cold now. Puts down his sandwich, giving up the pretense that he's interested in eating. He sees where this is going. He sees Jake's point. And he hates it.

"I get it," Jake sympathizes. "It sucks. But if you proactively call out what Reagan Hearst is doing, that he's trying to buy the favor of the incoming district attorney, then you become the hero again. You say anti-corruption work remains to be done—do it from the office you're in now. Start by taking a look at just what Hearst is trying to buy. Your backers and followers will respect you. And you live to run again in four years."

Bell just glares. There's a fleeting attempt to argue. "I'm running now."

"You're young. You've got plenty of time to get wherever you're going. But next time, you'll be more careful. You'll pay attention to who your friends are."

Jake pops the last bite of his Reuben into his mouth.

41

Stephen Gibson walks down the hall and revels in the deferential glances. As managing partner, he *should* be feared. Some like to rule with kindness—in his experience, though, an iron fist breeds better results. Not to mention that he enjoys inspiring said fear.

It's the end of the day and he's going to inspire such a feeling today not in his underlings, but his boss. Norman West needs to understand that Gibson could destroy him. He knocks on the door of Norman's office, wondering how many years it will take before this office is his.

"Come," is the gruff response from inside. What an arrogant fuck. Gibson can't wait to have this conversation.

He opens the door to find Norman at his desk—and Daria Barati sitting across from him. Plotting his demise, no doubt.

"Can we have a minute? Alone?"

"We can have a minute, but whatever you have to say, Daria can hear as well."

Gibson considers arguing the point but doesn't. If she wants to angle for power, it's time to fold her into the knowledge of what's transpired at this firm. Because that knowledge will drag her into the fallout, if there is any. So Gibson closes the door and moves to the couch. He chooses the couch because he wants to appear relaxed. He wants to *be* relaxed, but he's nervous and he's desperate not to let it show.

"You wanted to be brought up to speed," he says as casually as he can manage.

"Yes."

"I understand that desire. However, I would counsel that is a mistake."

He wants Norman to ask him why. Or at the very least, he wants Daria to chime in. Neither obliges. He has to push on, which he knows weakens the presentation. "*Not* filling you in insulates you. It's my way of protecting you and this firm."

He wants a reaction out of Norman. Assent. Anger. Disdain. *Something.* But Norman simply nods to Daria.

"If I may," she begins, "I think that's unwise, Stephen. I think that your actions, as managing partner, have already put this firm at risk. And if we're to *manage* that risk, we need to know what we're managing."

"No, you *want* to know. But I'm telling you, you shouldn't."

Norman enters the fray. "And I'm telling you that I reject that advice."

Daria gives him something else to think about. "When you engineered Jake West's removal from the firm, you correctly quoted chapter and verse of our bylaws. I would like to direct you back to those bylaws and suggest the same now applies to you. With the same result likely if you refuse to bring the two of us up to speed on what is going on at this firm."

It is abundantly clear to Gibson that Norman has thrown his lot in with Daria and has no interest in turning back. So much for playing nice. It was worth a shot.

"Whatever actions I may be found culpable of under those bylaws, they apply equally to the second named partner at this firm."

Norman abruptly stands. "Are you threatening me?"

"I'm stating fact. There are deals between you, and me, and Reagan Hearst, and the district attorney, all of which are best not spoken about, and certainly not revealed. I know I feel that way. I'm sure Bob Forrester feels that way—"

"Get out, Stephen. Now."

The only shock is that it's not Norman who says this—it's Daria. Regardless, he has done what he came to do. More words won't change that. To save face, to show he still has the upper hand, he wants to toss off a parting shot on the way out. But he can't think of one.

Bob Forrester's mouth is hanging slightly open as he gapes at his computer screen. An observer walking by might conclude he's watching porn, which at times he does. But this is better—he's viewing the results of a click-bait ad for "The 25 Best Golf Courses You Can Actually Play Right Now." Lush greens, mountains, oceans, pristine sand, blue skies. Porn he can actually make a reality.

"We need to talk."

His reverie is ruined by an angry Austin Bell. He hopes whatever this is doesn't prolong the end of the day—he was about to go hit some balls at Wilshire Country Club before heading home.

"I didn't hear you knock," Forrester says pointedly.

"I didn't," Bell shoots back as he comes in without invitation and closes the door behind him.

Forrester rises to his full six four. He's got a chiseled face, his hair only lightly salt-and-peppered, and he appears younger than his sixty-one years. As a white liberal in a diverse liberal city, he's managed to cobble together alliances that have taken him to the legal pinnacle of LA government. He's been elected—twice—because he's the living image of a man you'd want fighting for the city. For the people.

But in reality, he's not.

Forrester finds Bell irritating, but since he's likely to be the next DA of Los Angeles, he'll try to keep things civil. "This feels ominous, Austin. Or is it just theater?"

"Tell me about CLAAC," Bell says with no preamble.

Forrester takes a noncommittal moment to craft his response. "Tell me . . . what you want to know about CLAAC."

"I want to know if you know who's behind it. And why."

Again, Forrester wants to stall. He goes to the bar and pours himself a little cognac. He usually saves brandy for after dinner, but he likes what it says about him that he doesn't mind drinking it whenever he wants. In this instance, he's drinking it not so much because he wants it, but in order to make Bell wait. He wants to force Bell to appreciate the beautiful bottling of the Courvoisier XO. And he wants to use the time to figure out just how to put the genie back in the bottle.

Carrot or stick? That was the question turning round and round in Robert Forrester's head.

Norman West had reserved a table at Cecconi's, the West Hollywood branch of a Tuscan Italian restaurant started in London and now part of a chain owned by an American billionaire. It sits behind a high hedge wall that adds to the intended feeling of exclusivity. Their table was at the far end of the outdoor terrace, and there was no one within earshot, so Forrester knew that what was going to be discussed over branzino and pappardelle with a wild boar ragu was something either on the edges of the law, or beyond it. What he didn't know is if the approach was going to be with a carrot, offering him something enticing, or with a stick, threatening to destroy him for past misdeeds, of which there were far too many to count.

The answer was held in abeyance over cocktails and appetizers, but when the branzino arrived, when the fork was in Forrester's hand, ready to attack the succulent fish, the question came.

"Tell me, what are your plans, Bob?"

"Plans for what?"

"For when you get out?"

"I'm going to get my handicap to single digits. And I'm going to accomplish that at some of the most spectacular golf courses in the world."

"Really. That sounds marvelous. And while you're off galivanting, you're going to leave our fair city in whose hands, exactly?"

"Not mine to say. It's an elected position."

"Don't be naïve. You have the ability to anoint whomever you choose. Silverstein. Capuano. Bell."

Forrester had studied Norman for a minute, then took a forkful of fish and scooped some tomato and spinach to stall while his mind raced to parse what was really being discussed here.

"I'm assuming you have a favorite?" Forrester asked deferentially.

"My favorite is whoever can live up to your legacy."

If this had been a compliment, Forrester would have been flattered. But he knew what Norman was saying: he wanted someone who could be bought. Forrester had savored his fish to stall for time as he mulled over how to turn this conversation in the proper direction.

"Silverstein likes to dig. Into everything," Forrester offered.

"Which has made him enemies, which in turn makes him highly unelectable," Norman interjects. "Too many people have too many things buried that his digging might unearth."

It was a fair assessment. Russ Silverstein had molded himself into a righteous champion of the people. Which sounded good on paper, but elections are decided with money, and *the people* don't have money. Not the kind of stupid money corporations have. Not the kind of money rich men and women who work for said corporations have. The same people whose buried corruption might be dug up in a Silverstein administration. The fact that they were on the same page had encouraged Forrester to point him toward the path he'd assumed Norman had already decided on.

"Capuano is young," Forrester ventured. "He can be tough, but he's measured, and that balance could get him elected. But more than that, I like him because he has the least assets. And the most to gain." Forrester wasn't about to say the subtext out loud. That Capuano could use an infusion of cash.

"True enough. But I've tracked his record. He's a wild card. I don't like wild cards."

So Norman wanted Austin Bell. That was a problem. Like Silverstein, Bell cast himself as a reformer. But he'd done so without making enemies. He's a local, he's a lock in the Black community, close to a lock in the Hispanic community, and looks like a movie star. All of which would be good qualities in a

DA, but the problem with Bell was that he's his own man. Forrester was fairly sure he couldn't be bought, and there were no skeletons in the closet he was aware of. But he's also fairly sure Norman doesn't actually want an opinion.

"Austin Bell is a mistake." Forrester couldn't bring himself to stay silent.

"Why?"

"Because he can't be controlled."

"You mean *you* can't control him."

"You think you can?"

"I think *we* can, Bob. If we use our imagination. I think we can keep the trains running on time."

"And you need my help for that? I assume that's the purpose of this little meal?"

"We've had a productive relationship, Bob. Based on mutual interests. And while your time in office is coming to a close, our mutual interests will remain. We are, some might say, inexorably bound by those interests. My assessment is that Austin Bell will serve those interests moving forward. And I wanted to share that thought. And get *your* thoughts, of course. So that we move forward in lockstep."

Bob Forrester had studied Norman and was reassured that the man was as sharp as ever, had all his faculties intact, and had, no doubt, certain information he wasn't sharing. So if this was how Norman West wanted to play it, Forrester would go along. Because he couldn't have anything being exhumed after he left office that would interfere with his golf plans. Casa de Campo was calling.

Having stalled to pour his Courvoisier and ruminate, Forrester is now ready with his play to Bell. "I'm going to give you a piece of advice, Austin."

"Unsolicited advice. It must be my lucky day."

"You've always been too righteous for my taste."

"Not to quibble on semantics, but that's not advice."

"It is. I think it's a virtue for you. Particularly if you want to replace me, it's a good . . . vibe, is that what they say these days?"

"It's not a *vibe*, and that's still not advice."

"You think your shit doesn't stink?" Forrester's patience is running thin.

"I think you're ducking my question. CLAAC, Bob. You know it's Reagan Hearst. Now *I* know it. And I want to know what he gets in return for the donations. Or what he already got."

"What he got from me? Or what he expects from you?"

Bell is shocked that Forrester seems to be openly admitting it.

"Don't be so surprised. I know you're not wired—you wouldn't want to be because you have more exposure than I do. So let's just talk freely, shall we?"

"Please."

"My advice about your self-righteousness is that it has limits. It's a virtue with certain voting populations in our city. But if you run on that tack, and then it comes out that you yourself are part of the problem, it will backfire."

Bell sees the threat for what it is. "What have you done to implicate me in something I have nothing to do with?"

"I have forever tied you to Reagan Hearst and the success of Hearst Plaza."

"And why is that a problem?"

"Austin. You know better than to ask questions you don't want answers to. Leave yourself some deniability."

"If you don't tell me, I'll find out myself."

"I don't want us to be adversaries here. I'm rooting for you. I'm *voting* for you. Partly because you'll move heaven and earth to keep me protected. You have to."

Forrester sips his drink. He's glad he poured it, frankly, and that this is all coming to the fore. It makes him relax, knowing the cards are on the table. He can see Bell is absolutely livid.

"Have a drink, Austin. Try the cognac, it's good. It's good we're having this talk."

"I'm not enjoying this, Bob."

"No, I imagine what you've done doesn't sit well with you."

"I've done nothing."

"Austin. Really. In the last week alone, you've dropped charges on two cases, both directly involving Jake West. Two cases that appeared to be slam dunks."

"Someone tampered with evidence on the *Tiana Walker* case. A witness statement went missing. Never made it into discovery. Was that you?"

"It was *your* case. If something untoward was done, I'd say the prime suspect is you."

Forrester's tone implies—intentionally—something quite different. That Forrester is indeed the one who orchestrated this. He wants Bell to know. Bell needs to understand the lengths Forrester, and by extension his associates, will go. He almost feels bad for him.

"You're a great lawyer, Austin, but you're not running to be a lawyer. Like it or not, it's a political position. And if you want to be a real politician and not an ineffectual crusader, you'll have to learn to live with compromise. If you let this go, under your watch, Hearst Plaza gets built, jobs come to the city, investment, taxes. You'll be a hero. Hell, when it's all done, you could run for mayor. The sky's the limit."

Forrester sits back and drinks. It irks him to realize what he just said is true. He may have fucked Austin Bell right into higher office.

Bell gets up. Not angry. Not shouting. He goes to Forrester's bar and pours himself a taste of the Courvoisier. Sips it.

"You know what, Bob? I agree with you. It *is* good we had this talk."

Bell sets down his drink and leaves without another word. Forrester is happy with how the talk went, and yet . . . there was something unsettling in that last moment.

He pours himself a second round.

42

Grace is eating a slice of the Capricciosa and reading over Roger's shoulder as he goes over everything on the flash drive she got from Rich, and cross-references it with the same files as accessed by Stephen Gibson, Norman West, and Archie Thompson. It's a long shot, but it's these endless stretches of research that she specializes in as a paralegal, and she's seen the hard work turn a case. Which is why she ordered another round of pizza from DeSano, and this time sprang for the beer.

She watches Roger with growing admiration. He put in a full day at Thompson & West, then drove across town in Hollywood Bowl traffic to put in a second shift here in the strip mall offices because he understands the urgency they're facing: two men are dead, Jake and Javi were nearly killed as well, and the real powers behind everything that happened are still out there. Grace notes Roger's focus and how he works the keys are impressive. The fact that an IT guy has put his life on the line for this cause is even more so. She wishes she could fall for someone like him. Live a simple life with someone who made her the center of his world, which no doubt Roger would. But she's not built that way. Clearly, evidence shows she's more inclined to the self-destructive.

"Can I ask you a question?" Roger keeps typing, not wanting to make any eye contact during this conversation.

"Sure. Anything," Grace says.

"Why are you doing it? Giving up your job, working here, making enemies of people you'd probably want to hire you someday."

She watches as he keeps typing. Wondering what he's really asking.

"Does it matter?"

"Yes."

"Why?"

Roger stops typing and does something Grace has noticed he has a hard time doing—he meets her eyes.

"Because I'd hate if you're doing it for him." There's a long pause, then he continues. "Don't get me wrong. I like Jake. I respect him. I wouldn't be here if I didn't. But I think you could do anything. And he just seems . . . I don't think he'd be good for you."

She could be mad, but he's not being mean, or manipulative. She senses he really cares and is actually concerned about her well-being. Impulsively, she leans in and kisses him on the cheek. Clearly not what he had in mind—she sees his face fall. It's adorable.

"Roger, I'm doing it because it's right. I'm doing it to make up for all the aiding and abetting I've done on a thousand cases helping a thousand bad people do a thousand bad things to tens of thousands of others."

"Okay. Good." And he goes back to work.

Grace is impressed by him in this conversation. Maybe it's time to rethink her view of Roger Whitby. But as she's pondering that, he freezes, focuses intently on the screen, deciphering something. But from what's there, she can't tell what he's thinking.

"You got something . . . ?"

"Maybe."

He's putting up windows—one document, another document, comparing things.

"Roger?"

One more flurry of keystrokes, then he drags the cursor to put three windows side by side. "You want to know what a smoking gun looks like? It looks like *this*."

She leans over to see the documents he's pulled up. She scans from one to the next.

"You should keep breathing," Roger suggests.

She tries to do that as she digests what she's looking at. When its implications become clear, without thinking about what she's doing she kisses Roger full on the mouth. A long kiss, and how right it feels shocks her maybe more than it does him.

They both take a moment, digesting these feelings, savoring the moment. Then he tries to speak.

"You should . . . We should . . ."

"Call Jake. Yeah."

"That's not what I was going to say."

He kisses *her* this time. Grace relaxes into the moment, letting go, maybe for the first time in weeks. She feels good, maybe for the first time in weeks.

"*Now* you can call Jake." Roger grins.

They should, Grace thinks. And Jake's going to lose his mind. Grace's eyes fall back on one of the documents.

A memo. Written by Stephen Gibson, Managing Partner, Thompson & West.

43

Nine months earlier, that same memo, in paper form, was being waved around angrily by Reagan Hearst. "This is unacceptable."

He actually slammed it onto Gibson's chest. Gibson was pissed, but he took the document.

"It's a fraction of the lot. It's only thirty-two-hundred square feet," Gibson explained.

"It's in the middle of the property."

"So we build around it."

"We? Are you a builder now?"

"I just meant—"

"Do you realize the costs I've sunk into the design? That my financing is *based* on that design?"

"There are hiccups in these things all the time, Reagan—"

"I have you on board to make those go away."

"And I can. In time. But a lawsuit for eminent domain isn't the quick fix you want. The building's designated as a historical landmark—"

"The city council can overturn that."

"Yes, but you'll face the wrath of the public, which won't do your stock any favors."

"I don't care."

"Do your homework, Reagan. Think about what happened when Warner Brothers tried to raze The Formosa. Think about the outcry when someone wanted to demolish Taix in Echo Park."

"This is stupid. We're offering triple what it's worth. What the fuck is wrong with this guy?"

"Falcone's has been open since 1923. Horace Falcone's great-grandfather built the restaurant from the ground up, and Horace's greatest joy in life, his *only* joy in life, is going to work every day. Serving the regulars, chatting them up, talking about how things were back in the day."

"Offer him more."

"He doesn't *need* what we're offering. He wants to walk the floors where Charlie Chaplin ate dinner. Stand behind the bar where Clark Gable ordered drinks for very young women."

Reagan took stock of the pathetic man in front of him, talking to him like he's stupid. Horace Falcone had to be the dumbest man alive, but Gibson was giving him a run for his money.

"I've sunk everything into this. My father's legacy—it's *this*. If we delay, I lose my backing. And that can't happen. Hearst Plaza *has* to happen—now—or I'm . . . it has to happen."

"And it will. In time."

This was not what Reagan wanted to hear. "Do better. I'm giving you a week. Or I'm going to start interviewing other firms to take our business."

Gibson wanted to stand strong, but this was a hit he couldn't afford. Archie Thompson's recent move to step back from day-to-day operations had left the firm in financial trouble, because a number of his accounts had departed as a result. Gibson, newly minted as managing partner, was supposed to shore up the finances, not lose the biggest client. Not to mention the hit to his own income, which he couldn't afford now that Anne's threatening to divorce him and take him for half of everything. He really should have had a better prenup.

So he bit back his anger and offered Reagan this: "Let me work on it. I'm sure I can figure something out."

But five days later, Gibson had no answers. He'd put the firm's in-house investigator on Horace Falcone to see if there was some dirt to be found. And what black mark was on Horace's record? Absolutely nothing. The man was beloved—by everyone. And his fucking restaurant that he refused to sell under any circumstances sat smack in the center of the main building design of Hearst Plaza. Gibson had friends on the city council, but none of them would touch this with a ten-foot pole.

So when Cameron Bancroft arrived in his office for an update, Gibson was grateful that Reagan had sent an emissary. Because what he had to say, Reagan didn't want to hear. Once Cameron settled on the couch with an expensive Scotch, Gibson was ready to try and smooth the waters. But Cameron held up a hand to stop him.

"Let *me* start. Reagan has his mind set on doing this one way, and he's put you in a bind." This was a surprising development—he didn't expect Reagan's fixer to be so understanding. Maybe even an ally. "I've known him since high school; he's always been this way. He wants what he wants and expects people to make it so. He doesn't care what it takes."

"Probably why he's so successful," Gibson replied, though what he thought was that Reagan Hearst had been an asshole his whole life.

"So the trick is," Cameron continued, "finding creative ways to deliver for him. That's why he loves me. I'm . . . creative."

"You have a thought?" Gibson asked tentatively, wary of Cameron's tone.

"More . . . an observation." Cameron paused for effect, and then delivered his genius idea. "Accidents happen."

The malice on his face scared Gibson.

"Don't look so shocked." Cameron laughed. "I'm not suggesting anything that doesn't come out of your playbook."

"I'm not sure what you mean," Gibson said. And he really wasn't.

"Harrison Foods."

Gibson's heart was in his throat. Harrison Foods was a near disaster, but his role in it, the firm's role in it, had been effectively buried. He tried to keep his face blank.

"Don't worry, I'm not making a threat of exposure here. I'm asking a favor, really."

"A favor?"

"Yes. I'd like a name. The name of a person I suspect you may have had, shall we say, dealings with. Or perhaps your contacts at Harrison Foods have had said dealings. With this person who I suspect could render Falcone's a moot point."

Gibson did know said person. But if he gave Cameron Bancroft the name, he'd be crossing a line there was no coming back from. What he did on *Harrison* was a cover-up. This would make him fully culpable in whatever followed. Legally speaking, an accessory.

He should have said no, said he had no idea what Cameron was talking about. He should have let Reagan Hearst find another lawyer, someone who might be more willing to take the risk.

But Gibson worked hard to get here. So he didn't say no.

Gibson is ruminating on this memory from months earlier as he stares absently out his window. His office faces west; on a clear day he can make out the ocean. On a clear night, it's just dark, which matches his mood. He's sipping his third bourbon and beginning to loosen up. Maybe Jake has the right idea, maybe alcohol makes things better, or at least easier. Maybe inspiration will strike him in between sips of the amber liquid for what he should do to undermine Daria and take back his rightful place as Norman's number two. The direct threats seem to have gotten him nowhere.

His distraction is probably why he doesn't notice the commotion sooner, but he hears a woman yelling, "You can't go in there!" then footsteps, and he panics. Is someone coming to shoot him? Is this the world he's gotten himself into? He races to his desk, fumbles with the key to the locked drawer, and pulls out a Glock that he bought after a disgruntled client killed four people in the law firm on the twelfth floor. It seemed prudent at the time, a way he could be both protected and potentially heroic.

"Is that for me or for you?"

Seeing it's Jake in the doorway, Gibson isn't relieved and he doesn't put down the gun.

"Come on, Stevie—let's put that away. Tell Adrienne—" He turns to the young woman who covers reception on the late shift. "It *is* Adrienne, right?"

She started work just about when Jake stopped coming in, or he'd know for sure. The young woman nods mutely—she has now seen the gun and isn't sure what to do. The man is her boss, but he's currently brandishing a weapon.

"Tell Adrienne everything's fine—we're just going to talk."

Gibson lets out a breath and tells the young woman, "It's okay. You may go."

"You want me to call security?" she asks, deeply uncomfortable with the situation.

"Not unless you hear a gunshot," Gibson replies.

The joke is meant for Jake's benefit, but Adrienne is horrified.

"He's kidding," Jake reassures her. "He's not going to kill me. And I'm unarmed."

Adrienne backs out of the office without another word. Jake closes the door as Gibson puts the handgun back in the drawer.

"You ever actually fire that thing?"

"What do you want, Jake?"

"I want to help you." Gibson laughs at that, but Jake continues: "Seriously. I'm here to offer you a way out. It's all coming down around you, Stevie. Everything you've done, sanctioned, aided, abetted. But if you *resign* now, if you turn over evidence, I'm sure there's a great deal to be had. They'll want my father, they won't want you. No one wants you."

"How much have you had to drink?" Gibson spits at him, deflecting.

"From the smell in here, a lot less than you have. But I'm hoping you can focus through your haze. Are you listening?" Gibson just shakes his head, but Jake presses on once more. "You need a good lawyer. And I'm a great lawyer. You know that, even if you hate that it's true. Even if you resent that I'm twice the lawyer you are."

"Which is why your own father chose me over you to run this place."

"Archie Thompson chose you. My father merely acquiesced."

"Your father was the deciding vote."

"Because he realized something important about you. That you'd make a terrific fall guy. You really want to pick him over self-preservation?"

The fact that Jake is articulating things Gibson knows deep down does nothing to turn the tide.

"If this is the best you have, Jake? We're done here."

"Does my father have something on you? Is that the problem? Because I can help with that."

"You've got it backwards. *You're* the one who needs *my* help. You're drowning, Jake. If you stop this bullshit, I'll throw you a line and get you out of whatever mess you're in."

"Oh, I'm already out. And let me tell you—it's liberating being out from under Norman's thumb. Firing me—you did me a favor."

"I did the firm a favor."

"Let's stop dancing. The truth is coming out. What is Anne going to say when she finds out what you're involved in?"

"I don't know, Jake. What did Cara say when she learned what *you* were involved in?"

"She threw me out. That's my point exactly. You have to get in front of this."

"You're bluffing."

"I get it. You want to believe that. So let me help you. I won't tell you the details, that's confidential, but let's just say I can connect you to Milo Stapp. *And* I can connect you to Reagan Hearst and Cameron Bancroft."

He sees Gibson's stoic face droop just a little, though he recovers quickly.

"Here's the thing, Jake. In law school, we used to call what you're doing now the empty folder gambit. They use it on TV all the time. You wave a folder around in front of the guilty party, threatening to reveal evidence of their guilt. The problem with that is, it only works if the person is guilty."

"Though it's also true that if you're guilty, the best course of action is to deny," Jake counters. "We live in an age when that works far too often. But it won't work here. That said, you do have options. Maybe not great options, but you have some. For now. I haven't given this information to anyone."

"Put your invisible folder away, Jake. Time for you to go. Back wherever you crawl under these days."

Jake sees Gibson's agitated—he's done what he came for. Almost.

"One last thing, Stevie. Just for my personal curiosity. Did *you* try to have me killed? Or was that Dad?"

"Good night, Jake. Consider that an invitation to get the fuck out of my office."

"I'm going. But think about Anne, okay? Think about what you want to tell her. Because her hearing the truth from you before it comes out—it's really the only hope you have."

As Jake leaves, he realizes something: he needs to take his own advice.

44

Jake is sitting on the front steps of what once was his house. He can hear the birds that incessantly chirp all night long. He can hear the crickets, some of which live in the walls of his (former) house. Other than that, it's quiet. Pretty. Tranquil. Home.

He wants a drink. Needs a drink. Desperately. But he can't have one. That would invalidate what he's here to do. It's almost midnight, but in the upstairs bedroom, he sees a light is still on, so he picks up his phone and calls.

"I'm not bailing you out of jail," Cara answers.

Jake grins, both at her answering line and the fact that she answered at all.

"I'm not in jail."

"Drunk dialing?"

"I haven't had a drink in two days."

"Wow. Is there a chip for that?"

"Have *you* been drinking? Because you're over your quip quotient."

"Quip quotient? Seriously? I'm tired, Jake. If you need to talk, call your sponsor." She pauses, knowing the answer to her next question. "Do you even have a sponsor?"

"I was hoping *we* could talk."

"So talk."

"In person."

"You can't just come over in the middle of the night."

"I'm already on the front steps. Just come sit with me for a few minutes. You're up anyway."

Cara sighs. There's a long pause, then she hangs up without a word. But three minutes later, she's got sweats on as she comes out to join him. They used to do this, have late-night heart-to-hearts sitting here. She sits, then sizes him up. Probably assessing if he's really sober. She must conclude that he is, because he watches her eyes soften. He's always loved her brown eyes; it's as if he can see into her soul. And he knows she can see into his.

"I have a drinking problem."

"Breaking news."

"It's not news that I have a problem. It's news that I'm acknowledging it. I'm acknowledging that I told you I'm going to meetings, and while I went to a couple, that was only so I wouldn't be lying to you. So, to answer your question, no—I don't have a sponsor. But I'm going to go. I'm going to actually try this time."

"Okay. That's good."

"But that's not what I came to say." Jake pauses. He's truly scared right now, more scared than he was up in Morro Bay. "I came to say . . . I had an affair. With one of our paralegals. About a year ago. I think you know when."

She doesn't flinch, doesn't get angry, doesn't cry.

"You were right that night. I should have admitted it and begged your forgiveness. But even after it stopped, I was afraid, and I was drinking, and I was in a dark place, and . . ." He stops because she turns away. He hears his words from her point of view. "That's not an excuse. I did it. I was wrong. And I'm deeply sorry."

He lets that sit for a minute, the awful gulf between them widening, deepening.

"I want to come home, Cara. You know Aaron wants it—"

"He'd forgive you anything."

"Maybe. But even Chloe wants me to come home."

"You think because you took her to a bar, all is forgiven?" Jake is surprised. If Chloe told Cara about this, he'd have expected to be read the riot act. Cara follows the thought process on his face. "Yeah, she told me. And yeah, I get what you were going for. And yeah, it made a dent. But it's not as simple as that. She may want you back, but what she wants and what's good for her are not the same thing."

That old refrain coming back to bite him.

"That's true. But it's really not the point. The question is—what do *you* want, Cara?"

She doesn't answer. He tries to read her face, her body language, hoping to see that her want will win out over reason. Because if he's being honest with himself, something he isn't usually, Jake understands that him coming home wouldn't be good for her. He wants to anyway.

"It's okay. I don't need an answer. I just needed to be honest with you. Because I want to do better. Be better."

He wants to hold her. He wants to kiss her. Instead, he gets up.

"Good night, Cara."

He has to will himself not to look back, and by the time he's opened the car door, she's gone. He looks up to the bedroom window and watches as she turns out the light.

God, he wants a drink more than before. And despite what he just pledged to Cara, maybe he would have had one, but his phone rings. Javi.

"I'm not bailing you out of jail." Jake figures using Cara's answering line will get a laugh, but it doesn't.

"What are you talking about?"

"Nothing, sorry. It's late. What's up?" Jake asks.

"There's been a break-in. At our office."

The video is black-and-white and grainy. A man wearing a hoodie to shield his face, a man who can barely walk a straight line, nervously looks around. He tries to jimmy open the front door, but he can't. He reaches into his pocket, pulls out a hammer, again makes sure no one is watching, then slams the hammer into the glass front door. But the glass pane holds, and it must sting like hell because the hammer drops to the ground and the guy doubles over.

Then he retrieves the hammer, winds up, and hits the door with full force. This time the glass shatters into little pebble-like fragments. Hoodie Man reaches in through the jagged mess, unlocks the door, and slips inside.

Jake stares in disbelief. Is he watching the man who shot Rich? Is this the same hooded person that he saw disappear into the Metro? Did he return to finish what he started?

The second new security camera picks him up inside the office. Hoodie Man hunts around, desperately checking desks, using the flashlight on his phone. He's not finding whatever it is he thinks is here. He's getting worked up, and clearly getting hot, because he wipes his brow and doesn't seem to notice that the hood comes down.

But watching the video on a laptop, sitting in Jake's car, now parked outside Javi's downtown apartment, Javi and Jake notice. It's clearly Stephen Gibson searching their office, panicked, attempting to fix a problem he can't fix.

"He's wearing a hoodie," Jake says, his mind racing. "Do you think—"

"That he's the shooter? Look at him, Jake. He can't pull off a low-level break-in."

"No. I suppose not."

"I think this is just him taking the bait you laid out. What did you tell him we had?"

"I told him what we could link him to. Not Harrison, I want to save that. But what we're watching here, his panic? This says there's more than what we have."

On the video, Gibson has run out of options. Then he sees a bottle of tequila on the desk. He opens it. Jake thinks he's going to take a drink, maybe leave DNA behind. Instead, he pours it all over the desk.

"Now that is a waste of good tequila."

"It gets better."

Gibson digs around in his pocket for something. A matchbook. He strikes a match—it goes out. Another—it won't light. Finally, he takes four matches at the same time and ignites them; they flare, he drops the flaming mess, and when it hits the liquor, the desk practically explodes in fire.

"Wait—he burned us down?" Jake asks.

"Keep watching."

Gibson books it out of the room, but the flames quickly dissipate and die out.

"I guess we know why he hired people the other times. It's almost sad," Jake says.

"Almost."

"So now we call it in?"

"Are you kidding?" Javi sees Jake's confusion. "No. We save this."

45

The South Park Center's Penthouse and Sky Deck was chosen for the event because of the view. Specifically, the 360-degree view of downtown Los Angeles. If Austin Bell is going to talk about what LA means to him, his hopes and dreams for the city, he needs the city to be part of the event.

The evening is shaping up to be quite a spectacle. Free-flowing cocktails, a wide range of hot and cold hors d'oeuvres, stunning waitstaff serving it all. Serving the big-money donors, the stakeholders in the future of Los Angeles, who have come because they have been led to believe that this is the ticket to having an inside track when they need it. That's what has been promised by the Citizens of Los Angeles for Action and Change.

Bell tries to hide his disdain for the expensive clothes, the ungodly, ostentatious jewelry. He understands that as a politician you must serve your constituents, but these constituents are not *his*. They're people jumping aboard a bandwagon because they think he's going to win, and they've been told they will benefit.

In a corner of the ornately decorated room, he sees Reagan Hearst laughing at the story he's telling, and those around him are laughing too, probably not because the story is that funny, but because they recognize this is a man wielding power. Bell wonders what Reagan thinks about him. Does he think he owns Bell? Is that what he's been told?

"Ladies and gentlemen, our next district attorney—Austin Bell!" The overly tanned man whom people mostly remember from his starring role in a prime-time soap a dozen years ago applauds the man of the hour, and everyone turns as Bell moves to take center stage. They don't know what's about to hit them.

Bob Forrester is pleased. Obviously his little talk with Bell went well, because here they are, all systems go. He's thinking he may get a jump start on retirement. Reagan Hearst invited him to golf at Mayakoba next weekend, and why the hell not?

Gibson's at the bar with a bandage over his hand. He's got a story to explain it, but the story is a lie, and it's hard to say if he could pull off a lie just now—he's had way too much to drink. He's simultaneously watching and trying not to be seen watching Norman in a seemingly deep conversation with Daria Barati. His break-in yielded nothing to change his precarious position at the firm, except a deep cut on his right hand, one he didn't notice until he was back in the car. He worries that means he left his DNA behind at the scene of the crime, but knowing the LAPD as he does, he's fairly sure no resources will be put toward this. Especially not with Sioban McFadden on leave.

The event is packed with donors and press, so Sioban has an easy time keeping out of sight in a corner. While she is still technically on leave, she's here for a reason. She was invited. But the truth is, she wouldn't have missed it anyway. She is scanning the crowd and sees Jake has spotted her from across the room. He and Javi seem to be hiding in their own corner, but not from her. She knows what he's done to make this night happen, so she raises her glass to him. He shrugs and shows her—no drink. She's impressed, particularly in light of him having shot a man to death just days ago.

All of them turn their attention to the dais.

Bell takes in the crowd, and it occurs to him that he really could win the election. But he can't think about that now. He takes a sip of the water that's at the podium, then begins.

"Good evening. Thank you for coming, it's great to see everybody here. I'm guessing you came because you heard a little rumor that I have an announcement to make. The way I heard it, it was a lock that I was going to use this truly sumptuous event to make official the worst-kept secret in LA legal circles—that I intend to run for the Office of District Attorney for the City of Los Angeles." Bell uses his hands to indicate the city that sprawls beneath them. He has rehearsed this opening. He delivers it strongly, to enthusiastic applause.

"I love this city," he continues. "It has a real sense of history. Yes, it's a younger city than New York or Boston, but its history is palpable, nonetheless. William Mulholland. Frank Shaw. The Hat Squad. Charles Manson. Rodney King. Anthony Pellicano. Rampart."

The audience grows uneasy. This isn't the speech they were expecting.

"You might notice a theme here. And that theme is corruption. I'm sorry, I do love this city, but you can't escape that it was built—*is built*—on corruption."

He looks to Bob Forrester in the crowd. Bob appears to be in utter disbelief.

"So if I'm to take the mantle of fighting crime in this city, a city built on a bedrock of corruption, how do I do that? Because if I can't stand *against* that, if I can't stand up for the values I believe in—truth, justice, equity—I shouldn't be running at all. Am I right?"

He gives the audience a moment. They're still trying to figure out where he is going with this. A few "Hear! Hear!"s urge him on.

"I'll take that as a universal acceptance of my point. That the district attorney's office should stand for truth, and justice, and equity. That would be a pretty good campaign slogan, and it's truly what I want. What I believe."

He pauses here, partly for effect, but he's having trouble pushing forward. He's gotten to the hard part.

"And that's why today I will *not* announce my candidacy. Instead, I'm announcing my withdrawal of my name from consideration."

There are literal gasps in the room, but Bell holds up his hands for quiet.

"Let me explain why. It's been brought to my attention that there are contributions to my campaign that may not be violations of campaign finance law, but there's certainly the *appearance* of corruption. These violations suggest that one company—the Hearst Plaza Corporation—backed my campaign to the tune of $12.6 million. These violations suggest I owe a debt to that corporation, and that I cannot abide. So tomorrow, I will begin an investigation into that company and all of its associated companies."

Bell looks to Reagan Hearst, who seems to be trying to figure out what the best expression is to put on his face.

"Into the deals that were approved—by the current holder of the Office of District Attorney—to build the Hearst Plaza Project."

Bell focuses his attention on Forrester, drawing the audience to do the same. He's sure Bob wants to leave but is calculating that would be even worse for him.

"Into the legal firm of Thompson and West, which represents that project."

Norman West stands stock-still, and next to him Daria holds her composure as well—lawyers are highly trained to show no emotion when a case starts going south.

"And finally, there will be an investigation into the Citizens of Los Angeles for Action and Change, who have so generously sponsored tonight's event, and must think me most ungracious." The murmurs suggest Bell is correct about that. "But this is my city. I will stand up for it. And to do that, I must refuse any financial backing. I must walk away at even the appearance of corruption. So instead, I will use my *current* office as it was intended—to bring truth, justice, and equity to this situation."

People are masking panic, half of them likely trying to figure out if whatever corrupt things they have done will be caught up in this investigation.

"I will defer any further questions until I have gotten to the heart of this investigation. Until then . . . thank you all very much. Enjoy the rest of your evening."

Austin Bell steps away from the podium to let the chips fall where they may.

Jake and Javi emerge from their hidden corner to take in the resulting chaos. Reporters surround Austin Bell, ignoring his declaration that he won't talk, and they hunt Bob Forrester, but can't seem to find him. Jake watches with amusement as Reagan Hearst moves toward Norman, who works hard to keep his distance. Jake can't resist; he walks into the room just far enough to make sure his father sees him. When Norman finally turns in his direction, he doesn't get angry, doesn't seek Jake out, doesn't turn away. It's as if he's doing the math, seeing what his son has done behind the scenes to get to this point. All things that will make life hard for Norman, but his reaction is to simply nod.

Javi can't believe it. "You fuck him over, and now he respects you? That's some deep therapy shit."

"I need a drink," Jake replies, but then meets Javi's eyes. "I'm not going to have one. But I need one."

"You don't need one—you *want* one. And that's a step."

Sioban has found her way over to them. "Something tells me you two are having a good time. You might be the only ones."

Jake thinks she might be right. Over her shoulder he sees Daria at the bar, drinking. He wonders if tonight's events are a win or a loss for her.

"I thought you were on leave," Javi says.

"Funny story. There I was, sitting at the bar Jake introduced me to, deciding that there was nothing keeping me from getting drunk, when I get a call from tonight's keynote speaker. Who had had a rather unsettling lunch with our friend Jake here."

"I guess I really made an impression on him."

"I'd say so," Sioban says. "I think he kinda hates you."

"That's fair," Jake says. "Even so, I may have to vote for him. Next time around."

"In any event, he asked me to come tonight. Thought it would be good if I watched the various players, before he put me in charge of investigating them."

Jake and Javi share a look, then a nod.

"Something I'm missing?" Sioban asks.

"That investigation you're gonna be leading?" Javi says. "Jake and I may have a little something to help kick-start it."

"I'm all ears."

"We can do better than telling you," Jake says. "We'll show you. We have it on tape."

46

Two days later, Jake sits in the conference room of Thompson & West. He's indulging in the brief fantasy that this actually is his firm, that he's in charge. The truth is, he very much feels that way today, despite that he's offered up this expedited settlement meeting to officially sever his ties with the firm. After what happened the other night, he holds most of the cards in this meeting, even as Gibson keeps using the phrase "termination for cause." Given Gibson's late-night foray into breaking and entering, Jake knows he's scared about what could be revealed, so it's almost a certainty the terms they agree on for the equity buyout will be quite pleasing.

Jake is surprised that Gibson's been allowed to run point on this meeting. His father and Daria are here, as are Dan Arkin from Contracts and Helena Tsu from HR. Policy dictates their presence, but they're nothing more than a buffer against Jake claiming some misdeed or coercion down the line. Jake hasn't yet deduced what Norman and Daria have in mind by letting the meeting play out this way, but he doesn't really care. After today, the internal politics of Thompson & West will no longer be his concern.

Gibson has just finished a preamble so boring Jake isn't really listening.

"I'm sorry, I was a little bit distracted, Stevie. Is your hand okay? What happened there?"

Gibson absently rubs his bandaged hand. "I'm fine. Corkscrew got away from me. Bet you're familiar with that."

"I am. You sure that's what that was?"

Jake sees Gibson is unsettled by his implication, but he pushes on, rattling off terms.

"Let's continue. A current valuation of the equity shares suggests your capital contribution is worth six million dollars. However, as your father fronted your initial contribution, we are going to halve that. And then there's the matter of the litigation costs of the *Harrison Foods* case."

Gibson has just stepped exactly where Jake knew he would. "Ahh yes, the *Harrison* case. I have some thoughts about that as well."

"I'm sure you do, but if you want to spout conspiracies, I don't think anyone here has the time."

A knock on the glass doors from Kendall interrupts the meeting.

"Not now," Gibson snaps. "Are you not clear on 'do not disturb' after all this time?"

"Sorry—I have a Detective McFadden here to see you, Mr. Gibson."

"Tell her another time."

"I can't. She has a warrant."

Gibson's face goes pale. Kendall heads back down the hall as Sioban comes in, holding up a paper.

"Here's the warrant, if any of you want to check my work. But it's signed by Judge Eleanor Merrin. And she's quite good on the details, from what I hear."

Jake was not tipped off to *this* development, but he wonders if Sioban knew about the meeting and timed her arrival accordingly. Allowing him to have a front-row seat.

Daria moves toward Sioban, but Gibson beats her to the punch, snatching the warrant from her hands.

"Our files are all protected by attorney/client privilege—" he begins, but then stops.

"It's not a warrant for files, Mr. Gibson. It's a warrant for your arrest."

Gibson is frozen, reading the cover sheet, and Norman's had enough. He gets up and grabs the warrant. What he sees confuses him. It cites California Penal Code Section 459 in official language: *Every person who enters any house, room, apartment, tenement, shop, warehouse, store, mill, barn, stable, outhouse or other building, tent, vessel . . . with intent to commit grand or petit larceny or any felony is guilty of burglary.* It also cites criminal trespass under CPC 602(c), using similar legalese.

"Well, don't keep the rest of us in suspense," Jake says, gilding the lily.

Norman ignores him, turning his focus on Sioban. "Trespassing where?"

Sioban looks to Jake. *You wanna take this one?* Jake would love to deliver the final blow to Gibson, to pronounce sentence on the man who tried to burn down his office, which is actually the least of his crimes. But he has a better way to make Gibson squirm.

"You want to field that one, Stevie?"

Gibson tries to make himself taller as he faces off with Sioban. "Whatever you have, Detective, it's bullshit."

"But it's not," Jake says, drawing Gibson's attention back to him. "I know my current offices don't seem like much, but we did put up hidden security cameras. So imagine my shock when I saw your face as you dumped my very fine tequila and tried to set my office on fire. What were you trying to find, anyway? That 'evidence' I told you I had?"

Sioban decides to throw fuel on the fire. "Mr. West, the younger one here, was kind enough to share that video with the LAPD. We've verified its authenticity."

Gibson desperately tries to hold on to his appearance of strength. "My team of lawyers will have me out in an hour."

"Your team of lawyers may want to consider one thing," Sioban cautions. "Judge Merrin wasn't ready to sign off on other charges, but they will be coming. Mr. Bell assured me of that."

"*Other* charges?" Daria asks. It is quite clear that the job of cleaning up Gibson's mess is going to be vastly more expansive than she's been led to believe.

"Sorry," Sioban says, not sorry at all. "I have nothing I can offer you on that." Protocol does prevent her from saying more, but throwing Daria's words back in her face is a side benefit. There is, however, no such protocol to prevent Jake from plunging the knife in further. Maybe that's why Sioban served the subpoena while he was here.

"Maybe I can help clarify, Daria," Jake says. "I mean, it's not my investigation, but as someone who has been doing my civic duty and cooperating with the fine people of the LAPD and the district attorney's office, my guess as to what they may be gathering evidence on? Arson. Conspiracy to commit arson. Murder. Conspiracy to commit murder. Fraud. Conspiracy to commit fraud."

Gibson has no quip, no defense—he realizes anything he says now will be empty bluster. He looks weakly to Norman for help, but he is busy in nonverbal communication with Daria. With no words exchanged, an agreement is reached.

"Given all that, I think you're best served by outside counsel, Stephen," Daria says.

"You have no say here! Norman?!"

"Actually, she does," says the founding partner of the firm. "Pending a vote of the full partnership, Ms. Barati is the firm's new managing partner."

"Well, as I haven't signed my exit agreement yet," Jake offers, "I'm gonna go ahead and cast my vote in favor. I think Ms. Barati will be a huge step in the right direction."

Daria nods. It's all she can do; she can't be seen as being on Jake's side.

Sioban feels it's time to be done. "I'm assuming I don't need cuffs, Mr. Gibson?"

Seeing he has no allies here, Gibson musters all the dignity he can and simply walks past her out the door.

Sioban can't resist one more thing, directing her gaze on Daria. "And thank you, Ms. Barati, for all your help on that other matter." And she follows Gibson out.

After a long, awkward silence, which Jake enjoys, he realizes he'll have to wait to officially sever ties. Probably not a priority for Thompson & West today.

"Maybe it's best if we finish this up another time," Jake says. "You probably have things to discuss." And without waiting for a response, he leaves the conference room.

Heading down the hall, Jake wonders if he'll ever be back here. Chances are, they'll send him terms far exceeding what would be called for, and he'll accept. And while he's come to loathe this place, there was a time it was his playground. And that makes him just a little bit sad. His first reaction to that sadness is that he wants a drink. His second, as Javi pointed out, is that he doesn't need it.

He's almost at the lobby when he hears his father's voice. "Jake."

He could keep walking. He could leave his father wanting more. What could this be? A plea to stay? A rebuke? A threat? May as well find out. So he stops.

"I didn't know."

Jake isn't sure which part his father is trying to be absolved for. Burning down his office? Having Rich Kaplan killed? There are so many crimes, most of which he hasn't even been accused of. And Jake could engage, tease out which denial this is. But to what end?

"I hope that's true, Dad. I really hope that's true."

And Jake goes. Wishing he didn't want to believe him.

Sioban has chosen the R Bar once again. She's decided it will be her new go-to spot, since no cops she knows will ever come here. She's taken to using the password and not her badge to get in, and she's now on a first-name basis with the bartender and has a new signature drink. The Corpse Reviver. She tried it for the irony and stayed for the absinthe. She finds it calming. Knowing she's drinking something that in excess could kill her. At least that's the myth.

Jake slides in across from her. Takes in her orange-colored drink.

"What round is that?"

"A callback. I didn't think you were sober enough last time we were here to remember anything."

"I remember."

A cute server he knows well comes by. "What's your poison tonight?"

"I feel like mixing it up, Daphne. How about vodka and orange juice. Hold the vodka."

Both Daphne and Sioban do their best not to show surprise.

"Yup. A whole new me," Jake offers up, hoping this could be true.

"I'm all for reinvention." Daphne laughs, then nods at Sioban. "You good?"

She means the drink, but Sioban responds, "Yeah. It's been a good day, thanks. And I think it's about to get better."

Jake's intrigued by that tease. "You have news? Some breaking development in your battle to bring down the Death Star?"

"Maybe," she says cagily.

"Oooh. You're a tease."

"I am. And you're going to wish you were drinking something stronger when I tell you why you're here."

"You mean it's not a date? I'm crushed."

Sioban makes him wait until Daphne brings the orange juice. "I dressed it up a little. It has an orange slice wedged onto the glass, and a parasol."

"Just like a real grown-up," Jake says. Once Daphne's gone, Jake turns to Sioban, out of patience. "Okay. What are we drinking to?"

Sioban raises her glass. He follows suit.

"To Milo Stapp."

Sioban enjoys his confusion.

"You're not going to drink?"

"To a serial arsonist?"

"Well, sure, he's that. But he's also the one who's going to bring this case home."

"I thought I already did that."

"The problem is, we have lots of pieces. Gibson's memo. There's the case they're building up in Morro Bay on Cameron Bancroft. The hidden police report on Stapp in your *Harrison* case. But so far, nothing gives us your father, and certainly none of it gives us Reagan Hearst. Not directly. But we do have two people up to their necks in this. Stephen Gibson. And Milo Stapp. Bell is playing them off each other to see which one makes a better deal. Which one will sell out the bigger fish."

"Gibson's not going to deal. I hear he hired Paula Conroy to represent him. Fitting—I might dislike her even more than him."

"She does like to represent the worst of the worst," Sioban says, "but it's actually been mildly productive. He's indicated a willingness to give up Cameron Bancroft."

"He'll sell out a dead man, how useful. Is Stapp going to make a deal?"

"He is ready to play along. *Ish.*" She stops there, teeing up her news.

"There's a catch."

"It seems Milo Stapp has a condition."

Jake waits for everything he's put in motion to unravel.

"He needs a lawyer," she says evenly. "And he asked for you."

Jake is stunned. "*Me?* After we lied to him?"

"The crime he's in for now? Gibson refused to represent him when he was charged for that fire. So Milo blames *him* for his conviction. Gibson *and* your dad. He figures you'll want to help him stick it to them, given how they screwed you on *Harrison Foods*. Say what you want, but he did his homework."

Jake hates this man. This man responsible for so many deaths. Last time he saw him, Jake could barely contain his impulse to throw the weasel against the wall. Now he sips his orange juice as he considers Milo's terms. There are so many deaths to consider, but the one Jake can't let go of is Rich Kaplan. Milo Stapp didn't kill him. And someone needs to pay.

The drink's lack of kick is disappointing, but that just means Jake has a clear head when he accepts the deal. He'll represent one devil to bring down another.

47

At eleven a.m. the next morning, Jake is back in the meeting room at California State Prison, Corcoran. He's pacing, agitated—he's not sure how much of the agitation is his body rebelling against the ongoing absence of alcohol, how much is fear that what's about to happen is too good to be true, and how much is the fact that he's about to help a man who might accurately be called a mass murderer.

There's a paper bag sitting on the table, awaiting Milo Stapp's arrival. Sure enough, when the guard escorts him in, Milo's eyes go for the bag and he lights up. He sits and pulls out a sandwich wrapped in white paper, neatly sliced in half on a diagonal.

"Domingo's. Ohh man—this is worth anything."

Stapp takes a large bite into one half of the Italian roll stuffed with prosciutto, mozzarella, basil, tomatoes, and avocado. His eyes blissfully roll back in his head as he ingests the Monte Carlo sandwich. Jake watches him, disgusted. It makes him angry to see a man who's done so much damage get such pleasure, but it's the price that has to be paid if Jake wants to use him to right other wrongs. Stapp chews thoroughly, swallows it down, burps, then he's ready. "Okay—where do we start?"

"We start with the ground rules. I'm going to ask you questions. I'm going to determine the value of your information. And then I'll tell you what I think you may expect to get in exchange for your cooperation."

"And everything I tell you—"

"Covered by attorney/client privilege. I am not allowed to disclose the information or use it in any way without your say-so. If I do, any information that results from my disclosure becomes inadmissible against you."

"Awesome." Stapp takes another bite.

"Let's dive in then, Mr. Stapp. Shall we start at the beginning? The fire at Harrison Foods—you set that? Intentionally?"

Jake tries to keep his face impassive—his role is to represent Stapp here, not condemn him, but the screams of Estelle Guadalupe are echoing in his brain, sounds he's heard in his dreams on too many occasions to note. But here, Stapp doesn't seem gleeful or arrogant—he appears almost contrite.

"The place was supposed to be empty," he says. As if *he's* been wronged.

Jake lets that sit a moment before responding. "That's not what I asked."

"No, but you should know that. I'm not a monster."

Knowing the totality of fires Milo Stapp has set, and the cumulative damage done, and the lives lost, Jake is struck by a thought: Monsters can look very mundane.

"The whole point of the fire was they were losing money. They overinsured the place. But what they did in the meantime was they ramped up production, they were operating crews around the clock because they had to make money somehow. Kind of a right hand/left hand thing, I'm guessing. I was talking to the right hand. The left hand was focused on product."

"And who was the right hand?"

"It's not what Austin Bell wants to hear. I never talked to Edgar Harrison. I never talked to *any* lawyer. It was some guy I'd bet wasn't even on the payroll. So he couldn't be traced."

"Name?"

"Dave. Dave Smith. And before you say it, I know, it's not a real name. But in my line of work, that's kind of standard operating procedure."

"You were paid in cash?"

"Bitcoin." Milo grins at Jake's reaction. "It's the future, you should get on board. It's easy to move, untraceable, and they tend to overpay if you're willing to take it. I have a guy who can convert it when I need real cash, so it's all good by me."

"Then we can't trace the payment. What about after the fire? Anyone reach out to you? Complain about the . . . 'mishap'?"

"I told you, it wasn't my mishap, but the answer is no. No call. I felt shitty, but hell, like I said, that's on them."

Jake fights an impulse to crush Milo's skull. Instead, he decides to move on.

"The fire at Falcone's. Who approached you?"

"Cameron Bancroft."

"Directly?"

"Yup."

"Well, he's not alive to argue that point. He tell you how he got your name?"

"He did. He said he was working with the firm that repped Harrison Foods. I asked for a name, I wanted some level of assurance he was legit. He gave me two names: Stephen Gibson. And Norman West."

Jake's heart skips a beat. "You're sure about that?"

"I'm sure. Because I didn't know them—not personally, not then, so I had to check out who they were. Sure enough, I saw they repped Harrison, so it was kosher by me."

"He tell you why he wanted you to start this fire?"

"He did not."

"He didn't mention Reagan Hearst?"

"He did not."

"How about Hearst Plaza?"

"Let me give you a shortcut. He gave me squat. I assumed he had a beef with the restaurant guy. Whatever, I did the job. But then—" Milo pauses to take another bite, chew, savor, and finally swallow. "Then we get to the part of the story you're going to like. The reason Austin Bell is going to want to offer me the moon."

Milo Stapp counted four valets working at the entrance to the small, wooded cul-de-sac above Sunset. He parked his beater down the block, where he drew suspicious glances from the old homeowner who knew the car didn't belong there. But the guy was probably used to the help showing up to work these events blighting his Brentwood enclave on party nights.

Milo marveled at the cars that people freely turned over to strangers who could drive away and sell them off for parts—Ferraris and Sterlings and some with logos he couldn't identify. So much money. So much excess. Which is why he was here: to get his fair share.

One of the valets shot him a suspicious glance as he headed past their stand, but Milo told him he Ubered in and Reagan Hearst was expecting him. That was a lie—he would be the last person Reagan Hearst was expecting.

The party was centered in a yard cut into a canyon, stretching for acres. There were string lights in the trees, there were food stations and bar stations and people mingling all around. These people had a lot to celebrate, Stapp knew. Because the *LA Times* that morning trumpeted the groundbreaking on what was heralded as the biggest development in downtown Los Angeles since LA Live.

Before he made his move, Milo decided a snack was in order. A tray of Wagyu beef sliders went by and he snagged two, along with a martini flavored with something purple to wash it down. The martini was so refreshing and emboldening that he used a second one to wash down the first. Then, only then, did he scan the crowd and locate his target: the way-too-slick man with the way-too-slick hair. And just his luck, Cameron Bancroft was talking animatedly with a man Stapp recognized from the photo in the *Times*—Reagan Hearst himself. In person, he looked like even more of a prick.

Cameron noticed Stapp, tried to place who he was. When he figured it out, his expression darkened. He said something to Reagan and made his way toward Milo.

"Nice party," Stapp said as Cameron reached him.

Cameron grabbed his elbow, not a yank, but forceful enough to steer him away from anyone else. "What the fuck are you doing here?"

"Celebrating." His goal was to goad Cameron and he was succeeding.

"You can't be here."

"Why not? You wouldn't be here if it weren't for me."

"You were paid for your work."

"Well, yes and no. I was paid for work. But I believe I was given the job under false pretenses."

"What the fuck are you talking about?"

"You didn't mention you wanted the place to burn so you and your friends could buy it and then multiply its value a hundredfold. If I'd known the value of my work, the charge would have gone up immeasurably."

"Fuck off. We're done."

"You know what I notice about this party, Cameron? The high-end guest list. I bet there are lawyers and CEOs, probably celebrities. I don't know a lot of them. But there's one I do know. I know *that's* Bob Forrester over there, standing next to that stiff old guy and chatting up our host. So I have to ask—was the DA in on the deal? Is that why there was no investigation into the fire? Why it was ruled an accident?"

Cameron went sheet white but controlled his anger. He moved very closely into Stapp's space so he could speak quietly. "Your point is well-taken. Come see me tomorrow. Better yet, tell me where to find you. And we'll make an accommodation."

Stapp hesitated, not sure if he was being blown off or if he'd just won.

"Okay. But if you don't show? I could become a problem."

With his threat made, he turned to go and nearly bumped into a very attractive Hispanic woman leading a little girl across the grass. The woman stopped.

"Excuse me, sorry," the woman said, though it was not her fault.

Stapp nodded, but the woman was standing dead still. Milo turned back to see Cameron Bancroft's eyes were glued on the Hispanic woman. At the time, he assumed maybe Cameron had tried to hit on her or something, and that's why she was scared. But in retrospect, given what happened later, he knew what Cameron was thinking in that moment. He was wondering just how long Jacinta Castillo had been standing there. And what she overheard.

Jake digests the story. The Forrester piece, while circumstantial, will certainly whet Austin Bell's appetite. At the very least, it can be used to hasten Forrester's departure from office. And the story does bring in Reagan Hearst, though again circumstantially. Most telling, the story delivers a clear motive for the murder of Jacinta Castillo. Milo Stapp can't speak to what was in Cameron's head, but he places him and Jacinta together at the party at the exact moment a conspiracy was discussed. Not enough to convict Cameron, but they don't need to. He's dead.

Jake is relatively pleased that Milo's story connects so many of the pieces. But not all of them. There's one part missing. Or is it?

"The 'stiff old guy' you mentioned, the one with Bob Forrester and Reagan Hearst, toasting the fruits of your labor. Was that my father?"

"Well, I hadn't met him yet. I was telling you how I saw it that night."

"Was that my father?"

"Yes, Jake. Your father was there."

Jake takes a moment to process that. It's what he wants and what he dreads at the same time.

"You said you hadn't met him. Yet. When *did* you meet him?"

When Cameron Bancroft told Stapp the meeting following the party would be at the law offices of Thompson & West, Milo at first thought it was a joke. Cameron had stalled him for days, but Milo was in no hurry. The truth was, dropping a dime on Cameron Bancroft would be next to impossible without implicating himself, so he hadn't yet figured out how to do what he'd threatened. Then came the call.

At the time, looking out the firm's thirty-seventh-floor windows, what he didn't get was why he was *here*. An accommodation, as Cameron called it, would be in all of their interests. But this wasn't where deals like Stapp's were usually made.

Milo was ushered into the office of Stephen Gibson, Managing Partner—he knew this from the frosted lettering—and Cameron made what seemed like a formal introduction.

"Stephen Gibson, Milo Stapp," Cameron said genially.

Gibson's apoplectic response made Cameron's plan crystal clear—ambush. Gibson had no idea who Cameron was bringing to this meeting. "What the hell is this?!"

"This, my good friend, is insurance."

"No. We're done. You need to leave," Gibson insisted.

"We're not done, Stephen. And we are not leaving. Because our mutual friend here, the one whose name you gave me, would now like to be paid triple."

"I have no idea what you are referring to—"

"Shut up, Stephen!"

Cameron Bancroft turned so vicious it rendered Gibson mute, whether in fear of Cameron or in fear that the sudden shouting would be heard by his colleagues was hard to say.

"I have agreed to pay Mr. Stapp what he's asking," Cameron continued. "A large multiple of what he has been paid so far. In exchange, he is going to provide one last service for us—"

"Not for us, this was not for me—"

"Fine. You want to find some high ground, I don't care. I just need you to write up some nondisclosure thing that makes his silence mandatory, not optional."

Gibson was practically hyperventilating as he calculated how to respond to this thing he clearly didn't want to do. But before he spoke, the door opened and Stapp found the imposing figure of Norman West in the doorway. Stapp was struck by the man—he exuded power. He was almost regal. And Stapp instantly remembered him—he was the one chatting up Bob Forrester and Reagan Hearst at the party.

"Good to see you, Norman," Cameron said. "Please join us."

But Norman had clearly calculated some semblance of what was going on here. "No. I'm sure whatever it is, is way beyond my scope."

He shot a warning look at Gibson and left. Even Stapp understood Norman's message—*whatever this is, I am no part of it.*

Milo enjoys the expression on Jake's face. He can only imagine what this information means to him. "So how soon 'til I'm out of here?"

In this moment, Jake hates that his job is to make this monster's life easier.

"I'm not sure what you're thinking, Mr. Stapp, but let me paint a picture for you. Mr. Bell can link you to three arsons and nineteen murders. In the absence of mitigating factors, this is a death penalty case. And while you've told a lovely story today, Mr. Gibson—who knows how this game is played—is having a similar meeting with his own lawyer and placing the blame squarely on Cameron Bancroft. And on you."

"But I just gave you—"

"You gave me a dead man. Your link is to someone we don't need."

"I gave you—"

"Ammunition, yes. On Hearst Plaza, maybe that helps. On Quinton and Mariella Walker—those are the names of the children you burned alive, by the way—on that you may actually have much to offer as well, though again, you're claiming you were hired by a man who can't defend himself, and that means your value is debatable. But you can't give us Reagan Hearst. You can't give us Edgar Harrison. You can't give us Norman West. You're offering to give us a dead man and a guy named 'Dave Smith.' And I don't think either of them are going to buy your way out of multiple homicides."

Stapp sits back, unperturbed by Jake's tirade. "I don't think you like your father very much."

"Thanks, Dr. Freud."

"I also don't think you like me very much."

"What was your first clue?"

"Here's the thing, *Mr. West.* Mr. West *Junior.* If there's no deal on *Harrison*?

I give them nothing. And your father and Bob Forrester and Reagan Hearst and maybe even Stephen Gibson, the people who wanted all these things to happen? They walk. It sucks what happened, you may hate it, you may hate *me*. But let me state the obvious. I was just the match. *They* lit the fire."

Jake watches as this awful, awful man finishes his Monte Carlo. Despising the fact that Stapp has assessed the situation perfectly. If Jake wants truth, justice, and equity, those things Austin Bell talked about, he'll need to help Milo Stapp. He's just not sure he can live with that.

48

It's been nearly a year since Jake's seen Ramon Guadalupe, and two years since his wife Estelle's death. He doesn't know what to expect. A broken man? Unshaven, alcoholic, bitter? Jake's nervous as he opens the rusted gate and moves past the dead grass in the front yard of the four-unit apartment building that borders an alley, which in turn borders a chained-off empty lot in Boyle Heights. But when Ramon opens the front door and sees Jake, he smiles broadly. He's lost weight, he's rejuvenated, maybe even . . . happy?

"Jake! How the hell are you? You look like shit!" he says good-naturedly. "Come in. Manny's out; he'll be sorry to have missed you."

Jake enters the house and is startled to note that in contrast to the exterior, the place is bright and airy. The windows are open, there's a brand-new rug, it's been painted, there are plants everywhere, and prominently displayed are photos of the family that once was—Ramon and Estelle with their son Manny at different ages. But the display doesn't feel like a mausoleum, it feels warm. Alive.

Ramon picks up on Jake's confusion. "I know, last time you were here it was pretty dark, right? I was dark. We'd lost, and I didn't know how to move forward. I'd never had to picture my life without Estelle, and I didn't know what to do. But Manny needed me. So I had to kick myself in the ass and do something. I started hiking, running, hell I've even tried surfing. You ever surfed?"

"Once," Jake laughs. "Got a five-inch gash that needed stitches."

"Well, I recommend another try. It's life-altering."

Jake could use a little life-altering.

"I'm glad, Ramon. I'm glad my failing you didn't . . . That you've been able to move forward."

"You didn't fail me, Jake—you believed in me. And that's exactly what I needed. Not money from the lawsuit, but someone to believe what I *knew*. What really happened." He claps Jake on the back. "So, now that your wellness check is a success, can I get you a drink?"

"I'm sober."

"Good for you."

"Just a week in, so don't expect there to be much evidence."

"One day at a time. I know the drill. Caffeine okay? I can get you a Coke."

"I'm sober, not Amish," Jake says, laughing. "Yes, thanks."

By the time Ramon returns with two bottles of the good Mexican Coca-Cola, Jake is worried that his visit may have the opposite effect than intended. Is he about to derail all of Ramon's progress?

"Spit it out, man. Whatever you came to say. I can handle it."

"Okay. Here's the thing. I found the arsonist."

Ramon doesn't move for a moment, then sinks back into what's left of the cushioning on the worn tweed couch. Jake suddenly regrets that he came, that he has opened old wounds. But then Ramon exhales. "You're a fuckin' miracle worker, Jake."

Jake wants to make sure he's not overselling where things stand. "Well, it's a half miracle. We can't directly tie him to Edgar Harrison."

"Yet," Ramon says optimistically.

Jake feels better about having come, but he doesn't want a fast yes. If he's going to help Milo Stapp, he needs Ramon's blessing. One come to after appropriate deliberation.

"So here's the thing. I have to ask you a question."

"Anything."

"I want you to really think about this before you answer," Jake cautions. "I want to push to reopen the case. The lawsuit. Make sure there are consequences."

"But . . . ?"

"*But* I don't want to open old wounds. That's why I came to you first."

Ramon nods, then reaches over and picks up a gorgeous photo of Estelle from the old teak coffee table. He looks at his wife as if consulting her on this question.

"The wound will always be there, Jake. But you want to know what I want? What she would want?"

"I do."

"She'd want justice. You go and get that for her."

Sioban McFadden and Austin Bell are already in the booth when Jake slides in. They've chosen a generic coffee shop outside downtown LA where they're less likely to be recognized. Jake takes in Austin's demeanor—he's intent, professional. Jake knows the information he delivered over pastrami derailed a boatload of hopes and dreams, but instead of wallowing in self-pity, Bell has seized the opportunity to do the right thing. It's a rare trait these days, and it forces Jake to reevaluate all the harsh things he ever thought about Bell.

The waitress arrives, and Jake just orders coffee. When she's out of earshot, he begins. "You want to cut a deal with my client."

"I'll be the judge of that," Bell says. "Who does he give me? And no, Cameron Bancroft doesn't count."

"He'll give you much more on Gibson. Ties him to Falcone's and the Walkers and Jacinta Castillo."

"Keep going," Bell prods.

"Some on Reagan Hearst, but it's all circumstantial. He probably skates. My father—that one's touch and go."

"I'm not feeling overly generous based on your summary."

"He does give you one solid win. And that's why you're going to say yes." Jake waits a moment before delivering the main course on a silver platter. "Bob Forrester."

Bell sits back in the booth, digesting that. Calculating. Jake watches his body language change, and he realizes Bell may want to get Forrester almost as much as Jake wants to nail his father.

"Didn't see that one coming," Sioban says as she sips her Coke.

"There is a condition," Jake says.

"He wants another sandwich?" Sioban asks.

"It's not his condition. It's mine. On the Harrison fire, all he can really give up is some unnamed guy. Dave Smith. Doesn't matter. I want you to reopen the case. Find this Dave Smith, whoever he is, and tie him to Edgar Harrison. And if the evidence is there, to Thompson and West. Whoever was the point person."

"You want to resurrect your lawsuit."

"It's not about me. It's about Ramon Guadalupe. It's about his dead wife. It's about sixteen other dead people."

"I will look into—"

"No. Looking into is not good enough. I want a promise—from both of you—that you'll make this a priority. You do that, I think we can come to a deal on Milo Stapp."

"I'm in," Sioban says quickly. "But I need the power of the DA's office if I'm gonna push this. I'm not exactly popular in my own department at this particular moment."

They both turn to Bell, who considers—for a second. Bell offers his hand. "You're asking me to do what's right. That's a deal I can live with. Let's cut a deal for your arsonist."

They shake on it. Bell notes that Jake doesn't seem pleased. "You just extorted the district attorney's office to reopen a case that may make you millions. Maybe try a smile."

"Representing Milo Stapp is everything that makes people hate lawyers," Jake admits. "It's hard to stomach."

"We do have one thing that might make you feel better," Sioban says. She nudges Bell to expound on that.

"We do," Bell agrees. "But I believe Detective McFadden is the best one to deliver that news."

Jake focuses on Sioban. Waiting.

"You are no longer a person of interest in the shooting of Richard Kaplan."

Jake's relief is tempered by the fact that the mention of Rich's name calls up the image of that night. Of the carnage.

"Isn't that good news?" Sioban asks, seeing his odd reaction.

"It is. But then, I always knew I was innocent. And I had faith in the system."

"Well, that makes one of us," Sioban notes.

"Two," Bell says. "Let's just hope the system works as well on the rest of this."

49

A week ago, when she walked Detective McFadden into the conference room to arrest Stephen Gibson, Kendall Clark had an epiphany: she was working at a job she hates, working with lawyers, a breed she's come to hate. They're arrogant, they look down on her, they hit on her, they act entitled, they think they're smarter than everyone else, which is annoying even if they *are* smarter than everyone else, and as it turns out, some of them are just really bad people. She had enjoyed being able to say *I work at a law firm*, but her best day in recent memory had been serving papers on Reagan Hearst. She felt a surge of power in that moment, or excitement, but the berating she endured after wasn't fun at all.

So the question she faced was: What did she want? From a job, from life. She'd had trouble answering that for some time. High school was so much easier. She wanted to be a cheerleader. And she was. She wanted to date Matthew Callahan. And she did. She wanted to be class president. She got that, too. But four years at Northwestern hadn't inspired any revelations. Hadn't induced any life goals. She came home to LA, got a good job, but . . . now what?

Jake West had provided an answer in an offhand remark when she stamped his parking validation as he left that day. "If you get fired, you have a standing job offer with me."

"At the massage parlor?" she'd said.

"That's an unfair characterization," he'd argued with a laugh.

But as she walks through the recently replaced glass door in the mostly empty strip mall and takes in the lobby of Jake's office, "massage parlor" doesn't seem that far off. She shrugs it off. She's certainly not going to feel less-than here, or talked down to, or like she doesn't belong. This may not be a long-term answer, but for now it's something.

"Is it everything you imagined?" Jake asks.

"Everything and less," she jokes. "But fear not—your new receptionist is here to make it feel fractionally more legit."

Jake makes a strange face. "I'm sorry, there must've been a misunderstanding. We don't need a receptionist, Kendall." She's confused—he seems serious. "We do, however, need an office manager. And your first task in that new capacity is to find us a new office. One we can actually invite clients to."

Kendall feels a jolt of excitement. Of empowerment. *Office manager* has a nice ring to it. Her mother will like it.

"You thinking one of the Century City towers? Water Garden? Arts District downtown?"

"I'm thinking a step up from this. Honestly, two steps up, and with a short-term lease, because when the money starts flowing in, I'm all for the Arts District. I just have one general rule—it must be as far from Century City as possible."

"And as far from *here* as possible, I hope."

"I leave that decision in your very capable hands."

And he leaves her to it. She takes in the lobby once more. *Okay then, what the hell.* She sits down, pulls out her laptop, and gets to work.

Jake spends much of the day researching precedent for holding Thompson & West liable for all manner of ill deeds in all three cases he was mired in. Working to sublimate one addiction for another, Jake gets up to grab his fifth or six Diet Coke and notices Grace typing away in Conference Room A. He watches her, a bit puzzled at just what she's working on.

"I can feel you breathing," she says without stopping.

"I didn't want to disturb you. We get some new case no one told me about?"

"Nope." Her fingers fly over the keys for a minute more, then she hits a button with a flourish. "I just sent you a little something."

"Secret love note?" Her exasperated expression says, not funny. "Sorry. Do tell."

"It's your recommendation."

"What am I recommending?"

"Not what—who. Me. You're recommending me as a candidate for UCLA Law. This letter describes me in glowing terms and carries your signature over your heading as a senior partner at Thompson and West."

"You think that holds more sway than a founding partner at West, Alvarez and Associates?"

"You can't put Javi's name on the door until you live up to your promise to get them un-disbarred. Or *re-barred*. Regardless. I'm sorry to say that while I prefer the new firm, I'll go with establishment for now."

"No. I will not sign that letter."

"You are signing and you are sending, because I'm done waiting on this. I booked the LSATs for next weekend. By the way, I'll need the week off to study."

"Week off—yes. But I'm still not signing it—until I add about seventy superlatives."

"Read it, it has enough. I don't want to tread into territory where it appears anything less than professional."

Jake gets her point. "No one knows about that, Grace."

"No, no one *there* will. And we'll keep it that way by making the letter accurate to my genius, but not overdone. In any event, I thought it would be less embarrassing for you if I just did it for you. Like most of your legal work the past three years."

Despite the fact that this means Jake, or more accurately the law firm of West, Alvarez & Associates, may be on the hook for something approaching two hundred grand, he's actually moved. If you take away all the improper parts—which he knows he can't—it's been one of the most productive working relationships he's ever had. He wants this for her. She deserves this. And what her work has brought the fledgling firm more than justifies the expense.

"No snappy comeback to that?" Grace asks. "No quip? No suggestion that this calls for drinks?"

"I'm just happy for you. I took advantage—"

"Jake, no, we don't have to go there—"

"I just want you to know. You deserve this. You *earned* this. You're gonna kill it."

"Thank you."

This would naturally lead to a hug in most relationships, but Jake doesn't want to go there. Instead, he knows just how to cut the tension.

"Now—enough treacle. Time for a drink! To celebrate!"

"There's the Jake West we know and mock. And the moment does call for drinks." She looks down the hall. "But you're not invited."

That's when Javi brings Roger in. If Jake isn't mistaken, Roger's wearing cologne. And a tailored Italian shirt, slimming and extremely well pressed. His brown soft leather loafers are probably Italian too, and definitely haven't been worn before today.

"If it isn't Giorgio Armani," Jake says. "You sure you want to be seen consorting with the enemy?"

"You're no longer the enemy. I followed Kendall's lead," Roger says proudly. "I quit. Today was my last day."

"All the best people getting off the sinking ship. Congratulations." Jake is truly pleased that his father's firm will be losing something else. "I guess you and Grace both have things to celebrate."

"We all do," Roger says, his grin widening. "I brought you a parting gift."

"We love gifts," Javi notes, then looks to Jake. "Though I don't know anyone's given us one before."

"Let him get to the point," Grace urges.

"Okay," Roger says, trying to contain his excitement. He clears his throat. "So up in Morro Bay, Cameron Bancroft was killed. And I know you guys can connect him to the firm. But the *other* dead guy—Grace told me he was identified as Arvin Drudge. And she had an idea."

"I just told him to dig a little," Grace demurs. "He's the one who found it."

"Found what?" Javi asks.

"Arvin Drudge, a long time ago," Roger tells them, "was a client of Thompson and West."

Jake has to sit down. "A client of which attorney?"

"The interesting thing is that his file was wiped from the firm's records, so finding it was almost a miracle, but once upon a time we had microfiche files, so I checked into those—"

"Roger!" Jake snaps.

"It was Stephen Gibson. During his first year at the firm, he was doing some pro bono work that Arnie Thompson assigned to him. He got Arvin Drudge off on an armed robbery charge. And here's the good part. The gun he used in that case . . ." He pauses for emphasis. "A matte-black .44 Magnum. Same weapon used to kill Mr. Kaplan. Same as the gun you picked up off the ground that night."

Jake's head spins. A month ago he was a drunk pissing his life away in self-lubrication and self-pity. A month ago, Richie Kaplan was trying to do a good thing to impress a girl. It was Arvin Drudge who exploded both of their worlds.

"I'm no lawyer," Roger wraps up, "but you give that to Detective McFadden, doesn't Gibson become the prime suspect for soliciting the murder of Rich Kaplan?"

Jake is actually too stunned to answer. He knows Gibson is awful, knows he set fires that resulted in people dying, knows he tried to burn down these very offices. But the idea that he actually hired the guy to kill Richie . . .

"Holy *shit*!" Javi exclaims. "Jake. You did it! You did what you wanted to do!"

"What are you talking about?"

"You avenged Richie."

It takes Jake a moment, processing that information and its implications. "I shot the guy who killed Richie and I didn't even know it."

Jake should be happy about this, but he's just sad. Sad for his friend, for what happened to him, for cutting him off, even for driving him into the arms of his wife. He's sad for Tiana and her two dead children. And he's sad for Jacinta Castillo and Consuela Estrada and Estelle Guadalupe, none of whom he ever met, though he feels he knows Estelle. He has the overwhelming urge to go home and talk to Cara about all this, to hold her, to be held. But that can't happen.

Javi knows Jake well enough to move off the point. He needs to create a diversion.

"So . . . what's next, Roger?" Javi asks. "You've become a real badass. You going to law school, too? We could use you in a few years."

"Yes," Grace chimes in. "What's the thing you wouldn't tell me on the phone?"

"I'll tell you after drinks. And to be clear—we're not going back to Trunks."

The absurdity of that shakes Jake back to the moment.

"You took him to Trunks? Nice, I like that place."

"You like any place that serves drinks," Grace reminds him, and he can't argue. She grabs her purse. "Don't wait up, kids," she says as she and Roger head out.

The front door closes. Jake and Javi are alone in the sad office. Jake looks around, shaking his head. Javi realizes he's not thinking about the office, but he wants to cut the tension.

"Don't worry, Kendall will find us something spectacular."

"I don't know, it's growing on me." Jake almost means it.

"Don't get too attached. I saw a Buildings Department truck outside early this morning. They left this." Javi holds up a red paper: UNSAFE—DO NOT ENTER OR OCCUPY.

"You really know how to pick the spaces, don't you?"

"I was wondering why I got such a good deal."

"Isn't there something on there saying it's a crime to remove that notice?" Jake asks.

"I'm sure my lawyer can get me out of it." For effect, Javi ceremoniously shreds the red tag.

"So—they're going for drinks. What about us?" Jake asks. "Seems like we have things to celebrate too."

"You're not drinking, Jake. Stop trying to game the system."

Ironically, Jake hadn't been doing that. In that solitary moment, he wasn't thinking about a drink. Just about celebrating. He knows he has a long road ahead, but . . . it's a step.

50

From the rooftop lounge, they can see the beach. They can also see the traffic of Lincoln Boulevard if they face the other direction, but that means they're a short walk from the Metro, from bus lines, and most importantly, they're in the Santa Monica School District, which is good for Reggie. And while Tiana doesn't know anyone nearby, that's part of the attraction. It's a chance to start over. Because even though the charges were dropped, everyone in her old neighborhood sees her as a tragic figure who either killed or lost her children. She wants that behind her, and more importantly, she wants it behind Reggie.

Grace is the one who found the place, with Jake springing for first and last month's rent. After that, Tiana will be able to pay everything herself from her new job as a Store Sales Specialist at REI, not to mention whatever she gets from her lawsuit against the City of Los Angeles for hiding a witness statement that might've kept her out of jail. Jake promises that what she gets will be more than she can imagine.

Jake has spent the day helping them move in, and the physical work is cathartic—as is seeing how happy Reggie is. The nearby cliffs overlooking the beach are very much like the ones he loved so much in Cambria without having to drive three and a half hours to get there. But now, as they toast the new place from the rooftop, Jake sees Tiana is tearful.

He's brought her a drink—sparkling cider—and she wipes her eyes as she takes it.

"It's not fair."

"I know. Mariella and Quinton should be here," he says.

"Don't get me wrong, I'm grateful. But all of this, all of what I can do for Reggie now. It's not enough."

"No."

They stare out at the ocean, soaking in the moment. It's cold—not yet spring, and the wind off the ocean always makes Santa Monica ten degrees cooler than five miles inland. But Jake doesn't mind the bite of the wind. The vastness of the Pacific mesmerizes him. Watching waves break, watching surfers navigate the break, watching people living their lives fully. Having fun. He used to take his kids to the beach a ton—until he didn't. Another regret.

"What are *you* going to do now?" she asks him. "Other than make them pay for what they did to me?"

"I've got two kids of my own who deserve better than what I've done for them. I'm gonna have to fix that. If I can."

Reggie is not one for savoring the moment or the view—he wants to *do* something. He pulls on Tiana's arm. "You said we could go when we were all moved in."

"I sure did, little man," Tiana agrees.

Jake is intrigued. "Where are you going?"

"The beach. Duh," Reggie says.

Tiana swats him on the head in mock punishment for his attitude, but Jake laughs. "You know what, Reggie? That's a perfect idea."

There's something about the feel of wet sand between your toes that's restorative. Nineteen days sober, walking with Cara along the beach, watching Chloe and Aaron climb the rocks and hunt for crabs, Jake feels good. He feels a peace he hasn't experienced in years.

How could he have risked all this? And how can he get it back? He looks at Cara and sees that while he feels good, she seems sad. The hair on the back of his neck stands up.

"This is good, right?" Jake wills her to feel what he feels. To want what he wants.

"It's good to see *you* this way. It's good to see *them* this way."

"It's good to see *you* this way. You look beautiful. I'm not sure I tell you that enough."

She takes a long moment to digest the compliment. And then the bottom falls out.

"You should know . . . we have an offer on the house."

Jake feels like he's on a roller coaster cresting the top at high speed, about to get yanked downward. He feels like he could throw up all over the sand.

"It's a good offer."

"It's a good house," is all Jake can manage. "It's a house for a family. It's a place to live a life. You told me that. You told me you could see us there forever."

"I did. And I could. I wish I *still* could, Jake. I liked the life we had. But when I look at the house now? I don't see that anymore."

"I'm working hard. I'm going to meetings, *really* going. I have a sponsor."

Jake still wasn't fully sold on AA. He understood its value, its necessity—he just didn't want to believe he really needed it. Which Jesús told him was perfectly normal. He had chosen Jesús as his sponsor for three reasons. One, the fifty-two-year-old's story of how drinking cost him his family resonated with Jake. Two, Jesús eventually got his family back, and Jake was secretly hoping for some pointers. And third, and maybe most importantly, Jake knew he couldn't lie to the man. The guy has a bullshit meter that would have made him a damn fine attorney.

"That's great, Jake. But you have to do that for you, not for me. Maybe for the kids, that's fine. But the life I saw in that house—it's gone. I need a fresh start. Like what you said Tiana told you—it's time to leave the past behind."

"I don't want to be your past."

"You're always going to be in my life. In their lives. But it's time for me to figure out what my life's going to be."

"You know you could do anything. Be anything. Have . . . anyone."

"There's no one else, Jake."

"There will be. And I won't like it. I'll want you to be happy, but I won't like it."

There's a long moment. She's not sure how to manage his pain.

"We'll always have Paris," she offers.

The joke is funny, but it hurts. "I never took you to Paris."

"I know. But we'll always have the *idea* of Paris. The number of times you pitched me every detail of that trip, I feel like we were there."

"We could take the kids. Tomorrow. I could make it happen."

The hope on his face breaks her heart a little. She still loves him. But it's not enough. "*You* should take them. Sometime. But the trip we planned—that'll just be ours. Real or not, it's ours."

He sees the kids. Laughing. Happy. "I want to be a good father to them."

"You will, Jake. You're not your father."

He wants to find a better closing argument, turn the jury, win his case. He's done that a thousand times. But watching Cara now, he knows he has to concede the loss. Let go of the woman he loves most. So all he says in response is . . .

"That may be the nicest thing you've ever said to me."

And then he sprints into the cold, white foamy water breaking on the beach. Splashing the kids. Having fun. Heart broken.

EPILOGUE

The parties have gathered in the courtroom of the Honorable Eleanor Merrin for a hearing in the case of *The People of the State of California v. Stephen Gibson*. The hearing should be a formality—all indication is the judge will sign off on a plea deal for Stephen Gibson, J.D., on four charges. Burglary, criminal trespass, arson (for the fire he tried to set in Jake's office), and most notably, for solicitation of the murder of Richard Allen Kaplan. There may be other charges down the line, but those could be mired in the courts for years.

The press is out in force. The *LA Times* has decided the story has legs, and they've spent the past six months since Austin Bell's surprise non-announcement digging into all aspects of a case that touches on what they love—stories that highlight the disparities between rich and poor, the powerful and the powerless. And the story has indeed had no shortage of villains, another thing that sells papers or, in the modern era, online subscriptions.

At the prosecution table, Austin Bell is flanked by Cecilia Nevins, a rising star in the DA's office, who will rise further, given how well Bell has played everything. But everyone here is focused on the other side of the courtroom. At the defense table, Gibson tries to appear professional and innocent, but the late summer heat—or his fear about what's about to come—is making him perspire. The general effect is that he seems lost and alone and scared, even though sitting next to him is his expensive hired gun, Paula Conroy, in a suit probably worth at least three grand.

Jake wonders who's actually paying her bill. He and Javi have chosen, very purposely, to sit in the gallery on the prosecution side of the court. They don't need to be here at all, as there will be no witnesses and no testimony, but Jake has to see this through to the end. For himself. And for Rich.

"Mind if I join you?" Daria Barati slides in next to Jake.

"Come to watch the downfall of your predecessor?"

"I've come for the same reason you have. For Rich. I know you thought I'd be bad for him, but you want to hear something I never told anyone?" She takes Jake's lack of response as a go-ahead. "I really liked him. I might even have—" She stops herself. "He was a good person. And I needed that."

Jake takes solace in this. Happy that, at the end of his life, someone cared about Richie. Jake wasn't there for him, but someone was.

"You know what else I've been thinking?" Jake says. "All of the cases that fall from this case—Harrison, Tiana, Jacinta. You know who really solved it all?"

"Rich." Daria nods. "I was thinking the same thing."

"Maybe he could've been Clarence Darrow after all," Javi adds, and they all take a moment to actually smile about Richie. Giving him his final victory.

Jake pictures Richie in court, cross-examining a witness, coming into his own. The image from the BMW, the awful night this all started, beginning to recede. It's not gone, there are too many threads left to untangle. But he can think of the good along with the bad.

"So how's it going, being the Devil's right-hand man?" Jake asks, to change the subject. Apparently Thompson & West is in free fall. With Gibson's arrest and soon-to-be conviction, lawsuits being filed right and left against Hearst, against Harrison, and against the firm itself, lawyers have been jumping ship, looking for soft landings, and the poaching season for the best and the brightest has been a frenzy.

"I don't think you'd believe me if I told you."

"Try me."

"It's not bad. You father's a different man."

"It's an act."

"That's certainly possible, but at least it's a good performance. I think having to accept a censure from the bar association, from a group where he once chaired a committee—that was a tough pill to swallow. He's stepped up to settle on *Harrison*, you know that. He's made a lucrative offer to Horace Falcone. And he dropped Reagan Hearst as a client."

"He dropped Reagan?" Javi interjects. "I heard it was the other way around."

"I wasn't in the room where it happened, so I can't say," Daria answers. "But either way, they both need to steer clear of each other."

"And you think Dad really didn't know?" Jake asks. This still keeps him up at night.

"Didn't know about what?"

"About the fire that killed Tiana's kids. That it was his client behind it, and his managing partner who connected him with the arsonist."

"I'm sure he didn't know before the crime. I certainly hope he didn't know after."

"What about Rich? Dad must've been a part of that—he's the one who sent Richie to get me that night. It had to be so Arvin Drudge would know where to find him. And hey, if I got caught in the crossfire, or blamed . . ."

Jake doesn't want to believe this, and his father has of course denied it, but Jake keeps coming back to the fact that this is the likeliest scenario. His evidence is circumstantial, but that can be enough for a conviction. That said, it's not his case. Having to sit on the sidelines of the investigation into all these matters, having to let justice play out its excruciatingly slow march, has been hard. Which is why, even now, Jake's looking for a window into the truth he can't see. Looking for proof as pure as a 184 proof Bruichladdich X4 Quadruple-Distilled Whisky. But he can't have either that proof or the gloriously numbing alcohol.

"It's not his style, Jake. If your dad had known what Rich found, he would've threatened him or offered him something and it would've worked. That's the sad truth. Richie didn't have the stomach for a real fight. If I'd been honest with him about what your father wanted, or didn't want, this never would have happened."

There's logic in her words. Also, a depressing irony.

"And Tiana Walker would still be in prison and Stephen Gibson would be on to fucking over the next guy."

"True enough."

"All rise," the bailiff announces.

Jake stands, pondering Daria's words that almost make his father seem blameless. But lives have been destroyed, many lives, all in service of corporate profit, of Thompson & West and their clients. The dichotomy of the moment strikes him. Here, in this courtroom, this symbol of all that's right about the law, the proceedings are happening because of all that's wrong about the practice of law. The question remains: What is Jake going to do about that?

His musings end as Judge Merrin takes her seat on the bench and the gallery follows suit. It strikes Jake that Eleanor Merrin seems weary. This settlement has been fast-tracked; it's only been half a year since he last saw her, yet she looks a decade older. Perhaps it's because she loves the system and she's going to take no joy in sentencing a lawyer to prison.

As she scans the papers in front of her, Jake whispers another question at Daria. "How did Bell get Gibson to take the deal?"

"What I know or what I think?"

"I love a good conspiracy theory," Jake replies. Truer words were never spoken.

"Rumor has it Reagan Hearst is paying a huge sum to Gibson's wife, Anne. In exchange for Gibson not selling him out, and Anne not divorcing him."

Jake sees Anne Gibson sitting just behind her husband, looking like she'd rather be anywhere but here. Even from a distance, he can see some large chunks of jewelry. On her fingers, her wrist, her neck, her ears. The spoils of war.

"True love. Such a beautiful thing," Jake observes.

"Attorneys, approach please," Judge Merrin orders.

As Bell and Paula Conroy confer with Merrin, Daria whispers: "I have one more piece of news."

"I'm all ears."

"It's not for you."

She extends her arm past Jake and hands an envelope to Javi. He's dubious, but opens it and reads the letter inside. He takes a deep breath, then audibly exhales. Javi's not revealing anything, so Jake turns to Daria.

"You want to let me in on this?" Jake asks.

Daria shakes her head, but Javi hands him the letter, printed on letterhead from the State Bar of California. It outlines the reinstatement to the bar of one Javier Martín Alvarez.

"Wait—*I* was gonna do this." He turns to Daria. "How did you manage it?"

"I didn't. Your father did."

Jake takes a few seconds to move from anger to annoyance, then finally to elation for his friend. "I guess he really does like you."

But Javi knows better. "No, Jake. He did it for you."

Jake tries to make sense of that. He understands it, but he isn't sure how to feel. He doesn't want anything from his father, but Norman was smart enough to know that, so he did something Jake couldn't reject. It's genius. It's infuriating.

"He's trying," Daria says, finding herself in the odd role of peacemaker between father and son.

Jake can't settle on what to feel about this, but seeing the lawyers sealing the fate of Stephen Gibson, knowing that he'll spend a minimum of nine years in prison, is certainly reason to celebrate. Javi's resurrection is a far better one.

As Jake is leaving the courtroom, Austin Bell calls after him. They take a seat in the back row of the gallery to talk privately.

"Well done," Jake says. "You're gonna make a great DA."

"Says the man who made me pass up the job."

"Doing the right thing is hard."

"Maybe that'll be my campaign slogan."

"You did better than I could've hoped. Except for Reagan Hearst."

"He played things well. Kept his hands clean and bought off anyone who was a danger. And—that plaza *will* be good for the city."

"Maybe. I'll keep digging."

"If you find something, I'm all ears."

Jake nods, assuming they're done. "See you around, Austin. And thanks. For everything."

"Wait a minute. I didn't come over for you to thank me. I have an offer for you."

"You want me to be a prosecutor?"

Bell laughs. "I don't think you'd be particularly good in a political system, Jake. Playing outside the lines is how you thrive. The offer isn't for you. It's for you to take to Tiana Walker."

Austin hands Jake a piece of paper. Jake skims it—it's a settlement offer meant to compensate Tiana for the fact that Bob Forrester hid evidence in her case, keeping her in jail far longer than necessary. If she agrees not to sue, they'll pay her two million dollars.

"The city attorney okayed this?" Jake asks, surprised.

"I told them it was this or I was gonna start uncovering every corrupt thing Bob ever did, which would probably bankrupt the city coffers."

"Shouldn't you do that anyway?"

"Give me four years. *Then* I'll be in a position to do it. Capuano is going to play it safe for now. He thinks that's the ticket to success—not ruffling feathers."

"He's going to spend his four years in office looking over his shoulder at you."

"Yeah. Gonna be fun." Bell offers his hand. "We have a deal, Counselor?"

Jake shakes it. He and Tiana talked about possible numbers for this settlement. This is far more than either of them dreamed of.

As Bell leaves, Jake sees a redhead standing at the back door, waiting for him. Sioban, too, had to see everything through to the end.

"Satisfied?" she asks.

"Today? Yes. You?"

"I'd say so. Detective John Mackenzie decided to take early retirement."

"He's so young, though."

"It's amazing what an IA investigation does to your future plans."

"And Gantley?"

"He's proving to be the rare bird—a good cop. How's the new firm?"

"Well, we have a problem. I just lost my top investigator."

"Javi's leaving?"

"Got his license back. So if you want to make real money, we could use your talents."

"I'll have a think about it. When I get back."

"Going somewhere?"

"Dublin."

From the fire with which she says it, Jake immediately understands why she's going. "Brin Maloney won't know what hit him."

"We'll see if I can find him. Seems he's dropped out of sight. But your case made me think maybe it's never too late to right old wrongs."

"You'll get him."

"I hope so. I'll get him for whatever I can find. Someone once told me: We're all guilty. *Of something.*"

Jake is pleased that he's had a positive effect on her. They've come a long way from the interrogation room downtown, from her assuming he was just another corrupt lawyer doing awful things.

"So here's a weird question," Sioban tosses out as casually as she can manage. "Wanna come with?"

Jake takes that in. Not fully sure what she's asking.

"Looking for a lawyer? Or an accomplice?"

She seems to think about it. "Can't it be both?"

Acknowledgments

I want to thank the earliest readers of the manuscript—Phil and Carolyn Cowan—who convinced me I wasn't crazy for trying to write a novel. The next set of readers—Jennifer Cowan and Dena Klapperich—your enthusiasm helped me push forward, and your thoughts and notes helped get the book where it is. And a very special shout-out to Anthony Epling, who knows my writing as well as anyone, and whose notes are always spot-on.

I also want to thank Lynne Litt and the late Justin Peacock, friends and colleagues who went down this path before me, for their early advice.

I want to thank two lawyers who prove that lawyers aren't always what they are made out to be: my own lawyer, Bob Myman, who has helped guide my career for three decades now. And my first lawyer, the late Gene Rosenberg, who made me see at a very young age that lawyers could fight for what's right, even going up against big corporations that had more money and more power than you could imagine. Thanks also to a future lawyer, my son-in-law John Clark, who patiently indulged my questions about the minutiae of working at a big law firm. And I'm sure he will patiently indulge more questions on the next one.

I want to thank Dan Halsted and Nate Miller at Manage-ment for their encouragement to pursue this project. And a deep level of thanks and appreciation to Liz Parker and Emma Kapson at Verve, who read the manuscript, loved it, found a home for it, and walked me through this very new process. It has been a fairy-tale experience.

Last, but in no way least, I want to thank Ed Schlesinger at Gallery Books for seeing what I saw in this story and this world—and in Jake—and helping to take it to the next level. In addition, I want to thank Aimée Bell and Jennifer Bergstrom at Gallery for their excitement and support, and Stacey A. Sakal and Alessandra Lusardi for their meticulous notes, which pushed me to make everything line up and make sense. It made the book better. Thank you all.